KATYA

KATYA

LUCY CORES

ST. MARTIN'S PRESS
NEW YORK

 For information, write:
St. Martin's Press, Inc.
175 Fifth Ave.
New York, N.Y. 10010.
Manufactured in the United States of America

Library of Congress Cataloging in Publication Data

Cores, Lucy Michaella, 1914–
Katya.

I. Title.
PZ3.C8122Kat [PS3505.06673] 813'.5'2 79–22919
ISBN 0–312–45096–6

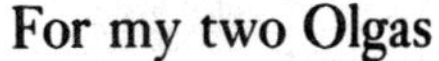

For my two Olgas

CHAPTER 1

Countess Vorontzov's reception, one of the first to mark the resumption of the social season after Lent, was an important social event in Petersburg. From eight o'clock onward carriages flowed ceaselessly along the Fontanka, stopping in front of the brilliantly lighted entrance of the ancient Vorontzov palace to discharge the guests.

"Another sad crush. It seems to me his lordship has been dispatching me to far too many of them lately."

The speaker, who had just alighted from a carriage emblazoned with the arms of the British embassy, was the Honorable George Graham, an attaché at the embassy, standing in for his superior, Lord Granville Leveson-Gower, a diplomat much in demand among the Petersburg hostesses because of his handsome looks and ingratiating ways. Graham, not the vainest of men, had dressed with considerable care for this occasion. He wore a frilled shirt, knee breeches and silk stockings and carried his chapeau bras under his arm, his sandy head bared to the bracing breezes of early spring.

His companion, also English, a plump and amiable old-timer who had once been a physician at the court of Catherine the Great, gave a comfortable chuckle.

"You'll not dislike this one, lad. There'll be at least one pleasant sight to compensate you . . . You have never been here before, I gather?"

"No, this is my first visit. You intrigue me, Doctor Rogerson. What am I to expect?"

"You'll see."

A footman in a violet and gold uniform preceded the two

gentlemen up the grand staircase decorated with miniature orange trees in delft tubs, and announced them. They entered a large white salon lined with columns. A grand piano standing under a huge mirror was just being vacated by one of Petersburg's more fashionable performers. Presently the applause was replaced by conversation, and powdered footmen began circulating among the guests, bearing trays with champagne glasses and cakes.

Graham surveyed the gathering through his lorgnette. It looked as though most of the fashionable world was present. He saw Marie Naryshkin, the emperor's current mistress, shining with complacent beauty. That she was accompanied by Adam Chartoryzhski, a young freethinker from Poland, would be of interest to his superior, he thought. There was also the usual sprinkling of Petersburg literati, among whom he saw the famous old historian Karamzin and the rising young court poet Zhukovski.

The scene was no different from those to be seen on the Continent. Even the fashions had improved in the last five years. The cumbersome German modes that Russians had favored during the recent reign of Paul I were gone, and today in the year of our Lord 1807 the women wore high-waisted, transparent gowns straight from Paris, while men of fashion, in their velvet jackets, tight-fitting tricot pants and waistcoats (once forbidden by Tsar Paul on the ground that they had caused the French revolution) could have come from—well, perhaps not quite Bond Street, Graham thought with the unconscious snobbery of an Englishman not too long ago arrived from London.

"Are you looking for Count Vorontzov? Do not trouble to do so," said Dr. Rogerson. "He seldom appears at these crushes. He is quite old, you know. Leaves it all to Countess Elena Petrovna."

He pointed out a handsome woman nearing forty who was holding court at the other end of the room. She wore a sumptuous yellow gown and turban so ablaze with jewels that Graham, used though he was to the proliferation of diamonds in the Russian court, couldn't help blinking. Two young girls dressed in identical figured white muslin gowns stood on either side of her. One was a pale, slender girl with fair ringlets. The other was the most beautiful girl Graham had ever seen, either in England or in Russia. The radiance of her beauty dazzled him from across the width of the room. He gazed entranced at the raven locks, the eyes as brilliant as stars under the delicately drawn black brows, the beautifully curved lips slightly parted to show small, pearly teeth.

"That is what I meant," said Dr. Rogerson with his rumbling laugh. "Well, shall I present you to Countess Vorontzov and her daughters?"

Graham nodded, eyes glazed. "Yes," he said, "immediately."

She was even lovelier at close range. The longest black eyelashes shaded her deliciously slanted eyes, giving them a velvety, caressing quality, and her black hair lay along her small, regally held head like bands of black satin. She had the dark yet sparkling beauty of a starlit night. Graham found it difficult to keep from looking at her as he was being presented to his hostess.

The countess greeted him graciously enough, though she was at first clearly disappointed by the absence of Lord Leveson-Gower. Her slight pique was allayed by hearing that he had been summoned to Kamennyi Ostrov, which was the spring residence of their imperial majesties.

"And now let me make you known to my young ladies," she said with a wave of her fan. The pale girl curtsied silently. The beauty, however, was chatting lightheartedly with a tall, handsome man whom Graham identified as Prince Dmitry Ivanitch Lunin, and didn't at once attend to her mother. The countess frowned.

"Well, Katya?" she said with some asperity. The girl turned her head and smiled at Graham, completing his subjugation.

"Katya," he thought rapturously. "What a delightful name."

The two girls were presented to him more formally as Lisaveta Vassilevna and Katerina Vassilevna. The Russian custom, dictating that a lady should sketch a kiss on the brow of any man kissing her hand, no matter how little known to her, brought her very close to Graham. As her quick, warm breath touched his hair, his heart missed a beat and tightened deliciously.

He was not given a chance to talk to her, however, as a group of Life Guardsmen resplendent in their scarlet uniforms surrounded her, shutting him out. He could merely listen to the sound of her pretty voice prattling to them about the ballet she had seen the night before. It had been Didelot's latest, *Zephyr and Flora*, and had contained some astonishing aerial effects.

"Absolutely enchanting! I am so glad I saw Flora's flight. Why, she was actually *wafted* across the stage in Zephyr's arms! However did they manage to do it?"

One of the officers began a labored technical explanation of the special machine devised by Didelot to produce this effect and was gallantly interrupted by another, a brash, mustachioed Hussar in a fur-trimmed baldrick. "Now *you* would need no special device to elevate you from the ground, mademoiselle. Angels have no need for machines . . ."

"Oh, Captain Kozlov!" The beauty laughed heartily at the inane compliment. "I could have done much better," Graham thought idiotically as the silvery sounds of her laughter sent a shiver up his spine.

Thwarted, he turned to her sister and began to make himself agreeable to her. Her replies were polite and rational, although sometimes monosyllabic. Her mother watched them with undisguised approval. Presently she too addressed the young lady, saying with a sort of determined playfulness: "Monsieur Field tells me you are doing wonders with your music, Lisa. Will you play for us?"

Her daughter looked at her in dismay. "Oh, no, maman—not after—" she indicated the previous performer, who was still receiving plaudits on the other side of the drawing room.

"Nonsense, child." Her mother turned her glittering smile on Graham. "I would have you know, Monsieur Graham, my Lisa is an accomplished pianist. Your famous countryman, Monsieur John Field, is teaching her, and he considers her his best pupil."

"I am fortunate indeed to have come in time to hear Mademoiselle Lisa perform," Graham rejoined politely.

The young lady answered his encouraging smile with a small, bleak one and, resigning herself to the inevitable, marched to the piano, shoulders drooping.

"Marie Antoinette on her way to the guillotine looked sprightlier," Prince Dmitry remarked, watching her through his lorgnette. His somewhat thin mouth set itself in sardonic lines. "Another one of the little martyrdoms fond mamas are apt to inflict on their daughters."

"Come, come, Dmitry," said the countess, sitting down on

the red morocco couch and tapping his faultlessly tailored sleeve lightly with her fan of Italian gauze. "The child must learn not to be so diffident about her accomplishments."

"I imagine she will, in time," said Prince Dmitry indifferently. "A pity."

"What a cynic you are, Dmitry."

That indeed was his reputation, Graham knew. A man in his early forties, rich, saturninely handsome, the prince was much in demand in the Petersburg salons, where he had made himself feared and respected as much for his savage wit as for his readiness to give satisfaction to anyone offended by it.

Meanwhile Lisa had seated herself at the piano, and after having announced in a hardly audible voice that she would play a selection from Monsieur Gluck's opera, *Orfeo ed Euridice*, she proceeded to do so.

Her performance turned out to be more or less what Graham had expected: technically faultless but lacking in either fire or pleasure. As he looked at her anxious little face, Graham found himself feeling sorry for her.

He ventured a glance at the other side of the room, where her lovely sister stood surrounded by her admirers, of whom, he noticed with pleasure, she was taking no notice as she listened to her sister's playing. The same brash Hussar to whose sallies she had been gaily responding just a short while before whispered something—another inane compliment, no doubt—in her ear, but all he received for his gallantry was a frown of displeasure and a hushing gesture.

Lisa finished her piece and, acknowledging the polite applause with a quick, nervous smile, half-rose in her seat, ready to leave the piano. Her mother's voice stopped her.

"Are you not going to play for us that charming Handel sonata you play so well, my darling?" the countess said cooingly. "Precisely what we should love to hear."

"But maman, I do not have it all by heart as yet."

"I know, my love, and that is why I had your music put on the piano . . . Well, *mon ange?*"

Reading her fate in her mother's implacably smiling face, Lisa dispiritedly sat down again. The tinkling notes chimed dutifully through the politely attentive salon.

She had only played a few bars when an incisive voice cut through the music.

"That will do, my child. The company has had enough of this damned tinkling, I believe."

Lisa's hands froze on the keys.

A tall old man, magnificently though carelessly dressed in a court costume from the days of Catherine the Great and wearing a white peruke, was making his way through the audience with the help of a cane.

There was no doubt in Graham's mind that this must be the master of the house, Count Vassily Vorontzov, one of Catherine the Great's "victorious eagles." And indeed he looked like an old eagle, molting a bit, perhaps, Graham thought, but still indomitably upright. A scar bisected one seamed cheek, and steely blue eyes glinted fiercely under the bristly white eyebrows.

"What we want," he continued, seating himself leisurely in the large chair that was immediately brought for him by the footmen in attendance, "is some gay music and some dancing to go with it. Katya?"

He turned his head, looking for her. The countess made an indecipherable sound, her hands tightening on her fan. Dull red patches swam up her neck and covered her handsome face.

"Yes, papa," said Katya, coming toward him.

"Tell your sister what you want her to play for you. You'll dance for us—something sprightly, mind, none of those die-away minuets."

As he spoke the footmen began to move the chairs back, presumably to make room for the performance. Apparently this was a procedure to which the household was accustomed.

Katya, however, made no move to enter the impromptu stage prepared for her. "I beg to be excused, papa."

"What?"

"I would rather not dance, papa."

The fierce eyes fastened on her with an ominous glint. "Why, what is it? Have you gone lame?"

"No, papa." Katya's chin went up. She had gone a shade paler but her black eyes met her father's unflinchingly. "I do not believe you realized it, papa, but Lisa has not yet finished playing her sonata."

Her voice rang clearly across the hushed room. At the piano Lisa gave a gasp, barely able to manage a desperate little head shake at her sister, who, without paying any attention to her, went on: "It would be wrong for me to dance until she—"

"I see," said the count gently. "Now that you have shown yourself to be a good sister, I suggest you attend to my request."

"No, papa, I could not . . ."

The redoubtable old gentleman regarded her with narrowed eyes. "You know, *dushenka*," the caressing word was at odds with the cold menace of the tone, "you are not too old to be whipped. Publicly. In front of this company."

Graham caught his breath. The words were uttered softly enough, but there was no doubt in his mind that the old man was quite capable of carrying out his threat.

The uneasy stir about him indicated that the other guests were likewise aware of this. Lisa put both hands to a face washed clear of color. Above them her dilated blue eyes gazed in terror at her father. Only Countess Vorontzov, seated rigidly on the couch, failed to show any signs of apprehension. In fact, Graham thought he could spot a certain gleam of pleasurable anticipation in her handsome, hard face.

Katya gave a reckless little laugh. "You can whip me till I die, papa, but dance I will not." With an infinitely graceful movement she sank down to her knees, bending her head and giving her pretty shoulders a little shake as if to bare them for the coming blow.

The count rose to his feet slowly, his face quite expressionless, and raised the gold-headed cane. Why, Graham said to himself, stunned, he is really going to do it; that cane is really going to come swishing down on those gracefully bowed shoulders. As he involuntarily made to step forward, he became aware of a detaining hand on his shoulder.

"I shouldn't, really," a voice drawled behind him, and, turning, he encountered Prince Dmitry Lunin's amused gaze.

Graham tried to shake off his grip, but the slender fingers grew suddenly steely, holding him back with unsuspected strength.

A harsh croak of laughter broke from the count. Lowering the cane, he reseated himself in his chair.

"Devil's daughter," he said with evident relish. A universal sigh of relief went through the salon. Prince Dmitry relinquished Graham's shoulder and helped himself to a pinch of snuff. His eyes met Graham's with a glint of amusement. "As a lifelong friend of the family," he said softly in impeccable

English, "I have been privileged to witness a few of these scenes. They both enjoy them, I assure you. I daresay it's hard for you to understand this . . ."

Graham, still shaken, said baldly: "Yes." He tried to transfer the scene he had witnessed into any of the English households he knew—even the egregious Devonshire House, where anything could happen and often did—and failed. This, he decided, could only take place in Russia.

The count had in the meanwhile turned his attention to his other daughter. "Well," he said to her irritably, "what are you waiting for? Finish your piece of nonsense." And as Lisa stared back at him mesmerized, "Did you hear me, girl? Hop to it."

Despite his indignation Graham couldn't help smiling as he listened to the bravura performance that followed. Lisa's fingers fairly flew over the keys, slurring and missing notes; never had Handel's staid sonata been accomplished in such jig time.

Katya, still on her knees, moved closer to her father's chair and kissed his hand. The count smiled grimly, his other hand patting her sleek, dark head. "Devil," he said again. Katya leaned back against his knee and with some complacency listened to her sister hurtling through her sonata. When it was over and the relieved audience had finished applauding, she looked up at her father through her long eyelashes, a tiny, roguish smile curving her perfect lips.

"What shall I dance, papa? The Russkaya? It's what you like best, isn't it?"

The count nodded, with another grim smile.

Without waiting to be told, Lisa began to play a Russian folk tune. Katya walked to the middle of the room, stood for a moment quite still, her hands clasped together, her eyelashes making dusky half-circles on her cheeks, and presently swayed into the dance, making the ceremonial low bows to the four sides which commonly introduce a Russian dance. The music warmed up and went faster, and so did she. Her black braids loosened and came down, her little feet in their white satin slippers drummed out the quickening tempo without missing a beat, her pliant young body swayed and bent like a birch tree in the wind. And as she danced, she was wildly, glowingly beautiful.

Graham noticed fleetingly that Lisa, now that the attention of the audience had been drawn elsewhere, was playing with a verve and relish that previously had been quite lacking. A faint smile of pleasure, as her quick fingers kept pace with Katya's flying feet, made her look like a different girl from the docile, well-bred performer of before. He noticed this briefly and then forgot all about her as Katya, circling the cleared space, flew by him, her trailing scarf brushing his cheek lightly.

And then she was back in the center of the room, spinning, black braids whipping about her, the white muslin of her skirt billowing in a froth about her slender ankles, until suddenly both she and the music stopped abruptly. She stood stock still, her bosom rising and falling lightly, one hand on her hip, the other upflung, the scarf fluttering down along the slender, uplifted arm like a banner coming to rest when the wind dies.

The count cracked his palms together. "That's my girl," he said strongly. "That's how it's done!" and leaned back smiling while the salon exploded in applause.

Afterward Graham stopped at the piano, where Lisa was quietly gathering her music together. He retrieved a fallen page and handed it to her. "Permit me to thank you for your performance, mademoiselle. I found it most enjoyable."

"You *did?*" The tone was frankly disbelieving, and Graham's lips twitched. He said: "It is true that I am not especially musical, but—"

"Oh, that would explain it," Lisa said simply. "Because I really played very badly. But thank you, Monsieur Graham. Anyhow."

Graham could not forbear an appreciative grin. "I suspect," he said, "both of us would have enjoyed the performance more if it had taken place before a smaller audience. Am I right?"

Lisa's blue eyes went to his in an arrested gaze. A faint flush pinkened her cheeks. "Yes," she said. "You are quite right." He waited politely for her to continue but she merely curtsied and slipped away without any further conversation.

Graham continued on his way, determined to speak to her sister, who, flushed and triumphant, was again holding court on the other side of the room. His way led him past a small clutch of dowagers. Putting together their powdered heads surmounted by awesome superstructures of frills and plumes, they were engaged in their favorite pastime of character assassination.

They were doing so in Russian, but Graham had no difficulty understanding them. He had a natural aptitude for languages and had been able to master this one, complicated as it was, quickly enough. Not that he had all that much opportunity to use it. The official language of the Petersburg *haut monde* was French, although any of its members could slip into German, Italian and English at will. Emperor Alexander himself, when Graham was presented to him on his arrival in Russia a year ago, had condescended to address him in unexceptionable English. The Honorable William Ponsonby, the other attaché in the British embassy, had assured Graham that the only Russian word one needed to know in Petersburg was *skorey!* ("faster") to be addressed to one's coachman. But then Ponsonby was a young man whose indolent habits made him totally unfit for diplomatic service and who was only tolerated in the embassy because his mother, Lady Henrietta Bessborough, had been Lord Leveson-Gower's mistress.

Graham, on the other hand, reckoned that it was just as well for a budding diplomat to know the language of the country where he was staying. He was often amused when his hosts resorted to their native tongue in front of him to share a confidence or communicate a private piece of gossip unfit for his ears, serenely sure that the foreigner would never understand such a barbaric language. This struck Graham as evidence of how little respect the Russians had for themselves as a people. Apparently Peter I, the Great Innovator, had impressed upon them for good and all the notion that West was best.

He realized presently that the ladies were discussing Katya.

"Have you ever seen the like, *ma chère?* Flouncing about like a ballerina, no shame, no decorum. Of course there is nothing poor Countess Elena Petrovna can do about it."

"No, he's the one who rules the roost. Well, if he likes to see his daughter behaving like a common—"

"Is it really so bad, *mesdames?*" The third old lady was apparently more tolerant. "Prince Alexis Orlov's daughter also dances for him and his friends."

"There is dancing and dancing. I don't mind seeing a *pas d'Espagne* or even a *pas de châle* if it is done with decorum and taste. But this one—why, she might be a gypsy!"

Spiteful old griffins, Graham thought indignantly, edging by them. Nevertheless the proper Englishman in him couldn't but agree that the beautiful Katya didn't dance like a lady of quality. The way she moved her hands and her shoulders was not what one would expect in a respectable salon: she had danced with the skill and abandon of gypsies he had seen performing at the regimental revels to which he had been invited by officer friends. All the more shame to the old despot who insisted on her doing so.

But even this faint caveat dissolved like frost in the strong sun when he was finally able to reach her side. Katya listened to his compliments graciously. She was still flushed with her exertions; her lips smiled unconsciously and a small pulse beat tempestuously at the base of her long, white throat. But though her black eyes smiled on him, Graham was only too well aware that to her he was merely a part of the general blur of admirers.

She paid a little more attention when, after praising her dancing, he expressed his admiration for her championship of her sister.

"It is unusual to see such friendship between sisters," he said. "Mine are always quarreling with each other."

"Really? How sad! Lisa and I have never had a quarrel. But then who could, with Lisa? She is such an angel." Dimpling delightfully, she added. "Me, I am not."

"No," Graham agreed before he thought. A delightful peal of laughter burst from her.

"How ungallant, Monsieur Graham. Would you compare me to a devil then, like papa? Or what?"

"I don't know." To his own ears his voice vibrated with unwonted earnestness. "To what would one compare the incomparable? To tell you the truth, mademoiselle, I have never encountered any being like you before."

And that got him a look of awareness before her attention was again taken away.

Graham went on to pay his respects to the old count, who on hearing his name drew his shaggy eyebrows together in a considering frown. "Graham," he said, reminiscently. "I seem to remember someone of that name on the English embassy staff during the reign of her late majesty, the glorious Catherine?"

"My uncle, the present Marquis of Lyndhurst, had been in Russia in that capacity in 1778, your excellency," Graham replied. "He was a mere John Graham then."

"Yes, of course. You remind me of him—a sandy-haired Englishman, phlegmatic like all your countrymen."

"My uncle would be delighted to know that you remember him."

"Nothing is wrong with my memory. I have one special

recollection about him . . ." His sunken eyes gleaming, he recounted it. It involved the late empress, who, as Graham knew by repute, had always had an eye out for presentable men and a rather imperious way of enlisting their services. Graham couldn't help a lurking grin as he thought of his stiff-rumped uncle trapped in that particular situation.

"He left soon after, and it is my firm opinion that he asked to be recalled." The count uttered a dry cackle. "All you Englishmen are afraid of women. Timid, proper fellows you are, incapable of honest passion . . ."

"You are hard on us, sir."

Could the censorious old rooster but know, he thought, the emotion that filled *this* Englishman's heart whenever he thought of his daughter, now laughing and glowing in the midst of her admirers without a thought for him.

Could this be love at first sight, he wondered—a phenomenon much described in the sentimental novels of the day but hitherto unknown to him. Graham's duties as attaché to the affable ambassador brought him into constant contact with the Petersburg upper class, and he performed the social functions required of him with ease and adroitness. The ladies of the Imperial Court were a flirtatious lot. He would receive many an implicit invitation during an assembly or a *raout*, and would sometimes embark on a discreet affair: although a serious-minded and conscientious young man, he was not a prig. But this could turn out to be something quite different and much more important.

The count seemed to notice the wistful glance the young man had involuntarily sent in his daughter's direction. All at once he laughed and clapped Graham on the shoulder.

"Well, well, John Graham's nephew. . . . You are welcome here anytime, my boy. Come and talk to me when you get tired of my countess's social nonsense. Can't stand it myself for longer than half an hour."

As if to illustrate the point, he got up from his chair and left the salon without any further ceremony.

On the way back from the reception, Graham took the opportunity of questioning Dr. Rogerson before dropping him off at his lodgings. He had been in the diplomatic service since he had left Oxford, and the process of noticing and classifying had become second nature to him; he couldn't help but notice certain significant discrepancies about the Vorontzov girls. They certainly had been sisterly with each other; yet they seemed to be too close in age to be sisters, unless they were twins, which they emphatically were not. Countess Vorontzov was "maman" to both of them; but he had perceived a marked difference in her behavior toward them. There had been an unmistakable motherliness toward the reserved Lisa that was quite lacking in her manner to the other girl. Even her insistence on Lisa's performing, however misguided, was indicative of a mother's ambition to see her child distinguish herself, and she had done her utmost to draw her into the conversation. True, there had been no need for that in Katya's case; her manner, her conversation had been delightfully free from constraint. However, that very freedom, which he found so enchanting, had seemed to displease the countess. All during the evening he had noticed dampening looks, a disapproving tightening of the lips and an expression of downright resentment as Katya was petted by the old count, whose favorite she evidently was.

Also, the two girls were addressed differently. Lisa was *countess;* her sister was *mademoiselle.* In England this would merely have meant that she was the younger one; not so in Russia, where all the members of a noble family had a right to the title.

As it turned out, his impression had been correct; in fact Mademoiselle Katerina (his heart rejected the formal title; to him she would always be Katya, lovely Katya) was an adopted daughter.

"A distant relation, one might say—not quite as distant from the count as from the countess," Dr. Rogerson had said with a wink. "The two girls have been brought up as sisters, which of course they are: Count Vorontzov makes no secret of the young lady being his natural daughter. He was quite a rake in his day, with many scandalous affairs to his credit. It is even said that he was extremely close to the late Empress Catherine at one time. This did him no good when Paul I succeeded her: Tsar Paul had a constitutional aversion to his mother's lovers. A considerable number of them landed in Siberia. But the count was a cagy 'un. He prudently kept out of sight and lived quietly—as indeed we all did here in Petersburg. Of course, with Alexander on the throne it's quite different—being a newcomer, you have no idea how very different."

"I believe I do have an idea." Upon arriving from Vienna he

had been told as much by the embassy old hands. He himself was aware of a lightness, a festive gaiety whenever one went to attend on the imperial family, and he had seen emotional Russians weep with joy, hailing the handsome young emperor to the skies whenever he appeared in public. "But as you were saying about Kat—about Mademoiselle Vorontzov?"

Dr. Rogerson shrugged. "No one really knows who her mother was. It is said that the child was a crim. con. of an affair with one Princess Lopukhin, and indeed there *is* a resemblance: all the Lopukhin females are dark, sultry creatures with a *beauté du diable.*" Dr. Rogerson helped himself to a pinch of snuff from an enamel box decorated with the monogram of the Empress Catherine picked out in diamonds, and gave a comfortable chuckle. "Got a leveler, didn't you, young Graham? Don't blame you in the least. The gal is a diamond of the first water."

CHAPTER 2

"Don't you ever dare do this again," Lisa said with fervor. The two girls in their nightrobes were seated side by side, having their hair brushed by their maids. "I almost died. I was sure you went too far that time. And it wasn't worth it, dearest. Indeed, it wasn't."

"Yes, it was. You've been practicing that sonata for weeks, you had it perfectly, I heard Monsieur Field say so. And then, just as you had a chance to show them . . ."

"But I didn't want to show them," Lisa protested, and as Katya made a small, incredulous sound, she added, "I never do, you know."

There was nothing Lisa liked less than performing; she lost all her pleasure in playing when she was faced with an audience. Her hands grew cold, her fingers tangled and all she cared about was finishing the burdensome ordeal as soon as she could. It occurred to her that the young Englishman who had spoken to her at her mother's reception understood something of the way she felt: his smile, at once humorous and compassionate, had seemed to indicate this. But Katya would never understand. In fact, it was always very hard for her to understand anyone feeling other than she did. Hence her valorous defiance of their father's terrifying rage in order to procure for Lisa something she had not even wanted.

And yet that very lack of imagination on her part was something that Lisa found endearing. She leaned toward her sister and hugged her. "You are good to me, darling."

Katya's answering hug, as always, was tempestuous. "You're my own little white mouse and I won't let anyone hurt you."

"But I die every time you defy papa."

Katya merely shrugged her shoulders. "I'm not afraid of him."

"You're not afraid of anything, that's the trouble," said the nurse, intervening in her young mistresses' conversation with the freedom allowable to so old a servant. "Better if you were, my little falcon." She made a protective sign of the cross over Katya's dark head. "May He shield and protect you."

"Well, He has so far," Katya remarked.

And that was the truth. Time and again she would brave their father's famous rages that terrorized the whole household, and Lisa would tremblingly wait for her to be demolished. But as often as not, instead of turning his wrath on Katya, the count would regard her with a strange wistfulness. "Just like her mother," he would say. "That was another daughter of Satan." Of course there was no knowing how long this resemblance to the unknown mother would go on serving Katya in good stead.

Lisa let the nurse braid her fair hair for the night and, putting on her bed jacket and muslin nightcap, went over to the corner where the ikons hung, illuminated by a perpetually burning taper, and knelt down for her nightly prayers.

Before long Katya, similarly clad for the night, joined her, but only briefly. Kneeling at Lisa's side, she gabbled a low-voiced prayer, ran on tiptoe to her bed, leaped into it, and presently was asleep, curled up into a ball like a kitten.

Lisa stayed on her knees, praying, for a long time. She was deeply religious, and prayer had always been a time of unburdening and refreshment for her. As she prayed, she felt her soul cleansed of the day's worries and distresses, so that when at the end she said, "Thy will be done, amen," she felt truly at peace. There were certain requests she always humbly addressed to the Almighty, and she did so again. She prayed to be enabled to love her father and not merely to fear him; she prayed that Katya would remain safe from his wrath; and also that her mother's age-old dislike of Katya would be turned to love.

Lisa had always known, sadly, that her mother hated Katya. From childhood she had known that whenever the countess said "she" with a certain hard, bitter inflection, this meant her sister. The countess resented everything about Katya: her beauty, her lighthearted ways, and most of all the fact that she indubitably was her father's favorite. In spite of her illegitimate birth, she had been brought up on exactly the same footing as her legitimate sister from the very day she had been brought into Vorontzov's household. Such were the count's orders, and he was never disobeyed.

Lisa had been only three years old when Katya came. But she remembered that day very well. She had been quietly playing in the nursery when her father entered, carrying a bundle of fur from between the folds of which a pair of bright black eyes peeped out. "I've brought you a present, Lisanka," he had said, laughing, and laid it down on the bed. The fur cloak had fallen open, disclosing a ravishingly pretty little girl of about her own age. "A little sister for you. You are to love her."

"Oh, yes, papa," Lisa had uttered, enchanted with her gift. She had no difficulty obeying her father's behest. The new arrival had responded in kind; she was an affectionate little thing, ready to love anyone who loved her.

As they grew up, the two little girls clung to each other as if they were both orphans, which in a way they were. In a noble Russian household, growing children were virtually brought up by the servants in charge of them. Lisa's mother, whose social ambitions and activities filled her entire life, paid as little attention to her own daughter as she did to the resented changeling. As a result, Lisa's considerable capacity for affection was expended on her sprightly, black-eyed little sister, who was her constant companion and with whom she shared everything. Her parents had very little reality for her; the countess was a glittering and perfumed being into whose scented presence she was allowed for a few minutes every day; the count was even more remote, a seldom-seen God-like personage that frowned and thundered at her terrifyingly. The comfortable reality was to be found away from them, in the nursery; she was content to get her share of love from the fond old nanny who petted and cosseted her and from the tempestuous bundle of affection and temper that was Katya.

By the time Lisa was old enough to be noticed by her mother and to take her place in her social scheme, the pattern had been set, and the bonds of mutual love between the two sisters had become unbreakable. Her mother's fretful accusation of "I believe you love her more than me," was nothing less than the truth.

Countess Elena Petrovna Vorontzov, thirty years junior to her husband, had always harbored great social ambitions, aspiring to be one of the leaders of the Petersburg fashionable set. During the bleak years of Paul's reign, this ambition had perforce lain dormant. After Alexander's accession to the throne, it was fully gratified. When she herself wasn't entertaining, she was constantly out in the world rushing cometlike from one brilliant affair to the other, the two girls trailing in her triumphant wake. The old count, in spite of his scorn for what he acidly called female henheadedness, was not ill pleased to see his daughters take their proper place in society. He made no secret of the fact that he particularly desired this for Katya.

"I want her to see and be seen," he told the resentful countess. "Puts everyone in the shade, doesn't she? And enjoys doing so, the minx . . . Now, her sister couldn't care less; she would rather stay home with her nose stuck in a book or playing the piano."

That was perfectly true. Lisa hated those loud and glittering affairs and would droop with fatigue and boredom as the evening wore on, while Katya, her sparkling loveliness undiminished by hours of dancing, was still romping though a country dance with every appearance of enjoyment. But however tedious she found these occasions, Lisa never begged off: to stay home while Katya went out to reap social triumphs would certainly have exposed Katya to the full measure of her mother's resentment. This was not a one-sided sacrifice: Katya, on her part, never quite lost sight of her sister, and whenever she recognized the white look of exhaustion on Lisa's resolutely smiling face, would insist upon going home immediately, in total disregard of her dance partners' anguished protests.

Lisa finished her prayers and slipped into bed, calling to the maid to blow out the candle. But she lay for a long time staring into the darkness. The young Englishman with the kind smile kept coming into her mind. She didn't know why it was that she found the memory so pleasant. It was a particularly charming smile, she decided sleepily, with his rather thin lips curling up at the corners just as though he found everything around him endearingly amusing. And his gray eyes had smiled, too, with great kindness. But then those gray eyes had turned from her, their expression altering, a blindly fascinated look filling them as he gazed at Katya.

And she had felt strangely bereft, as if a ray of sunlight that had been warming her had shifted, taking its comfort and warmth elsewhere.

Being noticed and then forgotten because Katya was there was not a novel experience for Lisa. It happened all the time without giving her a moment's pang. In fact, since she didn't care for any of the young men who came to the house, it merely amused her. Nor did it give her any satisfaction to know that many of these same young men, after being jarred off their course by Katya's blinding beauty, would eventually return to pay court to her: Katya might be an enchantress, but it was Lisa who was the legitimate daughter—the heiress, since there were no sons, to the Vorontzov estate.

Needless to say it was the countess who minded this state of affairs and couldn't prevent herself from inveighing darkly against her stepdaughter's encroaching, scheming nature.

"Scheming? Katya? Oh, maman!"

"Well, if you are too stupid to see it . . . Upon my word, Lisa, it's almost as if you gloried in being outshone by her. Why, she deliberately goes out to turn everyone's head, which is a singularly disgusting thing for anyone in her position to do."

"Maman, I assure you it isn't so at all. You are mistaken."

What her mother could never understand—and Lisa by now had despaired of making it clear to her—was that Katya's flirtations were performed almost automatically, with the same impersonal charm with which a Kolossova would smile upon her audience from the stage of the Opera House. Katya couldn't distinguish one admirer from another; for her they were a background, an audience. If she liked one better than the rest, as often as not it was because he was a more satisfactory partner to stand up with at a ball.

The fact was that Katya's one all-consuming passion was dancing. Monsieur Duroc, a retired old ballet master, hired when the two girls were still children, had instructed them in all the current dances from the stately polonaise to the lively mazurka, which was just beginning to come into fashion. They had mastered the intricacies of the cotillion and were considered among the best pupils. But the little dancing master's eyes had always lighted with special approval when he watched Katya's performance. She had taken to dancing as though it were her special element, something that she had been born and bred to. Although she hated discipline of any kind, her lithe young body submitted happily to the stern disciplines of the ballet, which she insisted on being taught as well as the more usual forms of social dance. Monsieur Duroc was at first dubious about the propriety of instructing a young lady in a dance which was only practiced by the lower classes for the enjoyment of the higher. But after it had been made clear to him (by the count; the countess had icily disassociated herself from anything so unsuitable) that there would be no objections, he was only too delighted to do so.

As a little girl, Katya used to say, "I will never marry. When I grow up, I will be a dancer." If it had been possible for a daughter of Count Vorontzov to do so, she would gladly have given up her social successes to be a lowly pupil at Didelot's Imperial Ballet School.

A childish conceit—but it was often borne in on Lisa that for all her seductive ways, her beloved sister was still a child at seventeen. Lisa couldn't see her falling in love with any of her admirers: she was as incapable of a serious emotion as a butterfly. Whereas, lacking as she herself was in the pleasant art of flirtation, Lisa often felt a longing, a readiness for something serious, something that would claim her whole heart. Instinctively she knew that if she were to fall in love, it would be no light affair but an enduring passion.

It hadn't happened yet, which was why Lisa, in spite of her mother's repinings, had been perfectly content to be eclipsed by her sister. Last night, however, had been a little different. She had suddenly felt that she would give anything to be the one on whom Monsieur Graham's gray eyes were arrested with that dazzled look.

But then what is there about me to dazzle a man, she thought, lying in her bed as straight and motionless as an arrow. With faint wryness she repeated to herself the endearments Katya was fond of lavishing upon her: my little white mouse, my dear little brown sparrow, my little dove. Who would look upon any of these with a bird of paradise strutting by?

And yet there had been kindness in his eyes. Everyone is dazzled by Katya at first. Perhaps after a while he will get used to her and see me! Comforted by the thought, she sighed and slept.

CHAPTER 3

But in the days that followed, Graham showed no signs of getting used to Katya. He was far too well bred to distinguish one sister from the other, but the look with which he followed Katya was unmistakable. At such times, Lisa thought with a painful compression of her heart, his self-possessed composure, so suitable to a young man holding a responsible post in the British embassy, melted away, and his face held the yearning look of a lovesick boy.

As for Katya, she treated him as she treated all the other young men who clustered around her. Sometimes she flirted with him outrageously, bringing him to the pinnacle of hope; only to plunge him into despair as her volatile attention was drawn elsewhere. Graham was a realistic young man. He would tell himself sternly that those deceptively soft looks of hers were merely an effect produced by the shadowy length of her improbable eyelashes, and signified nothing. Nevertheless, every time her eyes rested on him caressingly, his head would swim a little and he would find himself indulging in the wildest hopes.

He consoled himself with the thought that if he had not touched her heart, neither had anyone else. Occasionally she fancied a slight preference for a certain Captain Kozlov, a dashing young officer who, in the expectation of being sent to fight the Georgian tribes, had grown a pair of huge mustachios, affected Caucasian dress—high boots, furred baldric and all—and was for that reason a great favorite with the ladies. Graham, with a curling lip, apostrophized him mentally as a puppy and a straw-witted caper merchant, but it hurt him to the quick to see

Katya's eyes brighten whenever he approached and to watch the alacrity with which she accepted his invitation to a mazurka.

"How can she . . .?" He was not aware of speaking out loud and was quite startled when Lisa, who was standing near him, said earnestly in her soft voice: "She doesn't, really, Monsieur Graham. But Captain Kozlov dances the mazurka better than anyone else and Katya loves to stand up with a good partner."

"Are you sure, countess?" But before Lisa gave him any further encouragement, he recalled himself. He said, flushing, "What a fatuous fellow I am! Forgive me, countess, I don't know what I was thinking of. . . ! I am always amazed to hear how unexceptionably you speak English: no trace of an accent."

As Lisa acknowledged his compliment with a faint smile, he made haste to ask her hand for the cotillion.

By this time Graham had become a frequent and accepted visitor to Vorontzov palace. The old count had taken a liking to him and would often invite him to his apartments. There, surrounded by the martial mementos of his earlier years, the old soldier would talk about the Turkish wars in which he had distinguished himself. He would also dwell nostalgically on his memories of Catherine the Great, who to Graham's sedate ears was beginning to sound more and more like a proper old hellcat, rather in the style of Lady Henrietta Bessborough, who too had a predilection for younger men.

Prince Dmitry Lunin often made a third in these conversations. He was on a special footing in the Vorontzov household; the old count looked on him more or less as a son he never had, the countess valued him for the distinction he lent to her parties, and the young ladies treated him as an uncle too old to be involved in what he plainly regarded as their nursery activities, but glamorous in a distant way.

Graham found himself liking him, too. His reputation might be a murky one, replete with seductions and duels, but he looked and acted like a gentleman. His manners were impeccable, he was a superb horseman and excellent shot and he exuded an aura of tremendous elegance. His appearance was unmistakably Slavic. He had sharply canted cheekbones and eyes and a sinuous Russian mouth with secretively indented corners. Nevertheless, he reminded Graham of some redoubtable Corinthians he had known in London, and so far he had not encountered in him any of the peculiar behavior that he had learned to expect in his dealings with the Russian court.

It took a little maneuvering for Graham to keep abreast—and sometimes ahead—of the coterie of young men of fashion who dangled after the two sisters. Diplomatic training helped. Not content with merely asking Countess Lisa and Mademoiselle Katya to stand up with him at assemblies and balls (his performance in the ballroom being creditable but not remarkable), he elected to strive for the unusual. He persuaded the count to have his daughters' portrait painted by his friend Sir Robert Kerr Porter, the well-known painter and traveler who had just been appointed historical painter to the tsar. Sir Robert, an amiable man, welcomed him to the sittings to amuse his subjects, and even presented him with one of the preliminary sketches of Katya, caught in the full bloom of triumphant beauty, agreeing indulgently as he did so that she was indeed a nonpareil.

"Though I myself find her sister the more interesting of the two—to a painter, that is," he added with a twinkle, meeting Graham's astonished gaze. "Your Mademoiselle Katya's beauty is so palpable, so easy to capture that it offers no challenge. But her sister is not so simple. There are all manners of possibilities in that pale little face. It could be that of a saint or a martyr . . ."

"Yes, well, she is extremely religious," Graham said, somewhat blankly.

"There is a capacity for suffering, for strong feelings there—I have seen many such faces in Russia." He shook his handsome head reflectively. "Oh, there is a great deal in that quiet little countess."

Graham had a miniature made from the drawing and never parted from it, carrying it about in his vest pocket next to his heart.

He was also able to secure the young ladies' company at the ascension of a balloon, which took place in the grounds of the Cadet Corps Academy, with all the young warriors-to-be drawn up in martial ranks in their white and scarlet uniforms and by special dispensation allowed to cheer when the balloon rose up.

But his greatest coup was arranging a visit to the dancing school, where young girls and boys from the lower classes, many of them serfs, were being taught ballet. The success of this excursion surpassed his greatest expectations. Graham knew, of course, that Katya adored ballet, but was taken aback by the earnestness with which she thanked him: "The very thing I wanted most to see. How did you know?"

"By making a devout study of your desires," Graham told her. He lifted the small hand she had laid upon his sleeve and kissed it gently. "Have you not noticed, Mademoiselle Katya, what a great object it is with me to please you?"

"Oh, yes! So very obliging of you!" But although she let her hand linger in his, her attention had already slipped away from him. With deep concentration she was watching the young dancers being put through their paces by the renowned Monsieur Didelot, who upon learning of his distinguished visitors had come out to guide the class himself.

"How delightful!" she breathed rapturously, watching the foppish little maestro strolling slowly through the row of dancers, who moved gracefully from one attitude to another in response to his command, and occasionally tapping a faultily placed limb with his cane. "Oh, how I would love to be one of them!"

Just then the cane descended sharply on the ankles of one of the pupils not moving fast enough to obey a command, and Graham said, smiling, "Are you quite sure you would, Mademoiselle Katya?"

"Oh, *that*," Katya said impatiently. "That's nothing. She deserved it, for not attending properly."

Countess Elena Petrovna, who had accompanied her daughters to this event, carefully adjusted her Persian shawl across her shoulders and remarked to no one in particular: "If everybody who deserved a whipping got it . . ." Her eyes just barely grazed her stepdaughter's unconscious figure with a malevolent expression that vanished as soon as she realized that she was being observed.

Graham was well aware of the countess's dislike for her beautiful stepdaughter. Although she took good care to keep it hidden when the count was present—together with the rest of the household, she was in awe of him—it found expression in countless little snubs and setdowns, a never-stopping campaign to disparage her in the eyes of her admirers. But the full extent of it became apparent to him in an interview that took place in the countess's apartments the day after the felicitous visit to the ballet school. Invited to take tea with the countess in her apartments, Graham was not overly surprised to find that this was strategically timed to take place precisely while Katya was taking her dance lesson.

"Well, now that we are cozily by ourselves . . ." the countess began.

Graham's lips twitched at this slightly inaccurate introduction. Besides the countess and Lisa, who sat by her side quietly working on a piece of embroidery, the morning room held at least a dozen more people. Three or four faded, genteel pensioners sat around busily sewing and mending, bearing the obsequiously alert look common to their kind, ready to spring to their feet whenever the countess put out a languid hand for her handkerchief or dropped a reticule. The ancient majordomo in a white wig was bringing in a silver samovar, while several housemaids loaded a nearby table with pastries and hors d'oeuvres of all kinds. Around them there pranced a skinny, lavishly madeup creature of indeterminate sex: the house fool. Under the table Graham spied a couple of dwarfs, huge-headed and bedizened. A small blackamoor, in a saffron-colored turban, stood at the door holding a salver.

Altogether, Graham thought, it was the typical picture of a Russian noblewoman *chez elle*.

After a few minutes of inconsequential talk, the countess came to the point. "Since you seem to take such an interest in our Katya," she said, keeping her eyes studiously on her embroidery, "it is only right that you should know her antecedents. You are, of course, aware that she has been adopted into our family. What you may not know is that she is the count's natural daughter. My husband does not like to have this discussed, and in general his will is my law. Nevertheless, I feel that a young man of good birth showing an interest in her should know with whom he would be allying himself before he becomes too deeply involved. We all love our Katya, but there are certain traits, alien and deeply rooted. God knows if they can ever be eradicated . . ."

"Surely, countess," Graham said, smoothly interrupting her, "you needn't worry on that score. You must be aware that anyone knowing Mademoiselle Katya would not wish to alter her in any particular."

The countess shrugged her shoulders. Her needle stabbed viciously into her embroidery, and Lisa stirred uneasily by her side. "One can't help but wonder what your noble uncle would think of such an alliance."

"Ah, but that's one advantage of being in the junior branch," Graham rejoined. "One is able to marry to please oneself. And at any rate the young lady's attractions are so considerable as to offset any small disadvantages."

The countess gave a strident laugh. "My dear young man, I really don't know why you are telling me this," she said, unfairly but dexterously changing grounds. "What have I to do with this? The count is the one to decide. He may not want to part with his treasure yet. Oh, I daresay the time will come when he will find it necessary to make it worthwhile for some honest if deluded man to ally himself with our poor Katya, overlooking not only her illegitimacy but also such faults of character as would give any rational man pause—her vicious temper, her vulgar flirtations . . ."

"Maman," said Lisa softly but with great distress. Before Graham, pale with anger, had a chance to speak, she put down her embroidery and rose to face him.

"My mother is unjust," she said. Her voice faltered, but her blue eyes were steady on his. "There is neither viciousness nor vulgarity in my sister's character, only liveliness—and complete lack of pretense. Any man would be fortunate to win her love."

"Lisa!" the countess uttered, scandalized. "Well, upon my word!"

"I am sorry, maman, but I do love her and I won't have anyone—not even you—I can't bear it when you—" her voice trembled to a stop. Tears welled in her eyes; knuckling them like a child, she ran from the room, the blue sash of her dress streaming after her. The little blackamoor, rolling his eyes, flattened himself against the wall to let her pass.

Graham stared after her, forgetting for a moment his outraged anger at her mother. It was as though a pale pastel sketch had suddenly acquired color and depth; a person hitherto unsuspected had addressed him with firmness and dignity.

"Lisa is an angel," said the countess. "She is incapable of seeing evil in anyone. Now here is someone who's all goodness and sweetness—but all you men can see is vulgar good looks!"

Graham bowed coldly. "Unquestionably, Count Vorontzov is equally fortunate in both his daughters. . . . Your servant, madame." With this he took his leave.

Upon leaving her mother, Lisa sought refuge in her bedroom, casting herself upon her bed and finding relief for her feelings in a burst of tears. She wasn't quite sure why she was weeping. Part of it was the distress and fear that always overcame her when her mother revealed her true feelings about Katya. But for the countess to do so before Graham! She had a shaming feeling that her mother was not the only one who had exposed herself.

She was still weeping when Katya came bursting in, her cheeks as pink as peonies, her black braids flying. "So here you are! I've been looking for you everywhere. Oh, Lisa, I have had such a splendid lesson." She twirled ecstatically, her white dress ballooning about her. "Monsieur Duroc says . . . Lisa! What is it? You are crying!" She dropped to her knees next to the bed.

"It's nothing, I—" Lisa strove to hold back her tears, but they kept sliding down her pale cheeks.

"How nothing? You never cry for nothing! Did anyone hurt you? I'll kill them!"

Lisa produced a watery smile. It might have been the same fiery morsel of a child who years before would square off before a teasing boy cousin, crying, "Leave her alone or I'll kill you!"

"Really, it's nothing, dearest. A little argument with maman. Look, it's all over, no more tears."

She blew her nose and produced a firmer smile. Katya sat back on her heels and eyed her anxiously. "I simply can't bear it when you cry," she said with another of her tempestuous hugs. "You're such a silly dear little thing, and I do love you so. I won't let anyone hurt you."

"Now, you're the silly one." Lisa dropped a kiss on the silky, dark curls. "Who's going to hurt me?" She sat up straight and firmly wiped her eyes. "Katya, do you like Monsieur Graham?"

"Like him? Why, of course I do; he's nice."

"No, I mean, *really* like him. He's in love with you, you know."

"Yes, I know." Dimpling, she added with simplicity, "They all are, at one time or another."

"Yes, I know you flirt with all of them outrageously. But this is different; he really does love you. I think he'll probably be going to papa to ask for your hand."

"Oh, do you think so?" said Katya delighted. "That would be splendid fun."

"Yes, but do you love him?"

"I haven't thought about it."

"Well, think about it. And do, do love him, Katya. Please do love him." Her voice faltered.

"Well, I daresay I could," Katya said agreeably. "He is rather a dear, isn't he? A little too gentle and wellbred, though. The sort of man I would prefer would be—oh, someone tall and dark and rather sinister. Like Prince Dmitry, except of course he is much too old . . . Someone who would carry me off and beat me till I loved him."

"That's nonsense," Lisa said reasonably. "Why should you love him if he beats you? If I know you, you would hit him right back!"

Katya went into gales of laughter. Lisa smiled too, albeit somewhat mournfully.

"What nonsense we are talking! But never mind! Just look at this, Lisa." Katya leaped to her feet. Her expression changed, becoming serious, almost solemn. With her small feet in fifth position, she made a preparatory plié and then launched into three impeccable pirouettes, coming to rest on tiptoe, her slender arms arched gracefully above her head. "There," she said, "I wanted you to see this. Berylova does this in *Persis*, and Monsieur Duroc told me I do it as well as she."

With mingled exasperation and relief, Lisa saw that she had forgotten all about Graham.

•

Graham had not planned to declare himself until he had made sure of Katya's feelings toward him. But he was an extremely proper young man, and once the countess had provoked him to what was tantamount to a declaration, he could see nothing for it but to seek an audience with the count and make a formal offer for Katya. This he did at the very next opportunity.

The count heard him out silently with an occasional searching glance from beneath his shaggy white eyebrows. For a long time after Graham had finished, he sat without speaking, his thin fingers playing with a diamond-studded snuffbox decorated with the miniature of Catherine the Great. Finally he said, apparently talking to himself:

"Time flies. It flows away like a river, bearing you along. Only yesterday she was a romping child . . . To me she still is—I have forgotten that she has been growing up while I was getting old." And indeed there was the look of fragility about him that goes with age. The indomitable count suddenly looked very old indeed. He went on, talking to himself. "I have been remiss, indolent. I have not done what I should have done long ago. I have put things off—a national characteristic, I fear."

Without having the slightest idea of what he was talking about, Graham was inclined to agree with him on that score. He was only too well aware, in his dealings with the Russian officialdom on all levels, of the Russian habit of putting things off. It was a maddening characteristic—particularly, he reflected bitterly, since it was coupled with an equally inconvenient tendency to erupt unexpectedly into precipitate and unconsidered action. What was more, you could never predict which of the two they would favor. In fact, it was very difficult to tell what a Russian was thinking at any particular moment. Right now he would have given a great deal to know the thoughts of this particular Russian, whose face, beneath its old-fashioned snowy peruke, had frozen into an impassive Mongolian mask.

Emerging from his reverie, the count flashed a piercing look at Graham. "I don't know if you are aware that Katya is my natural daughter."

"I am aware, your excellency."

"I don't need to explain the circumstances of her birth to you or anyone." There was infinite arrogance in his voice. "She is the daughter of Count Vorontzov, and that makes her good enough for anyone." And upon Graham's quiet agreement, "I daresay you would like to know who her mother was?"

"Not unless you wish to tell me, sir. Was she as beautiful as her daughter?"

The count's grim features relaxed and he gave a curt little nod of approbation. "Yes. She too had a *beauté du diable*. She died giving birth to Katya. When they put the child in my arms, I wanted to strangle it because it killed its mother—and then it looked at me with its mother's eyes. . . . That is all I intend to tell you."

"I have no desire to pry into old secrets, your excellency," Graham said quietly. "It is as I have said. I love Mademoiselle Katya with all my heart. If I were given a hope of eventually gaining hers . . ." Absurdly his voice shook. Damn it, he said to himself angrily, being Russian is infectious, it seems. I am beginning to sound like one myself.

The count gave a grim little chuckle. "Aha," he said, "so the proper and phlegmatic Englishman is capable of emotion, after all. Well, we shall see. There is plenty of time. Katya is a mere child, for all her bold ways."

"I would wait as long as need be."

"Good. In the meanwhile—yes, you have my permission to address her. It would be well to find out how she feels about you. If she doesn't like you, you might as well give it up. You could flog her half to death and she wouldn't budge. Her mother was like that too. . . . I am glad you spoke to me, Graham. There is a certain measure I must take, a business I should have attended to long ago. The truth is it had gone completely out of my mind. I had forgotten that—never mind. I shall not put it off any longer.

He sounded abstracted again. As Graham respectfully took his leave, he couldn't help wondering just what the old man was talking about. He surmised that it had something to do with Katya's status.

He was not able to put this surmise to the test. When he came to the house the next day, he was greeted with the staggering news that the old count was dead. His valet, coming in at bedtime, had found him lifeless at his desk.

CHAPTER 4

In the days following the count's death, Graham, by now all too familiar with Russian ways, was not overly surprised to see the Vorontzov house become a scene of lively sociability, almost of festivity. Mourning cards, their sable borders suitably decorated with such explicit symbols of mortality as death skull and bones, went out to every noble family in Petersburg, and presently the Vorontzov rooms were crowded with commiserating visitors. The lights were shaded and conversations subdued as the countess, in sable habiliments, lay on the couch in the state bedroom with a black-bordered handkerchief in her hand and the two girls at her side, also dressed in mourning. Otherwise it seeemed no different from the usual Tuesday-night squeezes, and seemed to bear no relationship to the dead count lying on the bier in the next room.

Repelled as he was by this barbarous custom, Graham was well aware that if any of those ghastly convivialities had been omitted, the countess would have been convicted of indifference and disrespect to her husband's memory, and her status in high society considerably lowered. The emperor himself condescended to come to pay his respects to the man who had helped his imperial grandmother become known as Great—a visit that left the widow unable to suppress a gleam of ambitious joy that was quite at variance with her weeds of woe. Graham had no doubt that, once the period of mourning was over, she would resume her social rounds with even more zest than before—and enjoy them all the more for being no longer encumbered by the presence of a dictatorial husband thirty years her senior. There certainly had been no love in that marriage; only fear and resentment on one side and indifference on the other.

Others, however, sincerely mourned the old count. At the funeral services, which took place on the third day after his death as tradition commanded, a long line of mourners filed by the open coffin to pay their final respects. Prince Dmitry Lunin's impassive face bore signs of emotion as he gazed down at the stern old face made even sterner by death.

"We were old friends," he told Graham in his excellent English as they were leaving the church. "I became his aide de camp when I was less than twenty. Quite an unlicked cub I was—isn't that one of your felicitous expressions?—but I was licked into shape fast enough; he saw to that. I owe him a great deal. I think in some ways he regarded me as the son he never had. He had never fathered a son, strangely enough; only daughters, on both sides of the blanket—another of your telling expressions. . . ."

His eyes had turned thoughtfully to the two girls who were following the countess with candles in their hands, in the wake of the sumptuous coffin. As they passed him, Graham caught a glimpse of Lisa's face, tearless but drawn, her eyes wearing a dry look of sleeplessness. Katya on the other hand, was openly weeping. In the midst of his compassion, he could not help but marvel at her ability to shed copious tears without in the slightest impairing her beauty; tears merely rolled along her lovely cheeks like perfect pearls.

The old count's unexpected death affected the two sisters profoundly, but in different ways. Katya's was a simple, childish grief; Lisa's a little more complicated. She was unhappily aware of having been remiss in her feelings toward her father while he was alive. She had venerated and feared rather than loved him, and the consciousness of that lack of love tormented her now.

Her oversensitive conscience was also troubled by the involuntary pleasure she felt in Graham's presence while she was supposed to be immersed in grief. He was being equally attentive to both sisters, and she couldn't stop her heart from responding with timid joy to his efforts to console them.

"How good he is, how kind," she thought, her eyes wistfully lifted to his serious face. He was telling them earnestly that great as the shock must have been, at least they could be comforted by the thought that it must have been a quick, painless death, without any suffering.

It was very sweet to be comforted by him, and Lisa felt that it was pointless to tell him that the advantage of painless death was wholly overshadowed in her mind, as it would be in any devout Russian's, by the fact that he had died suddenly, encumbered by unconfessed sins and without the benefit of the last rites to help him on the lonely journey through purgatory that every departed soul must make before it faces its Maker. It was to help him through this terrible travail that Lisa had kept a sleepless vigil by the side of his coffin for two nights, adding her prayers to those of the officiating priest.

She listened silently to Graham as he told them about his own father, an ardent chess player, who at the conclusion of a hard-fought game said, "Checkmate," with a broad smile and immediately died, a happy man.

Katya sighed. "Yes, just like papa. He had been writing a letter; he finished it, signed his name and died. . . ."

Lisa looked at her, startled. "I didn't know that."

"Well, that's how it was. Timofey told nanny and she told me. He said that papa must have died right after signing the letter, because the pen was right by his hand and the signature was still s-smudged. . . ." Katya's voice wavered.

"And he—Timofey, I mean—had no idea what the letter was about?" Graham's voice was eager. Katya shook her head.

Lisa looked at him wonderingly: this curiosity was unlike him. And indeed he himself immediately recognized the impropriety of such a question and apologized for it.

"It's just that the last actions of the revered dead," he went on smoothly, "seem to be fraught with special significance; one can't help speculating on them."

"Yes," Lisa said slowly, "yes, that is so." All the same she was for some reason sure that he was not being quite open with them; that there was something else on his mind. She went on: "You are right, Monsieur Graham. There must be a special meaning in the last actions of a person about to die, whether he knows it or not."

It occurred to her that God, in His supreme mercy, might very well arrange for a dying man to make his last act something of an important and redeeming quality, an act of charity or grace that would make up for his dying unshriven. Ardently she hoped that it was so for her father.

But to her surprise, when she timidly ventured to ask her mother about the content of the count's last letter, the countess merely looked at her, at first blankly, then with growing anger. "Letter? Who told you about a letter? Did that old fool Timofey dare . . .?" Her eyes narrowed in a look that presaged no good to her late husband's valet.

"Dare? You mean dare to read it?" Lisa asked bewildered by her mother's fury. "Yes, that would have been very wrong of him. But maman, he couldn't, he doesn't know how to read. He merely saw that it was there."

The countess was silent, continuing to stare at her with an unfathomable expression. Finally she said: "It was nothing of consequence. Something he began and didn't finish." Her tone precluded any further conversation on the subject.

Lisa desisted. But she was puzzled. As it happened, she had spoken to Timofey herself, before approaching her mother, and according to him, the count had finished and signed that letter. "I know his excellency's signature—each letter like the stroke of an ax—only instead of that curlicue he puts on the last letter of his blessed name, the pen just went straggling down the page. That's when his soul must have taken flight. . . ."

"And you don't know what it was about, Timofey?"

"No; how should I, dear little countess? We are dark people, illiterate. Must have been an important letter, that's for sure. He would finish it if it took the whole night, he said, and no one was to bother him while he was at it. So I didn't dare to come in. Only when I saw that the candles had guttered down, I ventured—and there he was, my beloved master, with his blessed gray head on the desk, the pen fallen out of his dear hand . . ." The old valet's tears were flowing freely now.

Impossible that he had lied or was mistaken—yet there was her mother, equally positive, saying the letter was unfinished and of no consequence. It was idle to speculate about this, but the faint uneasiness about the whole episode persisted in Lisa's consciousness like a troublesome splinter.

Graham too had indulged in some speculation about the count's last letter. Remembering his words in their last interview—"a business I should have attended to long ago . . . I shall not put it off any longer"—he could not help but wonder whether that letter had something to do with Katya. No further mention of it was made to him, however. The will was read;

Katya had been left a generous competency, though, to his relief, not so large as to put her above his touch. More than that he did not know, and it would have been improper to make any further inquiries, however genuine his concern.

Nor did he feel that it was proper at the time of mourning to approach Katya with anything other than the most general expression of devotion. This very correct resolution, however, crumbled much sooner than he had expected.

He had gone to call and found Katya sitting alone in the drawing room, her cheek propped against her hand, as she mournfully contemplated the portrait of her dead father. The unwonted melancholy of her attitude struck him to the heart. Tears stood poised like small pearls at the ends of her ridiculously long eyelashes, and her black gown made her skin look dazzlingly white. Graham had never seen her look more beautiful.

Involuntarily he cried out, "Oh, how I love you," and brought upon himself a startled gaze from her brilliant black eyes.

"Forgive me," he said contritely, "I couldn't help it." He hesitated and then plunged on recklessly. "You know, Mademoiselle Katya, your father, before he died, gave me permission to address you."

"Oh, did he?" Katya said listlessly.

"I beg you to believe," Graham went on earnestly, "that it is not my purpose to plague you with declarations of love, no matter how deeply felt, when your thoughts are—must be—on other, sadder subjects. I merely want you to know how much I love you—how much I hope that one day you might bring yourself to think about it. Perhaps I am being presumptuous. . . ."

"Oh, no," Katya said, "I don't mind." Making an evident effort to rouse herself from her lethargy, she added, "I do thank you; I am very much obliged to you."

"Obliged! Oh, my lovely, adorable Katya!" He captured her small hand. It lay passive and warm in his grasp. "I won't press you now. If I only knew that there was hope, that you did not hold me in total aversion . . ."

"Aversion? Oh, no," Katya exclaimed impulsively. "How could I do so? You are a very nice man. And besides, if papa—if papa liked you . . ." All at once her lovely face convulsed into a grimace like a grief-stricken child's, and she began crying, noisily and helplessly.

"Don't," Graham said distracted. "Don't cry, my beautiful one, I can't bear it."

Falling on his knees, he drew her into his arms. Katya laid her head on his shoulder and went on weeping.

It was thus that the countess, coming into the drawing room with Lisa, found them.

"Well, upon my word," she cried, her eyes lighting on Katya with unconcealed contempt. "Really, Katya, it is unbelievable that you—yes, even you—could be so forgetful of the proprieties."

Graham gently relinquished the weeping girl and rose to his feet. "I must proffer my humblest apologies . . ." he began.

But the countess, paying no attention, went on flaying her victim. "And your father not a week in his grave!"

"Maman, I beg of you," Lisa said in a low voice, moving protectively toward her sister.

"No, Lisa, I won't have it, not in my house. If she thinks she can go on as she pleases, just because her father isn't here to scold her . . ."

"Oh," Katya cried, springing to her feet, "if only he were! I wouldn't mind if he scolded me or even beat me. I would dance for him whatever he wanted till I dropped . . . Oh, just to see him again!" A fresh onslaught of tears overwhelming her, she went running out of the room. Lisa made to follow her and stopped, indecisive, her troubled eyes on Graham, who said immediately:

"The fault is entirely mine."

"I daresay you were consoling her," said the countess, with something disagreeably near a sneer.

How I dislike that woman, Graham thought. Making sure that none of the dislike showed on his face, he went on, calmly, "On the contrary, I fear I pained Mademoiselle Katya by a reference to her father, who, as I told her, permitted me, just before his death, to address my suit to her."

"You have certainly found an inappropriate time for it." The countess's voice was icy.

Graham bowed slightly. "I am aware. But there was a reason for my precipitateness. A possibility has arisen of my being sent to Vienna within the not-so-distant future," he said, smoothly improvising on the spot. He was marginally aware of a gasp of, he supposed, surprise from Lisa. "I was perhaps unduly anxious for that reason to secure some understanding of your daughter's feeling toward me . . ."

"And it seems you have."

Graham bowed again. "At least she is now aware of mine. I agree that it was improper to express them so impetuously at this place and time. Pray accept my apologies."

As he kissed Lisa's hand in the course of taking his leave, after having performed a similar civility for her mother, he was startled to feel how cold it was. He looked up at her with intrigued attention and was startled anew by the still pallor of her face. She could barely manage the pleasant little smile she always had for him. For a moment he wondered if he had offended her, and then the reason for it dawned on him. "I am threatening to take her beloved sister away from her, to another country," he thought, enlightened. "Of course, she must wish me at the devil."

As he quitted the drawing room, he was momentarily aware of trepidation—would she oppose his suit?—and then dismissed the thought as unworthy. No, there was not a selfish bone in Lisa's body. Whatever her feelings, she would never stand in the way of her sister's happiness. The countess, spiteful termagant that she was, was the one to fear. He wouldn't put it past her to wreck his hopes out of sheer dislike for her stepdaughter.

He would have been vastly relieved if he could have been there to see the countess's reaction to his proposal. For a while she had paced the room, her lips vindictively thinned, her ringed fingers plucking at the fringe of her black silk shawl. But as Lisa watched with anxiety, her face cleared. She said slowly to herself, "Perhaps it might be better that way. As long as she is out of my sight, so that I don't have to see her hateful face wherever I go."

A look of distress crossed Lisa's face, but she remained silent. The countess went on thinking aloud. "And if he were to leave Russia, which seems to be a pretty sure thing, as he puts it, and to take her with him. . . . Well, and why are you sniveling?"

"I shall miss her so," Lisa said softly, applying the handkerchief to wipe away the tears that had welled in her eyes despite all efforts to control herself.

The countess shook her head in disbelief. "This defies credence! To think that you don't mind being totally eclipsed by her vulgar good looks! Why, I have lost count of the young fools who run after her with their tongues hanging out, like dogs after a bitch in heat." Like most Russian ladies, Countess Elena Petrovna talked elegant French when she was out in society; her way of expressing herself in the bosom of her family when she relaxed into Russian was far less refined. "The trouble with you, Lisa, is that you have no dignity and no sense of your own worth. 'I'll miss her so!' Well, you'll get over that when you start going out into society again and find how pleasant it is not to be eternally playing second fiddle."

"I have never minded Katya's success," Lisa said. "And I don't believe I shall want to go out into society if she isn't with me. . . ." A sigh escaped her. "Vienna seems so far away. . . ."

"So it is," the countess said with considerable satisfaction.

"I wonder how Katya will like it away from everything she knows and loves . . . away from me. We have never been parted before . . . But of course she will have her husband and that would make up for everything, would it not? For me it would. I shouldn't care about anything, not leaving Russia or living in a strange land if I could only be with him—" She stopped abruptly, a deep blush spreading over her face, and added hastily: "I mean with the man I loved, if ever I did love anyone . . ."

The countess, unimpressed by this caveat, fixed her with her slightly prominent eyes and said slowly, "So that's the way it is!"

"I don't know what you mean, maman," Lisa protested, blushing even more painfully.

The countess sighed. "It is just as I have said. You have no sense of dignity, Lisa. You set a very low price on yourself. You are a Countess Vorontzov, an heiress in your own right. Isn't it just like you to fall in love with someone totally unsuitable: a younger son, without any expectations other than being a flunky in a British embassy . . ."

"He's not! He's highly valued! Lord Leveson-Gower himself was telling me the other day—" She checked herself and continued quietly. "At any rate, the question doesn't even arise, does it, maman? He loves Katya."

"Yes indeed, and for *her*," the familiar, hateful emphasis was back in her voice, "for her he is certainly good enough. Far better than she deserves, the nameless spawn of a—" She broke off. "And the most important thing is that your father wanted this alliance," she went on. There was a different note in her voice now, as she mentioned the dead count; conciliatory, almost placatory. "He said so himself, didn't he? That he favored young Graham's suit? Needless to say, his wishes are sacred to me. I shall do the best I can for his daughter, unworthy as she is of consideration . . ." She leveled another curious and censorious look at Lisa. "And even this—the fact that *she* has stolen the man you love, however unsuitable he is—even that doesn't make you dislike her? No, I see it doesn't. You are too spineless. I am the one who has minded your humiliation all these years. Not even a spark of resentment out of you. Well, you are a saint, Lisa, fit to be canonized!"

In the days that followed Lisa felt very unlike a saint. Try as she would, she couldn't help feeling a new onslaught of misery as she saw the young Englishman accepted as a successful suitor for her sister's hand. Stepan the footman took his hat and gloves with an understanding smirk, and there was much animated gossip behind the stairs whenever he called. The countess, with unusual complaisance, went out of her way to leave them alone. Lisa once overheard her discussing the situation with a friend. "There is nothing official, of course, *ma chère*, since we are still in mourning, but since I am convinced that this is what my beloved husband would have wished"—again that oddly conciliating note had entered her voice—"I daresay we could call it an understanding."

What troubled Lisa was the feeling that her volatile sister was not perfectly cognizant of the existence of such an "understanding." There was no doubt that she was fond of Graham—who wouldn't be? Lisa thought sadly—but a sense of any special attachment was somehow lacking. Katya seemed to forget all about him when he wasn't there. And surely if she shared his feelings, she couldn't have been so heartfelt in lamentations when she learned of the imminent departure of another admirer, the dashing Captain Kozlov, who had at last received his orders and was getting ready to go to the Caucasus to fight the recalcitrant tribesmen there. Katya had expressed her regrets at seeing him go repeatedly and unrestrainedly, apparently quite unaware of how this affected Graham.

But when Lisa, moved by his evident distress, rebuked Katya for causing it, the latter looked at her in astonishment. "But of course I am sorry that Kozlov is going. He is so amusing to talk to. And the very best dancer—no one dances mazurkas like him!"

"Yes, but, my love, do consider Monsieur Graham's feelings. It must pain him to hear you going on so about another man."

Katya shrugged her pretty shoulders and looked rebellious. "We are not betrothed, after all."

"No, because of papa's death. But he loves you so much, and you have encouraged him to believe that you'll marry him. If it's a mistake—if you don't intend to do so—"

"Oh, I suppose I do. Papa wanted it, after all." Her voice trembled. "If papa wanted me to marry a bear, I would do so!"

"Well, Monsieur Graham is not a bear," Lisa said with some asperity. "He is a kind and excellent young man—"

"Yes, I know, he is a dear. I daresay I'll marry him eventually. But until I do, he does not own me; no one does." Her eyes flashed. "I'll behave as I please."

"And it pleases you to be unkind and thoughtless?" Lisa spoke coldly, and Katya, unaccustomed to this tone from her gentle sister, looked alarmed and expressed contrition.

"And I promise I shall be very good—after we are betrothed."

Altogether her attitude seemed to be that of a child who promises to behave after school begins, but until then. . . ! Lisa couldn't help feeling resentment on Graham's behalf. If I were the one he chose, she thought, how different it would be! I would have no eyes for anyone else. I would be living only for the day when I was his . . . Sometimes, when she saw the hungry and dazzled look with which he followed Katya's every movement, she couldn't help feeling for the first time in her life that perhaps her beloved sister did not deserve such adoration.

It was because of these disturbing feelings that Lisa resolved to go away and make a few days' retreat at a nearby convent.

She had done this every year since she was a child and had always loved the quiet time in a clean white cell, a time of contemplation and prayer unhampered by the outside world. Afterward there would always be a sense of great peace, a lifting of fears and uncertainties. She would return to everyday life cleansed and strengthened.

She couldn't help wondering, as she made preparations for her departure, whether this mightn't be the answer for her. Since God had not seen fit, in His wisdom, to give her the only man she could love, why not sever all connections with the shallow, artificial world that both bored and disgusted her, and retire to that other life? Vividly she could see herself, staff in hand, all her earthly possessions in a small bag slung over her shoulder, wandering through Russia like those devout pilgrims who so often used to break their journeys in the Vorontzov country home; coming back to prayer and contemplation in her cell. The more she thought, the more enviable this seemed to her.

Of course this would have to wait until Katya was married and gone away. Katya had very strong feelings on the subject. She looked upon Lisa's retreats with resentment and suspicion, regarding them as a sort of jail sentence visited upon her sister for some unspecified crime. The fact that these retreats were voluntary made no difference to her somewhat illogical mind.

This time, it seemed, she was more than usually distressed by her sister's departure. She tried to persuade her to stay home and, that failing, offered to go along. Lisa laughed and petted her out of this unlikely notion.

"But you won't stay away long, will you? Promise me that you won't," Katya begged, childlike.

"My love, what a to-do about a week's separation!"

"I don't know, I just have such a feeling *here*," she pressed her hand to her heart, "that you shouldn't go."

"Good heavens, how absurd!" Looking more closely at her sister's face, she saw trouble there. "What is it, dearest? What is making you so uneasy?"

"I don't know," Katya muttered. She looked down, twisting her slender fingers together. "Parasha was telling my fortune the other day. She said there's a big change in store for me, a complete turnabout . . ."

"Well, and so there will be, eventually." Lisa managed a smile. "A journey over the water, no doubt? To a foreign country?" she gibed gently. "Amazing how the servants know everything that goes on in the house."

But Katya shook her head, unsmiling. "No, she said this would be something else, something that will come upon me suddenly like a thunderclap. She saw it in the tea leaves and in the poured wax."

"Well, whatever it is, it won't happen till I come back."

As a matter of fact, Parasha's prediction came true soon after Lisa left. It began not in the Vorontzov Palace but in the elegant building on the Millionnaya Avenue that housed the British Embassy, and it took the form of an innocuous-appearing letter from England. Graham glanced at it, at first casually, then with stunned bewilderment, rereading it several times before he finally took in its contents.

An hour later he was in the Vorontzov drawing room, translating the family solicitor's stilted English into French for Katya's benefit.

"It is my mournful duty to communicate to you the sad news that both your cousins were killed within a few days of each other, Captain Gareth Graham being felled by cannon fire from a French privateer that his ship was pursuing and Mr. Guy Graham a victim of a riding accident. Lord Lyndhurst is naturally prostrated by these misfortunes, but cognizant of his duty to the family, he asked me to communicate to you the news that you, as future Lord Lyndhurst—"

"Future Lord Lyndhurst? You?" Katya's eyes were as round as saucers.

"Yes, since I am the eldest son in our branch of the family, it seems that the title will revert to me upon my uncle's death. It is the strangest thing." He began to fold the document mechanically, his sandy eyebrows clamped together in a perplexed frown. "My poor uncle. He has always been on the outs with my father and never liked our family, and now to have to accept me as his heir. . . . The solicitor tells me that he has been quite ill for a long time, and now this blow—he fears he may not survive his sons for very long."

"And then you will be Lord Lyndhurst," Katya cried. Unfeelingly she clapped her hands. "How splendid for you."

"No, it would only be splendid if you would consent to be Lady Lyndhurst." He caught her hands in his. "You must marry me immediately. Katya, my lovely Katya, say you will."

"Immediately?" The lovely, vivid face before him clouded

over. "You said you wouldn't press me. You know you did."

"I know, I know, it is infamous that I should hurry you in any way, but what am I to do? This change in my prospects means that I must go to England as soon as possible. Pray believe that I have no wish to do so. I am most loath to leave Lord Leveson-Gower with the Napoleon situation at this crucial stage and no one to rely on but that ass Ponsonby, who is incapable of rising from his bed until three in the afternoon. And I can't bear to leave you."

"But I am still in mourning for papa. I couldn't possibly . . ."

"I think under the circumstances it is permissible to overlook the conventions. How could I go to England without you? Why, I even wrote home promising my sisters to bring back a Russian bride." He went on, after a moment's hesitation, "But it isn't only my selfish desire to make you mine. There is another reason that makes me reluctant to leave you. Forgive me, but is it not true that since your father's death there has been a—well, a change? You are no longer as valued in this house as you should be."

Katya returned his troubled look with an unclouded one. "You mean maman, I suppose. Well, it is true that maman has never liked me. But then I have never loved her as a daughter should, either. So it doesn't really matter, does it?"

Graham couldn't help shaking his head over his love's lack of perception. Her sister has a much better understanding of her situation, he thought. He had noticed Lisa's anxious watchfulness, her sensitiveness to the slights and snubs that had passed unnoticed over Katya's unconscious head but were surely only too indicative of things to come.

It was not just the countess. There was a subtle change in most of the servants' attitude to her, as if they were conscious of her changed position now that the count was not there, and those who served the countess directly were sometimes downright insolent. A few days ago, before Lisa had left for her retreat, one of the countess's numerous female pensioners, a distant relative, had quite pointedly ignored Katya, who had spoken to her. It was Lisa who had said to her with gentle dignity, "My sister has just asked you a question, Anna Ivanovna. Are you unable to answer her?" The soft, aloof voice had brought the offending lady up short; she had reddened and stammered and finally bowed herself out of the room. Graham, remembering this episode, was conscious of wonder and gratitude. Diffident and retiring as Lisa was, she would never be found wanting when those she loved needed her. But would she be able to stand up effectively against her mother's unconquerable dislike for Katya, which was bound to get even stronger as time went on?

He said to Katya earnestly, "No, you are not regarded here as you should be. You do not have here the consequence that would be yours in England as my wife—and eventually as Lady Lyndhurst. I know this would mean nothing to you without love, but I hope, I earnestly hope . . ."

"Oh, I think it would be most amusing to be Lady Lyndhurst," Katya assured him. "But to live in England, so far from Russia! Lisa and I always planned to go traveling together, but this is different. I don't even know English very well; not the way Lisa does."

"My own love, that signifies nothing . . ."

"Lisa has been at me to learn English, but . . ." Her brilliant eyes sought Graham's questioningly. "Do you suppose Lisa could come to live with us?"

"Nothing would give me greater pleasure," Graham told her. "I regard her as my sister already."

"Oh, then," Katya brightened visibly, "then . . . Oh how I wish she were here instead of in the convent. I could ask her what she thought about this."

"I am sure," Graham put in adroitly, "she would approve of my plans for us."

"Would she? Yes, I daresay she would. She wants me to marry you. . . . Well, then, I suppose it must be so."

Graham kissed her hands, and then, emboldened, her lips. She did not repulse him, and he was filled with delight. "I am the happiest man in the world," he said, "and I shall be the most envied man in England."

He told himself that his happiness was complete now. If there was a tiny voice inside him pointing out that her agreement was not totally wholehearted and that the one thing that clinched it was the possibly doubtful prospect of Lisa's joining them in England, he drowned it out quickly. An understandable maidenly reluctance . . . a natural attachment to her country and her sister . . . surely in time these would be overcome and she would love him unconditionally. She couldn't do otherwise when he loved her so!

CHAPTER 5

Ordinarily Katya went to sleep as soon as her head touched the pillow. But tonight she found it difficult to do so. A vague uneasiness filled her, making her toss and turn and come wide awake with a galvanic start just as she was on the verge of dropping off to sleep. It was two days now since Graham's unexpected announcement, and she still had not come to a final decision even though everyone seemed to take it for granted that she had.

Marriage to Graham had never been a reality to her, just one of several pleasant options to be decided on at leisure. She had thought she very well might—she supposed she eventually would—marry Graham, of whom she was quite fond, particularly since her father had apparently wanted her to do so. But now the possibility was fairly likely to become reality, and all at once she was faced with the prospect of seeing her life completely changed. "Parasha knew what she was talking about," she thought ruefully. "Just like a thunderbolt!"

Not that the prospect was altogether displeasing. She was particularly tickled by the idea of becoming Lady Lyndhurst. Even now Katya couldn't help giggling as she remembered the stunned expression on her stepmother's face when she was apprised of this.

"You? Lady Lyndhurst?" Her lips had puckered on the title as if she had bitten into a sour apple, and Katya hadn't been able to forgo a little preening.

"Yes, maman, because I will be—what is it I will be, Graham? The letter said you will be the Most Noble the Marquis of Lyndhurst, and that means I will be what?"

"Your Ladyship will be the Marchioness of Lyndhurst," Graham had said, smiling at her.

"Simply unbelievable. Oh, but I can't wait to tell Lisa. She has been countess all along, but I shall be marchioness and that is much grander! Oh, dear me, how very droll this is!"

Even as she went into peals of laughter, she perceived that the countess was far from amused. But she had been pleasant enough, saying smoothly to Graham that under the circumstances she had no objection to an earlier marriage.

"Of course, we shall miss our dear Katya, though I daresay her exalted new position will put us all out of that heedless little head." She had tapped Katya smilingly on the cheek with her fan. "I daresay she can't wait to be off to England."

Katya had stared at her outraged. "How can you say that, maman! When you know how much I hate to leave Russia. Why, if I thought that this meant I would never return—or never see my dear Lisa—why, why, nothing would make up for that. I should be utterly miserable. I would give up the whole thing!"

Her voice had trembled with indignant tears, and maman had tapped her on the cheek with her fan again and said, still with that indulgent smile that stopped short of her eyes, "Come, come, child. You don't want Monsieur Graham to think that you care so little for him . . ."

But I do care for him, Katya thought, flinging herself about angrily in her bed. I don't want to pain him; it's just that I want to go to Vienna—no, it's London now!—as little as I would want to go to Caucasus with Captain Kozlov, who came to say good-bye yesterday and looked so very sad. That's the trouble with people loving you; you hate to pain them. . . . Oh, I wish Lisa were here to sort it all out for me, the way she always does.

She was conscious of a grievance against Lisa for being away in a convent precisely at the time she was needed here. "I know what," she decided, "I will send Fyodor the coachman to the convent with a message for Lisa, tell her how badly I need her, and she will come back immediately and we'll talk, and she'll tell me exactly what to do."

Soothed by the thought, she finally fell asleep.

It seemed to her that she had been asleep for less than a minute when she felt herself being shaken awake. She opened her eyes on a darkness that was just barely tinged by dawn and saw a figure standing by her bedside.

"What is it?" she mumbled sleepily. "What do you want, nanny?"

Even as she asked, she realized that it couldn't be their ancient nurse, who had accompanied Lisa to the convent. She took a harder look at the silent figure by her bed and presently recognized the countess's own maid, Arina, a forbidding creature of grenadierlike stature and dour countenance. She was generally disliked in the Vorontzov household for her repellent ways, but the countess valued her not only for her uncanny gift for dressing hair as well as any French hairdresser, but also for her total devotion. She never had anything to do with the young ladies, and Katya was both puzzled and alarmed to see her by her bedside.

"What is it?" she demanded, now wholly awake. "Is there something wrong?"

The maid said impassively: "You are to get up and dress, Katerina Vassilevna."

"Dress?"

"Yes, ma'am. You will be leaving for the country in half an hour. Those are her grace's orders."

For a moment Katya was convinced that she wasn't awake but, on the contrary, had just embarked on an especially senseless nightmare.

"Maman's orders? Have you gone mad?"

"No, ma'am. My lady wants you to get dressed and be ready to leave for the country immediately."

"For the country? I don't understand! With Lisa away. . . ?" A sudden fear struck at her. "Is there something wrong with Lisa?"

"As to that, I can't tell you, ma'am. Her grace the countess sent me to tell you . . ."

But Katya, no longer paying attention to her, had leaped out of bed and was simultaneously elbowing herself into her dressing gown and pushing her small feet into her Turkish slippers. The next moment she was flying down the corridor toward the countess's apartments, Arina stalking woodenly behind her.

The countess, who, still in her peignoir, was seated at her desk, writing, looked up as Katya came bursting in.

"Maman, what is happening? Why are we going to the country? I can't understand this. Is it Lisa? Has something happened?" She broke off as the countess turned upon her a look of cold and implacable hatred.

"How dare you come into my room like this?" Her voice held a note Katya had never heard before, and despite herself she flinched.

"But, maman . . ."

"And don't call me maman. To think that for years I had to submit to being called mother by a creature like you, you wretched serf's spawn!" She laughed, a hateful grinding sound, as Katya stood before her, turned to stone. "Oh, yes, I know what everyone, including myself, thought. A result of your father's indiscretion with someone from our own circle—perhaps even higher. He saw to it that we all believed that. Well, it's all a lie. Your mother was nothing—a dirty peasant, a debauched dancing girl from a serf ballet troupe, a *serf!* And that's what you are—a serf!"

"But this can't be so," Katya stammered. "My father . . ."

The countess smiled. "In his lifetime you were his serf as well as his daughter. He never did anything to change this; he was content to let you stay a serf. And now that he is dead, that's all you are!"

Katya stared at her tormentor with dilated eyes. "I don't believe it. He loved me—he wouldn't have left me to your mercy like that." As a sort of illumination came to her, she blurted out, "That letter—the letter that Timofey saw him writing and that you are keeping so secret from all of us—it was about me, wasn't it? He did try to do something about me before he died! And you—what did you do with the letter?"

Twin red spots burned on the countess's cheekbones. "Be quiet! Do you know what happens to impertinent serfs? They can be whipped to death. My mother had a housemaid whipped to death because she had spilled coffee on her favorite dress. And you are my serf, my chattel, with whom I can do what I want!"

"You have hated me all these years," Katya said wonderingly. "I knew you weren't fond of me, but you *hated* me . . ." She lifted her chin. "Well, what will you do to me now? Have me killed as your mother did her housemaid?"

"There's no need for melodrama," said the countess coldly.

"We live in more enlightened times now, and I have too much respect for your late father's memory, in spite of all I have had to suffer from him. You will be taken to where you came from and stay the rest of your life where you belong, with your own kinfolk."

"My kinfolk?" A vague curiosity rose up in her. Immediately another feeling supervened. "But Lisa is my kinfolk. My sister."

"My daughter will no longer be contaminated by association with you. She need no longer endure playing second fiddle to a miserable serf girl, seeing the man she loves stolen away from her—"

Katya's eyes opened wide in outrage. "You are lying. I have never in my life done so. I would rather die than—"

"Really, your ladyship?" Special venom informed her voice as she pronounced the title. She leaned forward, stabbing Katya with her angry eyes. "I would have kept to myself the discovery so discreditable to all of us," she said. "I would even have let you make a good marriage! But when I saw you not only stealing the only man my daughter cared for but actually profiting by it, being elevated so ludicrously above your station . . . No, indeed, my dear marchioness-to-be, that I really couldn't tolerate. I knew the time had come to scotch you and your pretensions."

"My sister loves Graham? I don't believe it. You are just saying so to hurt me—and to justify yourself. Lisa would have told me. My sister and I never keep anything from each other!"

"You are not to call Lisa your sister," the countess said coldly. "There will be no further contact between you and my daughter. Now go and do what you are told. It's time for you to start getting used to your station in life."

Katya didn't move. She said, looking at her stepmother steadily, "But she *is* my sister. You are not my mother and you have always hated me. I know it now. But Lisa and I are sisters and we love each other. She will always remain my sister and nothing you can do will change that."

Not answering, the countess turned back to her desk and resumed writing. She said over her shoulder, addressing Arina, who had been standing at the door impassively listening to the conversation:

"Send Fyodor up to me. I want to give him his last instructions and the letter which he is to deliver to the village headman when he leaves his prize there. Meanwhile you take her back to her room and see to it that she is dressed and ready to go in twenty minutes. You know what to do. . . . Well, what are you waiting for? Take her away."

With a swift, lithe movement, Katya stepped back, evading the abigail's grasp. "You lay a hand on me," she said, between her teeth, her black eyes burning dangerously, "and I will kill you." At that moment she had an uncanny resemblance to her dead father.

Head high, without another glance at the countess, she left the room.

CHAPTER 6

"No," Lisa said stubbornly. "I can't believe this. It simply can't be so."

"What do you mean, it can't be so?" Countess Vorontzov's voice shook with exasperation. At that moment, Lisa was sure, only Graham's presence was preventing her mother from boxing her ears. "It *is* so. Your beloved Katya has disgraced herself by running away with that impossible Captain Kozlov—I've never had any use for him, he and his great mustachios!—and is now on the way to the Caucasus with him. And don't say again that Katya wouldn't. It's time you learned what she is like. You have always been blind to her faults—and if I may say so, that holds true of you too, my dear sir," she added acidulously to Graham.

"I am only too aware of my blindness," Graham said steadily. Lisa stole a quick look at him and her heart turned over at the look of suppressed misery on his drawn face. "I have always known, of course, that Katya's feelings for me weren't—couldn't have been—equal to mine. But I did feel that at least she looked upon me as a friend—enough so that she would tell me about any previous attachment . . ."

"But there wasn't any!" Lisa broke in. "I would have known if there had been. We always tell each other everything. There are no secrets between us."

But of course there were—on her side, at least. The thought of it brought faint color to her cheeks and made her look away quickly.

"Unfortunately you were away at the time, countess," Graham pointed out wearily.

"And that's another thing. Not to wait for me! To take such a step without talking to me, without leaving a word for me. . . ."

Again she relived the first minutes of her return from the convent: the empty rooms of their suite shrieking Katya's absence, the servants' sidelong frightened glances, and finally the unbelievable revelation. She hadn't believed it then, and she didn't now.

"But she did send you a message with Ivan the Coachman," said the countess. "As I told you many times before. And you heard him yourself, as did Monsieur Graham . . . If the stupid fool had come to me directly after he had taken her to Captain Kozlov's lodgings . . . Well, it's done now; no use repining."

"But I can't understand why." Lisa twisted her slender hands together. She was aware that she was merely adding to her mother's irritation and Graham's misery, but she couldn't stop. "As I understand it, immediately after learning of Monsieur Graham's great new prospects—not that that would weigh with Katya . . ."

"Wouldn't it, though!" An angry laugh escaped her mother. "She positively flaunted herself at the prospect of being a marchioness. I never saw anything so vulgar." She agitated her black fan as though to waft away all traces of Katya's regrettable vulgarity.

Graham's lips tightened. He said coldly: "She merely expressed her pleasure at my good fortune in her usual enchantingly lively manner . . . But as you say, Countess Lisa, it didn't weigh with her—unfortunately for me." He rose from his chair, evidently eager to escape.

Lisa looked at him incredulously.

"And yet you see no incongruity in this? Monsieur Graham, my sister is an impulsive girl, granted, but this is beyond everything! One day she exults in being the future marchioness of Lyndhurst, and the next morning she runs away with an impecunious young officer who, I know, means nothing to her!"

The countess closed her fan with a snap. "Enough of this! Lisa, you are distressing Monsieur Graham needlessly. . . ."

"Monsieur Graham," Lisa persisted, disregarding her, "how can you accept it? Can't you see that there must be some terrible mistake?" Graham, who had risen to his feet, looked down at her with weary wonder, and she realized that in all their acquaintance she had never spoken to him at such length with such feeling. "You say you know Katya's feelings were unequal to yours. And indeed it's true, Katya is still a child in many ways, and incapable of great passion. But then, on the other hand, to believe that she was suddenly seized by such a passion for a young man who had previously meant nothing to her that she would leave everything and everybody—ah, no, impossible!"

"Lisa! You forget yourself!"

But there was a sudden, arrested look on Graham's face. "Are you sure of that? Perhaps the news that he was leaving Petersburg with his regiment . . ."

"But we have known about *that* forever, and Katya never minded, except for losing a good dancing partner. That's all it was. I assure you, she liked you much better."

"But then . . ." There was bewilderment in Graham's voice. "Are you sure?" His voice changed, livened. "For that does indeed make a difference."

"Perfectly sure, Monsieur Graham. No, something must have happened—something terrible. . . ."

Graham said, half to himself, "Something that took place after I saw her last. . . ." He was silent, his sandy brows drawn together. Presently his face grew stony. With horrified conjecture Lisa followed his gaze as it turned, coldly accusing, on her mother. The countess, caught unaware in that bleak gaze, flushed a dull crimson and looked downward, her hands tightening on her furled fan.

"Madame," Graham said, "have you been quite open with us?"

In the midst of her distress, Lisa's heart leaped irrationally at that "us."

There was a pause. Then the countess sighed and lifted a pair of candid eyes to him. "No," she said, "not quite . . . I had hoped to conceal our disgrace from you. Unfortunately Lisa has made it impossible." She gave her daughter a fulminating glare. "No, our ambitious little Katya would never of her own accord have renounced the great catch you turned out to be, Monsieur Graham. But that marriage could never take place. You know of Katya's illegitimacy. But her antecedents have turned out to be much worse than anything we could have expected."

The young people listened, horrified, as, not without relish, the countess explained the exact nature of those antecedents.

The two sisters hadn't begun to speculate about the identity of Katya's unknown mother until they had emerged into girlhood. One day when Katya was twelve she had come to her sister in great excitement: "I know who she is—I know who my mother is." It appeared she had overheard two of the countess's bosom friends discussing her resemblance to Princess Eudoxie Lopukhin, a brilliant beauty not in her first youth whose dark good looks were indeed reminiscent of Katya's. They spoke of the count's marked attentions to her in the days gone by—"And at precisely the right time, my dear. Thirteen years ago—Emperor Paul had just come to the throne. Her husband had to take her to the country and everyone knew why . . ." The countess's entrance stopped their conversation. But Katya had heard enough to make her perfectly sure.

"And what's more, Lisanka," her black eyes had blazed with excitement, "she is coming tonight, to the reception!"

That evening had found the two girls at their usual observation post whenever the Vorontzovs entertained: at the top of the staircase on the second floor, peering through the railing at the arriving guests. They were still in pigtails and not allowed below except for a brief appearance with their governess. It was then that Katya had conceived the daring notion of talking to Princess Eudoxie.

"Katya!" Lisa had been appalled. "You can't do that. Imagine how she would feel."

"But if I'm her daughter . . ."

"She couldn't have wanted you," Lisa had pointed out reasonably, "if she allowed papa to take you away from her."

But Katya refused to give up her project. "That doesn't signify; papa probably *made* her give me up. And of course I'll never tell anyone else, just her—it'll be our secret. I just want her to know that I know that she is my mother . . ."

"Nonsense," a voice drawled behind them. The two girls whirled around, startled. So intent had they been on their discussion that they hadn't heard the approach of Prince Dmitry Lunin, who had been closeted with the count and was now on his way down to join the other guests.

He loomed above them, a slight, amused smile lighting up his saturnine face. Lisa, who had always been daunted by the air of tremendous elegance and power that emanated from this particular grown-up, started up, ready to run away. But Katya, quite unintimidated, merely scowled at him: "Why nonsense? If she is really my mother . . ."

"Well, she isn't," said Prince Dmitry. "Your mother is no longer alive."

Katya's warm little paw found Lisa's and closed on it hard; two huge round tears suspended themselves on her long eyelashes. Prince Dmitry looked at her with some compunction. "Yes, she died when you were born. I am sorry to distress you, little one, but I really can't have you embarrassing innocent ladies by claiming them as mothers. Besides, I am sure you prefer knowing the truth."

Katya had nodded desolately. "I wish I knew what she was like, though."

"Oh, as to that—you merely need to wait four more years and look in your mirror. . . . Possibly," his voice altered subtly, "you may not even need to wait that long." He leveled a lorgnette at the vivid little face lifted to him. Lisa, vaguely uneasy, thought she saw in his dark eyes the merest shadow of the look with which he was inexplicably able to make grown-up ladies blush and bridle.

Katya had immediately cheered up. "She was pretty, then? Like me?" she inquired artlessly.

"Yes, quite beautiful. And you are a little baggage." With that he flicked a careless finger along her cheek and left them, strolling elegantly down the marble staircase. . . .

So the beautiful mother had been a serf! Incredulously Lisa listened to the countess saying to an equally incredulous Graham:

"So you see, Katya knew that you would have to be told. I made that clear to her when she begged me to keep it quiet," the countess said with relish. "The future Marquis Lyndhurst could not be allowed to marry a serf girl's daughter."

"Oh, my poor Katya," Lisa whispered.

"The future Marquis of Lyndhurst should have been allowed to have a choice in the matter," Graham said. A small triangle of muscle bunched hard in the corner of his mouth.

The countess looked at him with disdainful amazement. "I do not know how it is in England, but would you really have had a choice, your social position being what it is? Katya understood *that* well enough. Oh, she was a bit crestfallen at first, to be sure, but then she said, 'It doesn't matter whom I marry. If it can't be an earl, at least it'll have to be a good dancing partner . . .'" Lisa saw Graham flinch minutely at this authentic touch of Katya. "Well, she took her own way out, it appears. Katya had always been arrogant. She evidently could not bear to stay here where she used to lord it over everyone, now that everything is changed."

Lisa looked at her wonderingly. "But nothing *is* changed," she said. "She is still my sister."

"And my betrothed," Graham said. "I love Katya; but even if I didn't, I would still be honor-bound to her if she would have me."

The countess's black-silk-clad shoulders lifted in a shrug. "Follow her, then. By now I should imagine it's too late. She is probably married to that scapegrace. Or perhaps not," she added with an unkind laugh. "In that case—again, I don't know how it is in England and how an old family like yours would welcome a tarnished bride. Here in Russia virginity is as important as good birth. But do as you will. I daresay you will call him out. It won't bring her back and it will cause a great deal of scandal, but by all means do so if it pleases you. . . . And now if you will excuse me, I feel a migraine coming on. . . ." Her dismissing look took in Lisa as well as Graham, and they went out together silently.

"Monsieur Graham . . ." Lisa checked herself. "Am I addressing you correctly?" she asked diffidently. "Or are you a lord now?"

"No, not quite yet. I'm merely the heir to the title. In England we don't get the title until we have actually succeeded to it; there can be many a slip between the cup and the lip, as you have seen in the case of my own family. . . ."

They were seated in Lisa's own little reception room, where she had asked him to attend her after they had taken leave of her mother. This was something Lisa would never have done except under special circumstances, and doing so even now had thrown her into confusion. She was aware that Graham was talking about his title in order to help her recover. She looked at him in timid gratitude. There was a furrow between his sandy brows that hadn't been there before, and her fingers twitched, aching to smooth it out. She said: "Monsieur Graham, I am desperately worried about Katya."

He nodded. "So am I. I think I shall have to go to Caucasus after all. No, don't be concerned, I don't intend to call Captain Kozlov out; it would be a mean thing to try to kill a man your sister prefers to me. But certain circumstances might arise. . . ." Meeting her painfully questioning look, he said with difficulty: "According to the regulations, the officers of the imperial army cannot marry without permission. If Kozlov married Katya without such a permission—and obviously there has been no time to get it—he will most likely be punished by house arrest; and if he hasn't yet. . . . In any case, she will need a friend to stand by her. I should have done this before. I blame myself for accepting your mother's story so unquestioningly. But I suppose I have all along felt uncertain about Katya's sentiments for me. That evening she made it quite clear that, my new honors notwithstanding, she didn't really want to accompany me to England. It was only by assuring her that you would be persuaded to make your home with us that I was able to make her consent."

"Oh, Katya!" Lisa breathed with exasperation. "You know, she can really be impossible!"

"It wasn't hard, under the circumstances, for me to accept her preferring someone else—particularly Captain Kozlov, a far more dashing man than I could ever be," he said with a twisted smile. "But now, thanks to you, I can see another interpretation. Her act might have been one of desperation. The effects of such a disclosure upon a gently brought up young girl like Katya . . ."

Lisa nodded mutely. Yes, she could imagine that interview, the malicious joy with which her mother flayed her sister, finally able to inflict the worst wound of all on the girl she hated.

"But she should have trusted me. The disclosure of her origin would not have made any difference: an English gentleman does *not* cry off from an engagement . . . And anyhow," he finished boyishly, "I love her still. I can't bear to think of her in trouble."

"Oh," Lisa cried, "oh, how good, how very good you are, Monsieur Graham!" Faithful, true to the core, honorable—suddenly she was sorrowfully, happily proud of him.

"No," he said, "no, I beg of you. . . . And now I think I must go. There are many things to do."

"No, wait." She leaned toward him, her hands clasped together. "Monsieur Graham, I am still not sure that there has not been some—mistake."

The last word came with difficulty. In spite of everything she couldn't bring herself to share with him—it was too shaming!—her growing conviction that her mother was lying. Not about Katya's low birth; that had a ring of truth. But nothing else did. She couldn't explain what made her so sure of it: a certain suspect shininess in her mother's eyes, a sort of sliding glibness in her voice. And there was something else. She went on with growing earnestness:

"I do know my sister very well. I can understand her changing her mind about—oh, anything; yes, even running away on an impulse. But not like this. We are more attached to each other than most sisters. I think I love Katya more than anyone else in the world" (always excepting one, she thought) "and she loves me equally. She would never leave me like this, without a word. Why, she couldn't bear to grieve me so! There would have to be a letter!"

She was so sure of it that in her mind she could see it, scrawled in Katya's uneven handwriting, hurried and crisscrossed, perhaps with some tear spots puckering the paper, telling her all about it. "And since it hasn't been produced, I *know* that there has been . . ." again she faltered, "some terrible mistake."

Graham's gray eyes never left hers as she spoke. It was just another proof of his kindness, she thought gratefully, that he didn't force her to spell out the exact nature of her doubts.

He said, "But I understand there *was* a message for you, a verbal one that that coachman of yours brought after he had taken Katya to Kozlov's lodgings."

"A casual good-bye uttered as a sort of afterthought, as though she were going for an outing? Oh, no, never."

Graham thought it over, worry deepening the new wrinkle between his brows. "Your mother had him there to tell his story to me, you know. I assure you I couldn't have misunderstood him: I understand Russian quite well."

"But not the Russians, perhaps?" Lisa inquired diffidently. "It must be hard to tell if people are lying in a language that is foreign to you. Haven't you found it so?"

"Constantly," Graham said, a tired little smile breaking from him. "You think, then, that he was lying?"

Lisa was silent for a while, turning over and over again in her slender fingers a knickknack of porphyry she had picked up from the table. Finally she said, "Monsieur Graham, I am going to send for Ivan again. Perhaps if you were here while I talk to him . . ."

Ivan the coachman, a tall, strapping pillar of a man wearing the traditional dark blue full-skirted coat, was presently ushered into the room. He brought with him a variety of stable smells, and he stood stock still in the middle of the white and gilt room, smiling nervously and clutching his cap in his great red hands as though afraid that a movement from him would release further horsey aroma. But he retold his story glibly enough: how early at dawn the gracious young lady Katerina Vassilevna had come down to the stables all by herself and had commanded him to get the carriage ready, and put her portmanteau in it.

"How did she look? What did she say?"

"I wouldn't know how she looked, ma'am. It's not up to us, lowly serfs that we are, to see how our betters look. As for saying anything, here's what she said: 'Ivan, take me to the Voznessenskaya Street where the Spassovski Regiment is stationed.' Well, I know the street. I've often gone there to take invitations to the gentlemen of the regiment. So when we get there, she says to me: 'Ivan, find out in which house Captain Kozlov is staying.' So I did. And then she sent me home and went into that house."

"And she didn't give you a letter for me?"

"No, my gracious young lady, nothing like that. Just, she says, 'Tell my sister not to worry, I am off to find my happiness with the man I love . . .'"

"Or perhaps tell you with whom she left such a letter?"

"No, ma'am, nothing like that."

"Why didn't you tell them at home immediately about this?" Graham asked in Russian, his eyes narrowed on the coachman's stolid red face. The small blue eyes met his unblinkingly.

"Why, your honor, that was my great fault and mistake. The young lady gave me ten rubles, see, not to say anything for a while, to give them a chance to get away, like, so that's what I did, said nothing till I was asked. Yes, a great fault and a great mistake that was, and little good it did me! Her grace the countess had me beaten for it, twenty lashes, so I couldn't move for a day. . . ." He rubbed his back with a lugubrious grimace. From behind the door leading to Lisa's bedroom there came a high giggle, immediately smothered. Not paying attention to it, he finished stolidly: "And it served me right for the fool I was."

"And that was all? You haven't left anything out? Think, Ivan . . . God will punish you if you left anything out."

"But I haven't, ma'am. As I said, so it was."

"Tell us again," Graham suggested gently. "Maybe you'll remember something else."

"Yes, your honor. Early that morning Katerina Vassilevna comes down. . . ." Wooden-faced, he launched again into his recital.

After he had left, Lisa said thoughtfully: "Servants don't usually look you straight in the face the way he did, not even blinking, when you talk to them. When they do, it is because they are not telling the truth."

Graham agreed with her. "I have now heard him tell this story three times and each time he told it exactly the same way, not changing a syllable. Did you observe, Countess Lisa, when he spoke of the whipping, he rubbed himself with exactly the same gesture? As though he had rehearsed it."

Lisa frowned; there had been something else, something marginal; it just brushed the side of her mind and was gone. "Yes, he's lying. But why should he? Unless . . ." She broke off again, unable to utter what was in her mind. A look of intelligence told her that Graham was thinking along the same lines. She went on: "I don't think there is any use trying to find out more from him. Not even whipping him again would do it. And anyhow, I couldn't; it's too hateful."

She knew, of course, that servants were constantly being flogged for their transgressions, and that this was taken for granted by everyone, including the servants themselves. But she had always hated it; the very thought filled her with nervous disgust. When her little maid Parasha came to her weeping bitterly because her sweetheart, the footman Aleksei, was being soundly whipped in the stables where such punishments usually took place, she herself had been close to tears as she comforted her. That memory reminded her of something else. She turned to the door to her bedroom, calling: "Mavrushka, come here, I want you."

The maid came in from the bedroom, closing the door carefully behind her and bobbing a curtsy. She was a pert, snub-nosed girl, a gossip and a giggler—but surely not heartless enough to giggle at a fellow servant's punishment.

"Was it you laughing before, Mavrushka?"

The girl curtsied again, eyeing her young mistress with comic alarm. "Forgive me in your goodness, Miss Lisa, I meant no harm. I didn't mean to listen. I was just going by with the pillows and I . . ."

"It wasn't very kind of you to laugh at Ivan being beaten. I thought you were fond of him."

"Begging your pardon, ma'am . . ." Another irresistible giggle escaped Mavrushka. She muffled it with both hands. "It was just his saying he couldn't move for a day. Pretty spry he was that same night!"

"After twenty lashes? I was quite sorry for him."

"Well, you don't need to be, madam dear, he was just making himself important, like. Twenty lashes—why, there wasn't a mark on him, the braggart!"

"How do you know?"

Mavrushka threw her apron over her face and ran out of the room.

Lisa turned quickly to Graham. "There now! Do you see?"

"Yes, I see," Graham responded. Ordinarily the impropriety of their mutual understanding would have embarrassed both of them. But no vestige of a blush colored Lisa's cheeks; she was too much in earnest to be concerned with the indelicate details of chambermaid amours. She had finally come across a small roughness, a sign of a loose thread in the smooth tissue of secrecy that shrouded her sister's flight. By working away at it, she might unravel more.

Graham rose abruptly from his chair and paced the room. Feeling Lisa's questioning eyes on him, he stopped in front of her and took her hand. "No use wrapping it up in clean linen," he said apologetically. "We are both aware of your mother's feelings toward Katya. The fact that that oaf went unpunished might simply mean that your mother was not displeased with what he did."

And it might mean much more than that. Lisa's fingers tightened unconsciously on his. "Monsieur Graham," she said in a low voice, "I beg of you not to go immediately in pursuit of Captain Kozlov. Wait a little. Let me make more inquiries. I feel certain that Katya left a letter for me with one of the servants, who is afraid to give it to me. When I have it, we'll know exactly what—"

"I couldn't leave immediately in any case," Graham said slowly. "For one, I must apply to the ambassador for a leave of absence; and then I don't know where Kozlov's regiment will be stationed. All this will take time."

Lisa sighed with relief. "And meanwhile I will send out the word that if anyone has such a letter, they will find me grateful, and that I won't tell anyone about it. Most of the servants are quite fond of me, I think, and will not like to see me in distress."

CHAPTER 7

During the next three days no one came forward to tell Lisa anything about her lost sister. She was aware of sympathetic looks following her, and she occasionally overheard the compassionate murmur of "Poor little countess, misses her sister so," but there was nothing else. It was inconceivable that her heedless romp of a sister had been able to steal out of the house in such secrecy that even her personal maid Parasha knew nothing about it. And yet this seemed to be the case.

The servants who had waited on the two girls were fond of them. Lisa particularly had a gift of drawing confidences from them without pressing; the maids, and sometimes even the footmen, would come to her with their troubles, telling her of homesickness, of hearing bad news from their villages, of being unjustly treated by their superiors. Lisa would listen and try to do whatever she could; hearing their diffident thanks—"Thank you for listening to me, *matushka*, it's like a weight lifted from my heart to talk to you, poor orphan that I am"—she would feel a sorrowful kinship with them. But now they looked at her with wooden faces, disclaiming all knowledge. They *knew;* she was sure of that. Her perception heightened by anxiety, she felt as though all the faces around her were stamped with secret knowledge; it was there in the way these faces closed up when she talked with them, in the way their voices sounded when they answered her questions with a low voiced "No'm, there's nothing I know." Nothing less than an edict from above could have reduced an ordinarily gossipy and gregarious crew to this stubborn silence. They must have been told not to talk on pain of punishment.

Lisa was aware that punishment for disobedience could be

terrible indeed: certainly bad enough to outweigh their obvious sympathy for her distress. House serfs who didn't give satisfaction could be sent away to one of the family's outlying villages to do hard work, or even to Siberia. They could be married off regardless of their inclinations; they could be flogged or sold like chattel. They were, in fact, chattel. The owner's power over them was absolute. Lisa had listened to these stories with revulsion; and was delighted to hear that Emperor Alexander, that good-hearted young monarch, was considering putting an end to serfdom. But now for the first time as she looked at the closed-up faces around her she began to understand the exact nature of being a serf.

And Katya was a serf now. The thought came to her with a heart-stopping shock. In a panic she pushed it away from her. Of course, in Katya's case, it was merely a legality, a grotesque mischance easy to remedy. The possibility of her being actually treated as a serf was bizarre, impossible to envision. Or was it? Would her mother. . . ? No, she couldn't, she wouldn't; monstrous even to think of it! She might have known about Katya's resolve to run away and pretended not to know, might have even encouraged the elopement, but surely nothing else.

Kneeling down in the corner where the devotional candle burned before the ikon, Lisa repeated the prayer she made every night. "Preserve her, Mother of God, keep her safe." She prayed long and earnestly. The Virgin's small, dark face seemed to stir with compassion in the flickering candlelight.

Afterward she wandered restlessly through her apartments. The sunny rooms seemed infinitely sad now that they were unenlivened by Katya's gay voice, her ringing laughter. Every bit of them breathed and spoke of her. The very walls, papered to resemble a lilac grove, were a product of her whim (they had had to send to Paris for the paper!); her bed, a hand's reach away from her own—how often, waking up in the morning, she would see her sister curled up like a kitten on her bed, with just her long black braid showing among the quilts.

Oh, Katya, black-eyed little sister, where are you? What has been done to you?

The little gilt French clock on the mantelpiece struck two. It was time to dress for dinner. Calling the maid Parasha to wait on her, Lisa wandered listlessly into the wardrobe room to choose a dress to wear for dinner. Katya's dresses were all there, except for the few she had taken along with her, and Lisa, opening the huge armoire that held them, fingered them wistfully, trying to find solace in the scent and texture that brought Katya back so vividly. At any moment, it seemed, Katya's ringing voice would demand one of them. "Parasha, love, take out the blue toile. What do you think, Lisa, shall I wear that or the white muslin with the open work?" Katya loved dressing up and refused to wear anything that didn't become her. She was even particular about her mourning clothes: "Papa wouldn't want me to look hideous!" There was a black sarsinet that she was particularly fond of . . .

Frozen, Lisa stared at that very dress, still hanging in the armoire, emitting a faint hint of Katya's favorite lilac scent. She took a deep breath and said casually, without turning around: "That was a poor job of packing you did, Parasha. You forgot to pack Katya's favorite black sarsinet."

The answer came immediately, "No, ma'am, that wasn't my fault, it was Arina who packed for Katerina Vassilevna—"

Breaking off with a squeak of dismay, she crammed her knuckles against her mouth and stared at Lisa aghast, her face going so pale that every freckle stood out like a copper penny.

"Arina?" Lisa turned slowly from the armoire. "What has *she* got to do with it?"

Her mother's grim abigail, who never came near them, packing for Katya?

The girl flung herself face down at her feet, "Lisaveta Vassilevna, don't ask me, don't make me tell you . . . I'll be whipped to death, they'll have no mercy on me!"

Lisa bent down to her. "You've got to tell me, Parasha, you must. No, don't be afraid. I won't tell anyone."

"She'll find out I talked; she'll know it was me."

"Parasha, look at me." The girl looked up at her like a rabbit in a trap. "I've never lied to you, have I? I promise that you won't suffer for this. But you must tell me; I have to know."

Resignation spread over Parasha's face.

"All I know, ma'am, dear, is, I wake up that night and Miss Katya isn't in her bed. But then straightaway she comes in, with Arina behind her. And Arina, she says to me, 'Get out of here, I'll take care of everything.' And she takes me by the shoulders and pushes me out into the corridor. 'Go to the maids' room, and not a word out of you, now or later, or it'll be the worse for you. All you know, the young lady's gone, you don't know how or where.' And afterward we were all told that her grace the countess doesn't want us to talk about Katerina Vassilevna's running away—one word, out of anyone, and they'll be in bad trouble. Oh, you're never going to tell Arina I told you, ma'am, she'll kill me, the hard-hearted bitch, saving your presence, your grace . . ."

"I won't, Parasha. I promised, didn't I?" Arina belonged to the countess, body and soul, a sort of female Mamluk, mute and devoted—no use questioning *her*. But that brought it all squarely to her mother's door. If Arina had supervised Katya's elopement, there was no doubt that the countess knew all about it. "But what I want you to do is take a note from me to Monsieur Graham at the British Embassy."

Sitting down at her escritoire, she dashed off a quick note asking Graham to meet her that afternoon in the Summer Garden.

"I have been aware from the beginning," Graham said slowly, "that your mother knew more about Katya's flight than she was willing to communicate to us. In fact, that she may have initiated it. This, of course, is the final proof."

The Summer Garden, through which they were walking, followed by Parasha at the proper distance, was almost deserted. Occasionally they encountered a solitary promenader, who, passing them, would give them a discreet and benevolent smile, taking them for a pair of lovers bent on their own special romantic business. Lisa found a painful pleasure in walking with him through these green alleys, her hand on his arm, his earnest face bent down to hers. The shadowy alleys were peaceful. Marble statues glowed white against the dark green foliage. Tree branches met, cathedral-like over their heads; occasionally a ray of the late-afternoon sun would spear obliquely through the leaves, making a gold patch on the sleeve of Graham's olive superfine jacket or the lavender muslin flounce of Lisa's walking dress.

Graham went on: "I think as you do; your mother deliberately disclosed to Katya the circumstances of her birth and then played on her sensibilities to encourage her to join her fate to that of Captain Kozlov."

"Yes, but . . ." Lisa stopped. She walked on silently, not

looking at him, her eyes on the tips of her small kid half-boots.

"Frankly, I don't see what good would be served in discussing this with Countess Vorontzov. I don't believe she will ever admit to committing such . . ." he hesitated and finished grimly, "such an impropriety. No need to waste time on recriminations. It's far better for me to start to Caucasus as soon as I can."

"Oh, no, pray don't," Lisa said quickly. Meeting a surprised look, she added haltingly, "I don't know how it is, but I feel so very sure that that would be the wrong thing to do."

"I can't wait here any longer." She felt the arm under her fingers grow rigid. "It drives me mad to stay here doing nothing . . ."

Lisa suppressed a sigh. She was aware of men's characteristic predilection for doing *something*, even if it was the wrong thing to do. There was nothing she could do to prevent it; she couldn't confide to him, without further proof, her profound, intuitive conviction that somehow they were being deliberately pointed in the wrong direction. Nor could she bring herself to voice the chilling suspicion that, in spite of anything she said to herself, kept seeping into her mind: that Katya was perhaps sent away.

"Unfortunately," Graham resumed, "it isn't as easy as I had envisioned. There has been a change in our relations with Russia, as you must know. I don't know how it came about, but there it is: all at once Bonaparte is on his way to becoming Emperor Alexander's great and good friend. The ambassador foresees the declaration of a French-Russian entente. Under the circumstances a British diplomat wanting to know where a particular regiment is stationed is bound to arouse some baseless suspicions. However, I do have friends in the general staff from whom I expect to hear shortly. I shall keep you posted. Meanwhile, allow me to express my boundless admiration, Countess Lisa, for everything that you have done and for the unexceptionable way you have borne these painful revelations."

There was unmistakable warmth in his voice, and Lisa's heartbeat accelerated. But immediately she repressed the joyful response. All she was to him was someone who could aid him in finding Katya: he didn't really see her as a person. And that is how it should be, she told herself fiercely; it's silly and wicked to expect more. He is for Katya, not me; he is here to help me to save Katya.

Lisa came back from her rendezvous to find Prince Dmitry Lunin's English carriage drawn up before their house, the three perfectly matched Orlov coursers fretting splendidly in the coachman's competent grip. Prince Dmitry himself came over to hand her out of her carriage. He had just come from an audience at the Annichkov Palace and was magnificent in his regimentals, the star of the order of St. Andrew blazing on his chest.

"Well, Lisa," he said escorting her into the house, "we're quite in the suds, aren't we? No news from Caucasus, I daresay."

"No, Prince," Lisa said. For a moment she considered telling him what she had learned, but she gave the idea up almost immediately. Prince Dmitry had intimidated her since childhood, and today there was something specially forbidding about his aspect. His face was impassive as always, but a slight, dangerous glitter in his dark eyes warned her away from any idea of confiding in him.

"No, I didn't think so." He gave a short, sharp laugh. "Far too busy with other matters. The scenery is especially absorbing. . . . Announce me to the countess," he said to the footman, and with a slight bow he left Lisa.

If there was anything in which Prince Dmitry excelled, it was the art of concealing his feelings. As he entered the state bedroom in which the countess habitually received condolence calls—lights properly dimmed and curtains drawn—no one could have guessed from his enigmatic countenance how very angry he was. He bowed with his accustomed elegance over the hand the countess extended to him from the couch on which she was reclining. She was still in mourning and would continue to be so for the next few months, but her black satin was fashionably cut and relieved by a necklace of opals set in diamonds. The prince leveled a critical lorgnette on them. "Opals are almost the only gems that do not look well on black," he remarked. "Apart from that trifling error in judgment, my dear Elena, you look very handsome. How very fortunate that black becomes you!"

The countess acknowledged the compliment with a reserved smile. "You haven't visited us for a long time, Dmitry. I hope you bring me some interesting news from the outside world. I do not get out, as you know."

"Nothing very particular," said Prince Dmitry, seating himself. "We seem to be changing our alliances. Lord Leveson-Gower is most unhappy. . . . By the way, I understand young Graham is going to Caucasus."

"Is he really?" The countess's face clouded over. "I do not understand the English. One would think mere pride would prevent this ridiculous expedition. All Lisa's fault. If it were not for her, he would be in England now, I daresay, making himself useful to his poor uncle. I don't understand my daughter."

That was no less than the truth, the prince thought. The trouble with Elena was that she lacked imagination. To anyone else who knew Lisa, her response to her sister's disappearance would have been predictable. He said with a slight smile, "One wonders what he hopes to find in Caucasus."

The countess threw him a sharp look. She said indifferently: "By the time he gets there, it is very possible that the silly girl will have changed protectors. She is extremely volatile, as you know. Once one starts on that road. . . ." she shrugged her shoulders, dismissing the subject. Picking up a small, gem-encrusted mirror from the little table next to her couch, she surveyed herself critically. "You have made me quite uneasy about the necklace, Dmitry. And you are perfectly right, of course, you wretch. Opals do not go with black; I must change them straightaway." She raised her hands to her neck, fumbling at the catch.

"What a rare thing it is to find a persuadable woman," Prince Dmitry observed. "About Graham, however. I know that breed: irredeemably obstinate. Once he is on the trail he'll follow it to Caucasus and back if necessary. I am considering saving him the trouble and sending him straight to the village of Krasnoye near Velikiya Luki in the Pskov Province."

The countess's hands jerked violently at the necklace and a small stream of gems cascaded to the floor. The little blackamoor stationed by the door left his post to crawl on the floor, gathering them up. His mistress did not give them a look.

"You're a devil, Dmitry. How did you—?" she stopped. "I am not admitting anything."

"You don't need to, to me, *chère amie*," he reassured her

gently. "As for your question: in the first place, the story of flight to Caucasus did not ring true to me; second, as the late count's lifetime friend, I have the advantage of knowing where Katya came from, so it seemed possible that that would be her ultimate disposition. I had one of my men go down to the Pskov village and check up there. You will be glad to know that Katya is settling down comfortably with her family."

"Would that she would settle comfortably in nethermost hell," the countess said bitterly. She looked at him, challenge in her eyes. "Are you going to tell the Englishman?"

"Perhaps. It depends." Flipping open a gold and enamel snuffbox surmounted by a miniature of Catherine II, he helped himself delicately to snuff. "I feel the boy is longheaded enough to work it out for himself. That Caucasus story won't hold water, you know; it's very ramshackle indeed . . ."

"Well, even if he does find out about Krasnoye, he will probably get there too late," said the countess, somewhat reassured. "She will have been married off by then, I daresay, according to my instructions."

The prince's long fingers paused on the snuffbox. After a moment he clicked it shut.

The countess's eyes were not on him at that moment or she would have been quite frightened by the look that flashed momentarily out of his dark eyes. She went on: "What can he do about that then? After all, she is my serf, my property to dispose of as I will."

"You haven't thought it out properly, my dear Elena. He can go back to Petersburg with a rather scandalous tale. It might make it difficult for you to reappear in society after you're through mourning, don't you think?"

"I shall deny everything." The countess's face grew heavy with obstinacy. "Surely my word stands for something in Petersburg, against that of a mere foreigner."

"Against his unsupported word—yes, perhaps." He conducted another pinch of snuff to his well-shaped nose.

The countess's bosom heaved tempestuously. "Are you telling me that you would support him? A lifelong friend of my husband discrediting his widow—that would be too bad of you, Dmitry."

"Yes, almost as bad, my dear Elena, as his widow packing off his natural daughter to an obscure village before his ashes are cold. But I do not propose to do anything inconsistent with my friendship with Count Vorontzov. However, these stories do have a way of spreading. This one might even reach the emperor's ears . . ."

"I don't care. Are you suggesting that I should bring her back? Never! That Englishman shall not have her. The Marchioness of Lyndhurst, indeed! Before that happens, I would—I would have her—" She stopped. "It *has* been done, you know."

Prince Dmitry surveyed her in silence for a minute, taking in the high, violent color and the uncontrolled hatred blazing in her eyes. Then he said lightly, "All your family has a penchant for extreme measures, *ma chère*. Very unsettling and quite unnecessary. There are, after all, other ways of dealing with disagreeable situations."

"What?" the countess said, looking at him fixedly.

A slight smile appeared on Prince Dmitry's ambiguous lips. "You might give her to me."

"To you?"

"Yes, why not? I will undertake to take care of her future." His smile widened and was after a moment reflected on the countess's face.

"So that's how it is," she said, beginning to laugh.

CHAPTER 8

The next morning after Lisa's rendezvous with Graham, one of the footmen came to tell Lisa that Timofey, her father's old valet, was asking for her. "All upset he was, left his bed, wandered up and down looking for your grace . . . Now he's gone back to the count's bedroom. He's there all the time now, like an old dog on his master's grave, forgets to eat and drink. . . ." The footman shook his head sagely. "Won't last long."

Lisa went to see Timofey and found him asleep on his pallet in the count's dressing room, covered by his master's old campaign cloak. She put her hand on his frail shoulder, and the old man, immediately awakening, started scrambling to his feet.

"No, don't," Lisa said, pressing him back gently. "You just rest, Timofeyushka, don't mind me. . . . What was it you wanted to tell me?"

The old man looked at her vacantly. Since the count's death he had indeed deteriorated pitifully, becoming a mere ghost of the soldierly old man he had been. "Thank you, little countess, for coming to see me. I'm not long for this world, dearie, I'll be going to join him soon, and a good thing too. . . . But there was something." His eyes grew vaguer still.

"Yes, Timofeyushka, something that you wanted to tell me."

"Yes, yes, *matushka*, something important, I have to tell you . . . But what was it?"

His face puckered up with distress. Lisa waited, holding his shriveled old hand. But when he began to talk, it was merely about the good old days, when the count was helping beat the Turks for Empress Catherine, when he was hobnobbing with glorious commanders like Suvorov of blessed memory and carousing with Count Alexis Orlov. Lisa listened to his ramblings patiently, smothering her disappointment; she had thought that perhaps he had something to tell her about Katya.

But just as she gently tried to free her hand from his clasp, it strengthened. His expression changed, became stern, and he said in an unexpectedly strong voice: "What is happening here? I hear them, I hear them; they think I'm asleep, but I still hear them talking."

"About Katya, Timofeyushka? You know they say she ran away with Captain Kozlov."

"Nonsense," said the old man irritably. "Don't listen to them, little countess . . ." Gathering all his strength, he raised himself on his elbow.

"Ivan the coachman says he took her there, but I don't believe him."

"No, don't . . ." The old man took a deep breath. "Never mind Ivan—he says what he's told."

"Yes, that's what I thought too, Timofeyushka."

"Fyodor is the one. He was sent away the whole of last week, nobody knows where. The same day as Katyusha left. Where did he go, then? Eh? And Arina, too. She went with them."

Lisa bent down to him eagerly. "You think they took Katya?"

Timofey nodded, his old face full of intelligence. But in another moment it had drained away, leaving his face slack with senility. His eyes closed; his white head sank back on the pillow. He was asleep again, and all Lisa's efforts to rouse him failed.

Fyodor the coachman, busy applying fomentation to the sprained hock of one of the matched gray geldings used to draw the countess's landau, looked up to see the slim figure of his young mistress confronting him.

"Fyodor," Lisa said, "where did you take my sister?"

Immediately she knew that her suspicions were correct. The bearded face before her dissolved into a mask of terror and guilt. The bucket of foul-smelling liniment fell out of his hands, but Lisa, intent on the cowering figure before her, didn't even bother to lift her skirt out of the way.

"Tell me!"

"Lisaveta Vassilevna, your grace, have mercy on me, I can't, I can't . . ."

"Fyodor, our Savior above sees everything. Tell me!"

And for a moment it seemed as though he might do so. He took a deep breath; his mouth opened. Then he thought better of it. An impenetrable film seemed to come over his eyes. Looking down, he muttered: "There's nothing I can tell you, ma'am. We're dark people, your slaves; we do what we're told."

"Where did you go for a whole week?"

"Where I was sent, little countess."

"With my sister?"

"That I know nothing about, madam."

"Then I'll ask my mother about it."

"As you will, madam, but as for me, I can't tell you anything." A light band of sweat sprang out on his low forehead. In spite of herself Lisa felt sorry for him. She said coldly: "I'll make it clear to my mother that I couldn't get anything out of you," and left him.

That same afternoon Graham arrived at the Vorontzov residence to tell Lisa that he had obtained the information he needed and was ready to leave. He was told by the footman that Countess Lisa was with her mother. "If you will please to wait, sir." The servant's face was wooden, but Graham thought he noticed a suppressed note of excitement in the expressionless voice.

"I'll wait on both ladies," he said. "They are expecting me. Announce me, please."

As soon as he heard the countess's voice raised in anger, he realized that there was a scene in the making. Lisa must have faced her with what she knew, after all. His overriding concern for one sister suddenly shifted to the other: the sensitive, timid little thing facing her redoubtable mother! Not waiting to be announced, he brushed past the footman and entered the salon, to hear the countess say: "To think of my own flesh and blood turning on me!"

He was right, then. The countess was raging up and down the room with an ominous rustle of her stiff black satin at every turn, while Lisa stood stock still, her hand to her cheek.

"And for whom? For a spawn of a peasant whore? But she has always been between us from the very beginning." And as Lisa lowered her hand, disclosing a red imprint of a slap on her pale cheek, "Look, look what she made me do! All her fault!" Her voice wavered with self-pity and Graham was filled with cold, loathing rage. That brute of a woman!

At that moment the countess saw Graham; and the sight of him seemed to inflame her further. "Didn't I tell you that we aren't receiving anyone?" she flung at the terrified footman.

"You mustn't blame the poor chap," Graham said. "He did tell me, but since I felt that you were probably discussing Katya . . ."

The footman withdrew silently, closing the door behind him.

"You can't exclude Monsieur Graham, maman," Lisa said. "He has a right to know everything concerning Katya. It seems, Monsieur Graham, that Katya did not run away with Captain Kozlov, after all. She was sent away."

For a moment Graham didn't trust himself to speak. "Where?" he brought out finally in a strangled voice.

"I don't know."

"Nor will you, ever," said the countess. "But I assure you—and you," her dark eyes flicked briefly toward Graham, "that it is better so—better for all of us."

"Really, maman? To send her away like chattel?" Each word fell as soft and chill as a snowflake. "You told me once that it was an object with you to follow my father's wishes. Is this how you do it?"

"Oh, your father." The countess's voice was suddenly weary. She caught Lisa's hand and drew her closer, seeming to forget Graham's presence. There seemed, strangely, to be a pleading note in her voice as she went on: "I was in love with your father when he married me. He was much older than I, but so splendid, so handsome, he put all the younger men in the shade. We were very happy together at first. He went away when I was two months pregnant. When he came back, he was quite different: he no longer cared for me, because he had fallen in love with another woman."

Lisa listened quietly, her head bowed, her hand lying unresponsive in her mother's urgent clutch. Consumed though he was with rage and anxiety, Graham forced himself to stay silent. He was diplomat enough to know that the countess would be easier to deal with in that gentler mood that is often attendant on reminiscence.

"No, wait; listen; I want you to understand me. He told me

that it was so, without excuses or explanations. I was young and passionate; I raged at him, wanting to know who that secret serpent was who stole him from me. There was a terrible scene, and I lost my baby; a son it would have been, someone to carry on his name. Well, that was the end. Our whole family is proud and vengeful," the countess said, with what seemed like odious complacency to Graham. "I never forgave your father. I was glad, when you came, that you were a girl and not the son he wanted. . . . And then he brought the whore's child to be reared together with you, and I had to bear that for all these years. I had to look on while that black-eyed bitch robbed you of what was your due, just as her mother robbed me, stealing your father's love, and men's admiration, and then, then, at the very last, the very worst—"

"Maman!" Lisa's pale face flamed scarlet. "I beg of you!"

Graham's lips tightened. It was plain that that damned harpy was distressing Lisa by referring to a secret attachment, obviously to someone who had preferred Katya. He suspected that this happened rather often: not everyone could immediately recognize Lisa's attractions, rooted in character rather than appearance. Not that she was plain: there was a pleasing delicacy about her features. And from the very beginning he had liked her smile, shy yet with a hint of mischief in it. He had often seen it break forth at precisely the absurdities that ticked him too. But of course she was dimmed by her spectacular sister. And that was another thing: amazing that the disproportionate admiration gleaned by Katya did not arouse jealousy or envy in her heart. But there was nothing petty or ungenerous in Lisa's nature. Once she loved someone, it appeared, she did so unstintingly.

"No, no, I won't say anything, child. But you understand now how it was with me, don't you?"

Lisa sighed. "I am sorry that you had been unhappy with papa—that he had been so cruel to you, maman. But Katya is not to blame for those old mistakes."

"Still thinking of that wretched girl." Contempt crept into her mother's manner. She flung Lisa's hand away. "You certainly haven't inherited any of our family pride, Lisa. You remind me of your Grand Aunt Lisaveta—just such another meek creature with milk in her veins. Perhaps it was a mistake to name you after her. But you will thank me someday. And you," she said to Graham, suddenly remembering his presence, "you too should be grateful to me for saving you from a disastrous marriage."

"I am vastly obliged," Graham said icily, "and will be even more so when you tell me where my fiancée is."

The countess's milder mood disappeared. Her face hardened; her considerable bosom heaved. "Never," she said, again. "Never!" And turning on her daughter, who now regarded her with undisguised horror, "How dare you look at me so, after all I have told you. Don't you feel for me?"

"I feel for Katya," Lisa said steadily. "To be sent away from those who love her, to be utterly dispossessed, all in revenge for a past in which she had no part—no, maman, that is a sin. Bad enough for her to have learned of her situation—"

"Which was not of my making, let me remind you!"

"You could alter it, however, by freeing her."

The countess gave her an incredulous smile. "I? If her father didn't, why should I?"

"Yes, most remiss of him," Graham said. "It demonstrates the horror of serfdom in a very particular way, doesn't it? I understand Emperor Alexander is seriously considering abolishing it. A story like that, if recounted to him, would certainly strengthen that resolve."

"You too!" the countess uttered, the two syllables imbued with fear as well as venom. She glared at him in outrage. And then a lightning change came over her features. She said with unexpected mildness, "I told you before that it was better for Katya, too. And so it is. I did this to protect her."

Lisa broke the disbelieving silence, inquiring baldly: "From what?"

The countess dabbed at her lips with her scented handkerchief. "I am not Katya's owner. Her mother was Dmitry Lunin's serf. He is the one who owns her. Dmitry was my husband's aide in the Turkish wars; they were great friends. When your father took a fancy to the trollop, he gave her to him."

A sort of horrified intelligence lit Lisa's face. "I remember now! He said he knew Katya's mother."

The countess's smile was disagreeable. "I daresay he did.

Men are disgusting, aren't they? . . . At any rate he handed her over to my husband. Not that any papers were signed; it was all very casual, I understand."

"Casual, indeed." Graham's eyes blazed. "And that's how it was left? Nothing further done about it?"

"Not that I know of," the countess said.

And that was only to be expected. A characteristically Russian transaction! The old man, criminally dilatory, died leaving his favorite daughter the serf of one of Petersburg's most notorious rakes. Damn him, Graham thought savagely, damn them all for their slovenly, feckless, destructive ways.

"At any rate, since Katya seems to have the faculty of arousing men's worst instincts, I judged it safer to put her out of her owner's reach."

Setting his jaw, Graham forced himself to consider this new development. He immediately discounted the countess's pious concern for Katya's virtue. Prince Dmitry, congratulating him on his betrothal, had shown no traces of any special interest, let alone ungovernable passion, for Katya, merely adding to his felicitations the hope that Graham would be able to manage his fiery little bride. "An occasional beating might do the trick," he had said. "But you Englishmen are too polite for that." Besides, he might be an acknowledged rake and totally unscrupulous with women, but he also was a gentleman. Inconceivable that he would ever assert his property rights to his old friend's daughter.

But Lisa apparently thought otherwise. There was dismay in her expressive face as she asked quickly, "Maman, he doesn't know where Katya is, does he? You did not tell him?"

"No, I did not," the countess answered shortly.

"That would be too cruel, too terrible! Oh, maman, are you sure?"

"I didn't, I promise you. Don't you believe me? I swear to it." Turning to the opulent bank of ikons in the corner of the room, she made a slow, solemn sign of the cross. "I swear by the Holy Virgin that I didn't tell Dmitry where I sent Katya. There, do you believe me now, you two?"

Lisa let out an inheld breath. Graham made a curt bow.

Russians, in their heartfelt, passionate way, were redoubtable fabulists; that much he had learned in his job. They lied creatively, fluently, looking you straight in the eye with a candid, limpid gaze. But even the worst liars, when they wanted to be believed in spite of their record, would resort to the solemn oath sworn on an ikon. Such oaths were not taken lightly. Whatever other lies she had told, it could be taken for granted that the countess had not disclosed Katya's whereabouts to Prince Dmitry.

The difficulty was that she also refused to disclose it to them. Her face set, she repeated over and over again that Katya was where she belonged, that she was safe there, and that consequently there was no reason to worry about her. Graham, fighting down a savage desire to choke it out of her, did his utmost to sound reasonable, representing to her that surely Katya would be far safer in Petersburg, among people who knew her.

"Or else," Lisa put in, "why not send her to Aunt Aline in Moscow? She would protect Katya if you are unable or," her soft mouth tightened, "unwilling to do so." She was referring, Graham knew, to the widowed Princess Mourovtsev, the late count's sister, known and respected in Moscow as an old-time crony of the Mother Empress. "I entreat you to tell me where Katya is so that I can go there and give her whatever protection I can until she is brought back."

The countess's eyes flashed. "Nothing can force me to do so. Oh, saints above, aid me! Don't you realize, you stupid girl, that I did it all for you? Are you planning to undo it, like the little fool you are? Well, I won't let you. And that is my final word. Leave me, both of you!"

But Lisa didn't budge. "Very well, maman," she said quietly. "You have committed a great sin in sending Katya away, and I believe you know that yourself. But if you have committed it for my sake, then I am guilty too. Unless Katya is recovered, I shall have to expiate our common guilt. I will join a convent and spend the rest of my days praying for our salvation."

There was unflinching determination in her low voice. Staring at her, Graham knew beyond a doubt that she meant every word.

He saw now that he had never had an inkling of Lisa's quality. Whenever Katya talked about her, it was with protective love, using pet names that diminished her, so that he had always thought of her as timid and dependent. For the first time he recognized her for what she was—a mild but resolute personality, her sensibility propped by rectitude.

He remembered Sir Robert Kerr Porter saying to him: ". . . that pale little face could be that of a saint or a martyr . . ."

The countess gaped, her throat working. "No! You wouldn't!" she uttered in a failing voice.

But it was obvious to Graham that she too knew that Lisa indubitably would.

It was borne in on him that what he was witnessing with his astonished British eyes was the special Russian form of moral blackmail. He only hoped, fervently, that it would work.

CHAPTER 9

When the Vorontzov family had gone on a visit to Moscow, it had taken more than two weeks for the caravan of ten coaches to make the trip of 728 versts. Katya, hurrying south with all the dispatch that could be afforded by the speediest of troikas from the Vorontzov stables, reached her unwelcome destination in a quarter of that time. They made the minimum of stops, with short overnight layovers. It was the end of August, and their progress along the summer-dried roads was swift.

At first Katya had contemplated escape. Where to? She didn't know; it was merely an enraged desire to frustrate her stepmother's plans. But she soon gave up that idea. She might have been able to give the slip to Fyodor, the morose, elderly coachman in charge, or the young undergroom. But she knew very well there was no chance of escaping the grim surveillance of Arina, who silently waited on her, refused to answer any questions and saw to it that the others did likewise.

There was only one other way to deal with the situation and Katya did that. She slept through most of the journey, an easy thing to do in the *kibitka*, a vehicle that resembled nothing as much as a cradle on wheels.

She roused herself when they finally rolled into the village of Krasnoye in the late afternoon. Their arrival brought the whole village into the dusty street to stare at them. As Fyodor stopped the horses, it suddenly occurred to Katya that any one of those small, straw-thatched wooden cubes might be her future home.

Katya had visited peasant homes before: small, squalid dwellings consisting of a single room with a bench circling the walls, to be used for sleeping by the entire family. She remembered queasily the all-pervasive odor of cabbage and pitch. Would she be immured in one of those? She told herself staunchly that it didn't matter. *They can't keep me where I don't want to be; they can kill me but they can't keep me.*

But Fyodor had merely stopped to ask directions. After receiving them he started the horses up again, to her intense relief, and urged them on, away from the village. They drove up the hill and, passing through a lime alley, came out in front of a sizeable manor house with a columned front, which was surrounded by several smaller structures. Fyodor made for one of those outbuildings, from which a group of people, evidently alerted by the rattle of the wheels, had emerged. He addressed them generally:

"Are you the Golovins, the caretakers?"

"That's us, brother." The speaker was a smallish old man in his seventies, with lively black eyes in a seamed face. He wore a white smock with a rope for a belt. He was accompanied by a plump woman with two children, a boy and a girl, burrowing into her skirts. "And who might you be?"

As Katya looked at them, an extraordinary feeling rose up in her; somehow some part of her recognized the old man and the woman. She leaped lightly out of the carriage and faced them.

A gasp greeted her. "Lord save us," said the old man, crossing himself. "Tatyana! My own dear daughter come back to us!"

Fyodor handed the reins to the undergroom and ponderously climbed down from his seat. Arina followed suit, taking her place grenadierlike behind Katya.

"Are you Tikhon Golovin?" Fyodor demanded and, getting a nod, propped up his whip against the wall and began to grope in the pockets of his voluminous coat. "Then, old man, this is your granddaughter Katerina Vassilevna, and I have here a letter explaining all about it."

A brilliant smile illumined the old man's wrinkled face. "Why, of course. Who else could she be but my granddaughter, and her the image of her mother! Welcome here, my darling—I mean, your ladyship. Have you come to visit your mother's kin? I never expected the Lord to bestow such a blessing upon me."

"It's all here in the letter her grace wrote," Fyodor said, finally bringing that document out and carefully shaking it open. "It'll tell you all about it, old man, if you read it."

"How, read it? We're unlearned people here, brother. If it's to be read, you must be the one to read it."

"No, not I." Fyodor scratched his head. "You better get the priest, or still better, the headman. I am supposed to leave this with him before going back."

"The headman, Stepanitch, is out in the fields. As for the priest—well, I wouldn't trouble him: this is his time for drinking, and when he drinks, he can't read the Scriptures, let alone a letter!"

"Oh, give it to me," Katya said impatiently, snatching the letter out of the coachman's thick fingers. "I am not going to stand here and wait while you are looking for either of them."

She read aloud the lines in which her stepmother expressed her will that the girl Katerina, the illegitimate daughter of the late Tatyana Golovin, a serf, was henceforth to live with her mother's family in the village Krasnoye, and that this same Katerina was to dress and be treated according to her low station . . . And furthermore. . . .

Not bothering to read further, Katya crumpled the letter between her fingers and flung it to the ground, from where Fyodor hastily retrieved it. Her eyes moved to the woman who now approached her timidly, with the two children still clinging to her skirts. And again that stab of recognition pierced her. Somehow she knew how this woman would smile at her without parting her lips, covering her mouth shyly as she did so. Katya said uncertainly: "I know you, don't I?"

"Well you might, your ladyship, my darling, I'm your auntie Praskovya. I nursed you after my sister died, looked after you for three years, until his grace your father took you from us." The woman bowed low as she spoke; apparently the information in the countess's letter had not yet penetrated her understanding. "I loved you like my own, couldn't love these children more than I loved you . . ."

"Can you show me where I can change and wash, auntie?" Katya asked. "And tell them," she nodded at the servants, "where to put my things."

"This way please, ma'am," said her aunt to Arina, who silently followed her into the cottage carrying Katya's portmanteau.

Katya turned to Fyodor. "Wait here while I write a message to my sister."

But Fyodor shook his head. "No, miss, the mistress told us not to take any letters to countess Lisa from you. And you, old man," he turned to the old peasant who was silently taking it all in, "you're not to let the young lady write any letters."

"Not very likely she would, there being no pen or ink in the cottage," the old man observed.

"Well, then, see to it that she doesn't get them elsewhere."

"Ekh, brother," said the old man, suddenly assuming an unconvincing posture of extreme decrepitude. "I'm far too old to be a good jailer. Can hardly take care of myself, let alone a sprightly young female . . ."

"Well, see to it anyhow, and I'll tell the same thing to the headman when I give him the letter from her grace."

"Then—then would you at least tell her—tell my sister where I am," Katya faltered.

Another stolid headshake answered her. Katya flushed with anger. "Very well then," she said, "you can get yourself out of my sight, you sullen disobliging brute!" And upon Fyodor's muttering something about feeding the horses, "you can do that in the village. I don't want you here another minute!"

As he hesitated, she snatched up the whip that he had left standing by the door and advanced on him, her slim, imperious figure so menacing that both Fyodor and Arina, who had meanwhile come out of the cottage, beat a hasty retreat before her. Katya threw the whip after them and swept into the cottage, her head high. She stood rigidly in the middle of the room, her cheeks flaming, her chin up. Only when she heard the clatter of the wheels diminishing in the distance did her feelings overcome her; she burst into tears, sinking down on the bench.

"Don't cry, my poor little one, my darling." Plumping down next to Katya, her aunt drew her head onto her capacious bosom. "Oh, the wickedness of it. God will punish them for tormenting a poor orphan!"

"I don't mean to cry," Katya sobbed. "It's just that I am so tired . . . And oh, I want Lisa—I do so want my sister."

Her aunt continued rocking her and uttering endearments. The two children drew closer, round-eyed, and the little girl timidly put her hand on Katya's knee. "Don't cry, pretty lady," she said softly.

Presently her grandfather joined them. For a minute he looked silently at the weeping girl, chewing his lips. Then, laying his gnarled hand on her head, he said, with rough kindness, "Well, my dearie, no use moaning and wailing; won't change anything. Have to take whatever the good Lord sends you, whether you will or no. Could be worse, I daresay."

As she looked up into her newfound relative's twinkling eyes, Katya saw the kindness in them and felt inclined to agree, particularly when she remembered her previous fears.

She looked around her, drying her eyes. No doubt about it, her present quarters were far superior to the usual peasant *izba.* She was in a relatively spacious room, large enough not to be dwarfed by the huge, white-plastered stove. It was immaculately clean. Neither cockroaches nor other insects lurked among the sturdy beams and window frames. Bunches of dried herbs hung from the walls, giving off a faint, pleasant aroma, and the floor was swept. A small lamp burned in the corner under a large silver-framed ikon. Altogether there was an air of prosperity all around her. Particularly reassuring was the sight of two doors leading to other rooms: it appeared that this family, at least, would not be all sleeping in the same room.

The old man nodded. "Aye, a nice house," he said with evident pleasure. "Used to be the serfs' quarters. Upward of twenty maidens sat here spinning under my old woman's eyes, ten years she's gone now, God rest her soul . . . And the old count dead, too! That's what we heard, but we weren't sure that it was so, not until now." His small, wiry hand stirred reassuringly in Katya's tangled curls. "We'll get along," he said, "granddaughter."

"Yes, grandfather." Katya answered. The term came easily to her lips. It was as though she had known the old man all her life.

"Ah, but it's a sad day for her, poor orphan," said her aunt.

"Maybe so, but it's a happy one for me," said her father bracingly. "You stop clucking over her like a hen over a single chick, Praskovya, and give her something to eat. That'll be more like, eh, my girl?"

For the first time Katya became aware of a strong pang of hunger. "Oh, yes. Only I'd like to change first: I feel so dirty," she said, looking down with distaste at her traveling habit, lamentably dusty and wrinkled.

But when she opened her portmanteau, which had been placed in her aunt's little room, she was outraged to find that none of her dresses had been packed in it. There were only bundles of blue jersey and rough linen, such as were routinely issued to the household. The countess really did intend her to dress according to her new station in life, it appeared.

"Never you mind, my darling," Aunt Praskovya said. "I'll

sew such shifts and sarafans for you out of this, nobody will look better than you in the whole Pskov province, little beauty that you are!"

"But what am I to do in the meanwhile? I can't bear to wear this another minute," Katya said, close to tears again.

"You just wait, love!"

Dropping to her knees, her aunt groped under the bedstead and presently dragged out a long, low, wooden coffer, out of which she took a beautifully embroidered linen shift. "Your mother's," she said. "I've been keeping her dresses ever since she died, God rest her soul. Couldn't get into them myself, any more than a cow could," she gave a comfortable chuckle, "but I thought I'd keep it for my Annushka here," she nodded at the little girl who had followed them and was hanging back, shyly chewing at the end of her coal-black pigtail. "Our Tatyana was like you, thin as a reed, a waist you could span with your two hands, like any lady. . . ."

Katya put on the shift with mingled feelings of reverence and wonder. A memory came back to her: Prince Dmitry saying with his lazy smile, "Look at yourself in the mirror four years from now . . ." "Oh, I want to see," she said, and from habit looked around for the oversize cheval mirror that stood in her own bedroom. But there was nothing here but a tiny square mirror hanging from a nail in the wall.

"Just look at her," said her grandfather, when she came out. "Tatyana to the last eyelash!" His eyes moistened and, turning to the ikon in the corner, he crossed himself devoutly. "Thanks be to the Holy Virgin for rejoicing my old eyes. . . . Nor is a new granddaughter the only windfall I got today." Reaching into the bosom of his rough linen blouse, he pulled out a small leather bag chinking with money. "That besom of a female gave it to me for your upkeep."

In the romantic novels Katya had been reading, an offer of money from one's wicked rich relatives was usually spurned by the virtuous poor ones. Nevertheless, Katya didn't think any less of her grandfather when, after hefting the little bag pleasurably in his hand, he didn't pitch it out the window but replaced it with every sign of satisfaction.

"We'll find good use for it, you and I, my dolly. . . . Now go ahead and fall to, like a good girl. Look, I've brought you some fresh honey from my beehive. And then you can tell me all about it; a round tale is better told on a full stomach."

Waking up in the darkness, Katya didn't know for a moment where she was. Then it all came back to her. She was in the little cell of a room that her grandfather had given up to her, saying, "An old body like me is more comfortable on the stove, which is where I sleep winters." And off he went, taking his featherbed with him. Tired to the bone, Katya had gone to sleep the minute her head touched the pillow, unimpeded by the extraordinary hardness of the pallet on which she slept. Now that she was awake, her body, accustomed to the softness of her own bed, twisted and turned painfully, unable to find a comfortable spot on the pallet.

"Not at all the right sort of bed for the future Marchioness of Lyndhurst," she thought wryly. A sense of incredulity seized her. Was it really possible that only a few days ago she had been the affianced bride of a ducal heir? True, that had seemed unreal to her even at the time. And now, with something like dismay she realized that even Graham himself no longer seemed very real to her. But I *was* fond of him, she thought, and tried to visualize his frank gray eyes, fixed on her so adoringly, or the way his mouth would twitch when he was amused. But his image was steadily receding, and try as she would she couldn't hold it back. The truth was that he had been very shallowly rooted in her heart, and the storm that had displaced her had torn him out all too easily.

And then she forgot all about him as her thoughts went to Lisa. Could it be that she would never see her again?

"There will be no further contact ever between you and my daughter," maman had said. (How odd that she still thought of that cold woman with hating eyes as maman! But then all these years that term didn't really mean mother to her, it was simply a formal way to address her father's wife. Whereas grandfather became grandfather as soon as she laid eyes on him.) It was quite evident that she meant every word of this. What lying tale had been concocted for Lisa's benefit? She remembered that odious Arina snatching her clothes out of her armoire. But they hadn't been taken along. Most likely they had been hidden to give the impression that she had run away. Yes, that was probably the story Lisa would hear on coming back from her retreat.

But surely Lisa would know that she would never leave her like that, without a word of explanation. Surely she would see through whatever lies they told her, and ask questions, and not rest till she found out the truth.

Oh my darling sister, my dear little mouse, will you be able to do it? Or will you just stay there in misery, with your heart breaking for me, as mine is for you?

Unless. . . . This was the hour of the night when human resistance is low and doubts begin to creep out of the darkness like cold little snakes, invading the steadiest of hearts. That vicious lie maman had uttered—that Lisa loved Graham—what if that was true? What if Lisa did love him, and Katya had taken him from her, and now Lisa, far from missing her, was glad to find her gone? Katya's lips trembled. Now, indeed, for the first time in her unclouded, merry life, she felt like what Aunt Praskovya had called her: a poor orphan.

Far away a cock crowed. The dense darkness around her lightened by an imperceptible shade; a faint premonition of dawn stole into the shadows. Katya drew a deep breath. It just wasn't true. She would have known about Graham; Lisa would have told her, they had never had secrets from each other. And besides, hadn't Lisa been the one to urge her from the beginning to marry Graham? Without her exhortations she probably wouldn't have accepted him. No, doubting Lisa was a sin. She was her own beloved sister, nothing could change that. Eventually, somehow, somewhere, they would be reunited. . . . Once she had come to that certainty, the heaviness in her heart lifted. Katya sighed, turned over on her hard bed and went back to sleep, ignoring the growing clamor of the village cocks greeting the dawn.

Youth and summertime make everything bearable. For the next few days Katya was not unhappy in her new situation. In fact there were many aspects that she positively enjoyed. The clothes she wore suited her. Her body felt free and untrammeled in her linen shifts and capacious sarafans; it was nice not to be held in anywhere. It was also a strange new experience not to be attended by a footman or a maid wherever she went. At home she would have had to practice her harpsichord and study English in preparation for her life in England; she would have been expected to be present at the interminable condolence visits, primly seated in her chair for hours on end. At least so far, here she had no duties and was allowed to roam wherever she wanted.

She got used to the changes in her daily routine: to going to bed early by the light of the birchwood splinter (tallow candles were used sparingly for special occasions only) and rising at dawn, which was when the family's day started; to eating simple peasant fare like kasha and cabbage soup with black bread (which she found she vastly preferred to the white bread she was used to) and washing it all down with draughts of *kvas*. Luckily, it agreed with her.

She was getting used to all kinds of inconveniences. While she could never get used to Lisa's absence, she very quickly began to love her new relations. Her aunt Praskovya was a tenderhearted, sweet-tempered woman, recently widowed. Her ample reserve of affection, lavished on her children and old father, immediately expanded to take Katya in; she pampered and coddled her niece extravagantly. Katya also enjoyed the children: the stolid, tow-headed Petya and the lively, black-eyed Annushka, who followed her around wherever she went, unable to believe that this fairytale person was indeed their cousin Katya. They showed her their favorite haunts in the neglected old park: the secret grotto, almost overgrown with weeds; the hollow groves of lilac, as huge as forts, the green branches weighted with fragrant purple tassels. She played hide-and-seek with them, told them fairy tales and insisted on them sleeping in her little bedroom. The sound of their even breathing at night alleviated her loneliness as well as the sadness that still came at night.

Of course, the most important person in that household was her grandfather, Tikhon Golovin. Never in her life had Katya met anyone so imbued with energy. The old man was busy the whole day long, moving as briskly as a boy as he tended his domain. The estate gardens had been allowed to deteriorate, but he kept up the vegetable garden in the back of his cottage, and all of it thrived for him. He had a light hand with the bees, and every day sallied forth with netting around his head and a pot in his hand to bring back a piece of honeycomb dripping with sweet, thick amber. Even when he sat on the little porch sunning himself, his gnarled fingers were busy, whittling a wooden spoon, fashioning a toy. The day after Katya's arrival he made her a pair of bast slippers to wear instead of the kid boots she had worn with her town clothes; her feet were too tender for her to go barefoot. Those *lapti* fitted her little feet to perfection.

Not only his family but the entire village felt the impact of his wiry, lively, astringent personality. He was constantly being called on for advice. Stepanitch the headman himself dropped in the very next day and stayed for a long conversation, presumably about important village matters. Later a peasant came up the hill leading a horse that he was considering buying: what did Tikhon Yeremeitch think of the creature? Tikhon ran his hands knowledgeably over its flanks and legs and pronounced it a good buy.

Tikhon had been left in charge of the big house, and it was his custom to make a weekly tour of inspection, accompanied by his family. He did so the day after Katya's arrival, taking her along with him.

The manor house was much smaller and simpler than the palace near Peterhof to which they used to retire every summer. But its rooms were capacious, with tall ceilings and high windows. It had a shrouded, melancholy look, like a castle with a spell on it, haunted by phantoms and memories. The furniture was wrapped up in baize and the pictures covered over by netting against the dust. As they stepped into the library, Katya wondered if she could find something lively to read among the austere ranks of goldbound volumes; she regretted bitterly not having been able to take along her unfinished copy of *Pamela* by Mr. Richardson. Her eyes brightened as she saw an ornate crystal inkwell and quill pen on the writing desk. However, she immediately gave up the idea of using these writing implements. Even if she could find fresh ink to replace the dried dregs in the inkwell, there was no way to get the letter sent. All she would accomplish would be to cause trouble for her grandfather.

In the meanwhile Tikhon was carefully unveiling one of the shrouded portraits that hung in the library. He pulled away the netting and a beautiful, dark-eyed woman in a peasant costume looked at them out of the gilt frame, smiling a mysterious and seductive smile. Katya had the oddest sensation of looking in a mirror.

"Yes, that's her," Tikhon said. "That's your mother, my Tatyana. His grace your father sent for an artist from Moscow to paint her. And after he finished, she had that same painter make a miniature of the count himself, so she could look at it when he wasn't with her. Always kept it in her bedroom."

Katya found the picture there, a much younger and more dashing version of her father than she remembered. It stood on the little inlaid table next to the bed, which was a huge affair shaped in the form of a swan and hung about with velvet draperies, now sadly faded, with only the underside of the folds to show its former rich green blue.

"Should have been laid away," Praskovya remarked, fingering the dusty fabric, "only after Tatyana died, his grace commanded that the room be shut, no one to come in; leave it just as it is, don't lay a finger on it. I just try to keep it dusted, like. . . ."

"It's a lovely room," Katya said. And indeed the bedroom was furnished as richly as that of the countess in Petersburg. The furniture was made of Karelian birch. A huge lacquered coffer, fantastically painted with peacocks and swans, stood under the window.

"Yes," said Tikhon, "she lived like a princess, Tatyana did. Everything she wanted, his grace your father got for her. Tatyana loved swans, so he had a local man make this bed for her—a wonder at woodworking, that man was, could make anything he set his mind to. The count sent for him later, but I hear he didn't stay in Petersburg long, his grace not liking to look at anyone that reminded him of Tatyana. And he had had the same man build her the theater. I'll take you there . . ."

"A real theater?" Katya asked, saucer-eyed.

"Yes, they had all kinds of shows there; mostly dancing shows. That's what our Tatyana liked to do best, dance. Your father had a whole troupe made up for her, brought in people from Krasnoye and from his other villages; thirty men and women altogether. They were there to set her off, like."

"Are they still here in the village?"

"No, that they aren't. When Tatyana died, he sent them away. Somebody told me that he gave them all to Empress Catherine—she was still alive then—for her dancing theater." The old man shook his head. "To think of it, thirty people given away like they were performing monkeys. . . . The count had had a foreign dancing master brought here who taught them all kinds of dancing. Funny kinds, not like our Russian dances. A queer thing—the musicians would strike up and all of them would go high up on their toes, like they were puppets jerked up by their strings, and that's how they would dance, never coming down."

"Ballet!" Katya cried, delighted. "Was it like this?" Rising up on her toes, she did a *bourrée* across the room.

"Lord save us, Tatyana all over again!" Praskovya cried. The old man said nothing, but the expression on his face brought back another memory to Katya; the old count coming in during her lessons and silently watching her going through her steps with a wistful expression that sat oddly on his imperious, craggy face.

From the manor house they went on to another building. To Katya's joy it turned out to be a gem of a miniature theater, with gilt sconces on cream-colored walls and a painted ceiling on which three goddesses doffed their veils for the benefit of a puzzled Paris with an apple in his hand. The gilt was sadly tarnished, the crimson curtain faded, and spiderwebs covered the entrances to the miniature loges.

"This is where his grace the count used to sit and watch Tatyana," Tikhon said, pointing to the central loge with the Vorontzov coat of arms embossed on it. "Sometimes he would have a few friends with him, old cronies of his from his regiment. General Suvorov came once, Count Alexis Orlov, too—a great man he was in his time. I heard he was the one put the empress on the throne. . . . Well, after the performance he had everybody lined up before him, men holding out their hats, women their aprons, and he just walked along tossing in gold rubles for everyone except Tatyana: her he gave a diamond ring from his finger. That's how they were in those days. . . ."

"Was Prince Lunin ever there?" Katya asked. "He told me he knew my mother."

"Prince Dmitry Lunin? Oh, yes, your father was mighty fond of him and had him visiting time and again. . . . But never any of the neighbors. 'Won't have any of them provincial woodenheads gaping at you,' he says."

"I wouldn't have liked that," Katya observed thoughtfully. "I want people to see me when I dance—not just one or two but a whole audience."

"Looks like you take after your mother," Tikhon said. "That's what she wanted, too. When the count wasn't there, she would have everybody in the village in to look at her dancing. Once the count came back unexpectedly and oh, my, wasn't he mad! They all ran like rabbits, and he was going to have all the men flogged." Tikhon grinned suddenly. "Well, my Tatyana gave as good as she got. She stood up to him. Nothing in the world she was afraid of. Oh, she was a bold one, she was! There's gypsy blood in our family, comes out one way or another in every generation. There's always one special one, with special looks. Like your mother, and now you, and little Annushka here looks like she might be another one. That's how come I know all about horses—it's in our blood; and that's how Tatyana got her dancing and her temper, too . . . If she didn't want to do anything—whew! 'Kill me, if you will,' she would say, 'but you can't force me.' And he'd storm at her, his grace would. I'd be shaking in my boots listening, thinking he'll send her away for certain, and that'll be the end of our good life. Next thing you know, it's over, and he's petting and cherishing her like as if nothing's happened. . . ."

"Yes, his grace your father really loved our Tatyana, and that's the truth," Praskovya said. "When your mother died, he was like a wild man. Shut up the house, sent all the house serfs away and went away himself. We didn't see him again until he came back and took you away from us."

"That's right," Tikhon said. "Might have been better for you, Katyusha, if he had loved her less and thought about her baby more. If he had stayed here long enough to see you baptized and give you his name, you wouldn't be in the pickle you're in now—that's the law. But he couldn't wait to get away. Well, that's how the gentry are: like to pamper themselves in their griefs as well as in their pleasures. . . ."

Katya found the steps that led to the stage and mounted them. She stood in front of the footlights and looked about her. The perspective was unfamiliar. This was the first time she had been on a stage; whenever she had danced before it had been in the salon, on the same level as the spectators. But once she found herself on that special elevation that, however slight, draws once and for all the definite line between performer and audience, it was as though a sort of illumination had descended on her. She knew now exactly what she wanted to do.

Her face solemn, with a slow, hieratic movement she crossed

her arms on her breast. Her head lifted proudly and her lithe young body stretched as, with one small foot remaining firmly on the ground, the other rose upward.

"Look," Annushka shrilled, enchanted. "Standing on one leg like a crane! How long can you stay that way?"

"Forever, if need be," Katya said. "That's an *arabesque.*"

But it was more than that. It was a ritual of dedication, a sign that she now committed herself to a once-impossible dream.

CHAPTER 10

The most endearing thing about her grandfather Tikhon, Katya thought, was his abiding interest in her. He seemed to want to know everything about his new granddaughter down to the last detail; and never tired of asking questions about her previous existence. What was even more remarkable was that he made Katya feel that she could say anything to him. He would sit on the stoop, blinking in the fierce late-August sunlight and whittling away at a piece of wood, and listen attentively while Katya confided to him her dream of becoming a prima ballerina.

This was a resolution quite unlike the childish fantasies she had indulged in with Lisa in Petersburg. Then she had been a daughter of Prince Vorontzov, a *jeune fille bien elevée*, and as such could never perform except for the delectation of family friends or in front of select audiences at charity benefits, even then confining herself to well-bred *pas de châle* and spiritless *pas d'Espagne*. Now, of course, it was different. The fantasy had become a reality for her as soon as she had stepped onto the miniature stage of the little theater her father had built for her mother. How odd, she thought, that it was precisely the disastrous reversal of her fortunes that could make it possible for her to do what she liked to do best.

Tikhon saw nothing wrong about her ambition and asked her all sorts of intelligent questions. She told him at length about the imperial ballet school, run by the balletmaster Didelot, to which talented children from the lower classes were admitted. "I have no patience with my father. If he had only put me into that school when I was six instead of bringing me up as though I were a countess! I would have been taught by Didelot himself.

Why, by now I daresay I would have been a prima ballerina like Berylova." She was referring to a well-known ballerina who had started life as a serf and was freed by imperial decree as a member of the imperial troupe. "I would have been the toast of Petersburg by now. Petersburg, you know, is the only place for ballet; it's even called the home of ballet."

Tikhon scratched his head thoughtfully. "What about Mother Moscow? Don't they have any of that nonsense there?"

"I understand that they have *very* bad style." Katya said this with all the scorn of the born Petersburgian for the more provincial Moscow. "There might be a change coming, however. Something my dear old Monsieur Duroc told me." She frowned, trying to remember the disassociated bits of ballet gossip the old ballet master used to pour into her willing ears. "There has been talk of making the Moscow ballet company over. Moscow noblemen are great balletomanes." She paused, thinking it over. "Now, if I were to meet one of them and he were to fall in love with me and make me a prima ballerina . . ."

"Yes, if." Tikhon shook his head. "If my granny had whiskers, she'd be my grandpa."

Nevertheless, she could see that he was considering the possibility. There was no shocking Tikhon. It occurred to Katya that a virtuous peasant out of the modern novel would probably be still bemoaning his daughter's loss of virtue. Tikhon, an unflinching realist, thought that, everything considered, his daughter Tatyana had done very well for herself, and he only hoped that his granddaughter would have equally good luck. Katya herself couldn't help thinking that it had been an excellent arrangement, particularly when she compared it to the state of well-bred boredom in which her father and stepmother had lived together. To live with someone who loved you and let you dance all you wanted—how could anything be more desirable, she thought.

The news of Tikhon Golovin's newly arrived relative inevitably spread to the village; there began to be an influx of curious villagers to his cottage. Some of the women brought gifts—a newly baked loaf of bread, a dish of berries, a basket of eggs, tidily covered over by an embroidered napkin; others merely hung around at a distance to catch a glimpse of Katya as she played with the children or picked raspberries in the bushes behind the vegetable garden. They were both curious and shy. When Katya would try to speak to them, they would melt out of sight, giggling and covering their mouths with their sleeves.

When the Golovin family went to church—a neat white-washed structure with the usual bulbous roof—on the first Sunday after her arrival, she commanded more attention than Father Orofey, the red-nosed little priest who intoned the services with a nasal twang and looked a little unsteady on his feet. Later she was timorously greeted by the older women, who remembered her mother and marveled at Katya's strong resemblance to her.

She was particularly aware of being steadily observed both in church and elsewhere by the headman of the village, Stepanitch, a stocky, broad-shouldered man with a red, spade-shaped beard and small, blue eyes. She had caught him looking at her before when he had come to visit Tikhon, and had ascribed it to natural curiosity: after all, it isn't every day that one's master's daughter is sent down to one's village to live a peasant's life. But now there seemed to be something else in this steady, ruminative gaze. After a while it began to bother her, like the buzzing of a persistent fly.

She put it out of her mind after they had left the church. But it was brought back to her the next time he came to visit Tikhon. Like his first visit, this one dealt with village business. But although his manner was polite and he bowed low when she entered the room, she couldn't help but be conscious of that same heavy, ruminative gaze that followed her wherever she went, even as he and Tikhon went on discussing the good time for haying. It seemed that since one of Tikhon's gifts was his ability to predict the weather with uncanny accuracy, he was the person always consulted about the all-important timing of sowing and harvesting. He predicted a hot spell lasting far into September, with little rain, so that there was no need for immediate haying. Stepanitch listened to him respectfully, nodding and stroking his red beard, but his little eyes were still pursuing Katya.

"I don't like that Stepanitch," Katya told her grandfather later. "He stares so."

"And why shouldn't he stare at a wonder like you?" Tikhon

said chaffingly. "I daresay nothing like you has ever come his way before." But his face had darkened, and his smile was, it seemed to Katya, forced.

"Yes, I suppose so, but . . ." She was hard put to explain why it bothered her. "I don't know—it's as if he had a *right* to do so."

"Well, and so he has. A cat may look at a king, you know."

"I wouldn't mind a cat, but I mind *him*. You must tell him to stop it, grandfather."

"I'll give him a hint, Katyusha."

Apparently the hint took effect. The frank stares stopped, but they were replaced by something nearly as annoying: a sly and furtive sort of surveillance. Katya couldn't get rid of a feeling that he was secretly watching her all the time, looking away quickly before she could catch him.

Meanwhile, as August slid into September, Tikhon's prediction seemed to be coming true. Bright, hot days followed each other. The sleepy old park was permeated with heat, and Aunt Praskovya took Katya down to the river for a bath and a swim.

Sounds of laughter came to them from behind a copse of willows that masked a bend in the river, and they presently came upon a large group of women taking their bath in the cool stream. Praskovya went down to join them, calling out to friends. Katya hung back on the bank, frowning at the noisy congress of splashing, giggling women, some in their wet shifts, some naked. Her first impulse was to order them all away so that she could have her swim alone. And then it seemed to her a rather silly thing to do. With a sudden sense of freedom, she began to strip.

The women around her were a sturdy breed, wide of frame, with generous bosoms. Here in these informal surroundings their shyness was gone. As Katya undressed, she found herself being subjected to an embarrassingly thorough inspection. Little by little they began to make comments, not even bothering to lower their voices. It was as though this strange being that had alighted in their midst was so foreign and exotic that she couldn't understand what was being said about her.

"Look, Mashka, the little hands and feet!"

"And thin, thin like a thread; could break her in two at the waist!"

"And the hair—black like any tartar's!"

"Give over, women," said her aunt reprovingly. "Just listen to you, cackling like a gaggle of geese. You leave the maid alone, do!"

But the comments continued unabated.

"Look, the skin on her—white like a mermaid's . . . Shines in the dark like a mackerel, I'll wager."

"Yes, a regular *russalka*, a water hussy. . . ."

A timid little slap landed on Katya's bottom. She whirled around, turning fiercely on her assailant, who turned out to be a girl of about her own age, a blond, buxom creature with a long, fat braid falling on one plump shoulder. Meeting Katya's smoldering gaze, she flinched, stepped back and, tripping on a stone, sat down in the shallow water with a mighty splash. Looking up with a half-frightened grin on her snub face, her light eyelashes blinking comically, she explained: "Just wanted to find out if you *feel* like we do."

Katya stared down at her, scowling. From behind her came a murmur. "Ooh, look, like an angry white witch . . . Look out, Dunyasha!" And suddenly the humor of the situation overcame her and she broke into a ringing laugh, so loud and merry that an answering grin broke out on the apprehensive faces around her. Yanking the girl to her feet, Katya planted a resounding spank on her generous rear:—"Just to see how *you* feel!"—and, plunging into the water, swam away, the other girl splashing delightedly after her.

After this she became less of a wonder in the village. That same venturesome Dunyasha became a friend, coming up from the village to see her at every opportunity, often bringing an invitation from the other girls to come along berry picking or looking for mushrooms. Katya enjoyed these excursions. Everybody sang as naturally as birds in the midst of their labors: a voice would be raised in a song, another and then another would join in unexpected counterpoint. Later, after their baskets were full, there might be dancing in the cool of the evening, equally spontaneous. They would join hands and move around in a sedate circle as they sang. Suddenly the pace would change, the singing intensify, and one of the girl's would step out into the center of the circle and perform a more elaborate series of steps. Katya quite naturally became the leader of these *chorovods*, leading the dancing as though she had done it all her life. "Just as our Tatyana used to," said Praskovya in the tone of mingled sorrow and pride with which she always referred to Katya's mother.

She was coming home from one of those excursions when she met Stepanitch on the road. He was standing quite still, watching her come toward him, and the expression that had irritated her was back on his face. Katya frowned upon him:

"What is it, fellow? Why are you staring at me like this?"

"Why shouldn't I, my lady? I have a right to look at my promised bride, don't I?" he returned. He was swaying gently as he spoke, and Katya, who was about to pass him, couldn't help recoiling from the strong, spiritous fumes emanating from him.

"Why, you're drunk, you silly man!"

"Had to get drunk," he assured her seriously. "No other way of getting myself to talk to your ladyship." There was a mixture of servility and insolence in his speech. "Have been watching you, though—saw you dancing with the girls. Lord, but you're the prettiest filly ever came this way, and that's the truth. How about favoring us with a kiss, since you're my promised wife and all?"

As the bearded face advanced toward hers, Katya didn't move. Nevertheless, something about her expression seemed to sober him up and he drew back, dragging his hand downward across his face.

"Didn't mean to frighten you, missy," he said apologetically. "Still it's got to come out sometime."

"What has to come out? What are you talking about?"

But the headman had turned away and was unsteadily making his way back to the village. He called back to her over his shoulder: "You just ask your grandfather. He'll tell you all about it."

Katya watched his weaving figure out of sight and went home considerably perplexed.

Tikhon's face went bleak when she told him about this encounter. "So he came out with it, did he, the stupid ox. Well, not that I blame him! Must be working on his mind, too, no doubt about it . . ."

"But what is it, grandfather?"

Tikhon sighed. "Haven't told you this before. Why worry you before trouble comes? There were other orders besides the ones you know of in that letter her grace the countess sent here.

She wants to marry you off in the village. To someone in your own station of life, is what she wrote; the headman read it out to me."

"Marry me off?" Katya's voice rose high with incredulity. "But she can't."

"Yes, she can, my dearie, that's the wicked truth of it." Tikhon's face clouded over. "They can do anything they want to you if you're a serf; send you away anywhere, give you to the army for a soldier. Yes, and marry you off, too, to anyone they please. . . ."

Katya was speechless. This was a possibility that hadn't occurred to her. She, the pride of Petersburg balls, the betrothed bride of an heir to an English title, the future Marchioness of Lyndhurst, to be given as wife to one of the peasants who still took their hats off and bowed when they saw her—why, this was grotesque!

A horrible thought occurred to her. She said unsteadily: "And this Stepanitch—is he—am I—?" She couldn't bring the words out.

Tikhon nodded dismally. "Yes, that's it, my dearie. What she said in that letter, that old bitch, saving your presence, is that since you were used to better things and had had some high expectations—I guess marrying that Englishman is what she means—it is only fair that you should marry someone important in the village, so her command is that you should marry the headman. Stepanitch, that is. . . . She's really got her claws into you, ain't she?"

"Yes," Katya said tightly. Her hands curled at her sides as the depth of her stepmother's malice was borne in on her. "Well, I'd die first, grandfather."

"No need for talking that way, Katyusha. I'm not without weight in this village. That's the place your father gave me and that's the place I've kept. Pretty near everyone here has come to me. I've paid up their arrears, helped them out. Stepanitch himself owes me money! He's not going to be in a hurry to make an enemy out of me. It's not going to come to marriage, believe me. Not even her grace the countess can marry you off to a man already married."

"But he isn't, is he?"

"His wife died six months ago. But who's to know that? We're a distant village; nobody bothers us. You put that talk with that lout out of your mind. He didn't mean none of it: only it weighs on his mind, same as it does on mine, and seeing as how he was drunk . . . What Stepanitch wants is a dowry without a wife. He knows he'll be paid for his trouble. I've got plans, you see. And if they don't work out. . . ."

"Yes, what then, grandfather?"

Tikhon gave her his tight grin. "Why, then I'll make others. You leave the worrying to me, Katyusha." Katya, with perfect trust, was only too happy to do so.

Soon haying time was upon them, and Katya wanted to go out for it with the rest of the girls. Her grandfather lifted his eyebrows at her. "And how do you think you're going to keep up with the women, my Lady White Hands? They've been at it all their lives, and here you are fresh out of satins and silks and you think you can do it too, eh?"

"I know I can," Katya told him. Her grandfather had taken it for granted that her former life had been a totally inactive one, without any form of physical exercise. But Katya was accustomed to spending at least three hours every day hard at work on the arduous exercises necessary for ballet, and her young body had the toughness as well as the slenderness of a young sapling.

On the appointed day Katya went to join the crowd of peasant women who had gathered together in a field fragrant with newly mown hay. She was given a rake, and Dunyasha showed her how to hold it so as not to rub her hands raw.

"Have to get calluses here," she told her, presenting for Katya's inspection a broad palm with a ridge across the base of the fingers. "Your skin—why, it's like white curd, rub right off," she said, holding up Katya's small white hands and bestowing an enthusiastic kiss on each of them. Plump, good-natured Dunyasha had begun to worship her exotic new friend. Like the rest of the villagers, she was not quite clear about Katya's status or how to address her properly, alternating freely between an inaccurate "little countess" and an affectionate "dearie." Katya was fond of her: this naive attachment helped a little to fill the void left by her loss of Lisa.

That same keen sense of loss, which never quite left her, stabbed deeper as she looked at the busy scene about her. If Lisa were only here to share her new impressions, to enjoy this radiant, fragrant summer day with her!

She waited for Aunt Praskovya to finish winding some linen strips around her narrow palms as a further precaution against damage, and then she took her place in the line. Soon the rhythm of the work took over. All around her women moved with long, stroking movements that she tried to imitate, raking the mown grass into long, shining lines lying athwart the meadow. Their bright skirts had the vividness of wildflowers. Men followed them with pitchforks, tossing the grass into heaps. Presently broad, compact hayricks began to dot the field. The sun shone benignly above it all, making everything sparkle.

"Oh, what a day; it is God's gift, truly," said the older peasants, crossing themselves in gratitude.

At noon they broke off for a midday rest. "You come sit with us, little countess," Dunyasha said, seizing her hand and drawing her into the shadow of a tree at the edge of the meadow.

Katya greedily ate the lunch that Praskovya had packed for them. A communal sense of satisfaction as palpable as sunlight hung over the entire crowd, and for once she felt a part of it. Flushed with labor, warmed by the sun and the sense of comradeship with the others, she was quite happy. She listened to the songs that kept breaking out spontaneously among the groups and after a while became conscious of one of the voices raised beautifully above the rest: a male voice, velvety and powerful. A harmonious strum of strings accompanied it.

"There goes Vanya," said one of the girls.

A handsome, tall young man, his bright shirt half-open on his brown chest, was sitting on a hay cart a little distance away from them, lazily plucking at the strings of his balalaika as he sang. His reddish-blond curls were tousled, his bold blue eyes half-closed against the blazing sun. His voice was a resonant one; there was indolent strength in it and that special undercurrent of mixed wistfulness and recklessness that is typically Russian. Katya, listening to it with pleasure, decided that she preferred it to the highly trained voices of the Petersburg Opera.

"Yes, that's him, Vanya," Dunyasha said, with a giggle. "He is a one, Vanya is."

"What do you mean, Dunyasha?"

"Well, he just *is*, that's all."

After a while Katya thought she saw what Dunyasha meant. Girls kept going by him in a self-conscious way, addressing him in caressing little voices—"Vanya," they cooed, "Vanyechka . . ."—and getting a lazy, conquering smile in return. As she watched him, his eyes caught hers and opened wide. A quick, startled change came over his face, a response Katya was not unfamiliar with.

He broke off the song he had been singing and began another one, looking at her intently as he did so:

"Tis a snowstorm sweeping through the place,
A fair maiden follows it apace."

The beautiful voice thickened and throbbed.

"Won't you wait, my lovely, do, my beauty, wait,
Let me look upon you, let me know my fate."

Katya listened with undisguised pleasure and rewarded the singer with a quick, ravishing smile before looking away.

The whole village had turned out for the haying, and it was finished in the late afternoon. Some of the older people trudged home; but the young ones remained behind to sing and play games. Katya stayed, too.

It was decided to play *gorelki*, a game consisting of couples running hand in hand away from a single pursuer who tried to tag one of them, thereafter changing places with whichever of the couple was tagged.

The buxom Dunyasha ran with Katya; she was surprisingly quick on her feet, waving her free arm energetically as she kept pace with her fleet partner, and the two of them eluded all pursuers. Unaccountably she began to lag just as a new tag came after her. "Come on," Katya cried, pulling her behind a large hayrick. As the pursuer came after them, disdaining easier prey, Katya saw that it was the handsome young peasant with the alluring voice. Dunyasha squealed with excitement, as he tagged lightly on her shoulder. The girls unlinked hands, and Dunyasha, pouting, was sent on her way, the young man taking her place. His strong brown hand closed on Katya's and all at once, to her amazement, her heart skipped a beat. He smiled at her, his white teeth flashing.

"I won't let anyone catch us," he said. "From now on we stay together, my beauty."

Breathless and laughing, Katya leaned back against the sun-warmed wall of hay behind her, automatically casting up at her partner the same devastating look from under her long eyelashes that she had used to bewitch her Petersburg admirers. The next moment she found herself thoroughly and expertly kissed. Katya had been kissed before—hurried kisses stolen at balls, the respectful though deep-felt salutation bestowed upon her by Graham when they became betrothed. This was quite different. She was powerfully and relentlessly enfolded, another heart thudded against hers with strong, uneven hammer strokes, eager lips burned on hers. Never before had she been so sweetly and deeply kissed. She abandoned herself to this delightful new sensation.

She lay in his arms awhile after he had lifted his lips from hers, staring at the handsome, flushed face bent over hers, the smell of new-mown hay and sun and sweat pungent in her nostrils. Then reality flooded in on her and she became aware of voices in the distance.

The young man paid no attention to them. "What are you?" he asked in simple bewilderment. "What kind of a fairy-tale beauty, a tzar's daughter, Militrissa the beautiful? And here I've got you, I've captured you. . . ."

"Yes, but we can't stay here," Katya said prosaically. She leaned away from the powerful arms that still held her. "They're calling us."

"I'll never let you go, my golden bird."

"Yes, you will." Arching her slim back and placing her narrow palms against his chest, Katya pushed him away, sending him sprawling into the hay, and ran off, laughing.

On the way home Aunt Praskovya said casually but with a quick, sidelong glance in her direction, "That Vanya—a ne'er-do-well if there ever was one. Impudent, too, has to be watched every minute!"

Katya nodded absently. It *had* been impudent of him, she supposed, and she should be angry. However, she wasn't. It had been a remarkably pleasant experience, and Katya had to admit to herself that she was not at all averse to repeating it.

As she and her aunt approached the cottage, they heard angry voices issuing out of it.

"That's Stepanitch," Praskovya said, listening. Her concerned look went back to Katya. "Oh, Lord, what now? What is happening?"

They stood in the doorway listening.

"I'm disappointed in you, Stepanitch, my friend, that I am, and no two ways about it." That was Tikhon speaking. "Here I thought you were a reasonable, God-fearing man, no nonsense about you . . ."

"Well, I didn't ask for it," Stepanitch answered sullenly. "I didn't go around hankering to hitch up with the gentry; I'm the man to cut my cloth according to my measure. But here it is wished on me."

"You know it isn't fitting, Stepanitch."

"That's right, it isn't fitting, a simple man like me marrying the old count's by-blow, that's what I say to myself. And then I look at her running around in the field, and I say to myself, that's a pretty little piece there, and it's been given to you, like . . ."

"Why, you miserable old sinner!" Praskovya cried out, bursting into the room. "Do you think I'm going to let you touch my darling? She's not for you, do you hear?"

Katya followed her slowly. It was getting on toward evening. The last rays of the sun were coming in through the small window, bouncing off the bottle standing on the table between the two men.

The headman looked at her gloomily and glanced away. "It's no use yelling at me, Praskovya Tikhonovna. Like I said, I didn't ask for this—it was wished on me. We're dark people. We don't belong to ourselves; have to do what we're told."

"God sees everything you do, Stepanitch. He'll be there to punish you. You don't have to do everything you're told if there's a way around it." She faced him squarely, her arms akimbo. "And what about all the money my father has been giving you not to bother us, you lustful old goat?"

Tikhon sighed. "Bad enough if he were a goat, but he's a rabbit, too." He turned to Katya. "I didn't tell you all that time, my child; I kept some of the bad news from you. Her grace the countess has left other orders besides the ones you know of. Not only does she want to marry you off in the village, but a month is all she gave us. At the end of it, she says in that letter, she'll be sending here to see that her will has been done."

Katya was silent, her hands clapped to her cheeks. For some

reason this was much worse than the original revelation of her stepmother's plans for her. That had been a shock, of course, and she had been dismayed and infuriated; yet at the same time that arbitrary disposition of her person had seemed too grotesque to be real. It was the setting of the date that now made her alarmingly aware of the immediacy of danger. It was as though she had heard the click of a trap closing on her.

"Yeah," Stepanitch said with a gloomy sort of self-justification. "And it's getting on toward the end of the month. How am I, a headman, supposed to disobey a special order from the countess? Like as not there'll be someone here from Pskov to enforce it, like the time the folks in Makaryevo refused to do extra haying for the master. They'll manage a wedding if that's what the mistress wants, that's what they are there for."

"I'd like to see anyone try," Katya remarked, showing her small white teeth. "I'll scratch their eyes out."

Stepanitch gave her a sly and ominous look. "Never mind that, my lady," he said. "Girls have been taken by force to church before and married against their will, if that's what their masters wanted—aye, and bedded, too. As for the scratching out of eyes, the hands can be tied. . . ." He grinned unpleasantly, and Katya, watching him, stiffened.

When Katya got angry, she got angry all over, Lisa used to say. And indeed at this moment she felt consumed with anger; the heat of it spread all over her body. It crackled in her hair; it sharpened her vision so that she seemed to see its object with a special, deadly clarity.

"Listen to me, my friend," she said, and the special note in her voice wiped the grin off his face. "I suppose they can do it. They can tie my hands and drag me to the church and hold me down while Father Orofey performs the ceremony. But they cannot stop me from killing you as soon as my hands are untied. And that, I swear, I will do."

Stepanitch recoiled from her as though he had been scalded. "Do you hear her, old man? She means it, too!"

"Don't you worry, brother," said Tikhon soothingly. "I wouldn't let my granddaughter soil her white hands with your blood . . . But I'm an old man, more than three score and ten years, which is a man's allotted span, and I stand ready to do it for her rather than let you lay your dirty hands on her."

At that moment the two faces, the girl's and the old man's,

wore an identical, implacable look, and the headman cringed before it.

"That's a fine get-out!" There was a whine in his voice now. "Do you think I want to do it? I'm a simple man. I have no wish to deal with gentry in any manner or form. I have no desire to have a wife, who, every time I look at her, makes me think of the old count, so I have to get drunk when I want to talk to her, and who besides will cut my throat!" He gave Katya a look that was almost comical in its combination of resentment and cowardice. "But yet here are her grace's orders to me, like thunder out of the clear sky . . ."

"The countess is in Petersburg far away from the village, Stepanitch."

But now she didn't seem all that far away. Katya vividly saw again her stepmother's furious face, with all the accumulated hatred unleashed, and heard her hard voice saying: "You are my serf, my chattel. I can do anything I want with you."

". . . seems to me we have always been able to settle our own affairs by ourselves," Tikhon was saying, "and no one the wiser."

"That might have been before *she* came here, old man!" Stepanitch answered sullenly with a jerk of his head in Katya's direction. "Now it's different. There'll be a messenger sent here in a month's time to see whether her bidding is done, whether the girl is wedded to me. That's what her grace the countess says . . ."

For a moment Tikhon was silent. He looked suddenly old and frail; much too frail, Katya thought with a thin stab of fear, to cope with all that malicious power issuing from Petersburg. But in another moment he had recovered and was regarding the headman with amused disdain. "'The countess says!' The way you say it, it's like that letter is the Holy Scriptures, written down for evermore and aye, amen. You know what the gentry are like. Suppose you do what you're told and that's what you tell them at the end of the month. 'Oh, now, that wasn't what her grace meant at all, that was just in the heat of the moment. You just misunderstood it like the fool you are and there was no need for such a damned hurry, no need at all!' And in the end it gets taken out of your skin; you're the one gets punished for your pains. . . . Never heard of that happening, have you?"

From Stepanitch's expression it was clear that he had. "Well, so what do you think I should do, Tikhon Yeremeitch?" he asked in a chastened voice.

"Wait, that's what I say. Stall them along. All kinds of reasons can be given."

"That bit about being married already won't work, Tikhon Yeremeitch; they'll get to the rights of it immediately."

Tikhon gave him a slightly contemptuous look. "No, I can see you're not the man to carry it off, Stepanitch, my friend, and nor will I expect it from you . . . There are other ways. You can always say you're sick, you're going to ask permission to retire as headman—don't worry, I'll make it worth your while—and since her grace wanted Katya to marry someone important in the village . . . Or if it comes to that, tell the truth. Say you're in fear of your life. That'll give her grace something to think about; she wants to do it all on the quiet, and you can't hush up murder—it'll all have to come out . . ."

"And meanwhile I'll be in trouble, any which way."

"You'll be in less trouble the way I'm telling you. And you'll be paid for the trouble, never fear. It's the dowry you want rather than the bride, isn't it?"

At last Stepanitch left, and Tikhon sat down rather limply.

"Well, he'll think twice before trying to lead you to the altar, little Tartar that you are," he said, trying to smile.

"You were marvelous, grandfather."

"Yes, seems like we frightened him between us. How long he'll stay frightened—that's another matter." He sighed heavily and suddenly looked like a very worried old man at the end of his tether. "But at least it gives us time. We'll contrive something, never fear. We'll have to."

CHAPTER 11

The next day, when the family went on their weekly inspection tour of the big house, Tikhon went straight to Tatyana's bedroom. There he took a key from the bunch hanging at his belt and opened the large painted coffer at the window. A smell of camphor filled the room as he lifted the lid.

"There," he said, crossing himself. "First time since Tatyana died. 'Leave everything as it is'—those were your father's orders, Katyusha. But now is the time to disregard them, God willing."

"Tatyana's lady-clothes," said Praskovya, her mild eyes lighting up with pleasure as she peered into the box.

The clothes Katya saw were of a totally different order from the ones Praskovya had kept in their cottage. They were made of silk and velvet, trimmed with lace and gold braid. A dozen rich shawls of different colors lay among them, securely wrapped in silver paper, together with spools of shimmering gold ribbon and lace and plumed headdresses.

"Oh, how pretty," Katya said, lifting out a dress of blue taffeta as lustrously changeable as a pigeon's breast and lavishly trimmed with brilliants and pearls. "But what a silly style!" With curiosity she inspected the long, tight bodice coming to a point at the bottom and sternly stiffened by whalebone, the voluminous lace sleeves and the extravagant width of material gathered up for furbelows. There couldn't be a greater contrast between this cumbersome creation and the high-waisted, easily flowing Empire styles she was accustomed to wearing. She began to laugh. "Why, old Countess Golitzin still wears these gowns—*and* powders her hair."

"So did Tatyana, and looked as fine as any lady," Praskovya

said. "His grace your father liked her to dress up for the guests. She liked dressing up, too, but truth to tell, she felt much better in our own peasant wear."

"I don't blame her. It must have been so uncomfortable!" She pulled out a voluminous sable-trimmed cloak of raspberry-colored velvet. "And look at this. One could wear this to a masquerade." Wrapping it around herself, she peacocked over to the full-length cheval mirror to join Annushka, who was parading before it completely obliterated in a huge bokhara shawl with a sumptuous flowered border.

"Well, it's not a masquerade I have in mind," said Tikhon, "Seems to me there's enough material among all these fal-lals to make up a few dresses for Katyusha, eh, Praskovya?"

"But I already have plenty of mama's clothes, grandpa."

"I mean lady-clothes, girl, like the one you were delivered to us in. Since her grace your stepmother didn't see her way to outfitting you properly," he gave a sour grin, "looks like it's up to us, simple folk as we are."

"But grandfather, why should I wear lady-clothes here? It would be silly."

"Who said you'll be wearing them here? They'll be for later."

She understood at once. "You mean, for when I go to Moscow? To get into the dance company? Why, of course, grandfather. That's the only way out."

Tikhon gave her a sharp, appraising look from under his shaggy eyebrows. "Think you're good enough to please that Mr. Diddle-oh you're always talking about?"

"I think so. I've been practicing every day, you know that."

Every morning, rising early, she would go into the little theater that her father had built for her mother. There was a small room backstage with a barre and a pier mirror. There, stripped down to camisole and pantalettes, she would faithfully do the exercises that monsieur Duroc had taught her, going painstakingly through the *pliés* and the *battements*, and rehearsing the dance sequences she already knew.

"Anyhow, that doesn't arise—Didelot is in Petersburg and I shall be going to Moscow, and I am certainly as good as any Moscow dancer."

Tikhon nodded. "That's good. Know your trade and your fortune is made. . . . I want you to start sewing right away, Praskovya. Get those fal-lals ready for Katyusha. I like to be beforehand: this way if she has to leave in a hurry, she won't be standing here with her mouth open and nothing but a shift to put on."

"Leave in a hurry? But why?" A look at her grandfather's bleak face gave her the answer. She said slowly: "Do you think I'll have to? You said yesterday we had time . . ."

"So we do, and it's up to us to use it wisely, to get ready for whatever may come. I've always been one to look ahead. This way when the time comes for you to get out of here, you won't look like a runaway serf girl with a bundle on her back; you'll be traveling like a proper lady on the road to Moscow."

"Father!" Praskovya threw up her hands in dismay, letting the shimmering silks scatter at her feet. "Lord save us, you aren't thinking of letting Katyusha go to Moscow by herself?"

"Might have to." Tikhon's face grew a shade bleaker. "Better the wide road than a rotten marriage."

"But a child delicately raised, who never traveled unattended before—how will she manage?"

"Oh, I'll manage very well, auntie," Katya rejoined blithely. "After all, what can happen to me?"

"See," Praskovya mourned, "she doesn't even know the dangers around her, the poor lamb, in her innocence!"

"Stop croaking like a raven, woman." Tikhon said. "I know it all very well, no need to spell it out to me. No use repining: needs must go when the devil drives. . . . It's one way out; maybe the Lord will show us another. Meanwhile, you get busy on those dresses. Let everything else go. I want them ready as soon as possible."

Praskovya nodded. "I'll get some women to help me. We'll have them done in a trice."

"No, that you won't, Praskovya." Tikhon shook his head in exasperation. "No more sense than a hen, it seems like! Just you let the word spread around that there are lady's clothes being made for Katyusha, and we'll be in the soup for sure. No, you'll have to do it all yourself, no help for it."

Praskovya nodded, resigned.

"I can help you, auntie," Katya offered. Her relatives looked unflatteringly surprised.

"You mean they taught your ladyship something useful in Petersburg?" Tikhon inquired sarcastically.

"I can do the hemming, at least." She and Lisa had been

taught to sew and embroider and had spent many hours working over their hoops or hemming handkerchiefs.

"And so can Annushka. I taught her myself . . . Well with two such helpers we should be ready in jig time." Praskovya beamed on her, although somewhat tearfully. Clearly she was still oppressed by doubts about Katya's proposed journey. "Let's see what we have here . . . now this here celandine silk looks good. . . ."

Tikhon stumped out, leaving his womenfolk deep in consultation over the trunkful of fineries.

The next day Katya came in from gathering early-autumn raspberries to find a young man wearing country gentleman's clothes sitting at the table with her grandfather, putting away a plate of cabbage soup served up by her aunt.

"Have you been gathering berries, Katyusha?" Tikhon asked, at his most affable. "You've brought them just in time. His worship's carriage broke down as he did us the honor of passing through the village. Efrem the smith is working on it now, so I brought his worship here for a meal, there being no fit place for him in the village. This is my granddaughter, sir," he said to the young man.

The young man looked at Katya and his eyes glazed over. He was not an ill-looking young man, though somewhat on the weedy side; there was something weak and indeterminate about his face, with its longish nose and myopic, white-lashed eyes. Katya nodded to him graciously and said to Tikhon, "But you haven't introduced the gentleman to me, grandpa."

The young man bounded to his feet. "Feofil Petrovich Chirkin, a neighbor of yours, at your ser—" He broke off midword, bewildered, as he realized that these cultivated accents were emerging from the lips of a peasant girl who at the same time addressed the old peasant as grandfather.

"Now then, my girl," Tikhon said reprovingly, but with a twinkle. "You must forgive her, sir, she's just come from town. She isn't used to the right way of speaking to the gentry."

"Er, not at all—I mean yes, of course," said Chirkin gobblingly. Becoming aware of the absurdity of rising to his feet to acknowledge an introduction to a peasant girl as though she had been a lady, he reseated himself slowly.

Katya gave the berries to Aunt Praskovya and went outside to play with the children. Soon the carriage arrived, driven by a bearded coachman as countrified as his master. Chirkin emerged from the cottage and spent an unnecessarily long time discussing the repairs, even bestowing a slight kick with his booted foot to one of the wheels to convince himself that it was all right. His eyes kept straying to Katya even after he had finally climbed into his carriage.

"Do come back again, your worship," said Tikhon, who had followed him out of the cottage. "Plenty of good shooting here; the park is full of snipe and partridges . . . ! Katyusha, bring the pitcher of *kvas* for the gentleman to refresh himself with before leaving."

Katya demurely did his bidding. Chirkin's eyes glazed over even more and he almost missed his lips with the mug of *kvas*. "Er—good-bye," he said, handing it back to her, "and—er—thank you very much indeed."

"*Enchantée de vous servir, monsieur*," Katya said, curtesying. The coachman whipped up the horses. Her last view of young Chirkin was the sight of his astonished face goggling back at her over the top of his carriage until it disappeared over the hill. She began to laugh. "What a silly fellow! Who is he, anyhow?"

"Didn't you hear him? A neighbor. Lives a few miles away from here with his mama. His uncle is a governor hereabouts." An appeciative grin wrinkled up Tikhon's face. "You're a wicked puss, aren't you?" he said, looking at his granddaughter with approbation. "That did it—he'll be back for certain, see if he won't!"

Katya gave no further thought to this particular conquest. Her thoughts were engaged with her more troubling admirer. It seemed to her that Vanya was present wherever she went. He turned up at a berry-picking expedition, by tradition a purely female pursuit, where he was greeted with shrieks of indignation and pelted with berries. He held his ground, grinning, and was presently at Katya's side, helping her fill her basket. The sound of his voice lifted in song greeted her when she appeared at the village fair, and there he was accompanied by the inevitable balalaika, singing to an admiring group, his lively blue eyes on the watch for her. It was a homely enough little fair, consisting of a few stalls set up by traveling peddlers and an encampment of gypsy horse dealers and tinkers hawking their wares, but Katya, putting on her favorite sarafan of glowing red nankeen over a vividly embroidered blouse, and a *kokoshnik*, a headdress embroidered with seed pearls, was aware of a lift of excitement as though she were going to an Annichkov Palace gala. She had to admit to herself that she had dressed up in expectation of being seen and admired by the handsome young peasant who made her feel conscious of her beauty in a very special way.

There were other occasions; unconsciously she began to look out for them. Under the influence of this delightful new preoccupation, Katya's natural optimism reasserted itself. Her sense of ever-present danger receded. The shock she had suffered during her confrontation with Stepanitch faded, particularly since the headman was for the time being taking care to stay out of her way. With the incorrigible lightheartedness of youth she told herself that her grandfather would take care of everything, and put her situation not precisely out of her mind but to the back of it, where she could ignore it while she enjoyed herself.

Katya was only too used to pretty speeches from her swains; but no one in Petersburg had ever called her his sable-browed queen, his black-plumed swan. "Turn your eyes to me just once, burn my heart with your look," Vanya would whisper to her. "Walk over it with your little feet; I would gladly take death from you, my joy, my golden love-fever. . . ." Extravagant language, passionate and poetic, that reminded her of the fairy tales their nanny used to tell them: in such words did Ivan Tsarevich address the beautiful daughter of Koshchei the Immortal. Everything in Katya responded to these passionate endearments. As she listened to him and remembered his kisses, she wanted to purr like a cat.

By habit she would begin to think, "If only Lisa . . ." and then stop in mid-thought. Perhaps this particular experience was not one she would confide to Lisa, who would be sure to say, "Yes, but think of Monsieur Graham!" Just the way she used to when Katya would flirt too much with Captain Kozlov. Katya shrugged her shoulders: there wasn't much use thinking of Monsieur Graham, who was probably on his way to England by now, having been fed lies by her obliging stepmother.

One night something roused her from her sleep. The moonlight shining in through the small slit of her bedroom window had reached her bed, and it was as though a shining hand had touched her face, awakening her. Vanya's song was on her mind. She lay in her bed, smiling sleepily and repeating the words to herself:

"Won't you wait, my lovely, do, my beauty, wait,
Let me look upon you, let me know my fate. . . ."

Presently she realized that the song was not just in her mind. A barely audible strum of strings reached her from outside, a sound just above the even breathing of the sleeping children. All at once she was wide awake. Without another thought she slipped out of her bed, left her room and ran swiftly and noiselessly through the main room, where her grandfather snored peacefully on the stove. In a moment she was outside, looking intently about her. The sound came again, and Katya, moving as if in a dream, followed it into the black and silver garden. The strumming stopped. A tall figure, moon-silvered, moved in the darkness.

"Vanya?"

"I knew you'd hear. I knew you'll come out to me, my queen, my beauty," came the whisper. Her hand was taken, and she was drawn further back into the shadows.

She followed without demurring. All she knew was that the delightful sensations she had experienced at the mowing would be repeated and perhaps added to, and that seemed the most important thing in the world. With a shiver of pleasure she abandoned herself to his embrace, giving her lips to that fierce and searching kiss, feeling an agreeable weakness invade her entire body. It seemed only natural to be lifted from her feet and laid down on the warm grass, surrendering herself to an embrace that grew more exigent with each second. A fleeting thought passed through her mind: Where was this leading to? Very soon, she knew with exultation, she would find out. . . .

The sound of her name, repeated with angry urgency, broke through the spell. A light flashed jaggedly out of the darkness, and presently her grandfather walked into a patch of moonlight with a lantern in his hand. He shined the light grimly into their dazed faces before setting it down on the ground. The two young people scrambled to their feet in confusion.

"All right, then," said Tikhon sternly. "You get right back to the house, my girl. And as for you, you young Herod, I have a mind to give you a beating you won't forget."

"Tikhon Yeremeitch, I—"

"Never mind that. I know my name and my surname too, just like I know yours. Who do you think you are, prowling around decent Christian folks' houses corrupting young maidens, eh?" He was in a towering rage. Katya could see him clearly in the moonlight now. In his long nightshirt, from which his crooked old legs protruded, with his whiskers all abristle and his eyes glittering malignantly, he made Katya think of a *domovoy*, that redoubtable domestic demon that patrols the household at night.

"No, you just listen, old man. I didn't come here for that and that's God's truth. It's just like I've been drawn down here, like a spell has been cast on me. . . ."

Tikhon sniffed. "That's as it may be. All the same, you get back to your kennel, you impudent young dog, or it'll be the worse for you."

"Don't be so mean to him, grandpa," Katya interposed. "It's my fault too . . ."

"That's for sure," her grandfather agreed grimly.

"Tikhon Yeremeitch," a wild plea had entered the young man's voice, "give her to me, give her to me for a wife. I'll cherish her like the queen she is, work my hands to the bone. . . ."

"She's not for you," came the implacable answer.

"For whom, then? I'll tell you plain, old man, I'm not going to stand by and see her marrying anyone else."

"And who told you she would?"

"I know what's being planned. Stepanitch got drunk the other night in the tavern. He was saying . . ."

"In the tavern, eh? Well, that makes sense, seeing how you spend most of your time there, both you and he. What did he tell you, the loose-tongued windbag?"

"Just that she's got to stay here in the village, make her life here, that's the master's will. Well, then, why can't she make it with me, then? You would like that, wouldn't you, my love, my sable-browed queen? Tell him you would."

"She doesn't have to tell me any such thing. Nor you either, in the middle of the night, when decent folks are at home asleep, not prowling around like tomcats over the roofs. You want to ask her hand in marriage, you come in the daytime and I'll listen to you. Not that it'll be any use, either; she's not for you, my friend. Nor for anyone else, either, not in this village. Now off with you, d'you hear? As for you, my girl, you get back to the house if you don't want to feel my hand."

Katya found herself obeying meekly. It didn't occur to her either then or later to resent being ordered around in this peremptory manner by an illiterate old serf caretaker. He was her grandfather, justifiably annoyed with her.

The young man, somewhat heartened by that last assurance, cast one more longing gaze at Katya and went off into the night, his head hanging. Tikhon herded his errant granddaughter back to the cottage, scolding all the way. "This is a fine how-de-do. It's a good thing I was lying awake, cudgeling my brains about our troubles, and heard you sneaking out, or where would we be now? If this is what they teach you in Petersburg, my fine lady. . . ."

He let himself down on the bench, uttering a tired old man's groan. Katya perched herself next to him, tucking her slim feet under her. Not listening to his grumbling, she looked out into the moonlit night, thinking of how it had been.

Tikhon looked at her dreamy face and scowled. "You aren't thinking of marrying that great oaf out there, are you, by any chance, my lady?" he asked in a deceptively soft voice.

Katya jumped. Uncannily he had lifted the vagrant thought out of her mind. "I was just thinking—if it turns out that I have to stay here anyhow . . ."

The truth was that she wanted those arms around her again, that powerful yet tender mastery of her willing body, those deep, intoxicating kisses. An arrangement whereby this inflammatory lovemaking would be available to her whenever she wanted it couldn't be too bad, she thought.

The old man's eyes were understanding. "Ah, yes, my little one, it's the fever of youth, the hot young blood. Can lead to the worst mistakes if you let it. It all wears off and what do you have then? It's like a peddler is trying to sell you a length of goods, and the color is bright, the design is pretty. Good enough for the summer, but wear it a bit and it'll fall into rags, won't cover you decently, won't keep you warm in winter. . . ."

"Well, so you just get another one for winter!" Dimpling, Katya gave him an arch look.

"Another one for—" Tikhon repeated. Unexpectedly he broke out into an old man's laugh, his shoulders shaking, smiting his knees and emitting wheezing chortles until his face turned purple and Katya, alarmed, had to pound his back. "Another one for winter . . . That's a good one! You're a rogue, you are, Katyusha. No," he said, sobering up. "Unfortuantely all we God's servants get in this life is one length of cloth; has to do for all seasons. This Vanya—why, I wouldn't let any girl in the village come hear him. He's good to look at, sure enough, and he sings like a nightingale. But you go look at his cottage—it's the worst in the village, and he doesn't care enough to make it better. What he likes best is singing and running after the girls; and in between, where you'll find him is in the tavern drinking away his money . . . "There *had* been a faint whiskeyish taste in those kisses, Katya remembered. "That's his nature and his whole family's and it'll never change. You've been brought up in silks and satins; and we've been keeping our home clean and decent, so you don't know how it is. How would you like to live in a filthy hut, carrying out slops for yourself and taking care of a drunken husband?"

"Oh, no," said Katya, revolted.

"And besides," Tikhon pursued implacably "here you've been telling me all about Moscow and how you want to be a dancer, like Tatyana was. Did you mean it or were you telling fairy tales to yourself and me?"

"Of course I meant it," Katya answered heatedly. "That's all I do want. As for Vanya . . ." Despite herself she sighed. "Of course, that will not do, I can see that. I didn't really mean it. I was merely romancing a bit, grandpa." She added thoughtfully, "Anyhow, it isn't as if I wanted to *marry* . . ."

"No, I know what it is you want, missy," said her grandfather wrathfully. His small black eyes sharpened with suspicion. "He didn't have his way with you, did he? You're still a virgin?" And as Katya's eyes widened at this plain speaking, "All right, all right, I can see for myself nothing's happened."

Katya was silent, struck by the incongruity of the old man whose daughter had been his owner's concubine talking like any respectable old relative. Tikhon gave her a shrewd look.

"You're thinking of your mother, eh?" he said with uncanny perception. "Well, I kept my eye on my Tatyana. I saw that nobody touched her until his excellency your father came along. That's why he loved her as he did—because he was her first; she came to him untouched. Sounds calculating, don't it? Well, and so it is. When you've been put on the bottom of the ladder, you have to start scrambling up. That's the Lord's will; that's what he wants you to do. Use everything you have, don't squander it on the way. You stop scrambling, down you go in the mud. Nobody's going to help you; you have to do it all for yourself. You've been telling me about your sister. You think she'll have a care for you now you're down? Where is she now when you need her?"

"Don't you dare to say a word about my Lisa," said Katya, reddening with anger. "She's missing me as badly as I'm missing her. It isn't her fault that she doesn't know where I am!"

Tikhon shrugged, unconvinced. "All I know is that gentlefolk have a mighty short memory. Take his excellency your father; pretty near my son-in-law he was. No complaints about how he treated me while my daughter was alive. If not for him I wouldn't be what I am in the village today. And he talked about freeing all of us, that he did. But it was out of sight, out of mind with him. Once Tatyana was gone, he didn't even *want* to think of us. . . ."

Katya said indignantly, "Well, I think it was too bad and—and downright dishonorable of him."

She couldn't help thinking that her father had been remiss about her, too. He had loved her, he had pampered her, but he had never given a thought to her future. Her eyes stinging, she attempted to find an excuse for him. "He did try," she thought, remembering the unfinished letter, "with his last breath he tried." But she couldn't help thinking that it would have been better for him to have attended to her prospects before that last breath was taken. And here on the other hand was her grandfather, a lowly serf, worrying about her, protecting her from the results of what her father had left undone. A feeling of gratitude lifted her heart. She flung her arms around the old man's frail shoulders. "Oh, grandfather," she cried, "I do so love you."

"Well, and I love you too, dearie," Tikhon said, answering

her tempestuous hug. "You're my dear Tatyana's girl, flesh of my flesh. How not to love you? I'll take care of you, never fear. . . . Now go to bed, like a good girl."

This mutual affection notwithstanding, the very next day found them embroiled in a quarrel. About to go to the village, Katya was stopped by Tikhon, who sternly ordered her to stay home. "You've done enough lollygagging, my girl. How about staying home and giving your aunt a hand. She's wearing her eyes out sewing for you."

Katya reddened with anger. This attack was as unfair as it was unexpected, since she had just finished trimming a dress with Mechlin lace and had been praised by Praskovya for her neatness in doing so. She informed Tikhon of this with some dignity. "So since there's nothing else to do, and I promised Dunyasha to go walking . . ."

"Dunyasha, eh?"

"Yes, Dunyasha." Of course if by chance someone else was to join them . . . Her grandfather seemed to read her thought. His shaggy eyebrows coming together, he said grittily: "If you are sneaking off to meet that good-for-naught on the sly . . ."

Katya drew herself up. "It isn't my habit to sneak off," she rejoined haughtily. "If I do see Vanya, be assured it won't be on the sly. And if you think you can keep me penned up in the cottage, grandfather, as though I were a—a *cow* . . ."

Tikhon's scowl grew more pronounced. "Is that how it is, my lady? Too high and mighty to be told what's good for you, are you?" He slammed the cottage door shut and pointedly took a position in front of it. "Well, we'll see about that."

They glared at each other. It was borne in on Katya that her low-born grandfather was as much of a tyrant in his household as her aristocratic father had been. "Yes," she said, "we'll see about it," and, head high, went into her own room, also slamming the door.

There she was presently joined by her aunt. "Now then, Katyusha," she began conciliatingly.

"I am not going to be tyrannized by anyone, auntie."

"I know, I know." Her soft face puckered with distress, Praskovya put her arms about her niece's rigid shoulders. "It's not like father to be unjust. But he hasn't been sleeping nights lately with everything he has on his mind, so if he gets to be a mite irritable, it's not to be wondered at, seeing how he's getting on in years. . . ."

"Not sleeping nights," Katya repeated. She bit her lip. "On account of me, isn't it?"

"Well, yes, Katyusha, that's what has been on his mind, no denying it. Night and day he frets over our troubles, poor soul."

Katya was suddenly smitten by a distressful memory of coming on her grandfather in the midst of his prayers. Rather startled, since it was the middle of the day, she had tiptoed by respectfully, not without catching a few muttered phrases. "Help us in our dire need . . . Powerful enemies . . . No hope save in you. . . ." There had been something particularly pathetic in the sight of his turned-up soles as he prostrated himself before the ikon.

So Katya went to make her peace with Tikhon. "I know you're right about Vanya," she told him. Of course he was, she thought. No good could come from any more of these conflagrative meetings. "I'll keep out of his way, I promise."

Tikhon's face cleared. "That's my good girl." He patted her shoulder and added in gruff apology: "Didn't speak to you right, that I didn't. Your mother too could only stand a light hand on the reins. Getting old and cross-grained, I am, no doubt about that."

Katya swallowed. "I am sorry," she said in a constricted voice. "It looks as though I've brought you nothing but trouble in your old age, grandfather."

"Nonsense," Tikhon rejoined bracingly. "What you brought me is great joy: it's others who are giving us trouble."

"Is Stepanitch . . .?"

Tikhon shook his head. "When I get too old to handle that great oaf, I might as well get into my grave," he said bravely. But Katya could sense the trouble behind the defiant words. "Never mind him, my dolly. You just be a good girl and tend to your sewing. I'll see to it that nothing hurts you. I've got plans," he added mysteriously.

Faithful to her promise, Katya stuck close to home for the next few days, helping Praskovya sew her dresses. To her amazement, her modest aunt had turned out to be no mean seamstress. A thorough examination of the traveling dress Katya had worn upon her arrival to Krasnoye had immediately shown her how to transform the voluminous garments of twenty years ago into the scanty, high-bosomed modern garb. "Why, it's nothing but a little nightgown, when you look at it," she said scornfully, "with those dinky little sleeves and all. No trouble at all." Her red, work-worn hands moved with assurance, handling the rich materials. "I used to help the Frenchman his excellence your father had here to dress Tatyana. He showed me a lot, he did. I got to know how to cut the material and all, and mind you, those were no shifts with a little flounce sewed on, like this here. All sorts of furbelows and trains and farthingales we had, and the girls in the sewing room would be kept busy stitching and embroidering. Tatyana used to say to me, 'Pashenka, when his lordship gets tired of me . . .'"

"He never would have!" Katya exclaimed indignantly.

"No, it didn't look like that at the time, bu you can never tell with the gentry, my lovey. . . . Well, we'd be free, at any rate, and I could go to Moscow and set myself up as a sewing woman for one of the big dressmakers there. Or else sew costumes for the dance company, where Tatyana would be dancing. For that's what her heart was set on . . . But that's not how it turned out, is it?" Praskovya's buxom breast lifted with a gentle sigh. "Tatyana died, my darling sister, and the count went away and left us all. . . . And then I met my Andrey, may he rest in peace, and had the children, so it looks like what we planned wasn't what the good Lord had in mind for me. But it's still in my hands, that old skill. . . ."

"Never mind, auntie. When I become a prima ballerina, I'll send for you and you will design and sew all my costumes and become famous, too, a celebrated *modiste* known all over Russia."

"Lord save us, what next!"

"And me, too, I'll come too, won't I?" Annushka chimed in.

"Of course you will, my darling!" Katya gave her little cousin a quick hug. Annushka had been helping, too, stitching industriously at her side, with an occasional little yelp when she pricked her small fingers. As Katya looked at her dark head bent over her sewing, she remembered the times she and Lisa had spent together in similar occupation, sometimes chattering ceaselessly, sometimes in the comfortable silence of perfect companionship. She could almost see that fair head attentively inclined over the embroidery hoop, pale ringlets spilling over the frail white neck. *Oh, my little white mouse, my darling sister, I miss you so . . .* Her eyes misted over and she could no longer see Praskovya's clever fingers gathering a crimson velvet ribbon into a ruche around the neck of what was to be a fashionable walking dress of blue Berlin silk.

They had finished two dresses and put them in a small brassbound trunk ("A hope chest for you, my dearie," Praskovya said happily) and were starting on another one, a charmeuse tunic trimmed with pearl buttons over a straw-colored underdress, when they received a visit. One morning Tikhon's long-sighted eyes spotted a lone horseman cantering on the road to the manor house and immediately identified him.

"Yes, it's him, all right, Feofil Petrovich Chirkin himself, as ever was," he said, rubbing his hands gleefully. "Told you he'd come back, didn't I? And here he is. When I remember his face that last time when you let loose with your foreign fiddle-faddle! Knew for sure and certain then that he would be back for another look." He gave an exultant chuckle.

Katya too smiled dutifully, although she could not quite understand this disproportionate elation over the reappearance of a rather undistinguished personage whom she had in the meantime quite forgotten.

"He seems to ride well," she observed.

"Yes, left his carriage home this time, didn't he? Probably afraid his coachman will report his doings to his mother. He lives with her. Got several estates belonging to him scattered all over the Pskov province—Otradnoye is the nearest to us—but his mama insists on his living with her in Marinovka. She's the one that rules the roost. Not too strong in the head, the young squire is—but that's not such a bad thing. If you can be nose-led by one female, so you can be by another," he finished incomprehensibly.

The horseman approached at a brisk canter and indeed turned out to be Chirkin, wearing a riding jacket and buckskin breeches, his high boots twinkling with polish. He alighted from his horse in front of the cottage, and Tikhon, with a backward grin at his granddaughter, went out to greet him.

"Just passing by," said the young man. "Thought I'd stop and pay a visit to you, see how you are getting on, old man. Er—enjoyed your meal that time. Never get to eat *shchi* at home, mother says I have a delicate stomach . . . Never thought so myself, but there it is."

Tikhon, bowing low, respectfully expressed his hope that the peasant fare didn't damage his worship's delicate stomach.

"Not a bit of it, never felt as well in my life. . . . Er—and how is your granddaughter? Is she still with you? Eh?"

"Yes, indeed, and in good health, thanking you for your kind inquiry."

"That's splendid," said Chirkin, visibly brightening. "I mean to say, splendid for you. Must be a pleasant thing to have a granddaughter like her coming to stay with one . . . Would like it myself . . . Not that I have any granddaughters . . . Well, stands to reason, how could I? Not even married . . . What I meant was if I were you and had a granddaughter like yours . . ." Having thus talked himself into a corner, Chirkin stopped, took a breath and started over again. "Ah—a fine piece of property you have here. Beautiful park and all. Must have been—er—quite a splendid place in the old count's time . . ."

Tikhon agreed that it was so and asked whether his worship wished to walk through the grounds. "A bit overgrown since his grace's time, as you say, but there's still a lot to see, all manner of grand things, statues and grottoes and the like. My granddaughter knows every inch of it; she can show you everything . . . Katyusha!"

Katya obediently took the bemused young man on a tour of the gardens. She showed him one of the grottoes furnished with moss and seats hewn out of the rock, led him along her favorite winding path among the birch trees to the clearing where a granite statue of Catherine the Great was standing and through the overgrown alley of acacias, with its interspersed marble statues, most of which, unfortunately, showed signs of deterioration.

The young people were not alone on that walk, being accompanied not only by the two children but also by Dunyasha, who had wandered over from the village for a visit with her friend. The young squire was plainly intimidated by this retinue. Dunyasha in particular abashed him by giggling in her sleeve every time she caught his distracted eye.

He talked very little as he walked silently at Katya's side, his brow corrugated in bewilderment as he obviously tried to work out in his mind the disparity between Katya's looks and bearing and her relationship to the old peasant. It was all too much for him, and he was too timid to press for an explanation.

It was not until the end of the walk that he gathered a little courage and, assuming a nonchalant expression (as though saying to himself: "Come, this is silly, she's just a peasant girl after all"), awkwardly slid his arm around her waist. Katya, with difficulty repressing a desire to laugh, gave him a look of haughty displeasure and he immediately withdrew his arm.

"Lord save us," Dunyasha cried, after he had left them to ride home, "what a rabbit of a *barin*!"

"Yes, he is a funny one," Katya agreed. "Nothing like—" She broke off with an involuntary little sigh, thinking of her other suitor. Vanya had been anything but abashed in her presence; he had wooed her shamelessly, going his reckless way merrily and boldly, without giving a thought to the social differences between them. She had submitted to her grandfather's edict, knowing that he was right, and had tried not to think of Vanya. But often she would wake at night, her young body inflamed with longing, and toss restlessly in her bed, fancying that she was hearing the seductive jangle of balalaika strings outside the cottage.

As if picking up her thought, Dunyasha too sighed, her freckled face clouding over. "It's a pity and a shame about poor Vanya," she said sadly.

Katya looked down at her neat little *lapti*. "Why, what's the matter with him?" she asked with pretended indifference.

Dunyasha gave another gusty sigh. "He's been conscripted, that's what. Has to go into the tsar's army; no help for it. Our village sends three men every year. Well, poor soul, he's a bachelor, his brothers are married, so who but he—" She broke off, clapping her hands to her mouth. "I wasn't supposed to tell you," she gasped. "Tikhon Yeremeitch especially said not to say anything until afterward."

Katya stood stock still, shocked into silence. Gay, unruly Vanya a soldier! One of those inhuman perfectly matched automatons whom she used to see in Petersburg parading woodenly across the Mars Field, or standing motionless at attention in one of those military reviews that Emperor Alexander was so fond of. "Look how perfectly matched they are," she had said to Lisa, laughing. "Just like toy soldiers! Isn't it funny?"

"I don't find it so," Lisa had answered unsmilingly. "They aren't toys but God's creatures, after all."

A pang pierced her heart as she remembered this conversation. She cried out, "But he can't! I—I won't have it."

"Nothing to be done about it, little countess," Dunyasha answered with a sniffle. "If our masters were living here, it would be a different matter, it would be for them to decide whom to send and whom to keep. But the way it is, it's all left to the village *mir*, and they go about it as fair as they can, get all the likely men together and pick the three by lot. Vanya is the one who drew the unlucky billet, worse chance; must be God's will. His mother is weeping buckets; fit to die, poor soul. As for him," Dunyasha gave Katya a sidelong look, "well, he's putting a brave face on it. He says there's nothing for him here anyway, might as well go to the devil this way as any other."

"When is he going?"

"Tomorrow morning. The recruiting sergeant is already here. They don't linger around, carry the recruits off right away. Ekh, Vanya, Vanyushka," She was beginning to "give voice," the peasants' singsong lament in times of adversity. "What are they going to do to you, poor soul? Shave your head, they will, and take you far away, so we'll never see you again, never lay our eyes on your comely face, never hear you sing again, our nightingale!"

"Stop caterwauling, Dunyasha," Katya said impatiently. "Listen to me: I want you to go to his house and bring him here. Tell him I want to see him."

"Oh, but he isn't there now, dearie. He's at the pot house, with the rest of them. That's where he's been the whole day—drinking—and that's what he'll be doing till it's time to leave. That's what they always do, poor wretches. My uncle was taken last year. They had to pack him into the cart like a corpse, God forgive him, to take him to Pskov. . . ."

Katya thought it over. "I'll go to him myself," she said with decision.

"To the pot house? God forbid, little countess, it's not for the likes of you!"

Paying her no attention, Katya turned into the path that led to the village. Dunyasha ran after her.

"No, don't you do it, my dearie, Tikhon Yeremeitch won't like it."

Katya merely walked faster, her face set.

"He'll be mad at me, fiery mad," Dunyasha mourned, following her. "Fool that I am, I never know how to hold my tongue."

The pot house stood at a distance from the village, a small, square structure with a chimney rising out of its thatched roof. A sizeable crowd had gathered in front of it, making a circle from within which came the sound of a balalaika and of a voice Katya knew well, raised in song. She squeezed her way into the crowd.

The scene that she saw struck heavily upon her heart. Three men were rollicking drunkenly in the middle of the circle. Vanya was one of them. His bright red shirt was torn to the belt. Bare-chested, he paced back and forth, strumming discordantly on his instrument and singing a ribald song while the other two performed a sort of unsteady dance. His yellow curls had been shaved halfway down his head, as had the hair of the other recruits, and this gave his pallid face a strange, sinister look. Occasionally he would break into a dance step, hiking the balalaika high up in the air. There was a strange ungainliness about his movements, as though he were a puppet jerked on unseen strings, and his voice had lost its pleasing resonance and was merely loud.

The crowd looked on silently, with a sort of pitying intentness. Among them she saw Stepanitch leaning against the wall, looking down morosely. Next to him an elderly sergeant surveyed the spectacle with a half-tolerant, half-sardonic expression.

Katya watched it, too, hating everything about it but unable to tear herself away. Presently Vanya's bleary blues eyes fell on her. There was a blankness about them, and she wasn't even sure that he saw her. But for a moment his hands were still on the strings.

"Another glass of vodka, tapster!" he shouted. Twin bright red spots burned feverishly on his cheekbones.

"Enough, Vanyusha, you're barely standing up as it is," the headman said.

"What do you care, you redheaded devil? I'm paying, aren't I? Tomorrow I'm nothing, dog's meat: today I can still drink to—to . . ." Breaking off abruptly, he snatched a full glass of vodka from the tray that had been promptly brought to him from the pot house and drained it at a gulp. He dashed it to the ground and began singing again:

"Tis a snowstorm sweeping through the place . . ."

Both the words and the music were almost unrecognizable; the sweaty hands flattened the strings, the voice cracked.

Katya turned away and went home without a backward look, running all the way. When she got to their cottage, she went into her own little room, lay down on the bed and burst into tears. Her heart was aching. Now, she knew, she would not remember the young man as he had been, gay and indomitable with his conquering smile, his tender and burning kisses. Whenever she thought of him, she would only remember the pallid, sweat-bathed face and the cracked voice trying to frame the words of a love song.

CHAPTER 12

It was as though a signal had been given. All at once the weather changed, summer flowing away like water out of a cracked jar. The sky grew bleak; a chill wind started up. The villagers started dressing more warmly, putting on their *polushubki*, the rough mutton-skin jackets lined with fur, and Praskovya dipped into Tatyana's big coffer to bring out an embroidered leather surcoat for Katya to wear.

There was autumn in the air, and it was reflected in Katya's mood. She became silent and dejected, quite unlike her usual merry self, preferring to stay alone. The village had become hateful to her. Earlier it had been, in its humble way, a cheerful, comfortable place, made even more pleasing by Vanya's enlivening presence. Now that he and summer were gone, it began to seem dismal, almost sinister. The headman Stepanitch, watching her stealthily from a respectful distance, was a constant reminder of her predicament. Much as she loved her family, she began to long for escape.

The one thing that revived her sinking spirits was her dancing; she divided her time between helping Praskovya with the sewing and doggedly going through her dancing exercises in the little theater.

She was conscious at those times of an eerie feeling that she was not alone. Her reflection in the mirror seemed to become another presence, separated from herself; it watched over her efforts, smiling with approbation when she did well, and when she didn't, saying silently, with delicate dark brows drawn together, "Once again, little daughter."

In her gloomy mood the appearance of young Chirkin,

ordinarily an unfailing source of amusement, merely irritated her, and she retired to her room, fretfully refusing to come out and see him. Tikhon did not urge her to do so. After a brief reflection he nodded, saying to himself rather than to her, "Might work out better that way," and left her without explaining what he meant. Katya's incurious look out of the window showed him in earnest conversation with her disappointed admirer before the latter dejectedly went to the lower part of the park to shoot snipe.

Later, as she sat listlessly by the window hemming a round dress of twilled blue silk that Praskovya had finished, she overheard another conversation, this time between her grandfather and Chirkin's coachman, Matvey. In spite of his morose and intimidating looks, due mostly to a heavy beard growing way up along his cheeks and a pronounced wall eye, Matvey turned out to be unexpectedly talkative as he discussed his master's high-handed mother.

"Never loses sight of him, the old lady, clucks over him like a hen with a single chick. He does something she mislikes, doesn't she give him a headwashing! And he, the poor gentleman, just stands there hanging his head, not a word to say for himself. . . ." There was a silence and a glugging sound. "That's good vodka you have, old man."

"Yes, we have a good sort hereabouts. . . . It's a wonder she ever lets him out, sounds like."

"She checks up on him, that she does. Like today—she'll be asking me a lot of questions: what did the *barin* do? Where did he go?"

"And what'll you tell her, Matvey Andreitch, God's man that you are? Let me fill up your glass again."

"God's own truth is what I'll tell her. 'Shot snipe and partridges, like the last time.'" There was another glugging pause. "The last time he rode off by himself, she didn't like it a bit." Matvey's grumbling basso suddenly went falsetto. "'It's not fitting for you to go out unattended, *mon fees*!' That's Frenchy for my son. So that's how come we're here with the carriage. . . . She's got the poor lad so scared he doesn't dare lay an eye on a likely female. What she wants is for him to marry a young lady from an estate not too far from here, Archipov is the name of the family: plenty of money and ugly as sin, that's the type suits her best."

"And what about him, poor wretch? Does he stand up to her?"

"Wouldn't call it standing up, myself. More like weaseling out of the way real fast when it comes up. She keeps sending him there, see: 'Why don't you visit the Archipovs, Theophile?' That's her Frenchy name for him, but I say Feofil is Feofil, and a good name it is for him, not too quick on the uptake he is, poor fellow. 'Dear Eudoxie has been asking about you.' Well, let him have his fun meanwhile, I know why he is coming here, you old fox. What the old harpy doesn't know won't hurt her."

Katya, an unwilling listener to this conversation, began to feel extremely bored by it. Not so her grandfather, who kept drawing Matvey out with frequent applications of vodka until his master came back from his shooting and they went home.

"Like to know all about people," he told Katya afterward. "Listen to them long enough, they'll tell you everything you want to know. Now I know all about his worship, I'll know how to handle him when we get to see him again . . ."

"Why, what do you propose to do with him, grandfather?"

Tikhon didn't answer her question. "He'll be back, sure enough. I'll lay my life on it. Eh, Katyusha?" There was an unwonted anxiety in his voice, as though he was seeking reassurance.

Katya assured him, with some asperity, that it was a matter of complete indifference to her. But she couldn't help but see that this was not the case with her grandfather. Several times during the next few days she found him standing on the stoop and scanning the road with unmistakable concern. He seemed to grow more fidgety as time went on and heaved a huge sigh of relief when the traveling carriage with Matvey on the box drew up in front of the cottage one afternoon.

There was a distinct lack of cheer in the young landowner's manner as he greeted them. "Can't stay long," he told Tikhon ruefully. "Have been sent—that is, I am going on a long visit with some acquaintances," He sighed. "Matter of fact, mother's acquaintances. Must stay at least a week." Katya thought that she had never seen a man more reluctant to go for a visit. She remembered Matvey's mention of his mother's ruthless matchmaking and felt genuinely sorry for him. "Don't know if I'll be coming back. I mean—er—ever. Thought I'd like another walk in the park." His eyes swiveled to Katya. "Uncommon fond of that park. Delighted to have an opportunity to look at it before—er—giving it up."

Responding to the pathetic plea in his eyes, Katya, without being asked, volunteered to be his guide again.

As they walked slowly along the winding path in the shrubbery, Katya noticed that his manner toward her was now imbued with downright reverence. They were walking across an old-fashioned little bridge that spanned a stream when he addressed her with stammering diffidence:

"Er—Katya—Katerina Vassilevna—last time I was here, your grandfather told me your story, and I—"

"He did?"

"Must give vent to my feelings—deeply appreciate the delicacy of your situation. The thing is—with all due respect—know how you feel. Extremely disagreeable to be forced into a union with a person repellent to you—no matter how highly placed."

Katya looked at him with some bewilderment. Stepanitch, highly placed? She supposed he *could* be so considered within the framework of his village, but still. . . .

"Am aware that neither riches nor noble birth necessarily makes for a congenial partner . . ."

No, definitely not Stepanitch. What *did* grandfather tell him, Katya wondered.

"Must express my admiration," Chirkin resumed jerkily. "For a female—with all due respect—of such tender years and genteel upbringing to repulse the advances of—er—a dissolute nobleman, preferring to take refuge in a humble village—"

So that's what grandfather told him, Katya thought. I wonder why?

"—Shows an enviable degree of strong-mindedness. Wish I myself had it. However," his face clouded, "when one is subjected to constant pressure from a venerated parent with weak constitution, capable of making one's life hell if resisted. . . . But never mind that. Your grandfather—a worthy and respectable old man—has intimated that even here you are not safe from persecution . . ."

He looked at her inquiringly. Katya, not sure of her ground, contented herself with drawing a deep sigh and looking soulful.

"Merely want to say: command me in anything. Not much I can do—am aware of that—in fact, can't think at the moment of what I can do—but if something occurs to you, you need merely—er—pass it along. . . ."

Katya, considerably touched by this declaration, gave him a blinding smile. Her admirer's narrow chest swelled and he delivered a few more confused remarks, expressing his admiration for Katya and his contempt for the ramshackle nobleman whose odious persecution had sent her to this unsuitable existence.

"But I like being here," Katya protested. "Or at least I did until a short time ago."

"Gallant of you to say so. However, I am sure you must miss Petersburg. Gay life there—balls, assemblies, all sorts of entertainment unfortunately not to be found in the provinces . . . Eh?"

There was a wistful query in his voice. He looked at Katya with such innocent curiosity that she began to tell him something about her life in Petersburg, recounting its fashions and amusements much as she would tell fairy tales to her little cousins. He listened with childlike wonder and was rendered speechless when she told him about her presentation to Emperor Alexander and Empress Elizabeth.

"He is the most charming man you can imagine. His eyes are of positively celestial blue and his cheeks are pink and he has the loveliest golden whiskers—oh, he's an angel and we simply adored him, my sister and I . . . And I adored the empress too: she looks so much like my darling Lisa—the fair hair, you know, and the same mild manner and soft voice. Oh, and I do so miss her!" she cried, her voice breaking. Chirkin looked bewildered but sympathetic.

"Er—the empress?" he asked respectfully.

"Of course not. My sister Lisa. . . ."

By the time they came back to the cottage, the sun was nearing the horizon. Matvey, casting a fatherly look at them out of his one stable eye, proclaimed it to be too late to resume the journey. "Won't get there till late at night. A late guest is worse than a Tartar, they say. Perhaps if your honor were to stay here overnight . . ."

"Exactly what I thought," his master cried, only too delighted to put off his evil fate.

"This way we'll rise early, perhaps do a little shooting at our leisure before starting out on our way. . . . I daresay you can put the master up, old man?"

Tikhon assured him that he could do so without any trouble. "Open up a room in the main house, air it out. Praskovya will make you up a bed and you'll be as cozy as in Christ's bosom, your worship. And if you don't mind sharing our humble fare. . . ."

Chirkin, seated at the deal table (where Katya had joined him as a matter of course, and Tikhon upon being invited to do so) and partaking of the aforementioned humble fare served by Praskovya, looked radiantly happy. He did not do much talking, confining himself to watching Katya with spaniellike devotion.

Soon after supper Tikhon took him to the manor house, where Praskovya also repaired to make his bed. She returned to tell Katya that the gentleman was perfectly comfortable and that Tikhon was staying behind to make him even more so by means of the old count's brandy, which he was bringing up from the cellar. He was still there, presumably attending to his guest's comfort, when the rest of the family retired for the night.

Katya was awakened from her usual deep, dreamless sleep by a knocking at her door and her grandfather's voice peremptorily requiring her presence.

"What is it, grandather?"

"Never mind, you just come out." There was unwonted urgency in his voice. Katya threw a large shawl over her nightdress and stumbled out, sleepy-eyed.

Tikhon was not alone. Chirkin, still fully dressed, was standing in the middle of the room, seeming to waver in the fitful light provided by a wick floating in a saucerful of oil. As soon as he saw her, he fell down on his knees and said in a slightly slurred voice:

"Katerina Vassilevna, be mine."

"What?"

"Er—with all due respect—be mine."

"Is this a joke?" Katya turned angrily to Tikhon, who was busy lighting another lamp. "Grandpa, did you wake me up to listen to this silliness?"

But Tikhon shook his head at her. "Don't *you* be silly, girl. His worship is in earnest, looks like."

"Then he must be drunk." She took in the fact that Tikhon too was still dressed in his daytime clothes and was instantly suspicious. "Oh, my father's brandy." She glanced at the dark window. "Why, it must be far past midnight! Has he been drinking all this time, and you with him, grandfather? Shame on you!" She couldn't hold back a giggle. "You must be as drunk as owls, both of you."

"Don't be impudent, girl," Tikhon returned austerely. "I'm not a drinking man, and well you know it. As for his worship, well, who am I to prevent his taking a drop or so while he is doing me the honor of telling me how he feels about you?" With an expressionless face he added, "Mighty forceful and masterful, his worship is—wanted to talk to you, and no stopping him . . ."

"No stopping me," said Chirkin with considerable satisfaction.

Katya looked down on him and again fought back a desire to laugh. Vanya, drunk, had presented a savage and pitiable spectacle. Chirkin was merely absurd. She said to him, trying to sound stern; "Monsieur Chirkin, first of all, stop making yourself ridiculous and get off your knees. Then go back to bed and sleep it off. I am sure you'll forget it by morning."

Chirkin got up unsteadily. His insignificant face, with its blondish locks plastered to his temples, was flushed with a look of weak obstinacy. "Don't want to sleep it off," he protested. "Don't want to forget it, either. May be drunk but know what I want."

Looking with exasperation on his wavering figure, Katya perceived that he indeed meant it.

"Am resolved—with all due respect—to protect you from encro—encrosh—*unwanted* suitors . . . Beg you to be mine." He sagged at his knees, apparently intent on resuming his former position, and Katya hastily propped him up.

"Your worship, Feofil Petrovich," Tikhon's voice arrested him mid-crouch, "Lowly serf as I am, I am bound to ask you what it is you want with my granddaughter. It's all very well to say, 'Be mine,' and we are grateful for your condescension. But she is not one of your little village doxies, your worship, and you know it yourself. If not for the way things had fallen out for her, she wouldn't have even come in your worship's way."

"Wouldn't have even got a look at her," Chirkin agreed sadly.

"So if you are thinking of having your way with her, like the gentry is used to do . . ."

Chirkin shook his head and kept on shaking it. "Am an honest gentleman, not a dissolute nobleman. Don't want to have my way with her. Want to marry her." He went back to his knees.

"Well, if that's how it is," Tikhon said slowly, "if such indeed is your honorable plan and will . . ."

"Wait a minute," Katya said. Catching her grandfather by the sleeve, she drew him to the other end of the room, leaving the young man waiting obediently on his knees. "Grandfather, do you really expect me to marry this silly young man? Did you put him up to this nonsense?"

Tikhon nodded gloomily.

"Had to do it, Katyusha. You're as dear to me as my daughter was; there's nothing I would like better than to keep you here, feast my old eyes on your pretty face till my days are done. Looks like it ain't the good lord's will to let me have that joy. The month is pretty nearly up. Can't place any reliance on Stepanitch; can't even blame him for that—a man can't jump higher than he stands, like the proverb says. Better to get out while you can, rather than wait till they have you by the throat. This here," he nodded toward the waiting Chirkin, "is the best I could manage for you. . . ." He sighed. "And a hard time I had of it. Not till the last minute was I sure we had him."

He spoke with the weary pride of a skilled fisherman landing a large fish after a long struggle. Katya gazed at him with admiration.

"Grandfather, there is no one like you in the whole world!"

"Told you I'd take care of you, didn't I?" he returned with some complacence. "The best thing is you don't have to go to Moscow all on your own. That stuck in my craw, it did—sending a pretty young thing like you to travel all by yourself, without anyone to look after you."

"But I wasn't afraid, grandfather!"

"That's right—not enough sense for that," Tikhon said astringently. "Well, at least now I can sleep nights and not worry about *that*. . . . Well, Katyusha? How about it? I know he ain't no English earl. Not much to look at, either, and not too strong in the head, but that's all to the good, it seems to me. You can do whatever you want with him, tell him what you want, same as you would a child."

"Yes, poor man. He seems to think he is rescuing me from some dissolute nobleman!"

"Yes, that's what I told him, may the good Lord forgive me!

Had to explain your being here without telling him that you're a serf. Didn't like deceiving him, and he listening to me so trustful, but that's how it is in this sinful world—you want to get ahead, you keep some things to yourself. You can tell him the truth later, once you're spliced. Or you may not even have to. Seems to me what's sticking in her grace's craw is your getting that Englishman: she wanted him for her own daughter, it looks like. Now don't you break out in a temper, girl. I ain't saying that the young lady your sister wants him, but it's certain-sure from what you told me that the mother does, for her. Once she knows you're married and out of his reach, she won't bother you anymore, let you be. . . ."

"Do you really think so, grandfather?"

"Stands to reason, don't it? She don't want to bring her malice out in the open where it would stink in honest folk's nostrils." He spat eloquently. "How would it sound: here is the count not cold in his grave and she is sending his daughter to a village, marrying her off to a lowly serf. Not a story she would want to get out. That's why you had to be bundled out of Petersburg at night, nobody to see what she's done. . . ."

Katya was silent, considering it all. A plan, vague but audacious, and to her mind a distinct improvement on her grandfather's, began to surface in her mind.

A plaintive voice reached her from the other end of the room. "Katerina Vassilevna," it said, "be mine."

Her mind made up, Katya went back to him. "Very well, Monsieur Chirkin," she said. "I will marry you if you really want me to."

A beatific smile spread over the young man's face. Struggling to his feet, he caught Katya's hand and showered kisses on it. "Made me a happy man," he gasped rapturously. "Never knew before what happiness was. Well, stands to reason—never *have* been happy before. Intend to take you away immediately."

"Where to?" Katya asked practically. "Are you proposing to take me to Marinovka to meet your mother?"

A shudder convulsed Chirkin's reedy frame. "No, a bad idea. Would never let us marry. Rather die on the spot. Always threatens to do so when she doesn't like something." He added thoughtfully. "Never does, however."

"That sounds very disagreeable," Katya said, dubiously. "Are you sure . . .?"

"No need to trouble your lady mother," Tikhon interposed smoothly. "Surely a priest in your own village of Otradnoye will marry you to my Katyusha, if such is your will, since you are master there."

"So I am." Chirkin brightened up. "My own estate. Left me by my favorite uncle. Always liked it. A capital idea to get married there . . . Give us your blessing, old man."

Tikhon took the ikon from the wall with careful tenderness and lifted it over their bowed heads. "May the Holy Virgin bless you, may She save and preserve you. . . . You get ready, Katyusha. I'll go to the stables and wake Matvey up, tell him to get the carriage ready."

Praskovya helped her pack, making no attempt to check the tears that poured down her pleasant, wide-cheeked face as she put the newly made dresses into the little trunk. "God save us, and we didn't even finish that last dress," she exclaimed with distress. "You'll have to hem it without me, my darling. And I'll put in that sable jacket of Tatyana's, it will come handy later."

Katya embraced her. "Don't cry, auntie." But she was close to tears herself. "I don't want to leave you either. We won't be parting forever; I couldn't bear that."

"God grant it, my lovey. It's like losing Tatyana all over again . . . But there, my father knows what he is doing. It's all for the best. Well, no use hanging back. Let's get you dressed."

It was a strange sensation to dress like a lady again: to pull the hose onto her slim legs and thrust her small feet into the French kid half-boots she hadn't worn for nearly a month. As she put on her traveling dress, it occurred to Katya that the person who now wore it was quite different from the person who had worn it to Krasnoye.

Even without a mirror in which to check that conviction, Katya was sure that she must look different, with her skin tinged a golden brown and her hair allowed to grow unfashionably long. She twisted it up into a knot on top of her head, threw a cashmere shawl over her shoulders and was ready.

Praskovya sighed heavily, wiping her eyes. "Now you are a young lady again, not my Katyusha."

"Yes, I am; I always will be. And I hate wearing this dress; I've been so happy in my mother's clothes. Do put in my dear red sarafan and blouse with my other clothes, auntie. I can't bear to leave them behind."

When Katya came out into the other room, she found the coachman Matvey there, begging his master to consider what he was doing and not to bring ruin about their heads. "It's all very well to have your fun, and nobody would grudge that to you, your worship. But marriage? May the saints save and preserve us! Have you thought of your mother and what she'll have to say about this?"

The young man was beginning to show distinct signs of uneasiness; then Tikhon took a hand in the discussion. "That's exactly what I said to his worship. 'What will your lady mother say?' And his honor he says to me in his bold and masterful way, 'Let her keep her nose out of my business.'" There was a diabolic hint of admiration in his voice.

"Yes, let her keep her sharp old nose out of my business," repeated the pot-valiant Chirkin. With some effort he brought his thumb and second finger together and feebly snapped them. "And that goes for your nose too, Matveyushka, my friend."

Matvey, thus exhorted, lifted his eyes and hands heavenward. "Feofil Petrovich, what has gotten into your worship? Drunk as a sot, saving your presence, saying disrespectful things about your mother, running away with village doxies no better than—"

His voice died away as his eyes fell on the elegant apparition in the doorway.

"I am ready," said Katya, coming forward with an adorable smile for her bridegroom. "Take my trunk and portmanteau out, Matvey." She spoke as one who expects to be instantly obeyed, and automatically Matvey did so, shaking his bewildered head as he staggered out with her luggage.

Tikhon, who had been looking for something in his bed behind the stove, now came out with a small leather bag that Katya recognized. "Take a look at this, your worship. My girl is not only bringing you her youth and beauty but a dowry as well. You deal fairly with her, too, and God will bless you." He made a sign of the cross and stuffed the chinking little bag into Katya's reticule. "Time to go now. You should be away from here before you are seen."

"No, wait!" Snatching up one of the lamps Tikhon had lit, Katya ran back to her own room. The two children were sleeping peacefully. She kissed them gently, careful not to awaken them. "Good-bye, my darlings, I'll be back."

Outside they were all waiting for her, there faces dim white ovals in the darkness. The moon had moved toward the horizon and a fresh breeze was starting up. The horses stamped and neighed, eager to go.

Katya threw her arms around the old man "Oh, grandfather, I so don't want to leave you."

"Needs must when the devil drives." He gave her a quick, fierce hug and relinquished her. "Up you go, my lady."

"I'll come back," Katya cried, leaning out of the carriage. "Nothing will stop me. I'll come back to you, my dear ones!"

The carriage started up.

CHAPTER 13

Lisa set out on her journey to Krasnoye with a far larger retinue than that which had attended her sister: it consisted of two maids, eight menservants (including coachmen and postilions) and a trusted steward. This considerable cortege was escorted by Graham.

Lisa herself did not quite know how this great good fortune had come about. At first there had been utter and seemingly inalterable opposition to her going. The countess, upon being convinced that Lisa had meant what she said, had eventually capitulated and parted with the name of the village where Katya had been sent. But she had categorically refused to let Lisa go there.

"I will not let you go jaunting all over Russia. I told you I'll have the wretched girl brought back. Don't you trust me?"

Lisa didn't answer that question, merely bowing her head. No, she did not trust her mother at all as far as Katya was concerned. There would be delays, procrastinations, excuses—all in all, she had a dreadful conviction that if she left it to her mother to attend to Katya's return from exile, she might never see her sister again. She kept this conviction to herself, merely submitting in a low voice that she did not feel she could bear the anxiety of waiting for Katya to reappear. "And besides, maman, don't you think it would be far better if Katya went to Aunt Aline in Moscow? In that case surely I could go with her for a visit." But the countess was adamant in her refusal.

In the meanwhile Graham, apprised of Katya's whereabouts, stated his intention of starting out immediately. "I fear I might encounter difficulties there," he told Lisa. "Since I am not Katya's legal owner—though I hope to be, eventually," he added with a fleeting smile, "she might not be readily given up to me. It might come to me actually having to abduct her." A slight grimace of revulsion appeared on his face. Lisa guessed sympathetically that everything in his law-abiding soul rebelled at resorting to this melodramatic procedure. "Which I stand ready to do, little as I like it. Of course, if your mother could be persuaded to allow me to escort you. . . ."

To Lisa's intense astonishment, the countess, after giving this proposition some thought, quite unexpectedly agreed to it. "With you there to look after my Lisa, I shall be quite easy in my mind," she said to Graham, and her manner was gracious enough to offset the icy politeness with which Graham now addressed her. Thereafter there were no more objections and Lisa proceeded to pack frantically.

On the morning of her departure she went into her mother's bedroom to receive the maternal blessing for her journey. The countess was in bed, drinking chocolate. She put the cup down and, stretching out her shapely arms, embraced her daughter and made the sign of the cross over her. That done, she looked at her keenly.

"I know," she said, "you think I am a wicked woman."

"Oh, no, maman."

"Well, all of our family were always good haters," said the countess, not without satisfaction. "However, we have always taken care of our own. I have tried to do well by you."

"Yes, thank you, maman."

"And now I am giving you an opportunity to find your happiness. It's all up to you. I am persuaded it can be done: I have noticed certain looks lately . . ." Lisa, at a loss, looked at her questioningly, and her mother shrugged her shoulders in annoyance. "Well, go on, then, and God go with you."

Only after she was out of the front door did the meaning of these mysterious remarks penetrate Lisa's mind, bringing vivid color into her pale cheeks.

Graham had just arrived in his traveling chaise and was surveying the sizeable caravan that was awaiting departure in front of the Vorontzov palace with a frankly dubious air, plainly considering it too large for fast travel. Besides the luxurious post chaise with four horses harnessed abreast that was to accommodate Lisa and her two maids, there were three *kibitkas*, piled high with Lisa's baggage and all the necessary provisions for the trip, including kitchen utensils and victuals. He was engaged in conversation with one of the coachmen, but as Lisa called his name, he hurried to greet her.

"How charming you look, countess!" Lisa curtsied, murmuring her thanks. She had dressed with considerable care and was aware that the light mauve of her traveling dress suited her delicate coloring and the chip straw hat trimmed with ribbon of the same color framed her small face becomingly. "Your people," he added, "are being extremely uncomplimentary about my English carriage, which I have considered to be a tolerably satisfactory vehicle."

"You'll see, your honor," said Fyodor, who had climbed onto his box and was holding the reins of four horses securely in his huge fists. "A lot of you foreign gentlemen insist on using foreign carriages. Well, they may set out in them but they always finish the journey in ours. Russian carriages go best on Russian roads. You'll be lucky if it holds out to Pskov."

"We shall see," Graham said good-naturedly. He handed Lisa into her chaise and asked permission to join her in it. "We have a good deal to discuss, you know."

Lisa assented, not without a blush. She was wishing her mother had not made her embarrassing insinuation; it tarnished the innocent pleasure with which she had been looking forward to the days she would spend in Graham's company. She despatched Parasha and Marfushka to join Graham's valet in his chaise. The footmen sprang to their posts, Fyodor cracked his whip over the horses' heads, and the procession started off.

Graham's worry about their slow progress was quickly allayed. The carriages flew along the wooden road at the precipitous speed beloved by the Russian coachmen, disdaining to slow up for bad patches on the road or for bridges seemingly in need of repair. This was a totally new and somewhat unnerving experience for Graham, who had come to Petersburg by boat from Lübeck and had not had any opportunity for cross-country travel.

"I cannot credit this!" he gasped as Fyodor, drawing his four horses together into scarcely more space than was commonly occupied by two-wheelers, negotiated a passage alongside a slow-moving train of ten wagons without for a moment slackening the pace. "Why, this fellow would take the shine off our finest whipsters! But can this be kept up?"

The unnerving pace was kept up steadily for the whole of the journey. A lady of Lisa's rank traveling toward Moscow with a sizeable retinue was ordinarily expected to break her journey with leisurely overnight stops at the residences of friends along the way, and indeed Lisa had been charged by her mother with several messages to her putative hosts. However, Lisa, as impatient as Graham to get to their destination and fearful of being delayed by the civilities necessary on such visits, disregarded those instructions, preferring to stop in the official post houses. There the size and consequence of their cortege assured them the attention from the stationmaster that was conspicuously lacking toward less important travelers.

They found accommodations in a village near the post house where, as Lisa remarked ruefully, they spread themselves out like a tribe of traveling gypsies. Graham's eyes opened wide the first time they made a stop for the night. A huge trunk, taken down from one of the *kibitkas*, upon being opened turned magically into a large bedstead for Lisa. He twitted her gently about it, saying that this put him in mind of his aunt the Duchess of Lyndhurst, who never went anywhere, even to Brighton, without taking her own bed linen and her own plate. "But not even she went as far as to bring her own bed!" This bedstead was set up in the coach house, where the maids also laid down their pallets. It being a warm summer night, the rest of the domestics disposed themselves outside of the building. A bed was made up for Graham, on the leather couch in the post house, and he slept there until the onslaught of bugs drove him outside to seek refuge in his own chaise.

Both of them learned to look forward to these respites. There was a certain coziness about even the worst accommodations. Their retainers would bustle about, busily preparing their meals. Fresh eggs and milk would be obtained from local peasants, the samovar would be lit, and the two young people, relaxing in the makeshift comfort created for them, would have their conversations that had been made impossible during the day by the clattering, bone-rattling nature of their progress.

At first their conversations dealt largely with their plans for Katya. Those were simple enough. Upon arriving in Krasnoye, they would immediately set about extricating Katya from her unseemly exile. "Your presence, countess, will answer all questions and certainly do away with any need for abduction. I can't tell you how relieved I am! I hate melodramatic actions of any kind."

"I should imagine it would have been a most uncomfortable thing to do," Lisa agreed. "I suspect, however, that Katya would have enjoyed it to the hilt, silly girl!"

"Would she have?" Graham's face fell. "Yes, I daresay she would. I fear I am an unromantic sort of fellow." And as Lisa broke into laughter, "Now what have I said to amuse you?"

"Oh, Monsieur Graham, forgive me. But I can't help it, indeed I can't. Here you are going to Katya's rescue, you are planning to marry her with total disregard of the difference in your social positions—" (That was the next part of the plan—to go through a marriage ceremony as fast as it could be arranged, preferably right there in the village, with Lisa's presence to lend it respectability) "—and still you feel there has to be an abduction before you can allow yourself to be considered sufficiently romantic. One might think you had been reading the same novels as Katya. . . . Forgive me, I am being uncivil."

"But I don't at all mind being laughed at by you!" Graham sounded mildly surprised.

After that they planned to come back to Petersburg to arrange for the quickest possible return to England. "I don't believe any question of Katya's position will come up to plague us," Graham said. "Surely your mother won't raise it now."

"No, how should she? She is not even Katya's owner."

"Nor will Prince Lunin, I am convinced. I daresay he must have forgotten all the circumstances of his gallant gift of Katya's mother to Count Vorontzov." Graham's lip curled with distaste as he mentioned that disreputable transaction. "By the way, countess, I went to see him before we left. Your mother was still withholding the name of the village at that time, and it occurred to me that since he knew Katya's mother, he would know where she came from, and in all likelihood that was where Katya had been sent—to stay with her mother's people."

"And so she was. How clever of you to guess that. There is a grandfather and—oh!" Lisa broke off in dismay. "What did Prince Dmitry say?" she faltered. "Do you think he might have guessed why you were asking him those questions?"

"We are taught in diplomacy to make all inquiries most discreet and roundabout, countess. In the event, I didn't need to make them. I didn't find him at home." And as a sigh of relief broke from her: "You distrust and dislike him, do you not? Why is that?"

"But I don't." Lisa answered quickly. She felt it was unnecessary to tell Graham anything about the surely unreasonable fears that had been besetting her: the illogical conviction that if Prince Dmitry knew where Katya was *(But he didn't! Maman swore on the ikon!)* he would immediately post there to assert his rights to her. "There is no reason to. He is one of the most attractive men in Petersburg society, and he has always been very kind to me—and Katya."

The slight hesitation was not lost on Graham. He looked at her searchingly. "Do you feel that there was anything improper in his kindness to Katya?"

"No . . . He has always been the soul of propriety. But—I don't know—there was a certain look. I can't quite describe it to you. . . ."

It had been a reflective, weighing, strangely knowledgeable look, as if he knew all about Katya and yet expected to know even more. Whenever she caught it directed on her sister, it would make her uneasy. Sometimes she would even engage him in conversation, in spite of her shyness, in order to deflect it.

Needless to say Katya had never noticed it particularly and had flirted with Prince Dmitry as merrily and inconsequentially as she had with everyone else.

Graham gave a short, vexed laugh. "You don't need to describe it," he said. "I have encountered it before, wherever Katya appeared. As long as Prince Dmitry's admiration is confined to looks . . . You can't possibly think him capable of asserting his claims as a serf-owner to his friend's daughter! Why, he is a gentleman! Such an action would be certain to sink him in the eyes of society."

Lisa sighed. "Unfortunately, Prince Dmitry has never cared much for the opinion of society. That would not stop him if he were so minded. . . . But I agree! I don't believe that Katya would be in *that* sort of danger from him—not once she is married." And seeing Graham's puzzled frown, she explained painstakingly, "It is true that Prince Dmitry has very little respect for the sanctity of marriage. I don't think there is any married lady of consequence that he has not laid siege to. Once his name was even linked with Madame Naryshkin's, and I understand the emperor was very angry. So probably he will do his utmost to seduce Katya once she is a married woman. But to gain possession of her by asserting his rights as her owner—that would be downright mean and not at all the thing, do you see?"

"Just so," Graham replied gravely, his mouth twitching.

"Immoral Prince Dmitry may be, but mean he is not. So I do feel we are safe on that score. . . . Now what have I said to amuse you?"

"It's just your alarmingly clearheaded way of putting things. Pray forgive me!"

Lisa smiled. "I don't mind your laughing at me," she said demurely. Graham gave her an appreciative look.

"Well, Countess Lisa, you have laughed at me and I have laughed at you. It appears we are on the way to becoming fast friends."

"I hope so, Monsieur Graham."

"There is something I shall need from you—a firm promise to come to England. Your sister could not wish it more than I do. You will be my sister, too, you know."

"I shall do so gladly," Lisa said. "It will be a most enjoyable visit, I know."

No, it won't she said to herself silently. It will be a torment and a trial. With dismay she confessed to herself the twofold nature of her feelings about her sister's marriage. Beyond everything, she wanted Katya to be safe and happy; yet at the same time desolation and a sense of loss filled her heart. Lisa's small hands in their mauve kid gloves tightened on each other painfully. *It is God's will and I shall bear it silently, and with His help keep my trouble from them.*

"All I hope," Graham said soberly, "is that the relations between our two countries will stay friendly long enough to allow such a visit."

"Do you think they may not?"

"There is a definite drift toward Bonaparte, which began after the two emperors met on that raft on Tilsit, no doubt about that. A rift between Russia and England is a possibility that cannot be discounted. Lord Leveson-Gower is most disturbed by it . . ."

For the next half-hour Lisa listened attentively while her companion discoursed on Anglo-Russian relations. Afterward he gave her another, appreciative look and told her how useful, it had been to discuss this matter wth a Russian subject.

"Nothing, Countess Lisa, is more helpul than an intelligent listener."

That's what Katya must learn when she is married to him, Lisa said to herself: to listen intelligently. That's what I must teach her. . . .

As they sped south, coming ever nearer to their destination, Lisa's impatience to get to Katya became tinged with apprehension. She couldn't help but wonder how her sister was faring in her new circumstances. Would she be the same Katya when they saw her, or would they find her changed by her ordeal, her spirit broken by humiliation?

"It isn't just her living under conditions so different from what she has been used to," she said to Graham the night before they reached Krasnoye. "Discomfort is the least of it. But what if she has been mistreated? I can't bear to think of my Katya as otherwise than loved and cherished."

"Let us hope she is." Though it was plain that he was tormented by similar thoughts, Graham tried to reassure her. "I have noticed that there is much more genuine feeling among the lower classes than one would find in Petersburg high society."

"Yes, yes, that is quite true," Lisa answered eagerly. "The family ties are much closer. Why, I remember Parasha's father coming to see her all the way from their village, bringing her gifts and greetings from their family. He had walked all that distance to see her, and he couldn't even stay long; he had to get back in time for harvest. It was the most touching thing you can imagine, that simple old man trudging halfway across Russia for a glimpse of his daughter whom he loved. Pray God it may be so for Katya! And if not—well, we'll just have to make it up for her, won't we, Monsieur Graham?"

They arrived in Krasnoye in the late morning. Lisa looked about her, quivering with anticipation. Without knowing it she was undergoing the same sensations that Katya had felt upon her arrival. She, too, looked at the small, rough huts with dismay, remembering the inconvenience and squalor they had found in them as they traveled and wondering which one of those inadequate structures housed Katya.

The arrival of a caravan of four vehicles (Graham's chaise having broken down, as predicted, some distance before Pskov) produced a sensation in the village similar to that in a disrupted anthill. Peasants came crowding out of doors to stare at them. A stocky, redheaded man as potbellied as a Swedish stove approached the chaise in which Lisa and Graham were seated, bowing low at every step. He introduced himself in a shaking voice as the headman and wanted to know how he could serve their excellencies. When Lisa told him who she was, his already pasty complexion went lard-white and he fell on his knees.

"Your grace, have mercy on me, a poor slave. I did my best—if I did anything wrong. . . ."

"I am sure you haven't, my friend," Lisa said. For some reason the man's inexplicable agitation grated on her already tightened nerves. "I am not here to inquire into your wrongdoings. I want you to take me to my sister, Katerina Vassilevna, who has been staying in this village."

"Mercy, your grace!" The kneeling man now prostrated himself, beating his forehead on the ground. A terrible premonition squeezed Lisa's heart.

"What is it? Where is she? Take me to her instantly."

"I can't, your grace. She—she is no longer with us."

"What is he saying?" Graham demanded at her side, his usually adequate understanding of Russian defeated by the combination of local accent and mumbled utterance.

Lisa turned dazed eyes upon him. "He says—he says that Katya is—" She couldn't finish.

She had known it would be so. All along she had dimly felt that somehow they would be too late. But she had disregarded the knowledge; she had even allowed herself to enjoy the voyage, to be happy in Graham's company, while in the meanwhile Katya—Katya. . . . The dusty road, the surrounding *izbas* and the kneeling man began to revolve nauseatingly around her. As from a distance, she heard Graham's distressed, "Lisa!" and the receding mumble of the headman's explanation.

". . . Not my fault, so help me God. May He strike me dead on the spot if I know anything about it. All I know is that Tikhon Yeremeitch comes down and asks me if I have seen his granddaughter in the village, he couldn't find her anywhere around their cottage. So we started looking. But she wasn't anywhere to be found. We looked and looked all over, just couldn't believe that she had run away, but so it was. . . ."

Run away. The words were like a revivifying dash of cold

water in her face. Lisa opened her eyes on the dismayed, bearded face goggling up at her from the dust.

"My sister has—run away?"

"Yes, that's it, your grace, like I've been telling you. And it isn't my fault, as God is my witness, it's Tikhon Yeremeitch, her grandfather, who has had the care of her, and so I told his other grace, the prince. . . ."

Her strength returning to her, Lisa gently freed herself from Graham's supporting arm, and crossing herself, offered a brief but ardent prayer of thanksgiving. Katya wasn't dead. Everything else could be dealt with, even the dismaying fact that she wasn't there, that they had come too late to rescue her.

The headman was still babbling on. "And if your grace wants to punish me, that is your will and right, I being merely a slave, but seeing that his grace has already given me a beating. . . ."

"Wait," said Lisa. "Who was it who gave you a beating?"

"Well, maybe not quite a beating, just a few buffets, a heavy hand his grace has. . . ."

"Yes, but who? Let us have the name," Graham said sharply. But he already knew and so did Lisa.

"Why, sir, your grace, Prince Dmitry Lunin. He came here for Katerina Vassilevna. Showed us a paper, he did, a—" the headman gave an apologetic little cough, "—a deed of sale it was, with Countess Vorontzov's signature on it clear as clear. So it looked like Katerina Vassilevna no longer belonged to her grace your mother but to him. Mighty put out he was to find her gone, too."

CHAPTER 14

So this is Katya's family," Graham thought, "the people with whom she lived until three days ago." He observed them with curiosity. They seemed uncommunicative and frightened—probably the result of Prince Lunin's visit. It was to be hoped that even a scoundrel like Dmitry Lunin, bent on his ignoble mission, would hesitate to strike an old man as sickly and fragile as Tikhon Golovin, who could hardly drag himself off the stove to answer their questions. (Fyodor, busy attending to the carriage outside, could have confirmed this impression from his previous visit.) As for his daughter, the buxom Praskovya, there was no use talking to her; she was a mere Niobe for tears.

Graham did all the questioning, since Lisa seemed incapable of doing so. Both of them had been appalled by Prince Lunin's unprincipled behavior. ("To think that I had been blind enough to think him incapable of it," Graham told Lisa bitterly. "You were the one who had had the good sense to distrust him.") But Lisa had also suffered the additional shock of learning about her mother's perfidy. She seemed quite undone by it. Graham, disturbed by the sudden transformation of his charming and intelligent traveling companion into a pale, guilt-ridden wraith of a girl, tried to comfort her by pointing out that she could not be held responsible for her mother's malice. But she had shaken her head: "But I do feel responsible and I am, I am . . . You don't know . . ." She had broken off, her lips trembling. Hers was obviously a truly sensitive nature, Graham thought, bound to be profoundly affected by moral ugliness.

Graham was told the same story that he had already heard from the bailiff. They had missed Katya in the morning but thought little of it since she liked to go off by herself. As the day wore on, they began to worry and found that the bird had flown.

"And there was nothing she said before to indicate where she would be likely to go? Think, old man!"

A feeble shrug was his answer. "How would an old body like me know anything about that? She's a lively young girl, had her own ideas, I daresay, wouldn't tell me anything about it. Why should she, an old man like me?"

"But I thought you were supposed to watch her."

"Well, it's like I told her grace's servant that time when she was brought here—how am I going to watch a lively young thing like her? Can barely take care of myself. We looked after her the best we could: I guess it wasn't good enough." He glanced at Graham quickly from under his drooping eyelids. It was a remarkably shrewd and judging look, quite at odds with the rest of his demeanor. "You a foreigner of some sort, sir?" and as Graham nodded: "Thought you were, from your speech. English, perhaps?"

"Yes, I am an Englishman."

"You don't say. . . . Betrothed to her grace there, I daresay? Eh?" Tikhon said with a nod toward Lisa, who was seated at the deal table, silently listening to them.

"No, I'm not," Graham said shortly.

"I thought, since the pair of you was traveling together, if you forgive my boldness," Tikhon quavered.

"I am merely escorting the countess."

Tikhon shook his head mournfully. "Isn't the devil in it, though? Here her grace the young countess stops in the village out of the goodness of her heart, just to see how Katya is doing, so she can go back to her lady mother, give her a good report, and what must the silly wench do but take it into her head to run away?" Graham frowned; did he fancy it or was there some indefinable import in the old man's ramblings? Lisa, silent at her station, lifted her head and was staring at him intently, her slender brows lifted. "A crying shame it is. . . . And here is his grace Prince Lunin also looking for her. Perhaps if you were to meet him, put your heads together to figure out where she's gone to. . . ."

"Tikhon Yeremeitch," Lisa said quietly, "the reason I am here is because I want to find my sister as soon as possible."

"Your sister, is it?" the old man repeated tremulously. "Why, your grace, she is merely a serf, Katya is—how can a lady like you call her your sister?"

Lisa met his gaze steadily. "She is my beloved sister, whom I love more than anyone else in the world. And she has been badly and cruelly treated. What I want most in the world is to find her and see her married to Monsieur Graham, so that he can take her away from whatever danger she is facing. And the sooner the better . . . I mean it; indeed I do."

The old man in his turn contemplated her steadily. Finally he said: "Why yes, *matushka*, I can see you do, and I give praise to the Lord for your goodness and the love you bear my Katyusha." Graham stared unbelievingly. The fragile old man on the brink of senility, who had been dispensing inadequate information in a quavering voice a moment before, was gone. A totally different person stood in his place, the bent spine erect, energy sparking in every curl of the erstwhile drooping white beard. "And you're right, there's no time to lose. . . ."

Thus it was that less than two hours after reaching Krasnoye, Lisa and Graham were on the road again, making for the village of Otradnoye as fast as three fresh horses urged by Fyodor at top speed could take them. The rest of the cortege was left in Krasnoye to await their return. The horses had been provided for them by Tikhon, who, to Fyodor's astonishment, was able to round up some "good 'uns" for him out of the village herd.

"It'll take less than three hours," Tikhon had told them while they were waiting for the chaise to be reharnessed. "God is merciful; you might get to Otradnoye in time. Katya might just have decided to wait and look around her once she felt safe. As for him, poor gentleman, he's a timid soul: he'll do just as she wants." He produced a bleak grin. "That's what I said to Katya—this is the best I can do for you, my darling, and that's how it seemed at the time. Now, of course, it's a different story. If I had thought you'd be coming, little countess, and bringing his honor along for Katya, make sure I would have done differently."

"But you didn't think I would, did you, Tikhon?"

The old man shook his head gravely. "No, *matushka*, that was not the way I had it worked out in my head. And even when you came—bad doubts I had in my heart. I laid your mother's sins on you, and I crave your pardon for it." He bowed low before her, his gray head touching the ground, while Graham looked on wonderingly. Lisa, making haste to raise the old man from his obeisance, could only give silent thanks for her companion's imperfect understanding of Russian. "And the Lord punished me for it. If I had believed Katya, I would have waited for you and it all would have worked out—she would have been married to his honor there just like it had been meant from the first. . . ."

There were tears of vexation in his eyes, and Lisa, suppressing her own bitter disappointment, tried to console him. "Don't you blame yourself, Tikhon, you did the best you could. And besides, what about Prince Lunin? Suppose she had been here when he came?"

"Yes, diddled him good and proper, didn't I?" said Tikhon, cheering up at the recollection. "Lord knows he surprised me, sweeping in on us like a storm. Last time I saw him was near to twenty years ago. Even then he had an eye for the women—couldn't get his eyes off my Tatyana—and the other wenches, too, got plenty of attention from him; didn't scant any of them, the young rascal. A young lieutenant he was then, slim as a reed, hair like a raven's wing. Well, there's gray in it now. 'Getting on, aren't you, your grace,' I says to him. And he says to me, 'You too, my poor Tikhon,' and I can just see what's in his mind: 'Poor old codger, lost all his marbles, no getting any sense out of *him*. . . .' Well, he got no change out of me, and as for the folk down in the village, what could *they* tell him? They didn't know anything; I took good care of that."

Remembering this as they sped along the bumpy road, Lisa felt a rush of gratitude and affection for the old man. When she had first heard of Katya's flight, she had been tortured by the reflection that it might have been brought on by mistreatment. But now she knew that Katya's life in the village had been far from miserable. She might well have stayed there with her family until she was rescued, if the countess's machinations hadn't made it impossible. Lisa was again horrified and sickened by the extent of her mother's implacable hatred. As a result of it, the next time she saw Katya she might very well be married to a well-meaning bumpkin of a country squire on whom she would ordinarily not have wasted a look.

A sound came from Graham that was half-groan, half-expletive, and she knew that he was thinking the same thing. He said doggedly: "I am sure it is possible for such a marriage to be dissolved or held not to count, for the same iniquitous reason that my marriage with Katya could be held invalid if her owner chose to pursue it. A serf cannot marry without her owner's permission, after all!" He ground his teeth audibly. "Well, we shall see what to do when we get to that infernal village."

When they got to Otradnoye however, they found the same disappointment waiting for them as in Krasnoye. In this case the bird had not flown from the nest: exhaustive inquiries revealed that she had never alighted there. The manor house was shut up tight; the villagers looked at them with incomprehension amounting to idiocy; and the village priest, routed out of his parsonage, assured them with bewilderment that he had performed no marriage ceremony. He repeated what they had already heard in the village: that his honor Feofil Petrovich had occasionally visited but never lived here; and that his last visit had taken place more than a year ago. "Where you will likely find him, your excellencies, is in Marinovka—that's his lady mother's property and that's where he resides, with her." The priest gave a delicate little cough. "It is our understanding she keeps him pretty close to her side, doesn't let him out of her motherly presence. . . ."

There was nothing left to do but turn the horses around and go back to Krasnoye for a further consultation with Tikhon.

Their return was a melancholy one. The two maids, Parasha and Marfushka, who had been left in Krasnoye and had been eagerly waiting for Katya's return, immediately burst into tears and were joined by Praskovya and Dunyasha, who had come up from the village. Lamentations filled the air until Tikhon put a stop to it.

"Stop the wake, you silly females. Our Katyusha isn't dead, only missing." But his own face was wizened with anxiety as he turned to the young people. "Are you sure they aren't there? They might have been hiding from that mother of his."

Graham assured him that their search had been thorough.

During the gloomy ride back from Otradnoye, doubts had inevitably arisen in his mind: was it possible that they, like Prince Dmitry, had been sent on a wild-goose chase by the old man? But there was no doubting Tikhon's bewilderment and distress.

"Can't understand it, so help me God!" He walked up and down the room, his beard clutched in his gnarled hand, his forehead corrugated in a deep frown as he wrestled with the problem. "The devil's in it surely! That was the plan, plain and clear, just like I told you. They would go to Otradnoye, out of reach of that hellcat his mother, saving your presence. So what else could they have done? Beats me entirely, that does. Unless . . ." He broke off. A slow, doubting smile spread across his leathery face and he shook his head in awe. "That Katyusha—nothing scares her!"

Lisa's eyes widened. "Do you think . . .?"

"Darned if I don't," Tikhon rejoined, his grin broadening.

"What is it?" Graham demanded irritably. He was aware again, as he had been this morning, of the mysterious rapport between Lisa and the old man: they seemed to understand each other from a half-word. "What do you think happened?"

"That little devil of mine must have put some starch into that rabbit and insisted on their going to Marinovka and facing up to the old lady. I can't think of any other explanation. Now isn't it just like Katyusha, running right into trouble like that! Eh, little countess?"

"Yes, exactly like her," Lisa rejoined with feeling. "She prefers it that way." Her face lighted up with a smile to match the old man's grin. "Oh, grandfather, I am sure you are right!" With an effort she straightened her drooping shoulders. "Well—tell them to get the chaise ready again. How far is Marinovka from here?"

"About thirty miles, it is. You're thinking of starting out again, little countess? It's pretty near nighttime!"

"What else is to be done . . . ? I am ready, Monsieur Graham."

Graham looked at the small white face, smudged under the eyes with gray shadows of fatigue. All at once, to his dismay, he became conscious of an illogical resentment against his elusive love, who, unbeknownst to herself, was leading them such a chase. He said roughly: "You've been jolting back and forth on these damnable roads the whole day, and it's time to call a halt. I shall go by myself."

"But—but you can't! You need me with you!"

"I won't have you knocking yourself into flinders."

"It's better than staying here and—and waiting . . . If you can go, so can I!'

"Don't be stubborn, Lisa! Are you going to be as self-willed as your sister?"

Their conversation was in English. But Tikhon, his bright eyes plying from one to the other, seemed to have no trouble guessing what was being said. He broke in unceremoniously, "Now, little countess, you don't want to be getting ill just when Katya is going to need you. Both you young people look ready to drop where you are standing. What you need is a rest and a good meal. Have pity on yourself and on the horses, too. They're God's creatures as well."

"But—but what if we're too late?"

"That's foolishness," Tikhon said bracingly. "If they're already married, then it's already too late, whenever you start out. It's God's will, and we'll have to put up with it. But if we're right, and Katya's at Marinovka trying to get the old lady's blessing, she won't get it in a hurry, you may be sure of that. If you start out tomorrow before dawn, you'll be there in good time. Now you just stretch out and rest, little countess, and I'll send your women in to attend you."

"But what if Prince Dmitry . . .?"

"Don't you worry about him, *matushka*. He won't be looking for her *there*. The way he figures, she must be around here somewhere. After all, where can a helpless young maid go all by herself? Can't get far, that's for sure. Now you do what grandpa says, little countess. Make haste slowly, and you'll get farther."

Graham, going out of the cottage to issue orders to the servants, could not help but feel respect for the energy and authority emanating from the old peasant. He found himself submitting to it.

In no time at all he and Lisa were seated at the table, partaking not only of their own victuals but also of those provided by Praskovya, who joined their own servants in waiting on them at the table and tempted their appetites with pickled mushrooms and newly baked bread. To his pleasure, a faint color began to come back to Lisa's white cheeks, and the look of desperate strain left her face.

"Look, Monsieur Graham," she said, calling his attention to the two children who were peering at the company from behind the stove, as timid as a pair of scared little forest animals. The boy was a sturdy towhead of eight. But it was his older sister who captured Graham's attention, her huge black eyes and jet braids falling on her thin shoulders reminding him of Katya. "Exactly how Katya looked at that age," Lisa murmured, echoing his thought.

As she coaxed the children out of their refuge, Lisa had a special smile for the little girl. Her gentle smile and soft voice prevailed. In a short while both of them were leaning trustfully against her knees.

"They've been crying ever since they got up that morning and found her gone," their mother said, and wiped her own eyes with her apron.

"Well, don't you start keening again, woman," Tikhon said impatiently. "You'll see her again. The Lord has not sent me a granddaughter to solace my old age just to take her away again."

"Yes, father," said Praskovya, and obediently dried her tears. She glanced at Lisa timidly. "Do you indeed think you might be bringing her back again, little countess, so we can have a look at her pretty face? Because here is Prince Dmitry, God forgive him, ranging around the neighborhood like a wolf around a flock of sheep. Suppose he comes back saying he's got rights to our Katyusha, like he did before?"

"He can say he has rights all he wants," Graham assured her grimly, "but I'll be damned if he'll enforce them while I am here."

"Indeed he won't." Lisa said, with fire in her eyes. "It's a good thing after all, Monsieur Graham, that maman insisted on sending all that absurd retinue along with me. Now I am sure we have more men with us than he has!"

Tikhon gave her a droll look. "Mighty fierce you sound, little countess. Wouldn't have expected it from you."

"No, nor I." Graham suddenly felt cheerful. "But women are a practical lot, or do I mean unscrupulous?" he said, quizzing her with his eyes. "What I had in mind was in the nature of a single combat, but I'll welcome all the help I get!"

All in all, when they retired for the night it was in a more optimistic mood than either of them had expected.

The next morning found them up before dawn and off on their travels again.

"I feel thankful for one thing at least," Lisa said, leaning out of the carriage to wave good-bye to Tikhon, who was standing on the stoop with his daughter and grandchildren to wish them godspeed. "My misgivings—and yours, too, Monsieur Graham—have proved to be baseless, after all. Katya *was* loved and cherished here. She found her family and they are good, dear people. I thank the good Lord for that!" Crossing herself, she murmured a brief thanksgiving. After that she was silent for a long time, occupied with her own thoughts, while the chaise sped swiftly along the dusty road. Graham looked at her pensive profile, her sensitive lips parted in a serious smile and her long eyelashes casting a frail shadow on her white cheek. Tenderness stirred in his heart.

"What are you thinking of?" he asked softly. She looked up at him with a quick smile.

"Making plans for myself, I suppose. For after we have recovered Katya and you have taken her with you to England."

"I hope I needn't remind you that those plans must include your visit to England, as you promised."

"So kind," Lisa murmured. "But I was thinking of more permanent plans. What I had in mind was asking maman to let me have Krasnoye for my own. I am sure she will do so: I am perfectly willing to exchange all my inheritance for it. And then I shall make it my home, and Katya's family my own . . ." She nodded to herself. "Yes, that's exactly what I'll do. I used to think of taking the veil . . ."

"Good heavens," Graham exclaimed involuntarily.

"But now I don't intend to do so. I can do a great deal of good here and be happy. I shall quite enjoy living near Katya's family." The face she raised to him was calm and cheerful. "Why, I find myself already thinking of Tikhon as though he were my grandfather as well as Katya's. I must admit I've never liked anyone in my own family half as well. . . . And I'll adopt Annushka and raise her as though she were my daughter." Misinterpreting his dismayed silence, she added, "Of course, I shall not neglect to give them their freedom as my father did. They shall all be set free. Well, what do you think of my scheme, Monsieur Graham? Do you like it?"

"No, I don't," Graham answered baldly. "To talk at eighteen of retiring to the country—"

"But I have never liked living in Petersburg and leading a social life."

"To plan to adopt a daughter, just as though you were a superannuated spinster, long on the shelf—no, that's absurd. You have better things to look forward to. A happy marriage, children of your own. . . ."

Lisa shook her head. "I shall never marry," she said.

She said this with brisk cheerfulness, but there was a finality in her voice that silenced him. So, he thought, remembering her mother's gross hints, it *is* a serious attachment after all; and a hopeless one, besides. He was aware of a strong resentment toward that unknown clod who was too stupid to value Lisa and probably utterly undeserving of her love. But of course very few people would deserve it, he thought.

CHAPTER 15

The Marinovka manor house was a large, old-fashioned, wooden mansion with two wings encircling a courtyard and a Greek pediment precariously balanced on the slightly crooked pillars of the veranda. Lisa and Graham were greeted at the door by an ancient majordomo wearing a faded buff-and-gold livery and a yellowing wig. Upon being told that they wished to see Feofil Petrovich Chirkin, he bowed, took their visiting cards and disappeared, leaving them waiting in the antechamber. Presently he came back and conducted them into a drawing room, which was rather dark and crammed with the cumbrous furniture fashionable in the previous century.

An elderly lady swathed in a purple and green paisley shawl was seated in an armchair contemplating their visiting cards. She rose to greet them. She was a small, rotund person, who barely reached Lisa's shoulder, her shape reminiscent of the fat little samovars manufactured in Tula, with merrily twinkling small eyes and a host of dimples playing all over her round face.

She addressed them in the slightly rusty French of a provincial lady. "I am Anfisa Mikhailovna Chirkin, at your service. So delighted and honored, I assure you, countess!" She pronounced the title with special gratification as she returned Lisa's curtsy with a ceremonious one of her own.

"We were hoping, madame," Graham said, bowing, "to have the pleasure of seeing your son, Feofil Petrovich."

"Theophile?" Mme. Chirkin repeated genteelly. "Unfortunately he is not home at present. But I am always only too happy to entertain my son's friends, and it is a special pleasure to meet a neighbor, however distant . . . I am assuming, mademoiselle, that you are a connection of the Vorontzovs who own Krasnoye?" As Lisa, crushed by this new disappointment, assented mechanically, her hostess went on, "You will of course give me the pleasure of having tea with me." Not waiting for Lisa's response, she picked up a bell from the table next to her and brandished it vigorously, summoning a procession of servants who brought in a steaming samovar and trays loaded with all sorts of cakes and buns, together with jams of every possible description.

Mme. Chirkin began to pour tea, chattering without a stop as she did so. She called the countess's attention to the butter, whose freshness was the envy of all her neighbors, and urged Graham to sample the jams, particularly recommending the gooseberry jam, which was made according to her own secret recipe and was known throughout the whole province. Her small black eyes, as bright as jet buttons, plied busily between her two guests, alight with curiosity.

Lisa, mindful of good manners, forced herself to respond. But the delicacies pressed upon her seemed to stick in her throat and she felt a strong desire to burst into tears. All the disappointments of the past two days crowded in on her; she felt herself to be in the middle of a nightmare in which the person you seek eludes you, always staying tantalizingly just beyond reach. She gave a quick, sideways glance at her fellow sufferer and saw her own emotions accurately reflected on his face. Like her, he managed to keep a fixed, polite smile on his face and finally asked their hostess when her son was due back in Marinovka.

"I'm afraid I can't tell you that. But perhaps I may be of help. If you will state your business with my son . . ."

"I shouldn't dream of boring you with such dull stuff," Graham countered smoothly. "In fact it is unforgivable to be imposing on you as we are."

"Oh, no, not at all, I'm only too pleased . . ."

"We had sought Feofil Petrovich in Otradnoye, but he was unavailable . . ."

"Of course he was. It is his property, but he makes his home with his old mother, as a good son should." The shoe-button eyes were shiny with speculation. "So you actually went to Otradnoye to look for him? Dear me! You must want him rather badly."

Graham assured her with a touch of grimness that indeed they did. "But you do expect him to arrive here eventually?"

"Why, where else would he go? This is his home, after all," said Mme. Chirkin with a touch of tartness in her voice. "But as to when I expect him . . ." She gave them an arch look. "Shall I confide in you? You see, he has gone to visit our good friends the Archipovs, and I expect he will stay there as long as it will take him to come to an understanding with Mademoiselle Eudoxie Archipov, a charming young woman whom I hope to welcome here as my daughter-in-law." She paused smugly while her visitors bestirred themselves to offer congratulations. "And now, my dear countess, and you, Monsieur Graham, since I have been so confiding with you, parting with my dearest hopes as I did, I expect you to be equally open with me and tell me what business it is you have with my son."

Lisa gave Graham a despairing look. They had, it seemed, come to a blank wall, and she had no idea where to proceed next. For a moment she considered asking Mme. Chirkin for the Archipovs' address but immediately dismissed that unpromising idea. Surely it was inconceivable that Chirkin would take the girl with whom he had eloped to the house of still another prospective bride.

She asked faintly: "Is it possible that Monsieur Chirkin might be visiting some other friends of his?"

Mme. Chirkin frowned. "Impossible. His instructions were explicit." Her face hardening, she surveyed them with sudden suspicion. "And now I really must insist on being told your business with my son. You can't continue trifling with a mother's heart! What stupidity has he perpetrated? He hasn't been gambling, has he?"

"Not with me, madame," Graham hastened to reassure her. "In fact I have never had the pleasure of meeting your son, and neither has the countess."

The lady's considerable bosom began to heave alarmingly. "Then what is it? A fine pair you are! Coming uninvited to a lady's residence, making outrageous innuendos!"

"Indeed, you mistake us, madame. Pray believe that neither of us is accusing your son of any wrongdoing. On the contrary, we believe him to have been extremely—and as it turns out, needlessly—chivalrous."

"Chivalrous!" Real alarm flashed in Mme. Chirkin's small

eyes. Switching to Russian, she inquired shrilly, "What has he done now, that fool? Tell me at once!"

Lisa drew a deep breath. "Yes, I think we should," she said. "Madame Chirkin, we have every reason to believe that your son has married or is intending to marry my sister Katerina, whom he met while she was visiting Krasnoye. We were told that he was taking her to Otradnoye, to have the ceremony performed there. But since we didn't find them there . . ."

Mme. Chirkin sat in her chair as if frozen, unconscious of the tea that was trickling from a dangerously canted cup onto the lace trimming around her plump wrist. Her mouth was open, but not a sound issued out of it.

"In doing so," Lisa pursued, "I am sure he was impelled by the most virtuous and praiseworthy motives. He believed her to be in danger. Well, and so she is, but now that we are here to protect her—"

She broke off in dismay. Mme. Chirkin, still openmouthed, had not uttered a word, and her steadily purpling visage bore an alarming resemblance to that of a baby holding its breath in a temper tantrum. Lisa nervously considered picking up the nearest flower vase and emptying the water on their hostess's head. But before she had a chance to do so, Mme. Chirkin gulped sharply and gave utterance to a shriek so loud and piercing that they both clapped their hands to their ears.

"Married!" she screeched, flinging away her cup of tea and going as stiff as a board in her armchair. "Help! Murder! Help!"

Immediately a multitude of variegated femininity ranging from a barefooted kitchen maid to a genteelly aproned and coiffed companion erupted into the parlor and began to bustle frantically around their mistress, proffering water, smelling salts, pillows, calling upon the Lord for help, and generally behaving in such a well-trained manner that Lisa, watching them helplessly, could not help but feel that this was an exercise with which they were quite familiar.

"Throw them out," Mme. Chirkin screamed, flailing her arms about her. "Thieves, murderers, liars! Trifon, Mitka, protect your mistress!" And as two overgrown footmen who had joined the crowd hung back in bewilderment, "What are you waiting for? Throw them out, I say. They're nothing but imposters, a couple of gypsies who have wheedled their way in to kill me! Liars, murderers, imposters!"

Lisa stamped her small foot in exasperation. "This is silly. I am sure you know we are no imposters but exactly what we say we are. And you had better stop, Mme. Chirkin, before you do yourself harm."

"He can't be married! He daren't!"

"Well, and that's what we too are hoping," said Graham soothingly. "We know for a fact that he left Krasnoye intending to get married but—"

"Never! Never! I won't have it!"

"—But perhaps it could be prevented if we knew where to find them. So if you would stop—er—distressing yourself . . ."

But Mme. Chirkin was not listening. Her eyes dilated, she was staring wildly through the window, a quivering finger pointed at some horror unseen by anyone but her. The next moment she had leaped from her chair with remarkable energy for one so grievously afflicted and rushed out of the room, knocking her attendants right and left as she went. After a stunned moment Lisa and Graham followed her and found her on the veranda, glaring at a carriage that had just driven into the courtyard. A reedy young man got out of it, squared his rather narrow shoulders and, sighing audibly, went toward the house with lagging steps.

Mme. Chirkin rolled down the veranda steps with astonishing celerity and precipitated herself on the new arrival.

"Where is she? Bring her out, let me see that slut you married!"

The young man gave a gasp and stood silent, a picture of guilt, while the outraged mother pounded on his chest with her chubby little fists.

"Show her to me, let me see how she looks, the serpent!"

Her son seemed to collect himself. "Beg you not to distress yourself, maman. Haven't married anyone, serpent or otherwise."

"Don't lie to me. I know all about it. You picked up some doxy in Krasnoye and you're hiding her."

The name of Krasnoye having reduced the young man to a renewed state of terror, Mme. Chirkin pushed him out of the way and trotted over to the carriage. Graham, who had been watching the ludicrous scene from the veranda in petrified silence, here gave a smothered exclamation and hurried down the steps, reaching the vehicle at the same time as the embattled mother.

Lisa remained where she was. Unlike them, she entertained no hope that Katya was in that carriage and was not surprised when they turned back from it empty-handed.

Mme. Chirkin rounded on her luckless son. "Have you hidden her somewhere along the road instead of bringing her to your mother like a man?" she inquired. This was a possibility that had occurred to Lisa, and she awaited Chirkin's reply with some eagerness. As was to be expected, it was inconclusive, the young man persisting in his denial.

"Didn't hide anyone anywhere. No need to: didn't marry anyone. Fact is, don't intend to marry anyone," he added with feeble defiance.

Mme. Chirkin's eyes narrowed ominously. "Indeed? Come to think of it, why are you home and not at the Archipovs?"

"Never went there."

"And why not?"

"Don't like them. Never did like them. Any of them."

"Then if you weren't at the Archipovs, where have you been? In Krasnoye, marrying some doxy you found there?"

Chirkin shook his head doggedly. "Never married anyone. All a mistake. Ask Matvey." He motioned toward his coachman, who was dismounting from his box, cap in hand and an expression of bland inquiry on his bearded face. Mme. Chirkin swung to him.

"Well, what about it, Matvey? Where did the two of you hide her?"

"Hide whom, your grace Anfisa Mikhailovna?" Matvey asked, dodging the blow his mistress aimed at him with an adroitness that indicated long practice.

"Don't you trifle with me, you wall-eyed rascal. Her, you clod, the serpent who entrapped that idiot my son in Krasnoye."

"That I know nothing about, *matushka*. We did stop at Krasnoye, true enough, did a little shooting—the old park thereabouts is teeming with snipe and partridge same like a dog with fleas. Then we went on to Velikiya Luki."

"Velikiya Luki? Whatever for?"

"Well, ma'am, seems his honor had the fancy to visit his

excellency his uncle there." With a bow to his thwarted mistress and a definite over-to-you look at his master, he went to attend to the horses.

Mme. Chirkin, wearing a slightly stunned expression, was preparing to resume her inquisition when Graham forestalled her. "Monsieur Chirkin," he said, "what about Katya? I mean, Katerina Vassilevna? You must certainly know of her whereabouts: you left Krasnoye with her three days ago. I must insist on your telling me where she is now. In fact—"

Feofil Petrovich Chirkin slowly turned to face him. An expression of extreme dislike appeared on his undistinguished countenance.

"Don't have the honor of knowing you," he said woodenly. "Come to think of it, have no desire to do so."

"I am sorry for that," said Graham, considerably startled by this sudden display of hostility. "I merely desire to ask you some questions."

"Don't have to answer them."

"I suppose not, but . . ." Baffled, he tried another tack. "At least allow me to explain my position. I beg of you to accept my assurance that I bear you no rancor and indeed am full of admiration for your chivalry. However, since I am anxious to locate the lady you so kindly befriended—"

"Don't know anything about that. In fact, don't know anything about anything. What's more, have nothing to tell anyone."

Here, to make his feelings clear, Chirkin crossed his arms on his chest and shut his mouth tight.

"But perhaps you might tell *me*," Lisa said, in her turn, coming down the veranda steps and approaching him. She had been listening to the exchange with bewilderment, Chirkin's sudden obduracy remaining incomprehensible to her until, remembering something that Tikhon had told her, she thought she could perceive the reason for it. Clasping her hands together, she looked up at him pleadingly. "You couldn't be as cruel as to refuse an anxious sister any information about one who is so dear to her. If you knew how desperately concerned I have been about Katya . . ." Her voice trembled despite herself.

Chirkin stared at her, his eyes growing rounder and rounder. "Why," he blurted out, "you must be Lisa!"

"Then you know these odious people!" Mme. Chirkin exclaimed.

Her son threw her a hunted look. "Never saw them before in my life."

"Then how did you know her name is Lisa?"

"Lucky guess," answered the harassed young man. "Thought she looked like Lisa. Lots of people do." He turned back to Lisa. "Then—then he . . . ?" He indicated Graham, who, now that Lisa had taken a hand, had remained prudently silent, letting her handle it.

"A friend of the family who is escorting me in my search for my sister," Lisa answered firmly. She gave him a wavering smile. "It—it really is quite safe to tell us about Katya, Monsieur Chirkin."

Chirkin, his forehead wrinkled into folds, thought hard. "Delighted to meet you," he said finally. "Have always wanted to. However, I am unable to tell you anything about your sister. Otherwise, happy to oblige."

"But Monsieur Chirkin," Lisa began in despair and stopped as the whole right side of his face, which was averted from his mother's implacable gaze, suddenly underwent an alarming convulsion. For a moment she thought that he was suffering some sort of seizure. Only when the grimace was repeated did she realize that he was trying to tip them a wink.

She drew a deep breath. "I understand, Monsieur Chirkin. What do you suggest we do next?"

"I can answer that!" Mme. Chirkin cried. "You have made enough mischief here. Countess or no countess, I must ask you to leave and go back where you came from."

Her son's face cleared. "Er—exactly. Just what I meant to suggest myself." He looked at her hard, practically panting with significance.

"You can't mean," Lisa said quietly, "back to St. Petersburg?"

Chirkin shook his head violently. "Oh, no. I wouldn't. Not after you have come all this way. I mean—as long as you're already here, I'd go to Moscow. Always wanted to go there myself. Or if not, to talk about it. Er—in fact, would be delighted to talk to you about it."

Lisa remained silent as she cudgeled her brain to think of

another lead to give him. Graham stepped in. "Perhaps," he said to Lisa tentatively, "we ought to put up at a nearby inn—if Monsieur Chirkin would direct us to one—and see if we can learn something there."

Chirkin's brow cleared and he wrung Graham's hand enthusiastically. "Exactly so," he said. "There is a very good inn a few miles from here. It would be an excellent thing for you to stop there."

Graham, thus encouraged, went on probing delicately. "Perhaps you might join us for supper there?"

"Delighted to do so," Chirkin said firmly and again contorted his countenance into a huge wink.

"Well!" Mme. Chirkin broke out explosively a short while later. Their visitors had gone and her son was attending upon her submissively in the parlor where she had earlier entertained them. "I don't know what this is all about, but I assure you that I intend to get to the bottom of it. I expect a *full* explanation, Theophile!"

Chirkin blinked apologetically. "Can't do it. Er—expect to go out shortly."

"Theophile!" said his mother ominously. "Do you mean to keep secrets from your mother who loves you more than life itself? Because if you have forgotten your filial duty to that degree, it will avail you nothing. I will get it out of Matvey!"

"Er—I don't think so, maman."

"And why not, pray?"

"Because—with all due respect—I told him not to tell you anything."

Mme. Chirkin gasped in outrage. "Why, I'll have him whipped till the blood flows! No serf of mine is going to defy me!"

"No, maman. Er—Matvey is my serf, however. Wouldn't like to have him beaten."

"And what has that to do with it? I would like to remind you that this is my home and I am mistress here!"

"No question about that, maman. Never meant to dispute it." Chirkin gave a timid little cough. "Have decided to move to Otradnoye, instead. Intend to do so in the near future."

"What?" Mme. Chirkin clutched at her capacious bosom.

"I've always liked it. Everybody there looks upon me as

master. Well, it stands to reason: I *am* master there. Nobody to tell me what to do or—er—whom to marry. Think I'll like that—being my own master in my own place." His mild eyes dreamy, he contemplated this agreeable future, seemingly unaware that his parent had fallen down on the couch and was producing alarming sounds.

"Monster!" she finally brought out. "Are you going to stand there and watch me die?"

"No, maman," said Chirkin simply and left the room.

CHAPTER 16

At about the time Lisa was getting up after the night spent at Tikhon's cottage to make herself ready for their journey to Marinovka, her sister also woke up in an unfamiliar bed and stared vacantly about her in the gray light of dawn, for a moment not sure of her whereabouts.

It was very strange. She was lying fully dressed, her largest and warmest shawl tucked about her, on a roomy leather couch in a small unfamiliar room, which was certainly not a bedroom since it also contained a dining table and chairs. Piled up in a corner were her portmanteau and the small brassbound trunk holding the dresses her aunt had made for her.

She was, she realized, in a post house near Rzhev, where she had arrived last night in a somewhat ramshackle carriage obtained for her by her erstwhile bridegroom. The post house was more comfortable than most such establishments, being also a tavern, and Katya, after her jolting ride, had been only too happy to be accommodated for the night.

She lay quietly now, staring at the small, square window through whose stained panes the first light of dawn was beginning to creep, as she tried to assemble in her mind the kaleidoscopic events of the day before.

At this time yesterday—yesterday? It seemed ages ago, in a different lifetime!—she had been sitting wide awake in a carriage that trundled slowly along the dusty road, leaving the village behind. Beside her, Feofil Petrovich Chirkin lay fast asleep, his head lolling against the back of the carriage. Occasionally it would roll toward her and rest against her shoulder. Looking down on the dim white oval of his face,

Katya could make out its peaceful and childlike expression. His eyebrows were raised in an expression of mild amazement, a slight, whistling snore periodically bubbling out of his pursed lips.

A strong sense of disapproval seemed to waft backward to Katya from Matvey's dark figure looming on the box before her. He addressed no words to her but occasionally vented his feelings by cursing the horses, particularly the shaft horse, which for some reason seemed to have incurred his wrath and got a flick of the whip whenever it made a wrong move.

Katya's heart was sore with the pain of parting. It was the same pain she had felt a month ago when she knew that she would not see Lisa again. She would miss them all as she had missed Lisa: her loving and sentimental aunt, her frisky little cousins, her simple-hearted friend Dunyasha. Most of all, of course, she would miss her grandfather, who had loved her and protected her and schemed for her, and who was even closer to her heart than her father had ever been. But as a faint glow rose from the east, coloring the sky a pale green and peach, and stars began to wink out, despite herself a thrill of exhilaration, a sense of dawning adventure and new beginnings, leaped up in her heart.

Presently, as the sun came up over the horizon full and golden, presaging a bright autumn day, her companion woke up with a galvanic start and sat bolt upright in the carriage, looking around himself wildly. His bewildered eyes fell on Katya and he closed them for a moment, shaking his head vigorously as though to awaken himself completely. "Oh, my goodness," he said feebly as last night's events began to flood in on him.

His coachman twisted around on his box and looked down on him. "Good morning, Feofil Petrovich, sir. How does your honor feel this morning?" he inquired with heavy sarcasm. "Head aching a bit after last night? Is your honor having trouble remembering everything? Would you like me to help you out?"

"Don't be silly, Matvey," his master answered crossly. "I remember everything perfectly. Going to Otradnoye to get married. Live happily ever after."

Katya surveyed him. "I can't say you look very happy about it."

"In the evening, carousing, in the morning, tears," Matvey remarked pointedly.

Chirkin flushed. "Nothing of the sort. Er—delighted to oblige."

Katya hastily lifted a handkerchief to her irrepressibly twitching lips. In a stifled voice she said: "It *is* very obliging of you, Feofil Petrovich. But I do wish you looked happier about it."

Chirkin gave her an apologetic look. "Don't mean to look anything but divinely happy," he said. "However, a fellow can't help worrying about things."

"About your mother, I daresay," said Katya, forgiving him handsomely.

"That's it," Chirkin admitted. "Thinking how long it will be until she—er—learns the worst." He heaved a deep sigh.

"I shouldn't worry about that," Katya said cheerfully. "Well, at least not for another week. Aren't you supposed to be visiting with friends and paying court to the young lady there? I should imagine the longer you stay away, the better pleased your mama will be."

"So she will." Chirkin looked at Katya admiringly. "What a head you have!"

"Be all the madder when she finds out," Matvey put in gloomily.

"Nobody's asking you." Chirkin told him. "Thing is, we will be married by then; she can't do anything about that. And we'll just stay in Otradnoye. Er—for our honeymoon." Chirkin blushed and cheered up considerably. "Er—Katerina Vassilevna . . . Katya . . . Would you consider allowing me to kiss you?"

Katya obligingly offered her cheek, upon which he imprinted a respectful salute. "He *is* nice," she thought, touched by the beatific expression that spread over his face as he did so. "Even if he is foolish beyond permission."

"That's all very well," Matvey remarked, unimpressed by these civilities. "But you'll have to leave Otradnoye sometime. And staying there won't help; she'll find you there all right, course you down same like a borzoi bitch would a hare in the field."

"You stay out of this, Matvey! It's none of your business."

"Feofil Petrovich, your honor, I've been looking after you since childhood, seeing to it that you don't get into trouble, so how is it none of my business?"

Disregarding this appeal, Chirkin looked at Katya hopefully.

"Thought perhaps you could deal with my mother," he ventured hopefully. "Your grandfather—an excellent old man who—er—knows his onions—seemed to feel you could: said you could give back your own. . . ."

"I daresay I could," Katya answered. "Only it all seems like such a bore. Your mother sounds like a very disagreeable old lady and I'd probably have to fight with her all the time."

"That's right," Matvey interposed. "Morning, noon and night. What's more, if you think you can hold your own, missy, you're far wide of the mark. Her excellency Anfisa Mikhailovna can handle ten like you."

"Didn't I tell you to hold your tongue, Matvey?"

"And if you expect his honor here to help you out, I, his faithful servitor, am here to tell you you'd better think again."

Here the young man, tried beyond forbearance, lurched to his feet and belabored his faithful servitor about the shoulders.

"No, don't!" Katya cried, seizing his coattails and pulling him back to his seat. "Never mind him, Feofil Petrovich, but listen to me. I don't think my grandfather was entirely open with you. There are some things I ought to tell you . . ."

Chirkin interrupted her hastily. "No need to put yourself out," he said, blushing vividly. "Your grandfather mentioned the fact that your father, the late count—that is to say, I am perfectly aware that—that—"

"Oh, then you do know that I am illegitimate? I am so glad. I wasn't sure you did. . . . But you don't know the worst."

She launched into the explanation of her status. Her bridegroom listened, his eyes growing more and more round as he did so.

". . . So I should imagine if your mother finds out about my being a serf, both of us will be in even more trouble."

A low, protracted whistle came from the box. This time Chirkin did not bother to rebuke his henchman. He merely stared at Katya speechlessly, his mild blue eyes dilated with horror. Katya smiled at him.

"Feofil Petrovich, you don't really want to get married, do you?"

Chirkin was silent as dismay and chivalry fought for dominance in his troubled breast. Katya watched him sympathetically. She suspected, even appalled as he was by this new complication, that she still could get him to his village and through the ceremony if she were so minded. She wondered how he would decide.

Matvey, untroubled by any such conflict, snorted. "Not as weak-minded as that, we aren't!"

This ill-natured observation seemed to tip the scales. Chirkin lifted his chin. "Intend to go on as I started," he said, not without dignity. "Man of my word. Once I give a promise, I intend to go through with it, no matter what—er—the inconvenience."

"You *are* a dear," Katya said warmly, implanting an impulsive kiss on his surprised countenance. "But Matvey is right: it *would* be weak-minded. You don't really want to be married to me. And besides," she finished with devastating frankness, "I don't want to be married to you."

"Now you're making sense," said Matvey approvingly. "You just listen to the young woman, your honor, she knows what's what."

"But—but . . ." Chirkin stammered. "Why don't I just forget what you told me? I'm sure I could: have a shocking memory. And besides—swore on the ikon that I would marry you—promised it solemnly to your grandfather, an excellent old man, although apparently given to suppressing pertinent facts."

"Please don't hold it against him. He did so for my sake," Katya said, "hoping that you would protect me. And you still can, dear, kind Feofil Petrovich, only you don't need to marry me: just help me get to Moscow."

"To Moscow?"

"Yes, for that is where I want to go above all things."

"But why? Is there someone there whom you—er—know?" A faint glow of jealousy lit up Chirkin's downcast countenance.

Katya reassured him instantly. "Oh, no; nothing like that. I have relatives with whom I can stay and—why of course, I do! There's Aunt Aline!" she cried, recalling for the first time her father's sister; whom she had last seen five years ago. She shook her head at her ridiculous oversight: imagine forgetting that redoubtable dowager!

She fell silent as she considered this newly arisen alternative. There was no doubt that her Aunt Aline would be able to protect her against persecution—all the more so since there was no love lost between her and the countess. She would be quite safe in her house. But that would mean an end to all her dreams. She would resume her life as a *jeune fille biene élevée* in Aunt Aline's household. To be sure, now that her low birth was known she could not hope to be what she had been in Petersburg when her father was alive. Aunt Aline was strongly conscious of social distinctions. She would be a protégée, a young companion to her imperious relative, living a safe, humdrum life. Eventually a marriage would be arranged for her. A loveless one, of course. "I couldn't possibly feel for anyone what I had felt for poor Vanya," she said to herself. "And anyhow, I don't want to marry; I want to dance! I want to be a prima ballerina and bring an ecstatic audience clapping to their feet, as Kolossova does."

For a moment her fate hung in the balance as she weighed present safety against future glory. Inevitably the latter won.

She turned to her erstwhile bridegroom, who was watching her anxiously, and gave him a brilliant smile. "So you see, I'll be well taken care of in Moscow. And I shall never forget your kindness."

"But how—how can I. . . ?"

Matvey answered this question with alacrity. "Very simply, your honor. Instead of driving to Otradnoye, we'll make a turn right here and go on to Velikiya Luki, where you can get a *podorozhnaya* to Moscow."

Without waiting for further instructions he turned the horses about and struck off in a different direction.

"And the best of it," Katya said to herself with satisfaction as she watched daylight strengthening and spreading through her little room, "is that grandfather does not need to fret needlessly about my traveling alone—although I don't know why he should, in any case!—because he knows nothing about it. How amazed he will be when I write to him from Moscow! I wonder—"

At this point in her reflections Katya became aware of an ominous tickling sensation along the side of her neck, followed by a minute sting, and realized that she was being attacked by one of the pestiferous tribe that make life hell for the traveler even in the cleanest roadside inns.

"Ugh!" She left her couch with alacrity and after a hasty toilette came out into the waiting room.

Early as it was, the shiny brass samovar was already on the boil. After a cup of hot sweet tea, with a slice of fragrant homemade bread, she felt ready to resume her travels. She found the stationmaster and asked him how soon the horses would be ready.

It was then that she began to learn the realities of travel in Russia. Even as she waited for her carriage to be readied for her, three vehicles arrived one after the other and were sent on their way, while hers still waited in the yard, its shafts up in the air, while its driver lounged gloomily beside it, emptying a bottle of vodka. The first arrival was an official with a *feldjäger* in attendance, who immediately threatened the stationmaster with a beating on behalf of his master, thereby procuring immediate action. The other two travelers, being of only slightly less consequence, were also promptly served. Katya's bitter complaints were answered with a silent shrug. There was no need to point out that the change of horses was accomplished according to the importance of the customer.

Katya's equipage, a species of covered *kibitka*, was definitely lacking in consequence, and Chirkin, who had purchased it for her in Velikiya Luki, had been quite miserable about it. He had determined that Katya could not go by public conveyance, an inconvenient and unreliable method of transportation, but since the whole excursion was unforeseen, he did not have much money with him. After he had sent Matvey to buy a vehicle and hire a driver and horses, there was barely enough money left for the *podorozhnaya*, a document indicating their destination and listing their stops, which was necessary if they were to travel by post.

Chirkin had been silent all the way to the government office where this document was to be procured. It was a measure of his devotion to Katya that he had steeled himself to go there: Velikiya Luki, as it happened, was in the jurisdiction of a governor who was related to the Chirkins, and the possibility of meeting him was an unnerving one. And indeed so it fell out: the governor himself appeared on the steps just as Chirkin was about to enter the building with Katya on his arm. That affable official's "*Eh bien, mon vieux, qu'est-ce que tu fais ici?*" startled him so much that only Katya's hand on his arm stopped him from flight. His excellence was an amiable, well set-up man with a healthy complexion heightened to deep rose by the tightness of his high gold-braided collar and a roving eye which brightened as it fell on Katya.

"Introduce me," he said, not listening to Chirkin's halting explanations. The introduction was stammeringly made, and Katya took over before her escort had a chance to entangle himself further. She curtsied, smiled and was not astonished to see the familiar glaze come over the governor's eyes.

"Going to Moscow, eh?" The governor smiled at her paternally and held on longer than was strictly necessary to the small, gloved hand she extended to him. "Don't tell me, mademoiselle, that this unenterprising nephew of mine isn't making any effort to keep you here!"

"Oh, he tried his best," Katya rejoined lightheartedly. "If only my aunt were not expecting me in Moscow!" She pressed Chirkin's arm affectionately as she spoke, a gesture that did not escape his uncle's eye. He kissed her other hand, regretfully wished her a good journey, gave his speechless relative an approving dig in the ribs with the head of his cane, adding obscurely but jovially, "That's more like it, you young dog!" and departed with his retinue.

This encounter proved fortunate in more than one way. The clerk, who had witnessed it through the office window, bent himself double when they entered and made out the *podorozhnaya* without asking any of the embarrassing questions petty officials usually ask when they want to make themselves important. Its other result was that Chirkin's shoulders expanded under the glow of this approbation on the part of his uncle. Probably for the first time in his life, he felt himself to be a devil of a fellow.

His spirits fell with a thump when he saw the equipage procured by Matvey. For all his bumbling ways, Chirkin was a connoisseur of horseflesh, and it pierced him to the heart to see the hangdog troika harnessed to the battered *kibitka* Matvey had bought. "Not fit for a lady," he said, shaking his head sadly. "And here I've been relying on you, Matveyushka. Couldn't you do better for us?"

"Not with the money you gave me, sir," his henchman

replied tartly. "If you think you can do any better, you are welcome to try. After all, it's your honor who started the whole thing. . . ."

His tone had been distinctly insolent, but his master bore it with his usual mildness, merely blinking his whitish eyelashes apologetically.

"Not at all what I had in mind for you," he said to Katya dejectedly. "Unfortunately, not too full in the pocket at the moment." He sighed. "Trouble is, never do anything right. That's what my mother is always saying. Knows what she is talking about."

"No, she doesn't!" Katya's eyes sparkled dangerously. "I have no patience with you, Feofil Petrovich. Do nothing right, indeed! You saved me from a—a terrible fate, and you were ready to marry me in spite of everything, and you are sending me to Moscow. What you have done for me is—well, beyond everything! I value your kindness and goodness even if no one else does. And you," she turned on Matvey, "don't you ever dare to talk to him like that again or you'll have me to deal with!"

Matvey, correctly reading the threat in her dangerously narrowed eyes, beat a hasty retreat, muttering to himself, as Katya said to Chirkin: "I do hate to think of them bullying you after I am gone. Pray don't let them do so."

Chirkin's eyes clung to her, spaniellike. "I will endeavor not to . . . But—er—must you go? Couldn't we—er—hold by the original plan?"

"No, we can't. I must go on to Moscow. But Feofil Petrovich . . ." Taking his hand in both of hers, she looked at him earnestly. "There's another thing. That girl your mother wants you to marry—you don't really wish to do so, do you?"

Chirkin sighed. "My mother is the one who has set her heart on it. Feels very strongly about it."

"Then will you promise me not to let her marry you off? It doesn't have to happen, you know. After all, I would not be forced and I am a serf, so imagine how much easier it is for you. Oh, I daresay your mother will make a great fuss . . ."

Chirkin agreed sadly.

"But you needn't listen to her. Why don't you just go away?"

"Go away?"

"Yes, why not? You were going to Otradnoye for my sake, weren't you? Well, why not go there for your own?"

Chirkin seemed forcibly struck by this line of reasoning and was apparently preoccupied in thinking it over after the farewells had been said and Katya's inadequate carriage drove away.

The supply of horses at the post house being depleted for the time being, Katya was told that she would have to wait until the afternoon. She was close to tears at the prospect of the unrelieved tedium before her when it occurred to her that there was nothing now to keep her from writing to Lisa. Immeasurably cheered by this thought, she immediately called for writing implements and, seating herself at a small table by the window, embarked on a long letter recounting everything that had happened to her since she left Petersburg.

She was busily writing away when she heard a jingle of bells outside. The mob of hostlers idling in the courtyard sprang into activity as two carriages drove in. Presently two travelers entered the waiting room. The first one, a young man wearing a military cape, confronted the stationmaster with a cry of "Horses—and be quick about it!" Upon being told that no horses were available, he exploded into a volley of colorful military oaths to which Katya, lifting her head from her letter, listened with some interest. The other, a civilian, accepted his fate more philosophically, merely asking for some tea and sitting down at a table at the other end of the room to wait for it. Taking a book out of the pocket of his redingote, he became engrossed in it.

The first traveler had in the meantime thrown off his cape, revealing the dashing white and gold uniform of the Cavalry Guard. He was a presentable, fair-haired young man of a type that Katya knew only too well: there was always a small crowd of them besieging her at the Petersburg balls. Just now his handsome face was scarlet with rage.

"What do you mean there are no horses, fellow? You had better bestir yourself to find me a troika of proper ones or you'll get a taste of this," he said, with a threatening twitch of his riding crop.

"Not my fault, your honor! I would be only too glad to

supply you. Kill me if you wish, but there's not a horse to be had for another couple of hours. They were all used up this morning. Ask this young lady—she's been waiting for hours. I promise you, you'll be the first . . ."

The young officer swung around and saw Katya. His bold eyes lighted up. After a moment's hesitation he went over to her table.

"I beg your pardon, madame," he said, with a low bow. "I must apologize for my intemperate language. Allow me to assure you that I would not have indulged in it if I had been aware of your presence."

Katya gave him a dark look. "I don't care about that," she said. "What I find intolerable is that I have been waiting here since this morning, and now I hear that conscienceless fellow promising you my horses. It is too bad, indeed it is!"

"My dear lady, I would be desolate indeed if I were guilty of causing even a moment's inconvenience to such a vision of loveliness as I now see before me. . . ." His hand went upward to his mustache as he flashed a conquering smile.

"*Exactly* like Kozlov," Katya thought. Her stormy look dissolved in a reminiscent smile. The young man blinked. He said, "Let me see what can be done with that rascal of a stationmaster."

"Well, I don't know what you *can* do," Katya remarked. "There are just so many horses, after all. And if you are to take them. . . ." She looked at him sadly. Her lips quivered and a single, pearly tear rolled onto the tip of her eyelashes, emphasizing their ridiculous length. She waited for the effect of this maneuver.

"I beg of you not to distress yourself," the young officer exclaimed earnestly. "Please believe that if I were not proceeding on a matter of life and death—but it doesn't signify; I must and will attend to your interests before mine are served. I know these stationmasters. They are always sniveling about the lack of horses, but it's wonderful what can be done if you lean on them hard enough. I shall see to it immediately." He made a smart salute and left her, his spurs jingling. Presently his resonant voice could be heard outside, calling for the stationmaster, who had in the meantime disappeared.

"Well, we shall see," Katya thought. Her eyes strayed across the room to the other traveler. She surveyed him with mild curiosity, which presently became tinged with bewilderment. The young officer was familiar to her as a recognizable and predictable type. But there was a haunting familiarity about this man, too; somehow she knew him not as a type but as himself. And yet she could not place him. He was a slight, graceful man in his late thirties, soberly but becomingly dressed in dove gray with a dash of flamboyance about his cravat and embroidered waistcoat. There was a special elegance about him that teased at her memory. Looking up, he caught her eye and his mobile eyebrows rose slightly. He came to his feet and executed a bow of such polished grace that Katya was conscious of a throb of esthetic pleasure.

When the officer reentered, he reseated himself and quietly resumed his reading.

"Lieutenant Boris Gorin reporting," said the young officer with a jaunty salute. "I have extracted from the old scoundrel a promise that he will forthwith scour all the yards for horses. May I assure you, Mademoiselle—Mademoiselle—" He waited courteously for Katya to give her name. "Mademoiselle Vorontzov? I know of some Vorontzovs in St. Petersburg . . ."

"Distant relations," Katya said promptly. She wrinkled her small nose at herself: silly to give that name. She had done so without thinking because everything about Lieutenant Gorin brought back her Petersburg existence.

"Again accept my assurances, Mademoiselle Vorontzov, that if not for the special circumstances that call for my immediate presence in Moscow, I would be only too happy to surrender my horses for your convenience. Or my carriage—or indeed anything in my possession—and demand nothing in return except permission to kiss this charming little hand."

Katya's brows drew together. For some reason he sounded different from the way he had sounded when he had left her.

Katya had led a sheltered life in Petersburg and, to a certain extent, in Krasnoye. She was certainly aware of the difference of address due to a peasant and to a young lady. What eluded her was the gradations within the latter category: there were young ladies and young ladies. Those traveling in a ramshackle *kibitka* without a proper retinue to attend them were likely to belong to a certain class, into which the young officer would have been only too happy to place Katya. And yet he was not perfectly sure; there was something in her demeanor and her way of speaking that did not quite go with a little demimondaine in search of a protector; nor did the way her fine black brows had drawn together at the hint of familiarity in his address. He decided to proceed gently.

"I promise you that you shall not stay here one moment longer than is necessary. I understand you had to sleep here last night. I only hope that your maidservant was able to make you moderately comfortable."

"I haven't any," Katya said. She vouchsafed no explanation and, perversely, this very fact heightened his uncertainty, as did her offhand manner of thanking him for his kindness, as though she found nothing extraordinary in his efforts on her behalf. An imperious little thing, he thought, used to all manner of services. As well she might be with those looks.

He said, "Apparently we shall have to wait for another hour or so. I am about to order dinner. If you would do me the honor of joining me . . ."

Katya accepted the invitation without the slightest hesitation, just as she would have condescended to be taken in to supper at an assembly by a likely young man.

They talked for a while. Lieutenant Gorin told Katya that he was bound for his uncle's country place not far from Moscow. His uncle was on his last legs and anxious to see his nephew, who was also his heir, before he died. "This is the reason for my hurry," he told her, adding with engaging frankness that he had no desire to see the will changed at the last minute due to his remissness. Presently the stationmaster's wife, who looked after culinary matters, came in bowing and called them to dinner. Katya, who was getting hungry, rose promptly. As she took his proffered arm, young Gorin got a better view of her lovely, slim figure with its tiny waist and proud breasts. A voracious look came into his rather shallow, light-colored eyes.

"I have engaged one of their private rooms," he told her in a low voice, pressing her hand. "I felt you might be more comfortable that way."

As they passed the other gentleman on the way to the private room (it was the same one in which Katya had slept and still had her luggage in), he rose and bowed to Katya. And again that nagging sense of familiarity caught at Katya. She paused for a slight curtsy and a closer look at his smiling face, which, however, brought no further recognition.

The stationmaster's wife had served up a plentiful dinner of fish and soup with meat pies. Gorin's own valet waited on them, serving the dishes and pouring the wine, after which he discreetly withdrew from the room. The lieutenant drank a great deal and after a while began to take on the manners of a stage seducer, drinking toast after toast to Katya, praising her beauty and several times begging her permission to kiss her hands.

Toward the end of the meal, the stationmaster opened the door to announce that the lieutenant's carriage was being put to and would be ready to depart in half an hour.

Gorin rolled a wrathful eye in his direction. "Can't you see that this is not the time for such announcements, you fool! Now just take your head out of the door before I fling a plate at it!"

The stationmaster vanished, muttering apologies. Katya frowned. "That seems rather uncalled for," she remarked. "After he has done his utmost to procure horses for you."

"I know, I know. I have an unfortunate temper, loveliest Katerina Vassilevna. But I couldn't bear to have anyone encroach on the all too brief time we have together. . . . Is it really possible that I shall never see you again?"

"We may meet in Moscow."

"If you would graciously give me your address, I would immediately fly to your feet." He looked at her expectantly.

Katya shook her head. "I don't know where I will be," she told him, without realizing that by this artless statement she had finally placed herself irrevocably in a certain category. In the young man's experience, respectable young ladies knew where they were staying and that was with respectable relatives. Encouraged by this new revelation, he proceeded to take a risk.

"A suggestion, lovely lady. We are both going to Moscow, are we not? It galls me to think of you traveling in a rattle-trap more fit, if you will forgive me, for a traveling gypsy than for a young lady of your quality. I had my own coachman take a look at it. One wheel is cracked, he says, and the axle is not in the best of conditions. Your driver should have attended to this, but you know how those hirelings are. I myself would never travel otherwise than with my own people."

Katya agreed with him fervently. She would have given

anything for the presence of Fyodor, disobliging as he had been on their last trip together.

"Now take my Antropka," Gorin pursued. "A tiger on the road, a veritable tiger! He is bound to get me to Moscow in three days at the most. If you would do me the honor . . ." He broke off with an eloquent smile.

"The honor of what, Monsieur Gorin?"

"Of making use of my carriage—and me. I assure you, the offer is made in a spirit of deep respect, not to say veneration. An angel of loveliness like you should not travel through the country unprotected. I am not as impertinent as to inquire what brought about such a situation. I can only offer you my protection—the protection of an officer and a man of honor who will know how to value and—well, *protect* you . . ."

Katya listened in silence, her pretty head leaning against her hand and her large, lustrous eyes not moving from the flushed countenance of the young officer. She was thinking hard. The prospect of traveling in comfort and with speed rather than crawling ignominiously along bad roads was a tempting one. She took stock of her would-be protector. He had an open, reckless face and was quite handsome in a somewhat coarse way. His tightly curled blond hair and bold eyes made her think of Vanya. Yes, that would be how Vanya would look wearing a guardsman's uniform. Illogically it was that resemblance that made her come to a decision.

She had no doubt that somewhere along the road he would probably make love to her and wondered whether his lovemaking would be as pleasurable as Vanya's. If so, there would be no reason why she shouldn't yield to it. *And if I don't want to—* Katya's chin rose a trifle—*then I simply won't.*

Here the young man, who had been growing restless under her protracted, disconcerting scrutiny, broke the silence. "Well, *ma belle?* Don't keep me on tenterhooks. Say you will. I promise that you shall not regret it."

"Very well," Katya said, "I will go to Moscow with you."

"Famous! You have made me the happiest man in the world." Seizing her hand, he kissed it rapturously. "I can't believe my luck! To think that I have managed to find such a charming companion on such a tedious voyage. I hope you will not mind, *ma belle*, if I tell you that you are the most exquisite creature I have ever encountered. You put all the Petersburg beauties to shame. And here I have prided myself on knowing all the prettiest . . ." He paused infinitesimally, "girls in Petersburg. How is it possible that I missed you?"

"Perhaps we moved in different circles," Katya answered. She said this in all seriousness and was a little puzzled when he roared with laughter.

"And witty, too! Well, let us drink to this fortunate encounter!"

He emptied his glass and poured another. "And here is another fortunate circumstance," he exclaimed. "My uncle's illness! Now I shall be able to install you in his house without any questions asked. We shall be marvelously cozy there."

Katya frowned. "But I don't want to be installed in any house. I merely want to get to Moscow as quickly as possible."

The young man's face darkened. "There is someone waiting for you there, I suppose. Well, I promised to get you to Moscow and I will. It is essential to stop at my uncle's; but as soon as I have paid my respects to him and shown myself to be a dutiful nephew, I shall have you conveyed to Moscow. On my word as a gentleman and an officer."

"That will be very kind of you," Katya said, reassured.

"However, I warn you I shall do my utmost to persuade you to stay. That is perfectly in keeping with my promise, isn't it? And I flatter myself," a conquering smile dawned on his flushed face, "that I will be able to make you change your mind."

"Perhaps," Katya said and smiled at him across the rim of the glass of wine which she had been sipping abstemiously all through this conversation. This was badinage of the sort to which she was accustomed in Petersburg; it was thus that you answered a smitten young man when he tried to persuade you to walk out on the terrace with him.

The young man stared at her, his eyes suffused. "My God, but you are beautiful," he said. "You madden me." Leaping to his feet, he drew her into his arms and began to rain kisses on her astonished face.

Katya, in an experimental and receptive mood, submitted at first. In another moment she found, however, that all lovemaking is not the same and that she did not particularly care for Lieutenant Gorin's sort. Again a comparison to Vanya entered her mind, and it was borne in on her that the ignorant peasant, untutored in civilities, was far more delicate and sensitive in his handling of her than her present aristocratic wooer. Vanya had been powerful and insistent in his lovemaking; but there was also infinite tenderness in his touch. He never made her feel as uncomfortable or rumpled as she was feeling now.

Gorin's face, bending over hers, wore a disagreeably greedy look. His rough grasp hurt her. When she tried to push him away, he merely uttered a grunting little laugh and went on kissing her, holding her so tightly clamped against his body that she couldn't free her arms. Angry panic rose up in Katya. Turning her face away from his searching lips, she said in a fierce whisper: "Stop it, I don't want to!"

Vanya would have stopped immediately if she had wanted him to (but she never had; she would have followed that gentle and powerful lead to the end!). This one paid no attention. Pulling away the ruche at her neck, he laid her shoulders bare and proceeded to inflict even more voracious kisses on them; it was as though her skin intoxicated him. Finally freeing one hand, Katya caught up a handful of pomaded hair and yanked energetically, at the same time screaming at the top of her lungs. The pain and the sound brought him to himself and he let her go. Hissing and spitting like an angry cat, Katya retreated behind the table. Gorin lunged after her and stopped, awareness coming back to his red face. He gave an uncertain laugh.

"Come," he said, "all that commotion over a little kiss!"

Katya glared at him. She was profoundly furious. Never before in her life had she been so rudely handled.

"It's your own fault," Gorin said in a propitiating manner. "You are so damned beautiful."

"And you feel that that gives you a right to maul me?" Katya inquired wrathfully.

"I hadn't expected so much sensibility. Come, let us be friends again."

As he moved toward her, holding his arms out, Katya picked up a glass from the table and threw it. It missed him by an inch and went crashing against the door.

The next moment it opened to let in the elegant gentleman in gray.

His eyebrows lifted in eloquent silence as he surveyed the two disheveled young people. Gorin turned on him angrily:

"What the devil do you mean, sir, by intruding on our privacy?"

"My dear sir," the newcomer replied imperturbably, "much as I respect the inviolability of a closed door, the rules are, I fancy, suspended when one hears a lady screaming."

Gorin flushed. "It was nothing," he said shortly. "The young lady was startled."

"By a mouse, perhaps?" their visitor murmured.

Katya couldn't forbear a giggle, and the young officer scowled.

"May I request you to leave us to ourselves?"

The gentleman in gray turned to Katya, his mobile eyebrows raised questioningly. "Shall I do so, mademoiselle? Am I indeed to understand that you have recovered from your alarm?"

Katya assured him that she had and did not expect it to recur. "Now that I know what to expect," she added with a fulminating glance at her dining companion.

"Very well, mademoiselle. If you are—inconvenienced again, you shall find me outside waiting for a relay of horses, whenever our host shall find it practicable to bestow it upon me. You may be assured that you will find Pierre Philippe Truffaut ready to be of service." He swept her a bow of truly ineffable grace.

"Truffaut!" burst from Katya. "Of course!"

She had seen him last more than a year ago, coming to the footlights, flushed but stately after his performance of *Orfeo*, to bestow the same magnificent salute upon the wildly applauding audience. He had disappeared from view after that, and M. Duroc had told her that he had been sent to Paris for some specific purpose, which she could not for the moment remember. "I should have known immediately! No one else could bow so beautifully."

Truffaut smiled modestly, kissed his hand to her, bowed again and withdrew, shutting the door delicately behind him.

"Who is he then?" Gorin asked irritably.

"Assistant ballet master of the Petersburg Imperial Ballet," Katya told him. "One of Russia's best *premiers danseurs*. How silly of me not to recognize him immediately!"

"I can't say I did either, but then it's not the male dancers I watch when I go to the ballet." He grinned unwillingly. "And here I was about to call him out if he didn't leave us alone! Never mind that French mountebank. What a little Tartar you are, *ma belle.* Are you still angry with me? Deuce take it, what is a man to do when a ravishing little beauty like you smiles at him?"

Katya wasn't listening to him, her mind being solely on the exquisite gentleman who had just left them. There was something important that Monsieur Duroc had told her about him, some special reason for his going to France. She gave a gasp of excitement as it came back to her. If it was so, what a marvelous piece of luck!

She interrupted the young officer at the highest pitch of his propitiatory eloquence. "Pray stop apologizing, Lieutenant Gorin. It doesn't signify in the least and I forgive you. But I must tell you—"

"You are an angel, and I swear I shall make it up to you for being such a brute."

"That's very well, but—"

"I know exactly what you are about to say, and I promise on my honor as an officer that in the future you shall be handled as circumspectly as a piece of rare china—which you are, *ma belle.* I have never encountered such a piece of perfection as you in my entire—"

He broke off as his valet reentered the room, accompanied by the coachman, who informed him that the horses were harnessed and ready to go.

"Got real good 'uns this time," he added. "They tried to fob me off with some nags, but Antropka was too much for them. 'Only the best for his excellency,' I says, and that's what we got—prime cattle, after I pushed them around a little."

Gorin clapped him on the shoulder affectionately. "Yes, I know your ways, you villain."

Antropka grinned. He was a dark gypsy of a man whose deeply lined face bore an expression of reckless good nature. He was wearing the voluminous gold-braided tunic of fine blue wool that was the hallmark of the Petersburg coachmen driving for young men of fashion. These coachmen, Katya knew, were a breed apart, known for their expert but foolhardy driving. They won their masters' racing bets, aided them in their escapades, and afterward enabled them to escape pursuit by authorities, and were in turn as valued and cosseted as the spirited horses they drove. He said, "We should be starting right away, your excellency."

"Well, we're ready. The young lady is coming with us. Get her luggage out and see to it that it's securely strapped onto the carriage. It's right there, stacked up behind the couch, isn't it, *mon ange?*"

"I am not coming with you," Katya said.

There was a stunned silence. The young officer stared at her in disbelief. "You can't mean it!"

"But I do. I am sorry. I kept trying to tell you so, but you would not listen. You can put that trunk down," she said to the coachman who was about to hoist it onto his shoulder.

Gorin flushed darkly. "Am I to understand that you are discarding me as an escort?"

"Yes, that's it."

"And may I know why I am offered this affront?"

"Oh, don't be silly," Katya said, losing her patience. "I have no intention of affronting you. I have merely changed my mind."

"Merely. . . !" An extremely ugly look came over Gorin's face. "I perceive, mademoiselle," he said, speaking with the strangled courtesy of extreme rage, "you are ignorant of the proper way to treat an officer and a gentleman. To lead me on as you have and then to change your mind—"

Katya drew herself up. "I have a right to do so if I choose," she said haughtily. "I must say it seems odd to hear you talk of being a gentleman and an officer after the way you have behaved." She moved toward the door and was stopped by an iron grip on her wrist.

"I'll tell you what, my dear," Gorin said, "I do not choose to be dismissed in this summary manner by a little cocotte, no matter how superior an article. You have engaged yourself to come with me, and come with me you shall."

"How dare you!" Katya said, trying in vain to free herself. "Let me go!"

Gorin released her long enough to snatch his cape from his valet's hands. He threw it about her shoulders and, wrapping it closely about her with a swiftness and expertise that seemed to betoken a certain amount of practice, swung her up into his arms. For a moment Katya lay still, rigid with surprise. Then she began struggling with all the strength of her supple young body.

"You are mad," she gasped. "Put me down immediately."

A low laugh answered her. The grasp that held her was unexpectedly powerful. The enveloping cloak impeded her struggles and her indignant outcry was muffled by a ruthless hand clapped over her mouth.

She heard Antropka say admiringly, "Quite a handful that one is, your excellency."

"I'll handle her if you'll open the door for me and not stand there grinning, damn you."

Antropka did not do so immediately. "Does your excellency mean to take her to the carriage through the waiting room?"

"How else, you fool? There's no other way. Luckily it's empty—"

Antropka scratched his head. "Well, no, I wouldn't say so, sir."

"You mean that damned French caper master is there? Well, if he gets in the way—"

He broke off with an oath as Katya bit his hand. His hand momentarily removed, Katya filled her lungs for a scream. But it was muffled again, her abductor this time taking the precaution of using a fold of the cloak to do so. "Little vixen," he said giving her an ungentle shake. "It'll be a pleasure taming you!" He looked with a mixture of desire and anger into the black eyes blazing defiance at him. "Well, what are you waiting for, damn you? Let's go! You keep close to me, Antropka, and if anyone interferes, knock 'em down."

"Even the general?"

"Anyone who gets in the way, you fool!" He came to an abrupt stop. "What did you say? What general?"

"The one that has just arrived. He's right there in the waiting room giving the stationmaster proper hell."

Katya saw a thoughtful look coming to her abductor's face. It was one thing to stage an abduction in a practically deserted posting house, with no one of consequence to stop you; and quite another to carry a struggling young woman out under the nose of your superior, who among other things would expect you to stop and salute.

"Are you sure it's a general?"

"Yes, sir! A proper old 'un, with a mustache like a tomcat and a chestful of medals. What's more, he's got an eye for our horses; asked for your name and all. If he doesn't get waited on soon, I wouldn't put it past him to confiscate them. That's what I'd come to tell your excellency. Seems to me we should be getting out of here as fast as we can, and never mind the young lady . . ."

The next moment Katya found herself being unceremoniously dumped on the floor. The cape that enveloped her was twitched away, and Lieutenant Gorin went out the door without a backward look. His servants followed, Antropka giving her a broad wink as he carefully closed the door behind him.

Katya sat up and gazed after them balefully. A plate had slid off the table during the struggle and was lying beside her. She picked it up and hurled it at the door. This relieved her feelings somewhat. She was still furious, but her anger was now tempered with a great sense of relief.

She picked herself up from the floor and, after fastening the door against intrusions, began to repair her toilette. Her hair had come down and was hanging about her shoulders in disarray, and the ruche on her dress had been ripped away. She remembered how carefully Aunt Praskovya had sewn it on ("Just right for a young lady, my dearie!") and was furious all over again.

It seemed that her relatives' forebodings had been justified, she thought as she repaired the damage as best she could. Traveling alone was not as simple and safe as she had thought. Honesty compelled her to admit that she had brought it on herself. It was clear that something in her behavior, natural as it had seemed, had made the odious lieutenant take her for something she was not. On the other hand, a nicer man, she reasoned, would not have acted so outrageously with *anyone!* She should have known; there was something in his manner from the very beginning that should have warned her. She promised herself to be more careful in the future.

A conversation she had once had with Lisa came back to her. Her sister had been pleading Graham's cause, and Katya had told her lightheartedly that he was too nice, that she would have preferred someone more excitingly sinister ("like Prince Dmitry, only of course he is too old"), someone who would carry her off and force her into submission.

Lisa had laughed at her. And of course Lisa had been

perfectly right. She had come very close to being abducted, and she had not liked it at all. It had been a nasty, messy experience that had left her rumpled and furious. Prince Dmitry, she thought irrelevantly—for a moment she visualized his dark, arrogant face with astonishing clarity—would have managed it much better.

At this point she remembered the audacious plan she had formed in her mind before her trouble with Lieutenant Gorin. She gave a gasp of dismay: "Oh, Mother of God," she prayed, frantically struggling with her hair, which perversely refused to stay up, "oh, Holy Virgin, don't let him be gone!"

Flinging open the door, she quickly scanned the waiting room and was relieved beyond words to see M. Truffaut having a leisurely repast at his table. He saw her and rose from it to greet her. Katya hastened to him.

"Oh, Monsieur Truffaut, I am so glad to find you still here!"

There was no doubting the sincerity of this statement, and the ballet master's face lighted up in response. "How very charming of you to say so," he said, kissing her hand. "Indeed, I had expected to be gone by now, but it seems that my relay of horses has been preempted by his excellency."

Katya looked after the elderly general who was just leaving the tavern and silently invoked God's blessing on his unconscious head: it seemed she owed him more than just her deliverance from Gorin.

"Will you do me the honor of joining me, mademoiselle?" Truffaut said, drawing a chair out for her with the exquisite grace and courtesy she had already remarked. He ordered tea for her, discoursing easily on the surprisingly excellent qualities of tea to be found in post houses.

"Even in the worst accommodations one finds it to be strong and of a remarkable good flavor. Also, milk is of excellent quality. As for the home-baked bread—!" he kissed his fingers. "With those products in ample supply one can hope to survive—barely!—the exigencies of the road . . . May I know whom I have the honor of entertaining, mademoiselle?"

When Lieutenant Gorin had asked her that, Katya had thoughtlessly used her father's surname. This time she was more careful and introduced herself as Katerina Vassilevna Golovin. She added impulsively, "I must tell you how happy I am to meet you, Monsieur Truffaut. You are one of my favorite dancers, you know. I like your style so much more than that of Vestris. We saw him when he came to perform with the Petersburg ballet, and of course those *pirouettes* were magnificent, but I think he did too many of them."

"That is very perspicacious of you, mademoiselle." The ballet master's eyes were warm. "I assure you I can turn as well as Vestris, but I don't think *pirouettes* are everything. Ballet isn't all *pirouettes* and leaps and *entrechâts*. There is much more to it."

"Oh, I agree. Your performance in *Diane et Apollo* was what I considered perfection. I remember saying so to my sister. I am delighted to be able to say so to you in person. . . . Monsieur Truffaut, you *are* going to Moscow, aren't you?"

"Indeed I am, mademoiselle."

Katya, who had been holding her breath as she waited for his reply, let it out, deeply relieved. "I can't tell you how very happy that makes me. You see, I remembered being told that you had been sent to Paris to see how they produce their ballets, and then you were to go to Moscow to improve *that* company."

"That is true," M. Truffaut said. "And I assure you that I am looking toward that prospect with considerable trepidation. They write me that conditions are quite impossible."

As Katya was looking encouraging and sympathetic, he proceeded to enlarge upon this pessimistic statement. The Moscow troupe was so very bad, it seemed, that the only way to lift it up to acceptable standards was to send some of the lights of the Petersburg ballet to raise the lagging morale of the Moscow dancers and revive the interest of the Moscow ballet goers. He mentioned names which brought pleasure and awe to Katya's face: Auguste would be there, Berylova and Kolossova. (*"Kolossova!"* Katya breathed in rapture.) The corps de ballet was not up to strength, and there was even a dearth of *figurants*, the lowest category of dancers, who were used mostly in mob scenes and pageants. The director of the Imperial Ballet had charged him with stopping on the way to make a deal with a nobleman in Kaluga who had once been a tremendous balletomane but was willing to sell off his private company of serf dancers now that his enthusiasm had waned.

"But enough of me. It is charming of you to listen to me with such pretty attention, but I have no wish to bore you. I see your admirer has finally been given his horses and departed."

Katya sipped her tea slowly, her eyes reflective on him. She said, "I had thought to accompany him to Moscow, but I decided against it."

"So I perceive," said Truffaut with a hint of a smile on his well-shaped lips. "Allow me to congratulate you on your good sense in making that decision, mademoiselle. It would never have done. The young man, I could see, was totally lacking in *delicatesse*. I don't believe you would have enjoyed that journey."

Katya agreed with fervor. "Indeed not! It would have been a terrible mistake."

Truffaut's eyes were speculative on her. "I cannot help being curious, mademoiselle. If you'll forgive my saying so, I do not see you as a young lady who would make indiscriminate connections on the road. You must be remarkably anxious to get to Moscow."

"I am, very," Katya admitted. "It is most important for me to get there as soon as possible." She sighed deeply, watching him from under her long eyelashes. "It seems that I cannot do so on my own. My carriage appears to be falling apart, the driver I hired is drunk and I cannot make the stationmaster give me horses. It is all very annoying. That was why I had accepted Lieutenant Gorin's invitation. But I had not expected that he would turn out to be so impossible!"

Truffaut's intelligent gray eyes twinkled. "Ah, one has to have a strong head to withstand the effects of such beauty as yours. Young men of his age are generally greedy and undisciplined. I should imagine, mademoiselle, that you would find an older man—such as myself—far more civilized. At my age one is a man of the world; one knows that a relationship with a young lady of your superior character requires finesse."

"Monsieur Truffaut," Katya said, "are you suggesting that I should accompany you to Moscow?"

He bowed gracefully. "I am endeavoring, my dear Katerina Vassilevna, to impart my feelings of gratitude and delight should you decide to confer that honor upon me."

Katya was silent. This, of course, was precisely the offer she had been hoping for; from the first she had been resolved to profit by the heaven-sent chance that had put in her path the future *regisseur-en-chef* of the Moscow ballet. Nevertheless, remembering her recent ordeal, she hesitated. I must be very careful this time, she thought.

Putting her teacup down, she gave Truffaut a long, considering scrutiny to which he submitted with good grace, smiling a little. At the end of it she felt reassured. Truffaut awakened no apprehensions in her. There was humor and kindness in his face, and his offer had been made in the most delicate and reassuring terms possible. Reason told her that he too probably had certain expectations; but she was sure that he would not enforce them with the brutality and lack of savoir faire that she had resented in her previous suitor. "I am sure," she said to herself, "that he at least will not *rumple* me."

She said, "I shall be very happy to come with you, Monsieur Truffaut. It is quite clear that it is God's will for me to do so, or I wouldn't have met you on the road."

"I render Him my heartfelt thanks," Truffaut rejoined, beaming on her, "for bestowing upon me such an enchanting companion even for a brief time." He gave her a rueful smile. "Keeping in mind your haste to get to Moscow, I must suppose that there is a lover waiting for you there. Once we arrive, it will be good-bye to poor Truffaut!"

"Oh, no," Katya assured him earnestly. "You couldn't be more wrong. As a matter of fact, the reason I was going to Moscow was to meet you—although," she added punctiliously, "it is true that at the time I did not know it would be you, and I am so glad it is!"

Truffaut looked upward earnestly as if looking for guidance from above. "*Ma petite*," he said, "although I perceive that this statement is of a gratifyingly flattering nature, and I daresay I ought to accept it without question, even as the Israelites accepted manna from above, yet there is that in me that requires explanation. I do not quite understand."

"Why, it's very simple," Katya said. "I was going to Moscow to join the ballet there. And to meet you before I even get there—it almost seems as though it had been meant, doesn't it?"

"Yes, but . . ." said Truffaut.

"And what is more, now that I've met you all my hesitations are put to rest. I know that Moscow is not at all the thing. But it will be exactly right with you there."

"Yes, but . . ." said Truffaut.

"Although I daresay, from what you have told me, that it will take some time to whip it into shape, at the end it will be the sort of ballet troupe that no one will cavil at, and if Kolossova herself is not averse to taking a chance, I am sure I needn't be . . ."

Truffaut stopped her with an upflung palm. "Ah, no, *ma petite*. I see you have been utterly misled by those dreams. Another man would perhaps humor you in this delusion and seduce you with promises of glory. But I, Pierre Philippe Truffaut, am not a scoundrel of that sort. I would not seduce you by false promises. Ballet is a grueling and exigent craft. One cannot be a ballerina by merely wanting to be. It takes years of training . . ."

"I've had them," Katya said. "In fact, I have been studying ballet for years."

"You have?" said Truffaut rather faintly.

Katya leaned toward him, her black eyes holding his intently. "Monsieur Truffaut, if it turns out that I dance well enough, will you take me on?"

"*Ma petite*," said Truffaut gallantly, "you needn't worry about that. Your personal attractions are such that no man in his sound mind would hesitate a moment before taking you on."

"I suppose you mean as a mistress," Katya said calmly. "But that is not what I mean. I mean as a member of the Moscow ballet troupe. Will you—if I show you that I indeed do know how to dance?"

"*Entendu*," said Truffaut, amused. "When do you intend to show me this, *ma petite?*"

"Right now, if you wish. And right here." She looked around her and her brows contracted. "Oh dear, I wonder what can be done about music? I heard someone playing the balalaika; but they could only play a Russian song, and that's not what I want. I want to perform a classical variation. Well, no use repining. I can do it without music, if necessary."

There was now a gleam of genuine interest in Truffaut's eyes. He assured her that they could do better than that, and forthwith went to get his *pochette*, the miniature violin used by dance masters for their lessons.

By the time he had returned, Katya had everyone cleared out of the main room and was implacably pushing the stationmaster out the door. "It will be no longer than ten minutes," she told him.

"But supposing someone drives in!"

"Then you merely tell that person to wait, as you have been doing all along," Katya said, closing the door and turning the key on his protests. She faced Truffaut radiantly.

"I know exactly what I shall dance for you," she said. "The Diane variation from *Diane et Apollo.* I loved it so when I saw it with you dancing Apollo that I immediately learned the variation, and whenever I danced it I imagined I was dancing it with you. And here it has come to pass; I shall actually be dancing it for you. Isn't that extraordinary?"

Truffaut, somewhat dazed, agreed. He tuned his violin while Katya assumed the fifth position, raising her arms above her head in preparation. His look was immediately appreciative. The very way in which she made this preparation told him that her training had been excellent: everything was right—her small head was beautifully poised, her torso lifted and her raised arms formed a perfect oval over her head.

As he launched into the adagio, Katya began turning into the *arabesque penchée* which opens this variation. She stopped immediately and said angrily: "I can't perform like this!"

She quickly unbuttoned the dress, stepped out of it, and tossing it out of the way, resumed her former position.

Truffaut, consideraly shaken, regarded the slim vision in bodice and pantalettes that now faced him in perfect fifth position. His eyes roved appreciatively from the slender, rounded arms over the classically poised head to the snowy, virginal bosom half-bared above the camisole. An impatient exclamation from Katya brought him to himself and he began the adagio movement again.

Katya had chosen her dance wisely. Although the variation was short, it held all the elements that show a dancer's style and technique. Beginning with a gracefully held *arabesque penchée*, she went through a series of controlled, plastic movements, her arms floating gracefully, her body bending lithely, ending on one knee, holding an imaginary bow and aiming an imaginary arrow. Then as the music changed tempo, quickening to allegro, she circled the room in a series of *grand jetés.* A diagonal line of swift turns, strung out like pearls on a string, brought her to the middle of the room, where, after several impeccably performed stationary *pirouettes*, she went into an *arabesque*, her arms again poised as though holding bow and arrow. A great sense of exhilaration possessed her. Her lips curved into a triumphant smile, her eyes sparkled. As Truffaut finished the last few long-held notes of the variation, she held the pose perfectly, as immobile as the porcelain classical figure surmounting the French clock in their Petersburg drawing room.

He lowered his violin and looked at her, thunderstruck.

"*Incroyable!*" he murmured.

CHAPTER 17

Chirkin's story of his unsuccessful elopement had made it clear that Katya was bound for Moscow to seek their Aunt Aline's protection. Accordingly, Lisa had hoped that they would overtake her on the road. However, soon after they started out the fate that invariably befalls all vehicles traveling at speed on the dreadful Russian roads befell them, too, and they had to spend two days waiting near Velikiya Luki while a local wheelwright repaired their chaise. Thereafter they inquired for Katya wherever they stopped, but in vain; apparently their *marche-routes*, schedules indicating the post houses where they were to change horses, were different. The fact that they did not come across her *kibitka* on the road seemed to indicate that she must have reached Moscow before them. When after several more days of traveling the cortege drew up in front of the ancient palace on Nikitskaya where Princess Aline Mourovtsev lived, they fully expected to find Katya already there.

It was, however, an expectation tinged by a premonition of failure. Lisa had been disappointed so often that Katya was beginning to seem a beloved wraith who flitted tantalizingly before them, always evading the final contact. Don't let it be so again, she prayed silently.

A footman in a gray and gold uniform led them through an enfilade of rooms lighted by hanging lamps in the form of glass lanterns, to the portrait room, a large, pistachio-colored chamber lined by portraits of ancestors and royalty. Catherine the Great holding scepter and orb smiled graciously upon them from one wall; her son Paul in his Gatchina colonel's uniform glared from another. There was also a portrait of Lisa's father, and one of her aunt, both done in their younger days. Presently the princess herself sailed in.

The widowed Princess Aline Mourovtsev was a tall, corpulent woman in her late sixties. She affected old-fashioned styles, wearing dresses with hoops and powdering her graying locks before venturing out of her dressing room. Her majestic air was somewhat marred by a habitual myopic squint; her eyesight had recently grown worse, but she was unwilling to admit that and refused to wear glasses, depending solely on her lorgnette. She now directed that lorgnette on her niece.

"Lisanka, can it really be you?" she cried, enveloping her in a massive embrace. "I hardly recognize you. And no wonder. When did I see you last? Five years ago, wasn't it? And here you are, a grown-up young lady. What a surprise!"

Katya isn't here, Lisa thought, her heart sinking.

"Although I don't know why I should be surprised. I was, after all, expecting you." (Then she must be here, Lisa thought. Oh, why doesn't she come?) "Your mother wrote to me saying that you and your sister might be coming to Moscow. And here you are. But where is Katya? I thought you were inseparable, and here you are, not with Katya but with a young man," she peered at Graham nearsightedly, "whom I don't believe I know."

"Mr. George Graham of the British Embassy," Lisa said mechanically. Her heart was wrung with disappointment. Graham's face was bleak as he made his bow and kissed the plump hand the princess graciously extended to him.

The princess regarded the two of them with some shrewdness. "Now what is all this about? Your mother's letter was very odd indeed, very cold and brusque. I had thought at first that this was because I didn't come to the funeral of my brother Vassily, may he rest in peace. Absurd of her; I am far too old to drag my rheumatic bones to Petersburg. Your father wouldn't have come to my funeral, I assure you, nor would I have borne him any ill will for that. . . . But perhaps there is something else amiss? Come, out with it. I may be half-blind but I can see both of you are down in the mouth. You aren't eloping, by any chance?"

"No, of course not, dear madame," Lisa exclaimed. "Monsieur Graham has merely been kind enough to give me his escort to Moscow. In fact he is affianced to Katya and—Oh, my dear aunt, have you heard anything from Katya?"

The princess stared at her. "Why, should I have? You had better tell me the whole story."

She listened to it in disbelief, exclaiming and crossing herself all through the recital.

"Why," she interrupted, upon being told of Katya's parentage, "I remember Vassily telling me about that mistress of his he had set up at Krasnoye, a gypsy or something of that sort. He was quite mad about her, I can tell you, always singing her praises. And that's who Katya's mother was! *Epatant!*" She shook her powdered head in wonder.

She listened to the rest of the recital without any further interruptions. "Well," she inquired baldly, "where is she, then?"

"I don't know, *ma tante.*" Lisa's voice trembled. "And I am dreadfully worried about her, traveling alone, without protection . . . Oh, Graham, what do you suppose could have happened?"

Graham strove for a reassuring smile. "I should imagine precisely what happens to most vehicles on your unconscionable Russian roads. It has probably broken down and is being repaired in one of those roadside villages. In which case I should expect her to appear here in a day or so. And if she doesn't—"

"Yes, what then?"

"Only one thing to do then. Retrace our steps, stopping at every post house on the way and making exhaustive inquiries."

"Yes, yes, you are perfectly right, that is exactly what we should do."

"We?" Her aunt's eyebrows mounted to their powdered hairline. "No 'we' about this, my girl. If you think I am about to let you go gallivanting with this gentleman . . ."

"But I already have, *ma tante.* Surely if my mother raised no objection . . ."

"That is her business. But I am responsible for you now, and I shall brook no improprieties while you are under my roof."

In vain Lisa protested that surely the proprieties were fully observed with the mob of servants waiting upon them, and that she could not bear to sit home and wait, in ignorance of her sister's fate. The princess proved adamant, and so, to her indignation, did Graham.

"It really is neither fitting nor necessary for you to do so, Countess Lisa." During the last days of their journey, they had been addressing each other as Lisa and Graham, but Graham deemed it discreet to revert to more formal terms under the princess's censorious eye. "Your presence and authority as Katya's sister were necessary in Krasnoye, but that is no longer the case. I can do all the searching myself, without subjecting you to the rigors of travel."

Lisa sighed but submitted. The princess showed her approval of Graham by smiting him robustly across the shoulderblades.

"Very proper, young man. I must say, Katya is lucky in you."

As soon as Graham left Moscow, Lisa was conscious of the same nightmarish feeling that she had had in Petersburg, when she had come back from the convent to find Katya gone. Try as she might to be reasonable, she could not help the irrational conviction that Graham, upon quitting Moscow, had stepped into the same limbo in which Katya was wandering, and that she had lost them both. Every night she would dream of pursuing their receding forms through a cloudy and ominous landscape and, upon awaking, lie sleepless in her bed, whispering over and over again the familiar prayer of "Preserve them both from harm, Holy Mother of God, send them both back to me . . ."

This was, however, her private ordeal, and she did not let it show during the day, when she stoically kept her aunt company in all the social endeavors the latter devised, presumably in order to cheer up her niece.

Not a day passed without an entertainment of some sort. For all of her advanced years and occasional bouts of lumbago, Princess Mourovtsev was a devout partygoer. There was no social event of consequence at which she would not make an appearance rigged up in such antedeluvian splendor that she utterly eclipsed her quiet young niece. Lisa followed docilely in her wake when they went to the mammoth ball given by Count Alexis Orloff in his palace near the Kaluga gates. There she received condolences from that amiable giant, who used to know her father during the Turkish war; she watched him perform his favorite *tour de force* of rolling up a silver tray as though it were a page of silver paper, and listened to the performance of his famous horn orchestra, each member of which knew only one note.

They attended dinners that went on for four hours at a

stretch, and between dinner and supper made the rounds of the princess's dear friends. There was a visit to the theater to see a French play, and a quickly gotten up masquerade at their own house, a gay affair made especially so by the fact that all the servants participated, in masks, mingling and dancing with the gentry. Lisa derived some pleasure from dressing her two little maids, Parasha and Mavrushka, in her own finery and seeing them assiduously courted by some of the visiting beaus, while she herself escaped notice in a modest black domino.

The princess did all this ostensibly to keep Lisa's mind off her sister's situation. However, she defeated this kind objective by incessantly talking about it in private.

Moreover, she minced no words. Princess Mourovtsev was famous in Moscow society for her unbridled candor and never scrupled to say exactly what she thought of anyone, no matter what his or her rank. There was a legend that she once so enraged the late Emperor Paul that he tore her mobcap off her head and jumped up and down on it in his fury. Lisa had to listen to her pithy comments on everyone involved in the present situation: on Prince Dmitry Lunin's inexcusable viciousness ("They are all alike, these rakes, as they grow older!"); on her father's remissness in clarifying his illegitimate daughter's status ("Vassily always thought he was a law unto himself") and on her mother's disgraceful behavior ("A vengeful, unprincipled lot, all that family, and so I told your father when he offered for your mother.")

Nor did Katya escape censure. "I can't imagine why she never let me know of her situation. Don't you think I would have stood her friend? Isn't she my own brother's child? I understand that there was no way for her to do it while she was in that village. But once she was out—and I admire her going away with that squire; that was truly enterprising of her—why did she not write me then? She could have stayed on that estate with him and sent a courier to me with a letter, and I would have gone down there myself, lumbago or no, to rescue her. But no, what does she do but go off gallivanting by herself to Moscow. Probably thought it was the romantic thing to do. Understandable, of course. She has gypsy blood in her, and that's why she is roaming all over Russia instead of doing the rational thing."

Even as she tried to defend Katya, Lisa had found some solace in this line of thought: it was far more comforting to think of

Katya yielding to the call of her gypsy blood and heedlessly going a-roving than to consider other, dark alternatives.

"I wonder," the old lady pursued, "how that young Englishman feels about it. They are usually a rather proper lot. To have one's affianced bride not only turn out to have gypsy blood in her, but to act like one—one can't help but wonder what his sentiments are on the subject."

"His sentiments, *ma tante*," Lisa answered firmly, "are everything they should be."

"That's all very well, but I can't help thinking, my love, that you would be a much better choice for him. And if he does not realize it by now, I shall have a poor opinion of his understanding. You like him, too, don't you?"

She went on in that vein until Lisa, unable to bear it any longer, fled from the room, scarlet-faced.

Almost a week had elapsed when Lisa, coming down from her apartments, heard Graham's voice in the vestibule. She picked up her skirts and went flying down the grand staircase, her face radiant with surprise, as totally forgetful of her dignity as if she were again a girl of thirteen playing tag with her sister through the sedate halls of the Vorontzov palace.

"You're back at last!"

The young man turned to greet the flying figure, his own face opening up in joy. "Lisa." He made two swift strides toward the stairs and caught the hands that were stretched to him. "Sweet Lisa . . ."

"Oh, Graham, I missed you so."

"And I . . ." He broke off, the eager words dying on his lips. A bleak look came over his face. The glad color washed out of Lisa's cheeks, and she withdrew her hands from his. He made no attempt to retain them.

"And—Katya?" she said unsteadily. The terrible anxiety was back, and with it a great sense of guilt: iniquitous of her to forget her sister even for a moment, rejoicing in Graham's return! "You haven't found her? Not even a trace?"

"Well, yes. But . . ." He made a helpless gesture. "I don't know how to say this . . ."

Lisa saw that he looked desperately tired and discouraged, his hair slightly disheveled, his gray eyes rimmed with red.

"You shall say nothing until you have rested and had something to eat," she said. "Come with me, if you please."

She led him to the small withdrawing room, where she did her reading whenever her all too sociable aunt allowed her to. It was an airy and cozy room, with some of Lisa's favorite books stored behind the embroidered silk screen of the poplar bookcase. Voronikhin's peaceful landscapes of the environs of Moscow hung on the walls and a vase-shaped lamp poured a soft light through its milky glass shade. A tea table with inlaid top stood behind the fashionable treillage of tall hydrangeas. Lisa settled Graham at it and called for tea and refreshments.

Presently she sent away the servants and Graham began to tell her all about it.

He had proceeded north, as planned, stopping at all the post houses and making his inquiries, but without any results. "There seems to be an extraordinary amount of traveling going on, because the weather is still good; it is hard for the stationmasters to remember who has passed by. They are supposed to keep books with the travelers' names and destinations, but they neglect to do so, particularly when they are busy. So that the fact that Katya's name was not entered meant nothing, and I spent a good deal of time looking about the nearby villages in case there had been a breakdown. . . ."

Lisa listened patiently. It seemed to her that he was drawing out the recital because of a reluctance to tell her something he had learned. Stoically she waited for the bad news.

It was at a post house below Tver that he came across the first news of Katya. She had been there, and had stayed for a couple of hours waiting for a new relay of horses. The stationmaster was quite sure it had been she.

Lisa drew a deep breath. "Well? Tell me," she said steadily, sitting in her chair as straight and stiff as an arrow.

Graham glanced at her and away. He said heavily, "According to the stationmaster, she was traveling in the company of a gentleman who was bound for Moscow."

There was a silence. Lisa said almost inaudibly, "That's bad, isn't it?"

"Well . . ." Graham's smile was twisted. "It is—disturbing."

That had been as much as he could find out. It had happened nearly two weeks before, and the stationmaster, an elderly man harried and confused by the comings and goings of the travelers, could not remember which of the signatures in the book was that of Katya's companion. But he was quite certain that the two of them had been going to Moscow.

"Are you perfectly sure that it was Katya?" Lisa asked. "After all, as you yourself said, there was a great deal of confusion. The stationmaster could have made a mistake."

"He seemed sure of it, Lisa. The description fitted, and he had no doubts at all after I had shown him this." He brought out of his breast pocket an ivory oval with a portrait on it and gave it to Lisa, explaining: "I had a miniature made from the portrait of Katya that Sir Robert painted."

Katya looked up at them out of the gold frame, her enchanting smile curving her lovely mouth, the delicate wild-rose flush pinkening her cheeks, her black eyes velvety under the long eyelashes. They both looked at the miniature without speaking.

"I wish," Graham said suddenly, "I had one of you."

There was another silence, which Lisa broke. She spoke hesitatingly, her head down, unconsciously turning the smooth ivory oval over and over between her slim fingers. "I am certain," she said, "that it isn't the way it looks. There is something about Katya that makes men do for her what she wants done. Look what Monsieur Chirkin has done for her. She will always find someone who will help her without—well, without her being made to pay for it in any—degrading way. I know Katya; she is not only beautiful but also strong and fastidious. I have complete faith in her. And so must you."

Gordon's gray eyes held hers. It was an unreadable look, but she felt warmed by it, as though a ray of sunshine had alit and lingered on her. He looked away, almost, it seemed, with an effort.

"The thing is," he said heavily, "She is surely in Moscow now. That stop near Tver had taken place something like three weeks ago, and it takes less than three days to get from Tver to Moscow."

And she had not sought out Aunt Aline! Lisa clapped her hands to her cheeks. "But where is she, then? We must find her."

"Yes, we must." Graham's sandy brows drew together. His lips tightened. "One would need to be an insufferably priggish fellow, completely devoid of understanding," he said, as much to himself as to Lisa, "to blame your sister for any desperate measures she may have had to take in her extremity." His voice had a deeply considering note, as of one laboring to an unavoidable conclusion. "Katya knows nothing of our efforts to find her. As far as she knows, she is alone in the world, a victim of your pernicious system of serfdom. She is not to be blamed for a seeming impropriety—or for anything. I feel as I did when I thought she had eloped with Captain Kozlov. I still consider myself bound in honor to her."

He was repeating what he had said before, in Petersburg. But this time he did not add as he had then: *And besides, I still love her.* The thought flashed treacherously through Lisa's mind and was immediately banished. A wave of admiration and gratitude swelled up in her. "Oh," she cried, "you *are* good!" Impulsively she caught his hand in both of hers and kissed it.

Graham snatched it away, horrified. "Don't," he said. "You must not, my—you must not, Lisa. It is I who should. . . ." A wrenching sigh broke from him. He said, gloomily: "I understand how it is; I know what I must do. But I wish it were otherwise . . ."

It was then that the old princess swept in upon them and began to question Graham. Lisa had barely time to throw him an imploring look and get back a tiny, reassuring nod. His account of his travels was carefully censored and included no mention of the mysterious gentleman who was escorting Katya to Moscow. For all her raucous indiscretions in speech, Aunt Aline was a high stickler for propriety, and Lisa shrank at the thought of her comments if she knew Katya's latest adventure.

The old lady listened to Graham's account with a steadily darkening brow. "That settles it," she said. "I had hoped to keep our personal affairs to ourselves, but I see it will not do. Governor Bekleshev is a special friend of mine. I shall go to him tomorrow and ask for his help. We shall have to find Katya, come what may."

"Oh, yes," Lisa cried, "nothing is more important than finding Katya."

"I shall write to him straightaway to expect a visit tomorrow. Your efforts, my dear Monsieur Graham, have been most laudable," she went on, settling her large bulk at the small poplar desk in the corner and commencing to write. "But they're nothing to what a brace of *feldjägers* going about official business can do. They'll know just how to go about it. It's wonderful how much people can begin to remember when they are threatened with a beating. . . . The worst of it is that his excellency is like an old woman; you might as well have your private business shouted forth from the roof of St. Basil as tell it to him. I'll try to extract a promise of secrecy from him; he is a little afraid of me. But first things first." She wrote as she talked. Upon finishing her letter, she sealed it and rang for a footman to have it immediately taken to Count Bekleshev.

That done, she commanded the two young people to put Katya out of their minds for the evening.

"Nothing can be done until tomorrow, so there is no use thinking about it. It is a very good thing that you are here, Monsieur Graham. I shall expect you to take me and Lisa to the ballet tonight."

"But *ma tante*," Lisa said helplessly, "he has just come. And anyhow I was going to ask you to excuse me tonight."

"Nothing of the sort, my girl. No moping around: that is something I have no patience with. Besides, I hate going to the ballet alone. Prince Yusupov was kind enough to lend me his loge for tonight, which is most charming of him. I understand it is impossible to buy any tickets for this performance. We shall not stay for all of it, since we are also expected to look in on the Golitzin reception. Now, my good sir, you have less than an hour to make yourself presentable, so off with you!" She waved him away with a vigorous flourish of her oversize fan.

CHAPTER 18

This is my third day in Moscow," Katya wrote.

> Sometimes it appears to me that I am dreaming, but most of the time it is as though my life until now had been a dream. I had thought that I would just go on dancing as I had danced with Monsieur Duroc, but it is not like that at all. We practice and practice for hours, and I am so tired that if not for the pleasure of finally being able to write to you, my own dear mouse, I would be fast asleep in my bed.

This was her second letter to Lisa. The first one, started in the waiting room of the Rzhev post house and continued during the rest of her journey, she had sent as soon as she arrived in Moscow. She was writing this one late at night in her own room, which Truffaut had procured for her in Mme. Cornilov's little boarding house near the Arbat. It was drafty in the room, and she was grateful for the warmth of the huge, double-faced shawl which Praskovya had put into her trunk.

She wrote on:

> We are now rehearsing on stage for *Raoul the Bluebeard*, which will be performed in a few days. There are always people there to see us rehearse. Some of them are young officers, who ogle us outrageously while we dance and make appointments afterward. I pay them no attention whatsoever, although a few of them have tried to catch my attention and send me bouquets with notes pinned to them. I am far too tired after the rehearsal to go carousing with

officers as many of the girls do, and anyhow would not dream of doing so even if I had not made a bargain with Monsieur Truffaut.

"Oh, dear," Katya said, and dipping her quill deeper into the squat inkwell, carefully eradicated the last sentence. Much as she wanted to tell Lisa everything, it would not be advisable, she knew, to mention her bargain with the dapper ballet master, which she had made after she had danced for him.

After she had finished her *Diane* variation, made her reverence and taken the fifth position, in which a pupil customarily awaits the master's comments, Katya had stood before Truffaut perfectly unselfconsciously, having forgotten about her state of *déshabillé*. And indeed there was nothing in the impersonal, evaluating gaze bent upon her to remind her of the fact that she was still in her pantalettes and bodice. A tentative knock at the door brought them both out of their preoccupation. The impersonal look left his eyes, which now filled with a quite different sort of appreciation, and Katya, responding with a deep blush, snatched up her dress and hastily stepped into it. As she struggled with the buttons, her fingers grown awkward with haste, Truffaut strolled over to help her.

"Allow me," he said, stepping behind her. His fingers raced up the row of buttons with a nimbleness that bespoke infinite experience, and when he was through, he dropped a light kiss on the nape of her neck.

It was a far more civilized approach than the frantic assault of her military admirer. Katya, appreciating that, nevertheless felt a thrill of impatience at the diversion. She looked up at him questioningly over her shoulder.

"Well, Monsieur Truffaut?" she asked. "Will I do?"

A low laugh answered her. "Most certainly, you will do."

The knocking at the door had in the meanwhile grown louder. Dropping his hands from Katya's shoulders, Truffaut went to unlock it and let in the stationmaster, who, after one baffled look, scuttled to the kitchen, where he confided to his wife that the ways of the gentry were beyond his comprehension. "Not that I wouldn't have known exactly what to think, only that the gentleman never stopped playing the fiddle all the time the doors were closed, so it couldn't have been *that!*"

"What a fortunate man I am!" Truffaut went on expansively, throwing his arms out in an eloquent gesture. "How else would you call a man who quite unexpectedly finds a pearl of great price in a cowbarn? To think that I had been vexed because there were no horses for me! I might have gone on to Moscow quite unaware of the treasure I had left behind me if the gods had not been kind to me!"

Relieved, Katya gave him her blinding smile. "Then you do want me!"

"In every possible way!"

Katya thought this over. "You mean, not only as a dancer in your troupe, but also as your mistress?" she asked, determined to have everything spelled out.

Katya's forthrightness seemed to delight Truffaut. "Why, yes, *ma petite*. I must hope that that is your desire also. You will make me the happiest of men. And I—I shall strive to make you happy, too." Here Truffaut preened himself the tiniest bit. "Without undue boasting, I may say that I am accounted to be a skillful and considerate lover by the ladies who have favored me, as I hope you will. Nor would a connection with me be unprofitable in other ways. I can teach you a good deal—in dance as well as love. I am certain that I could make another Kolossova of you in time."

Katya gave him an appraising look. "In how much time?"

"Why as to that—*cela depend*. One does not become a prima ballerina overnight. You will start in the corps de ballet and go on from there. I shall do my best," he lifted her hand to his lips, "to make the time pass quickly."

Katya shook her head. "That is not good enough," she said decidedly. "You yourself have told me that there are not enough good dancers in Moscow. You would want me in the corps de ballet whether I slept with you or not, would you not?"

"Unromantic but true," Truffaut agreed with a rueful laugh.

"Well, then, if you want to sleep with me, you must do better than the corps de ballet for me."

Truffaut looked at her with mingled respect and amusement. "You are an extraordinary young woman," he said. "You say exactly what you mean, do you not? Well, then, so shall I. The thing is, my lovely Katerina Vassilevna—"

"You may call me Katya."

"—My delightful Katya, that I cannot make you a prima

ballerina with a wave of my baton, like a fairy godmother, no matter how great my inducement to do so. Nor is it merely ballet politics, though I shudder to think of the outcry that would be raised if I were to elevate an unknown newcomer too fast. Your talent and technique are redoubtable, but there is more than that to ballet. You can hope to become a ballerina of stature only after you have performed before an audience for a long time. You have never done so, have you, *ma petite?* You have only performed for your teacher, I am sure. What a delight you must have been to him!"

Katya looked at him with respect. That was quite true, of course. Her performances for her father's guests had never included ballet.

"You must develop in yourself a sense of audience," Truffaut pursued. "Establish a rapport with those who are watching you. Only thus will you acquire an ability to kindle in audiences that sacred fire which undoubtedly burns in you. Kolossova has that capacity and you will have it too—in time. But now you need your apprenticeship in the lowly corps de ballet. With your talent, it need not be long. Will you reward my ardor when you become a *coryphée*?"

Katya considered this. Dancers in that category belonged between the corps de ballet and the soloists, generally performing in groups of six and eight. She shook her head again. "I shall do so after I have my first solo."

The ballet master's face fell ludicrously. "*Parbleu*," he said. "I am a warm-blooded man. I don't know if I can wait that long."

"But it need not be that long! I do have technique, after all."

"You also have technique in bargaining," Truffaut observed. "Who taught it to you, I wonder?"

"My grandfather," Katya told him. "The dearest and wisest old man in the world. 'Use everything you have,' he said, 'do not squander it cheaply.' And that includes my virginity."

Truffaut clicked his tongue in annoyance. "*Voyons!*" he said. "A virgin! That always makes for trouble. Do you know, I sensed it, all evidence to the contrary. A certain *farouche* quality, a certain charming coltishness that is unmistakeable . . ." A twinkle came into his eyes. "So you propose to get as high a price as you can for your virgin favors, *ma petite* Katya?"

Katya nodded gravely. "I know it sounds odiously mercenary, and I'm sure if I were to fall in love I would abandon all such considerations. I almost did so once before . . . But I have not fallen in love with you, my dear sir, although I perceive that you are a very agreeable man as well as a great dancer. So I might as well try to do the best I can for myself. It need not be a very important solo," she added persuasively. "It could be a small variation—something of my own to do all by myself in the middle of the stage. Or even a *pas de deux* with someone important—like you . . . And then of course," she gave him an arch and caressing look from under her long eyelashes, "there is always the possibility that I might meanwhile fall in love with you, in which case—"

M. Truffaut, laughing helplessly, capitulated.

Writing to Lisa, Katya, unconsciously protective of her sister's feelings, stressed the glamorous and exciting aspects of her new situation, understating or even leaving out the less pleasing ones. When her first sight of Moscow burst upon her from Sparrow Hills, a fairyland of gleaming domes and cupolas piled upon each other like a dish of exotic gilded fruit, she had felt like a princess entering her own domain to live happily ever after. But then they descended into dusty, unpaved streets and stopped at a small wooden house not very much larger than Tikhon's cottage, with a scraggly birch tree in its minuscule yard. This was where she would board. She was introduced to her landlady, a capacious woman who dressed like a merchant's wife and moved, for all her comfortable bulk, as lightly as a dancer; which, Truffaut told Katya on their way to the theater, was indeed what she used to be before she retired and started keeping a boarding house for ballet dancers.

The old Pashkov Theater on Mokhovaya street was a huge building of no particular style, undistinguished without and grim within. There was another and better theater under construction on the Arbat Square, designed by the famous architect Karl Rossi, but it was not expected to be finished until 1808. Meanwhile all the plays, operas and ballets were rehearsed and produced in the antiquated barn, as Truffaut bitterly called it, which Pashkov, an avid balletomane, had erected for his own serf company and later donated to the Imperial Ballet.

The first rehearsal hall in which they stopped bore no resemblance to the elegant studio in Petersburg where Katya had seen Didelot train his pupils. It smelled of sweat, the floor was caked with rosin and the walls over the *barres* which went around three sides of the room bore the prints of many hands. A group of approximately twenty young girls and men wearing shabby tunics and much-mended tights were going through some steps while an elderly fiddler scraped away at his instrument in a corner. They were being directed by a young man holding a slim cane with which he marked time, occasionally stopping to brandish it like a weapon while he screeched abuse at the dancers, apostrophizing them as a herd of cows.

Truffaut shook his head to himself, his lips tightening. But he addressed the young man pleasantly enough as Monsieur Paul, begging his pardon for interrupting a class and introducing himself. The young man's scowl abated somewhat at this introduction, and he answered Truffaut's bow by an equally grand one.

"*Monsieur le directeur* shall be glad to hear of your arrival," he said. "We have been wondering when you would come."

Truffaut inquired whether any of the Petersburg contingent had arrived and was told that some of them had. "Not that there is much help to be obtained from *them*," said the young man, resuming his scowl. He was a sullen individual, Katya thought, with a disagreeable greenish complexion and a peevish mouth. "We are damnably shorthanded here, and I was hoping that Monsieur Auguste would rehearse the corps de ballet for *Bluebeard*, in which he is to appear with our own Madame L'Amirale. But he seemed reluctant to do so before your arrival, expecting you to make changes. Since I can't imagine what changes could be made in the opening scene of *Bluebeard*, which has been done the same way since time immemorial—" He shrugged his shoulders.

"No, he's perfectly right, Monsieur Paul," said Truffaut good-naturedly. "I do intend to make some changes—a little more miming and a little less marching."

Paul's acknowledging bow was made in a silence replete with bitter resignation. His eyes fell on Katya and his eyebrows rose interrogatively.

"Mademoiselle Katya Golovin is our latest addition to the corps de ballet," said Truffaut. "I am certain you will be pleased with her."

Katya sank down to the floor in a sumptuous reverence, which failed to impress the *regisseur*, who merely gave her a brief, jaundiced look.

"We have a full complement in that class, I believe," he said. "But of course we shall be delighted with any *arrangement* of yours, my dear Monsieur Truffaut . . ." There was the slightest insolent emphasis on the word.

"I daresay this was to be expected," the latter said to Katya ruefully after they left the rehearsal hall. "This puppy is a protégé of Baron Polonsky, who is in charge of the company here. The Moscow faction is bound to resent the Petersburg visitors, much as they need them."

"I don't like Monsieur Paul very much," Katya said. "He seems a most disagreeable man. Screaming at those poor dancers! I saw Didelot himself teaching a class, and he never treated them like that. And as for my own dear Monsieur Duroc . . ." Katya stopped. M. Duroc suddenly seemed very far away.

She followed Truffaut down the long corridor. He was in a somewhat gloomy mood. "Without a doubt," he said, "they will all be as difficult as they can be and endeavor to mortify me at every step. I shall be very miserable and," he gave her a drolly hopeful look, "much in need of consolation."

His next encounter with his colleagues, however, proved to be a more cheering one. There were two dancers rehearsing a *pas de deux*, with a group of inactive *coryphées* standing around them in graceful attitudes. As soon as his presence was noticed, the dancing stopped, and the entire company broke into applause, followed by deep *reverences* from the women and low bows from the men. The male performer, a tall, handsome man whose classical features were surmounted by a balding forehead, embraced Truffaut, exclaiming: "At last! You are overdue here, you trifler! Another day and I was going to send a complaint to Monsieur Naryshkin." He was referring, as Katya was to learn, to the general director of the Imperial Ballet in Petersburg.

Katya's eyes opened wide as she recognized Auguste, another of her Petersburg idols. His pronounced baldness came as a surprise, since the last time she had seen him, as Bacchus in *Bacchus and Ariadne* his noble head had been adorned by a luxuriant crop of glowing chestnut curls. She was equally surprised to learn that the plain young woman with a pug nose was Berylova, whom she had last seen as a distraught but lovely Andromeda.

Katya stood to one side, waiting to be introduced to these luminaries. After a while she realized with strong indignation that Truffaut was not going to present her. He went on talking to his friends, breaking off to call out to a middle-aged woman in a menial's dark dress with an apron who was waiting by the door, asking her to take Katya to the wardrobe mistress to be outfitted.

As Katya followed the woman out of the rehearsal hall, she began to realize that things were going to be somewhat different from what she had expected. She perceived the existence of a caste system every bit as stringent as that of the Imperial Court. In Petersburg the dancers would have been the ones to be presented to her; as Mademoiselle Katerina Vassilevna Vorontzov, a daughter of a noble family, she would have been the one to condescend to recognize them. But here she was merely Katya Golovin, a lowly new member of the corps de ballet. The thought was not an agreeable one. She comforted herself with the reflection that this situation would not last too long. Her glimpse, brief as it was, of the dancers practicing in M. Paul's class had shown her that she was as good as and probably better than they.

The wardrobe mistress gave Katya a pair of ballet slippers, a tunic and a pair of tights. Katya glanced at them and exclaimed: "But they are dirty! Someone else has been wearing them!"

The wardrobe mistress, a harassed elderly woman, sniffed. "And what of that? The way they are skimping money here, it's a wonder we have any old ones to hand out, let alone new ones. I am sorry that mademoiselle has been discommoded," she added sarcastically.

"But they haven't been washed!"

"Well, the good Lord bless us, here is a catastrophe! I am certain that neither Baron Polonsky, the director, nor Monsieur Sobakin, his assistant, nor even that new *regisseur* they imported from Petersburg would raise any objection to mademoiselle's washing them to her satisfaction."

"But they have holes!"

"Nor will they report to the governor of Moscow that you mended them."

"I don't know how to."

Finding no answer to this, the wardrobe mistress merely cast her eyes heavenward.

These same tights proved to be Katya's bane the next day. She had washed them out the night before in the cold water provided by a ewer in her room, with a result that they were still damp the next morning when she had to put them on. Moreover, being made of cotton, they wrinkled and sagged horridly at the knees. She also found that the holes fretted her tender toes unbearably, particularly when she did the *relevés*. In her extremity she thought of the expedient of putting them on over her own intact hose; which, to her despair, developed holes of their own at the end of the class.

Katya thought nostalgically of her own lovely silk tights—imported from Paris, too!—which were at this very moment uselessly reposing in her armoire in Petersburg, and resolved to ask Lisa in her next letter to send them as soon as possible.

Meanwhile she procured needle and thread and tried to mend the tights between classes. Her efforts were not very efficacious, since she had never mended anything before. Merely stitching the edges of the holes together produced a ridge which she could see would plague her as much as the hole itself.

Luckily the dresser Marina, who had taken her to the wardrobe mistress the day before, took pity on her and offered to mend her tights if she would leave them with her overnight.

Not even the discomfort of inadequate tights spoiled the pleasure of Katya's first class with Truffaut, which he gave on the morning after her arrival to acquaint himself with the material at hand. He was, she perceived, a superb teacher. His voice was gentle and he did not raise it, no matter what mistakes were made. As a result, pupils who had started the class looking frightened and strained drew a deep sigh of relief and thereafter redoubled their efforts to follow his soft-spoken instructions.

"What a lovely man—simply an angel from heaven," Katya's neighbor at the *barre* murmured fervently after he had corrected her and passed on to the next one.

In Katya's case, he had no significant corrections to make, merely raising her hand a little higher over her head as she made her *port de bras*. The touch was a gentle one but it didn't linger, and his smiling nod of approval was pleased but impersonal.

After class he approached her to scold her for her carelessness. "What are you about, standing in this draft uncovered? You will stiffen up and not be able to dance a step!"

He swathed her shawl around her. The gesture, though solicitous, was not romantic; what it reminded Katya of was Fyodor throwing a blanket over one of his treasured Orlov coursers. Later in the day she saw him applying a mixture of vodka and soap to someone else's injured ankle with equal care.

The class was resumed for three more hours, at the end of which Katya could barely stand on her feet. The way to the top, she reflected wearily, was not an easy one. Competence and grace were not enough; apparently you also had to have the endurance of an ox. The drafty rehearsal hall, permeated with the sweaty smell of twenty laboring bodies, was a far cry from the dainty little ballroom where she and Lisa had been taught dancing, and the grueling exercises to which she was being subjected were nothing like the reasonable workouts her healthy young body used to undergo so happily. This was real work, harsh and exacting. There was an ache along her shins and in the calves of her legs when she quitted the rehearsal hall and went to the dressing room, a large chamber with only the curtain separating the female from the male dancers.

With incredulity she learned as she prepared to go home that most of the dancers were expected to return that evening for a rehearsal onstage. "But that is impossible," she cried. "It cannot be so!"

The girl changing next to her shrugged her shoulders. "We do it all the time, dearie. We are always rehearsing for something. We shall be performing tomorrow night."

"But I thought *Bluebeard* was not until next week."

Her neighbor threw her a pitying glance. She was a small, stockily built girl with generously developed calves and thighs and the typically wide-cheeked, snub-nosed face of a Russian peasant. She reminded Katya somewhat of her friend Dunyasha back in Krasnoye. "You don't know much, do you? They call on us for all sorts of things: opera, divertissements before and after a play, everything. So of course we're always rehearsing. You will be doing it too after Monsieur Truffaut decides where he wants to use you." She gave Katya a curious look. "You're an odd one, *dushka*. We girls cannot make you out. You are fine at the *barre*, and you pick up any figure Monsieur Truffaut calls out faster than anyone here. But yet at the same time there's something different about you—it's like it's all new to you . . ."

"And so it is," Katya admitted frankly. "I have danced, but not in the Imperial Ballet."

"Fenya is right," another girl chimed in. "We have been wondering about you. Wherever did Truffaut pick you up?"

The first questioner had evinced friendly curiosity. But there was something impudent and spiteful about the other one, and Katya did not answer.

"What about it? Have you been with him long?"

"Leave her alone, Varvara," said the girl Fenya.

"I suppose I'd better, or she'll go complaining to Truffaut." Leaning forward, she shook Katya's shoulder lightly. "Is that what you are planning, *dushka?*"

"No," Katya said. "I can deal with you myself." Eyes narrowing, she bent on the girl the same look that had stopped Stepanitch in his tracks. The girl withdrew her hand as though she had been scalded.

"Well," she said, "mighty queenly airs we have! I do beg your pardon, Madame la Comtesse." She stalked off, her nose in the air.

This was the start of Katya's new sobriquet. Thereafter she was known as Little Countess, a nickname pronounced with sarcasm by those in the company who resented what they called her high and mighty airs, and affectionately by the good-natured Fenya and others who liked her despite them.

Tired as she was, Katya was looking forward to her morning class with M. Truffaut. But a disappointment was awaiting her. When she arrived at the theater the next morning, she found that that class was now being given by the disagreeable M. Paul of the greenish complexion and uncertain temper.

The class started inauspiciously. Finding the dresser Marina with whom she had left her tights to be mended took some time, and she immediately put herself in the wrong by coming in a few minutes late.

"Ah," said the odious young man mellifluously. "Mademoiselle Katya finally honors us with her presence. Would mademoiselle condescend to take her place in the middle group?" And as Katya, scarlet, hastened to do so, "lateness, my dear Mademoiselle Katya, is considered a cardinal sin in this company. I am certain that even your great friend Monsieur Truffaut would object to it."

Katya cast him a darkling look. "I am certain," she said, "that he would object even more to my coming to his class without my tights. I had none until a few minutes ago."

A titter, immediately suppressed, broke out among the dancers. The discomfited *regisseur* raked them with a baleful look. "*Commençons, alors, messieurs et mesdames.*"

The fiddler struck up a tune.

In a way the class was a triumph for Katya. She knew very well that the instructor was panting for an opportunity to find fault with her, and it became a point of honor not to give it to him. Her *battements* were crisp and swift, her *grands battements* soared and her *relevés* did not falter. When the class moved to the floor, she mastered her *enchaînements* very quickly. The only time he was able to find fault with her was toward the end of the class. Her weary arms had dropped momentarily from their classical half-circle, and he was immediately upon her, telling her that if she thought she was a candelabrum, he would be only too happy to supply the candles.

Altogether, M. Paul's method of teaching was quite different from Truffaut's. Truffaut did not find it necessary to compare his pupils to a herd of cows or to inquire sarcastically from some unfortunate dancer whether the appendage at the end of her leg was a foot or a flatiron. He used his cane to indicate a fault or at most to tap the offending limb lightly. M. Paul's cane was constantly descending viciously on a dancer's ankle for a misstep or an insufficiently high leap. "He had better not try it with me," Katya thought angrily.

By the time the class was over, she was soaked in perspiration. She drank thirstily the scalding hot tea but had no appetite for the kalach, the sweet Moscow bread that she ordinarily loved.

"You must eat, however," the friendly Fenya warned her. "You don't want to faint in class."

"And give that green-faced monster satisfaction? Never!"

Fenya laughed merrily. "Aye, that's just what he is, God forgive him; you've hit him off exactly. Well, never mind, we won't have him this afternoon. He is supposed to be training the new lot." She was referring to the consignment of serf dancers that Truffaut had bought earlier from the Kaluga landowner. They had been delivered to the theater that very morning by the latter's overseer: a pale, docile group that huddled together like sheep, starting convulsively at every command. "Monsieur Truffaut will rehearse us onstage instead. Isn't it wonderful? He is a blessed angel, he is, right out of heaven." Fenya's simple face shone with devotion.

"Oh, yes, I am so glad we are having him."

The class with Truffaut, however, did not materialze for Katya. On their way to the stage, the obnoxious M. Paul, lying in wait for her, neatly cut her out from her group and bore her off to the rehearsal hall where the new lot was awaiting him in fear and trembling.

"But I don't understand," Katya faltered, in the grip of deepest disappointment. "I thought I would be rehearsing with the corps de ballet for *Bluebeard* . . ."

"Permit me the privilege of putting you where I see fit, mademoiselle," her persecutor returned suavely. "I feel sure that you would be more comfortable with the *figurants*."

But Katya was anything but comfortable. M. Paul gave full vent to his cruelty in this timid assembly, and the atmosphere of anxiety that he generated grated on her nerves. The new arrivals, worn out by their trip and unnerved by the new situation, performed poorly, making mistake after mistake at the *barre* and on the floor. M. Paul's instructions, which were uttered in a vindictive screech, confused them even further; Katya could follow them, and M. Paul, proclaiming himself to be worn out by their obstinate stupidity, began to use her over and over again to demonstrate a step.

At first Katya was delighted to be so distinguished; but as time wore on, she realized that she was working more than anyone else in the classroom. She went on grimly, soaked in perspiration and conscious of pain beginning to shoot up her weary legs. Finally, after being told to repeat the same *enchâinement* for the eighth time, she demurred.

"I can't, M. Paul, I am too tired."

"Indeed!" The mentor's vindictive eyes lit up with pleasure. "Well, now, upon leaving this class, mademoiselle will be free to go on and enjoy the perfumed bath poured for her by her servitors. Just now, however, I must entreat her to demonstrate the step to her cloddish colleagues." His cane switched ominously and Katya lost her temper.

"I will not do so. It is not my fault that you can't get them to do the step properly, and I refuse to do your work for you!"

There was a frozen moment of silent incredulity. "You dare, you doxy!" he brought out finally. His cane whistled downward and landed stingingly across Katya's ankles.

She cried out with pain and outrage. As the cane was lifted for another blow, she wrenched it out of his hands, broke it in two and threw it on the floor.

A gasp came from the class. The *regisseur* stared at Katya speechless, his greenish eyes open to their utmost, as petrified as if she had suddenly turned into a man-eating tigress before his eyes.

At that moment Truffaut's voice was heard dulcetly inquiring what was happening, and he himself approached the combatants with his buoyant dancer's walk. A certain glint in his eyes told Katya that he knew very well what was happening and probably had even witnessed it; accordingly she felt no need to explain, but merely stood silent, her bosom rising and falling, her dark eyes stormy.

Her opponent had in the meanwhile found his voice. "Your insolent little protégée," he said in a quivering voice, "has just broken my baton."

Truffaut shook his head reprovingly. "That wasn't well done of you, *ma chère* Katya. Do you not know that without a baton in his hand to enable him to enforce his orders, an instructor is lost? You must immediately make your apologies to Monsieur Paul for rendering him helpless. . . . I am wondering, however," he went on, turning to the enraged *regisseur*, "what this little rebel is doing among the *figurants*? I was expecting to rehearse her with the rest of the corps de ballet for Saturday's performance of *Bluebeard.*"

M. Paul flushed dully. "Mademoiselle Katya being a newcomer—like this pack of incompetents," he added venomously, "I deemed it proper to put her in a group of her peers."

"But I am much better than they are," Katya broke in impetuously. "You know it yourself or you wouldn't have used me for demonstration. And they too would be much better than they are if you did not terrify them so that they are afraid to move."

"Insolence!" M. Paul's flushed face went several shades redder. "I can deal with thickheaded serfs without your advice, mademoiselle."

"Yes, extremely tactless," Truffaut agreed blandly. "More

apologies will be needed, I fear . . . However, the advice itself is not inappropriate. I myself have found it more profitable to encourage than to terrify when teaching. Moreover, *mon cher* Monsieur Paul, I venture to disagree with your description of this group." Steel entered his voice. "If they were thickheaded or incompetent, I would not have procured them, since we already have plenty of that commodity in this company. And as for being serfs—I wonder at you using it as a term of reproach. I am sure you are aware that the most luxuriant flowers of our art have blossomed from that soil. How many of us who have graduated from the Imperial School of Ballet did not have serfs for parents? I would like you to remember this, *mesdames et messieurs*," he continued, now addressing the class. "The days of your servitude are over. You are now, like the rest of us, servants only to the divine Terpsichore. Being an exigent goddess, she will demand much from you but will also have much to bestow. Serve her proudly and well, remembering that you are also serving another munificent master in the person of His Gracious Majesty, Tsar Alexander the First, our beloved sovereign by the grace of God. . . . And now, mademoiselle, make your various apologies to Monsieur Paul and follow me."

Katya was only too grateful to do so.

"Monsieur Truffaut," Katya said, as they walked down the corridor toward the stage. "You were simply magnificent. The way you spoke to that little monster—I am sorry, but he really is, you know!—and then what you said to the class. . . ." She almost told him how close to the bone his speech had been: as he spoke, she had almost felt that he was talking to her, that he *knew*. . . . He didn't, of course. The vague tale she had spun for his benefit had hinted at illegitimacy but certainly not serfdom; there had been no need to confide in him *that* far. She repeated fervently, "You were superb, Monsieur Truffaut. I loved you for what you said."

An injudicious remark! As soon as he heard it, Truffaut stopped stock still, swept Katya into his arms and, kissing her passionately, did his best to persuade her that given a chance, he would show himself to be superb in other ways besides making speeches. If this had happened earlier, Katya would have repulsed him indignantly. Now, however, she liked him so much that she would have liked nothing better than to find that she also loved him. Unfortunately, that convenient miracle didn't happen. As she submitted dutifully to his kisses, she found herself suddenly thinking wistfully of Vanya and how he made her feel. She was only too grateful when the appearance of a colleague made him stop.

"Well, my lovely one," Truffaut said as they sedately resumed their walk. "I hope you will not continue to be cruel but will consent to be mine in the very near future—tonight, say?—because otherwise I shall be so distracted that I will not be able to attend to my work."

"I think," Katya said, "we should keep to our bargain."

Truffaut was silent for a moment, his face clouding over. "Coyness becomes an absurdity after a while," he said, and there was resentment in his voice. "This is a ballet troupe and not a convent, *parbleu!*"

"Yes, but my grandfather said . . . ."

"Your grandfather be—blowed! That is to say, a worthy man, I am sure, but he could not have envisioned the circumstances. Don't you think that I would do my utmost for you even without that inducement held in front of me like a carrot in front of a donkey?"

Katya gave him a propitiatory smile. "Perhaps it is I," she said softly, "who needs an—an inducement."

Truffaut glowered a moment longer. Then his mobile face cleared and he gave a reluctant chuckle. "You are an unscrupulous, self-willed little rogue. I should be very angry with you if you weren't such a delicious morsel . . . Very well, sweet cruelty, it shall be as you wish."

"Dear Monsieur Truffaut!"

"I wish you would call me by my first name—as a pledge of future bliss, as it were. I must continue to be Monsieur Truffaut in public, of course. But if you were to call me Petya in private, it would give me great pleasure."

"But why Petya?" Katya inquired, puzzled.

"Because that is my name. I was born Pyotr Fillipovitch Trofimov. I only became Pierre Philippe Truffaut after I had left the Imperial School of Ballet."

"And I was so sure you were French. You talk and behave like a Frenchman."

"I spent three years studying in Paris under the incomparable Gardel, and I have just come back after a year's stay in France. I have been very careful to cultivate my Gallicisms, which I find very useful: a French accent commands a great deal of respect in Russia. Unfortunately," his lips curled derisively, "the Imperial Ballet's board of directors has a marked predilection for foreign dancers. In spite of the fact that a Russian-born performer is as good or better than his foreign colleague, the latter is much better paid and is treated with far more respect. It's a great shame and a disgrace to our profession, but so it is."

"Yes, simply terrible!" Katya agreed indignantly. She recalled Graham remarking upon the Russians' proclivity to underrate themselves, preferring anything foreign to the domestic product. It was so in clothes and in the use of the French language in society; apparently it was also true of ballet.

Graham! She had not thought of him for a long time. Another nice man, like M. Truffaut. Katya suffered a twinge of conscience as she realized that she had neglected to ask Lisa about him. She did so, conscientiously, when she wrote to Lisa again at the end of the week, before going on to more immediate matters.

> I was given my wages today. I shall not even tell you how much it was for fear of exciting your indignation—a ridiculous amount! I had to laugh when I found that a *child* is paid more than I am. The child is the little daughter of Mme. L'Amirale, a prima ballerina who is very popular in Moscow. She is known as *enfant accessoire* and dances such roles as Cupid and one of Medea's children in *Jason et Medée*. Her mother, by the way, plays Medea and slaughters her in the end—is that not comical? My salary would not keep me in pins in Petersburg but it suffices to pay my landlady for my board and daily hot water for my bath. I have it in the evening after classes, and I wish others did too: you have no idea how the rehearsal hall smells. You must not worry about me, however. I still have the "dowry" my dearest grandfather gave me. But I cannot imagine how the other dancers can exist on what they are paid. My dear M. Truffaut keeps helping them out. He is the kindest man alive. . . .

It occurred to Katya, as she finished writing, that this was the third letter she was sending to Lisa and that she had not yet got an answer. Surely—she counted the days off on her fingers—at least her first letter should have been answered by now. She was probably being unreasonable: letters were constantly lost or delayed in the mail; Lisa may have found it impossible to reply instantly. But Katya found it difficult to be reasonable: she wanted passionately some immediate indication that her sister was not lost to her.

It was only after the letter had been dispatched that another and more dismaying reason for Lisa's silence occurred to her. Suppose her letters had never reached Lisa; suppose that they had instead fallen into her stepmother's hands. Katya caught her breath, turning pale. How could she have been so abysmally stupid? But she just hadn't thought of it; all she had thought of was the exquisite pleasure of being at last able to communicate with her sister.

Panic overwhelmed her. Her stepmother's vindictiveness had pursued her to Krasnoye; surely it would overtake her in Moscow. Would she have to leave everything and run again? If only her grandfather were here! He would know what to do. That nimble brain of his would conjure a way out of the disaster.

Thinking of him calmed her. She could almost hear him saying: "No use running around like a sheep; better to stand still and think." She set her chin and tried to do so. Was it so certain that the countess would come after her? She remembered Tikhon's words on the night Chirkin had proposed to her. He had been convinced that she would be left well alone. "Can't bring her malice out in the open where people would see it," he had said. "That's why you had to be bundled out of Petersburg at night."

Presumably what was true of Petersburg would be equally true in Moscow; the countess would not care to have that story spread through the Moscow salons, particularly with Aunt Aline living here. As a last resort—the *very* last resort, Katya told herself—sanctuary could be found with her. Katya's panic abated and she began to feel safe again. Or rather almost safe. I suppose, she thought gloomily, I will never be really safe.

Immediately she contradicted herself. *Yes, I will! Monsieur Truffaut will give me a solo to dance and I will do it magnificently. I shall immediately become a ballerina and then a prima ballerina; my fame will spread all over Russia and the emperor will come to see me and grant my freedom and Lisa will be there and—*

She stopped short as another bleak possibility was borne in on her: the countess might very well leave her undisturbed in Moscow; but she would certainly destroy her letters to Lisa.

She cast about in her mind for ways to elude her stepmother's vigilance and presently hit upon one. Her next letter to Lisa would be addressed to Prince Dmitry Lunin, with a request to pass it on to her sister.

The strains of *Alexander, Elisaveta,* the new anthem that greeted the imperial couple wherever they appeared, rang out as they entered the ballroom. Prince Dmitry Lunin was one of the privileged band of courtiers that followed them. During the past year, with Russia's foreign policy undergoing an unexpected about-face, he had become quite important in the inner councils because of his earlier military experience in the Turkish wars and his special knowledge of England, where he had spent several years. He was now high in imperial favor.

However, he showed no special desire to stay close to the exalted source of it; as soon as he could, he left the crowd that buzzed respectfully around the emperor and stood by himself at a window, looking out at the chill October night. As often happened nowadays when he thought himself to be unobserved, his face wore the bleak look of one suffering from a deep disappointment or consumed by an overriding worry.

A fan tapped him lightly on the shoulder and he turned to confront Countess Vorontzov, resplendent in black lace and diamonds. It was now nearly three months after Count Vorontzov's death; while his widow still wore mourning, she had begun to go out in the world.

"You never come to see me now, Dmitry," she said. "I knew I would find you here or I would have written you a note asking you to come."

"I would have jettisoned all my burdensome duties to do so," Prince Dmitry rejoined politely, bowing over her lace-mittened hand. He wondered what was on her mind; there was a certain betraying glitter in her dark eyes.

"You look quite out of temper," she went on, "and no wonder, *mon pauvre* Dmitry!" There was a perceptible edge of malice in her voice. "To go all the way to Pskov to claim your property and find it gone!"

Prince Dmitry's lips tightened. His failure to find Katya had been galling to his arrogant and imperious nature; he had chafed under it ever since he had quitted the Pskov province, leaving his most trusted henchmen there to continue the search. He had had no choice in the matter; his absence from Petersburg at a critical time had been greeted by imperial displeasure, and a courier had been dispatched requiring him to return.

He said coldly: "My property, as you so obligingly put it, would have been available to me if not for your regrettable decision to bestow it on a yokel. You *will* overdo, Elena."

There was perceptible contempt in his voice, and the countess flushed. "The important thing—to *me*—is that Lisa did not find her, either. But it seems that I am in a position to aid you in your search."

If the countess expected a response to this statement, she was disappointed. Not a muscle moved on Prince Dmitry's impassive face, which retained its expression of polite indifference as the countess, extracting a letter from the beaded chatelaine hanging from her waist, handed it to him.

His face unreadable, Prince Dmitry looked down at Katya's hurried script crossing and recrossing the page. The countess's voice buzzed implacably in his ear.

"Isn't that typical? Exactly what I would have expected from her. Trust someone of her kind to find her proper level . . ."

"Damn the woman," he thought savagely. "If she would only go away!" He glanced at the bottom of the page and saw, written with some attempt at legibility, the words *Pashkov Theater*, *Mokhovaya Street*, *Moscow*.

"—A common ballet girl, and we know what *that* means. Wallowing in degradation and adoring every minute of it, if I know her. I wonder what her father would have thought! Well, I would leave her to it happily if I could count on her staying undetected. . . . What do you propose to do, Dmitry?"

"First of all, decipher this document."

"Well, I *told* you. She has managed to make her way to Moscow and creep into the Moscow ballet. She can't be permitted to stay there. I have just received a letter from my sister-in-law telling me that Lisa is now in Moscow. Still looking for the wretched girl, God help me! I don't care how long she goes on doing so, provided she doesn't find her . . ."

Prince Dmitry smiled. "Ah, yes," he said gently. "I understand she is being escorted by young Graham. Delightfully unconventional of you to permit this, Elena."

"My Lisa," said her mother, "is a saint, and utterly incapable of looking after her interests. If by some unforeseen chance she runs across her sister . . ."

"Yes, very awkward," said the prince, "particularly with young Graham in tow."

"Exactly so! Everything will start all over again. My poor child will again be cheated of her happiness by the little viper who has imposed on her all those years. Well, I am not going to permit it. I will do anything—anything—take any measures no matter how extreme to prevent it. Do you hear me, Dmitry? I have given you this information, and unless I have your assurance that you will act on it immediately, I will do so myself."

Prince Dmitry raised his eyes from the letter and fixed the countess with a somber look that was so full of cold, implacable anger that despite herself she flinched, her hand going to her throat. "I advise you not to," he said icily. "Allow me to remind you, Elena, that you are no longer Katya's owner."

The countess drew herself up. "And allow me to remind *you*, Dmitry, that I let you have the wretched girl only because I expected you to remove her from our sphere. Well, what do you intend to do about her? Are you going to let her stay where she is?"

"No," Prince Dmitry said reflectively. "That is not my intention."

"You *will* take measures, then?"

"I will take measures."

The countess gave him a hard look and seemed satisfied with what she saw. "I shall leave it to you, then. To be sure, you will find it harder in Moscow than it would have been in Krasnoye, but I am certain you will manage with your customary finesse."

Left by himself, the prince read and reread the letter with some relish, a small, sour grin tugging occasionally at his lips. Unfortunately, he could not leave Petersburg immediately. But at least he knew now where the fugitive was and where she presumably would still be when he would be free to attend to her.

CHAPTER 19

As soon as Katya stepped on the stage for the rehearsal, she realized how right Truffaut had been in proclaiming her unfit to make a professional appearance, in spite of her technique and talent. For one thing, performing on the raked stage was an unsettling experience in the full sense of the word; in the beginning she was terrified of sliding down into the footlights. It was reassuring to be part of a large group, where her mistakes were not so apparent.

In time the sensation of dancing on a mountain slope wore off, and the next day, when another rehearsal onstage took place, she found herself able to move around with more confidence.

However, she still did not feel entirely free from discomfort. In order to overcome it, she took to going onstage and practicing her steps there when no one was around. She was doing so one morning, trying to correct the imbalance that plagued her whenever she did her turns, when she became conscious of being watched and noticed the plump figure of the dresser Marina hovering in the wings. Katya gave her a friendly nod and essayed another turn, stamping her foot with vexation when it came out as badly as before.

"Yes, that's a hard one to do," said Marina sympathetically, shuffling onto the stage in her soft slippers. "Everyone has that trouble at first. The trick is to hold your arms closer to the body in second position."

She put down the piece of sewing she was holding, hitched up her decent gray skirt, went up on her slippered toes and executed as neat a turn as Katya had seen performed by any of the *solistes* in Truffaut's advanced class. Smiling at Katya's surprise, she added an *entrechât* for good measure and came down lightly, becoming once again the plump, sedate Marina.

Katya beheld this unexpected performance with stupefaction. It was as though a duck had turned into swan and back again within the space of a moment. Finally she found her voice: "You—why, you're a dancer, Marinushka!" No doubt about that; there was no mistaking the impeccable line, the fine style of an accomplished dancer that is never totally lost, no matter what the age.

Marina nodded, sighing. "Used to be," she said, "and not a bad one either. I studied under the late Angiolini, may he rest in peace. Great hopes of me he had, too. I remember when I danced Venus in *Acis and Galatea*. . . . Oh, well, that was long ago."

"But what happened?"

Marina shrugged her shoulders. "Old age," she said simply. "A dancer's life is a short one. If you take really good care of yourself, you can last until you're thirty-five—at the very most. I—well, I liked my food, and my drink too, if truth were told. So I put on weight. I used to have a waist smaller than yours; a child's hands could span it."

"But . . ." Katya looked wonderingly at the housemaid's dress Marina was wearing. "Couldn't you teach?"

"I'm no hand at teaching. All I knew how to do was dance. Once I could no longer do so . . ." She shrugged again. "At least I have my health," she went on more cheerfully. "When I said dancers have a short life, I didn't mean just as dancers. Plenty of us die young. The men are destroyed by the drink, like poor old Alexey." She was referring to the old porter who guarded the backstage entrance, watching the dancers passing by him with a lackluster eye. "Consumption is what gets the girls. Yes, it's a hard life, my dearie. Sometimes when I watch you young things dancing your hearts out. . . ." Not finishing, she sighed and shuffled offstage, leaving Katya prey to gloomy reflections.

Other casualties came to her mind. She had been hearing all around her hushed discussions about the sudden death of young Danilova, a talented dancer who had seemed likely to equal Kolossova. The day before, she had overheard Auguste complaining that he was beginning to be plagued by rheumatic twinges, like the famous ballet master Valbergh, whose version of *Zephyr and Flora* they were planning to perform.

Later, when her class joined her onstage for rehearsal, she anxiously scrutinized their flushed faces, looking for signs of hidden illness.

The idea kept haunting her for days to come. She found herself wondering whether M. Paul's green complexion and bad temper were not due to some latent disease, and the next time he addressed her in his usual style, she merely bent on him a look that was positively liquid with compassion, puzzling him considerably.

Even Kolossova, that incomparable ballerina, who had recently arrived from Petersburg in all her glory and was now gracefully passing through the steps of Vestris's *Gavotte* with Auguste—was she by virtue of her excellence immune to these unknown ills? Or was that ethereal, almost otherworldly grace a pressage of early death?

In time Katya's naturally optimistic disposition combined with the pressure of work to dissipate these gloomy thoughts, which came up only occasionally to plague her. But she began to have other things on her mind.

Even though she was in the midst of a never-ceasing bustle of classes and rehearsals and constantly surrounded by people, Katya found that she was quite lonely.

That had not been true at Krasnoye. There she had often been physically uncomfortable and apprehensive about her fate. But she had been surrounded by people who loved her and whom she loved. Here in Moscow great blocks of her time were filled with dancing, to the exclusion of all else. But in between there was no one she could talk to. A strict hierarchy reigned in the theater. There was little communication between the low- and high-ranking dancers. Soloists looked down on members of the corps de ballet. Prima ballerinas talked only to prima ballerinas. Katya fell in between the two categories; she was looked down upon by the higher echelons, and she was the Little Countess to the lower ranks, who saw her as an unfamiliar creature, somewhat mysterious and, for some inexplicable reason, a cut above them; at any rate, not a person with whom they could be totally at ease. She couldn't share in their inconsequential chatter or exchange ballet gossip and girlish confidences between classes. Even the good-natured and talkative Fenya was somewhat in awe of her.

Anyhow, she did not want any of them. She wanted Lisa.

She had always taken it for granted that once she was out of Krasnoye, it would be a simple matter to recover her sister: she would write and Lisa would answer and eventually come to her. But it hadn't turned out that way at all. There was no word, good or bad, coming from Petersburg. Her stepmother did not descend on Moscow, breathing vengeance; and there were no letters from Lisa. Katya did not even have the heart to write again; she had a dreadful feeling that her letters were being swallowed up in a black vacuum. Lisa was as inaccessible as she had been in Krasnoye, and the prospect of being reunited with her began to recede into the dim future. Perhaps they would never see each other again.

All this weighed heavily on Katya's spirits. Her only recourse was to immerse herself utterly in her work. While she was dancing she thought of nothing else and was able to forget her troubles. But afterward they crowded in on her again. Occasionally her spirits would sink so low that she would go off by herself and, sitting alone in some corner of the theater, with her mother's shawl drawn close about her, give herself over entirely to her unhappiness—a procedure very untypical of the gay, heedless Katya of other days.

It was on one of those infrequent occasions that she was discovered by Kolossova, who stopped and asked her in her soft voice: "Are you sad, *petite?* Why?"

Katya rose and curtsied. Caught unaware by this sympathetic query from one whom she regarded as a species of goddess, she blurted out: "I am lonely."

Gentle disapproval shadowed the great dancer's expressive face. "That is no reason to be sad. If one's *arabesque* is not of the highest, or one has scrambled a *pirouette*—then yes, that is indeed a cause for despair. But just because one is lonely—!" her exquisite shoulders moved up and down. "They tell me you aspire to be a great ballet dancer."

"Yes, like you, madame."

"Ah," said Kolossova matter of factly, "that will take a very long time, to be like me. And you must be prepared to be always lonely."

Katya gazed wistfully upon that small, plain face, which on occasion could be irradiated from within by such magical beauty. "Must it be so?"

"It is inevitable," said Kolossova, departing as lightly as a vision.

Katya's spirits rose. To be noticed by Kolossova herself! To have her comment on one's ambitions! She wondered who had told her about them and decided that it must have been Truffaut.

The amorous ballet master seemed to have postponed his pursuit of her for the time being. Presumably the situation that greeted him in Moscow required his entire attention.

"I am expected to be dancer, actor, ballet master, choreographer, administrator and teacher," he told Katya wryly. "All that for twenty-seven hundred rubles a year!"

In his capacity as a universal factotum, he was constantly in demand. He had to besiege the authorities for money to pay the dancers and refurbish the scenery. He was called upon to settle arguments and repair all the misfortunes that usually attend the reorganization of a theatrical company. The trunks with costumes that were supposed to be sent to Moscow from Petersburg had mysteriously disappeared on the way, and he had to make last-minute arrangements with Loques, the well-known Moscow costumer who, according to the Petersburg ballerinas, could not hope to measure up to their own dear M. Cherubino, who knew exactly how to clothe them. There was an obligatory patriotic ballet to be mounted within the month, and Katya, wandering into one of the rehearsal halls early one morning, was amazed to find him leading what looked like a regiment of soldiers through maneuvers more suitable to Champs de Mars than the theater; at that, only forty soldiers showed up for the military sequence instead of the necessary sixty that had been promised.

In the midst of that he also had to fight a running battle with the Moscow faction, which resented the Petersburg incursion, sabotaged his instructions and fought his innovations.

Katya had no doubt that once he was firmly in control he would again lay an assiduous and expert siege on her virtue. But she wondered whether meanwhile he was too busy to give due consideration to her career.

By this time she had already made her debut in *Bluebeard* as one of the obligatory rejoicing peasants and had felt perfectly at home on the stage, although at first the unexpected glare of the footlights almost undid her. Fifty bright lampions had been lit in front of the stage, and it had been as though an incandescent wall had risen in front of her, blinding her. She mechanically went through her first steps, seeing nothing but hearing and feeling an unseen audience stirring in front of her. Presently the luminous fog began to dissolve and she was able to catch glimpses of attentive faces, the shimmer of satin and silk gowns and glints of lorgnettes.

Since *Bluebeard* was a ballet especially designed for solo performances by the principals, the activity of the corps de ballet was confined to the simple wedding dance in the beginning and the rejoicing festivities at the end after the villainous Bluebeard (brilliantly danced by Auguste, for whom the ballet had been created) came to a well-deserved end. The festivities were more difficult, being done in a faster tempo and with several complicated *enchaînements*, but by then Katya was fully in control and able to go through the steps with the same verve and precision she had displayed at rehearsals. What was more, she enjoyed every minute of it.

The next day Truffaut congratulated her on her debut. "What a marvel you are, to be sure. I watched you very carefully, and I find it hard to believe that this was your first performance on the stage. You might have been doing this all your life."

"And that is exactly how I felt," Katya told him.

She looked at him expectantly. Surely he would tell her that she was now ready to move out of the anonymous ranks of the corps de ballet and take the next upward step. But he merely kissed her hand and went on to supervise Mme. L'Amirale's solo in *Jason et Medée*.

Katya looked after him thoughtfully. It seemed to her that he had taken to paying that lady a good deal of attention lately. This impression grew as time went on. Truffaut had always had an appreciative eye for the women in the company, treating even the lowliest figurante with the utmost gallantry. But his attentions to Mme. L'Amirale were beginning to acquire an alarming particularity. It wasn't only that he seemed to spend an unconscionable amount of time rehearsing her for her performance of *Jason et Medée;* but he did not do it in his customary impersonal manner. His every corrective touch was a caress. He smiled significantly into her eyes as he guided her through a double *pirouette*, and he held her waist in a loverlike grasp as she was doing the *arabesque*.

Katya was not the only one to notice this. Once she overheard the ill-natured Varvara remarking with considerble relish after a rehearsal: "Looks like someone is going to have her nose out of joint." She had darted a quick look in Katya's direction as she spoke.

Katya had loftily disregarded the taunt. But she had to confess to herself that indeed it looked as though Truffaut, possibly irked by her firm stand on their bargain, was finding consolation elsewhere. Not that he didn't continue to be charming to her, praising her in class and pressing her hand affectionately when he met her between classes. But his dalliance with the Moscow ballerina, whose darkly sullen good looks and serpentine locks made her seem particularly suitable for the role of Medea, began to take on the earmarks of a full-blown affair. Whenever she looked, she saw them talking earnestly and confidentially together, and once when she passed Mme. L'Amirale's dressing room and happened to glance in through the half-open door, there he was, enthusiastically showering passionate kisses on her opulent shoulders.

Katya had never known what jealousy was; nor had she ever worried about keeping her admirers. She enjoyed their adoration—particularly if they were good dancers—and if they drifted away, let them go without a sigh. But this was different. She began to watch Truffaut's infidelity with growing anxiety. In effect, she told herself grimly, Varvara was right: her nose *was* out of joint.

It had been reassuring, as she gave herself over to the exacting task of becoming a dancer, to know that Truffaut was there to look after her; that he was vitally interested in her advancement. She was no longer sure of this. If he was really losing interest in her, she might have to stay in the corps de ballet indefinitely, or at least much longer than she had expected. Her plan to achieve balletic heights in the shortest possible time and with the least trouble would be seriously disrupted. She began, with distaste, to consider other alternatives.

Meanwhile, preparations for the production of *Jason et Medée* went on, and the corps de ballet began to rehearse it on the stage. One afternoon a group of them including Katya was waiting in the wings for Mme. L'Amirale to leave the stage where she was rehearsing, with her little daughter and another "accessory child," the final scene where Medea kills her children. Her voice rose petulantly, asking for her knife, and an assistant *regisseur* hurried by them bearing the sacrificial dagger artistically stained red.

Katya, bored with watching this protracted infanticide, wandered to the back, where a small warm-up *barre* had been set up. As she began her exercises, she noticed with distaste that her tights were wrinkled again. Regretting for the thousandth time her inability to get the silk ones which never wrinkled or sagged, she began to pull them taut.

As she was doing so, Truffaut entered accompanied by the chief director himself. The two men stopped not far from her, continuing their conversation, and Katya had a chance to look at the exalted personage upon whom the company depended for its livelihood. She knew Baron Polonsky by sight: a plump, dandified man who would come to rehearsals in full regalia but never condescended to talk to the dancers, although he apparently liked to watch them. Rumor had it that he had a special predilection for legs and had become a patron of the ballet for the purpose of satisfying that passion.

After one quick look Katya paid the two men no further attention. She straightened up, did a deliberate, slow *grand développé*, and placed a beautifully arched foot on the *barre*. Then she hitched her tunic up to the hips (thereby affording the onlookers an unimpeded view of the outstretched shapely leg) and proceeded to smooth the wrinkles out of her tights, her hands slowly traveling from ankle to thigh with meditative, molding strokes. So intent was she on that operation that she did not seem to notice that the conversation going on near her had come to a sudden stop. Only when she was quite through did she look up to meet the baron's monocled stare. Lowering her eyelashes, she removed her foot from the *barre*, curtsied and made a confused apology in a shy little voice, then demurely walked away. As she did so, she heard the baron say in a hushed voice: "Now there's an ideal leg, Truffaut. If there is talent there to match it—" His voice dropped so low that she couldn't hear his next words, but she did hear Truffaut's carefully expressionless voice giving him her name.

Later that evening she was stopped by Truffaut as she was going home. He too was on his way out of the theater. He was wearing a uniform and carrying a sword, as senior members of the ballet were required to do on official occasions. From this she guessed that he was bound for one of the dinners to which he was constantly being summoned and which he detested because they took up his time, spoiled his digestion and produced nothing of consequence in return.

He looked pale and harassed and for the first time failed to give her his usual affectionate greeting.

"Well, *ma chère* Katya," he said with a forced smile, "you have certainly provided Baron Polonsky with a charming spectacle. He is quite captivated, it seems, and wants to see more of you."

Katya gave him a cold look. Her momentary triumph at capturing the director's attention had faded and she was feeling distinctly queasy: this was the first time she had deliberately exploited her attractions for a strictly utilitarian purpose. It was Truffaut's dereliction that had driven her to this, and unfair though it might be, she could not help feeling resentful.

Truffaut gave her a penetrating look. "Are you by any chance thinking of arranging another bargain, *ma belle?* You will not find the good baron quite as amenable as I was."

"No, I don't suppose he would be," Katya agreed glumly. "Besides, he is old and fat and disagreeable—I don't believe I could honestly promise to sleep with him no matter what he did for me. However, being able to 'captivate' him so easily makes me feel better. I am sure, if I look around, I will be able to do the same with someone more acceptable."

This was said with such pronounced lack of enthusiasm that Truffaut smiled despite himself. "Tell me, my child," he said gently, "why is it that you feel impelled to look around? Are you angry with me? Is it because I have not paid sufficient attention to you? Surely you must realize that it wasn't for lack of wanting to do so. But I have had no time for anything, hardly time to breathe . . ."

"You have time for Madame L'Amirale, however," Katya reminded him. She added hastily, "Pray do not think that I am complaining or reproaching you. You have already done a great deal for me without being—well—rewarded for it, and you have a right to bestow your affections wherever you wish. Madame L'Amirale is most attractive and an excellent dancer—though, to be sure, not to be compared to Kolossova."

Truffaut nodded. "That is the trouble, of course," he said. "It is one thing to hear that Kolossova is eclipsing everyone in Petersburg; but when she comes to Moscow and eclipses *you*—that is a different matter. The poor girl has been quite distracted . . ." He sighed. "The only way to manage Aurelie L'Amirale when she is having vapors is to make love to her. Otherwise she droops and pines and constantly sprains her ankles, so that performances must be postponed. I daresay at a pinch Beryllova could take her place, but L'Amirale is a superb Medea and I should not like anyone else to dance her role. Much easier to make love to her, I assure you!" He stopped and looked at Katya searchingly. A fatuous expression overspread his mobile countenance. "Why, you adorable child," he said with intense pleasure, "you were jealous!"

Katya was about to respond vehemently and devastatingly that she had been merely anxious about her future. But something told her—and this need for watching her words was also new—that that would not be the politic thing to do. She nodded and resigned herself to listening meekly while Truffaut told her tenderly what a goose she had been.

"Did you really think I was going to desert you? *Jamais de la vie!* Silly child, you do not deserve the surprise I have in store for you. I am going to take you out of Medea and put you in *Zephyr and Flora* with Kolossova."

Katya brightened. "How lovely—my favorite ballet!"

To think of dancing it with Kolossova, even as a humble member of the corps de ballet!

"You shall be dancing one of the six roses in the opening variation," Truffaut went on. "The red rose, I think. Yes, definitely the red rose. That is how I see you—a lovely crimson blossom whose hue delights the eye and whose perfume is intoxicating."

He kissed her hand lingeringly.

"I do look well in red," Katya agreed. "Not that I have had too much opportunity to wear it—it's much too exciting a color for a *jeune fille*. But I have a beautiful red sarafan—" She broke off, taking in the full import of what he had said. "One of *six* roses!"

"Yes. It is a *pas de six*. You are now a *coryphée*, my pretty one. Are you pleased?"

Katya sighed rapturously. "A *coryphée*! At last!"

Truffaut's eyebrows arched in gentle mockery. "What an impatient child you are. At last, indeed! One would think you have been lanquishing in the corps de ballet for an infinity of years."

"Well, it was beginning to seem so. I am so happy. Oh, dear sweet Monsieur Truffaut—Petya," she added in her softest voice. The smile that accompanied this was one of her most enchanting ones. Truffaut kissed her hand again even more lingeringly.

"If you smile at me like that, I shall forget all professional considerations and let *you* dance Flora instead of Kolossova."

Katya giggled. "No, I am not *quite* ready. Not yet," she added characteristically. "Do you know, I cannot remember a *pas de six* of roses in the beginning of *Flora*."

"There wasn't until I arranged it—especially for you."

Katya put her head to one side and regarded him quizzically. "What about the other five? Did you create it for them, too?"

"Ah, but I fully intend to subordinate them eventually to the red rose. If she proves herself worthy." He touched her cheek with a caressing finger. "*Au revoir*, my lovely one. Would I could avoid this cursed dinner. But I must be there in order to talk to the directors about a new ballet I have in mind. It is something very new and advanced and will, I imagine, terrify them at first. They are so afraid of any innovations here in Moscow. Too daring, they will say. Well, we must move with the times. When I first danced in *Acis and Galatea*, I did so in an eight-tiered wig, white stockings and shoes with red heels! Now *The New Werther* is being done in modern clothes. We show progress, do we not?"

The performance of *Zephyr and Flora* was not only a step forward for Katya; it was an event of importance for everyone concerned, being the first formal appearance by all the visiting Petersburg dancers. It was, besides, a benefit for Kolossova, who came down from Petersburg only on the understanding that one would be arranged so that she would be supported by the stellar Moscow performers. Altogether a gala affair, much glorified in the Moscow *News*, which printed the programs for all the ballets.

Truffaut was extremely annoyed by the way the announcement emphasized Flora's aerial flight with Zephyr. "A totally inartistic and unnecessary trick," he fumed. "Just like the Moscow *News* to mention it at such length. Didelot is the one who likes that sort of thing. As for me, I don't care for it and am removing it from the ballet. Besides, that infernal machine is not working properly, and I have no head for heights."

"You, Monsieur Truffaut? But I thought Auguste was dancing Zephyr."

"Unfortunately he caught a cold in one of those infernally drafty dressing rooms." Truffaut's face darkened. "There are more rooms provided for clowns at the fairs than here in the court theater for the dancers of the Imperial Ballet! It infuriates me. . . . At any rate, I shall be dancing Zephyr and probably paying more attention to the red rose than to Flora."

The week passed very quickly in an accelerating flurry of rehearsals, some of which took place late at night. While she was at work Katya had little time to think of anything but the impending performance. The bad times came when she returned to her boarding house and found that there were still no letters for her.

On the night of the performance, all the seats were sold out, and Truffaut, rightly interpreting this as a tribute to the Petersburg dancers, was wearing a broad smile. "A good omen," he said to Katya. "We shall have a magnificent debut. And you, too, *ma petite*. Go with God," he added, making a sign of the cross over her.

Katya went to the communal dressing room, where she suddenly realized with horror that she had to put on her makeup. In her one performance in *Bluebeard*, she had, in her simplicity, gone on without doing so. Since on that occasion she had been a member of the corps de ballet, mercifully placed in the back row, her remissness had not been noticed. This time, however, it was different; she would be performing in full view of the audience as one of the six *coryphées* and had to resemble the others in every particular.

The trouble was that she did not have the slightest idea of

how to go about it. While minutes ticked by, she sat in front of her mirror in mounting terror, looking helplessly at the collection of mysterious appurtenances of maquillage scattered before her, and would probably have gone on doing so until the time came to go onstage if the dresser Marina and Fenya had not realized her predicament and taken her in hand.

Between them they showed her how to use the moist sponge to whiten her neck and arms, using a smaller one to coat her entire face right up to the hairline. With the help of a rabbit's foot they shaded her cheeks with geranium red, and then powdered her face with rice powder. Luckily her brows were naturally dark and only needed to be elongated by being penciled slightly upward toward the temples.

The eyes, it turned out, needed considerable work. Marina shaded the lids with a purple pomade and drew a fine line along the edges of the eyelids at the base of the eyelashes. Then, melting what looked to Katya like black wax, she dabbed it on the ends of her upper lashes, pressing them upward with a thin stick until the wax hardened and made them fan up and out. Fenya completed the process by placing a dot of rouge in the inner corner of each eye. Her lips were painted a bright carmine. The nostrils were outlined with a fine line of pink; another touch of it was dabbed on the tip of her chin, the earlobes and the temples. A tinge of pink on the elbows and around the fingers and it was done.

"There now," says Fenya with satisfaction, "don't you look fine."

A bedizened stranger looked at Katya from the mirror with eyes that seemed twice their original size. She stared back dubiously.

"I look so odd," she said. "Like a merchant's wife at an Easter promenade. Will it really be all right?"

"You'll look lovely to the audience," Marina assured her, putting the wreath of roses carefully on her tightly coiffed black hair.

Just then the voice of the *regisseur* was heard summoning them to the stage. Katya rose, fluffed out the crimson petals of her rose costume, threw her warm shawl around her bare shoulders and left the dressing room, walking somewhat somnambulistically.

Still as if in a dream, she waited in the wings while the crew bustled about her, rearranging the set and preparing to raise the curtain. Kolossova passed her lightly, her flower-starred dress billowing about her, and Katya followed her together with the five other *coryphées*. Kolossova crossed herself—the others followed suit—and gave them a brief, reassuring smile as they arranged themselves around her. She seemed perfectly calm, although her small bosom rose and fell under the gauzy fabric. Katya's own heart beat tempestuously.

"This might be the most important night in my life," she thought as the curtain soared up.

CHAPTER 20

At precisely seven o'clock the princess's antiquated but gorgeous coach with the Mourovtsev arms on the doors awaited them at the lighted entrance. The princess, wrapped in a sable cloak and supported by two stalwart footmen, entered it, followed by Lisa and Graham. The latter had managed to array himself respectably in the comparatively short time allotted him, and his unexceptionable black frock coat and white satin waistcoat and breeches drew a nod of approbation from the old lady. "Well done," she said, "I like a man who is equal to social demands."

Graham bowed. "My diplomatic training has stood me in good stead," he said, smiling. "Lord Leveson-Gower expects his aides to be ready for anything at a minute's notice."

The performance started late. (Katya would have been able to enlighten them as to the reason: there were not enough *perruquiers* to go around.) It began with a mercifully short divertissement, featuring one of those garish and rather pointless extravaganzas that were characteristic of the Moscow ballets. Lisa paid no attention to it. Her thoughts were far away.

Before they left the palace, Aunt Aline had told her: "Try to cheer up, my dear. No point sinking into the dismals. Nothing can be done to help Katya until tomorrow, when we shall go to see the governor. Until then, why do you not pretend that all is well?"

Lisa had tried to follow this robust advice. All the way to the Pashkov Theater, she had played a little game, making believe that she was visiting her aunt by herself while Katya was safely elsewhere. After a while she enlarged the pretense: Graham was someone she had met at one of the exhausting affairs to which Aunt Aline had taken her—someone new, with whom she had immediately fallen in love. "And he too seems not indifferent," she went on, making believe that she was writing to Katya about someone her sister had never met. "I don't know much about these things, but I feel that he cares for me somewhat. He seems to like my looks—he complimented me on them." (And so he had, in fact. A speaking look had sped toward her from his gray eyes, followed by a quiet, "You are in great beauty tonight, Countess Lisa.") "He put my cloak around my shoulders with such tenderness! And I felt his hand tremble just a little when it touched mine. He gazes at me as though he likes doing so, as though everything I do pleases him. . . . Yes, dearest sister, I believe he does love me a little. . . ."

She could have gone on playing the fantastic game if it hadn't been ballet. But ballet meant Katya; it brought back Katya's childish, anticipatory pleasure before the curtain rose, her devoted attention to the performers, her gloved little hands applauding fiercely, her excited chatter afterward. It was a painfully clear memory, and the charming pretense crumbled as reality flooded in: Katya was lost somewhere, far away from her, and Graham, too, in a different way, was out of her reach.

She sat rigid and unseeing in her seat, responding mechanically to her aunt's comments, which were strident and uncomplimentary.

"Well, *batyushka*," the princess said to old Prince Yusupov, who came to the box to pay his compliments after the curtain came down, "you have promised me marvels now that this new ballet master of yours is here. But it seems to me exactly as before."

"You mustn't be impatient, Alina Andreyevna," Prince Yusupov said with a smile, kissing her hand. "Monsieur Truffaut has only been here two weeks, and I assure you there are changes already. This is our old Moscow stuff that you have been seeing. There is more to come."

"Well, I don't know if I can wait for it. My lumbago is beginning to trouble me. Perhaps we ought to go on to the Golitzins . . ."

Yusupov raised both hands in protest. "My dear princess, I beg you not to do so. Kolossova comes on next in *Zephyr and Flora*." (Katya's favorite ballet, Lisa thought with a pang.) "Not only is she as sublime as ever, but Monsieur Truffaut has improved vastly on the choreography. It is far better than Didelot's. Surely you would not deprive the young people of this spectacle."

"No, I suppose I should not do so," said the princess, reseating herself.

"I beg you not to stay on our account, *ma tante*," Lisa said.

"Well, I want to see Kolossova myself. But we shall leave immediately afterward."

The gold and crimson loops of the curtain winged upward, rising on a Watteau-like scene of a flowery clearing in the wood. In the middle of the stage nymphs and shepherdesses were performing a slow, circling dance. They were carrying flower-wreathed hoops which, being raised in the air, created a sort of revolving bower. Within it a cluster of still other dancers was seen; there were six of them, each dressed to represent a different variety of rose, making a crimson, pink, white and yellow bouquet. They were turned inward, away from the audience, arms raised gracefully, as they did homage to the goddess concealed in their midst.

The musicians broke into a faster tempo upon the entry of a male dancer with gauzy wings affixed to his shoulder blades, followed by a similarly dressed retinue. Stopping on the left side of the stage, he made several graceful, wafting motions with his arms, and the outer rim of the circling dancers went scattering away, lowering their hoops to the ground. Another imperious gesture wafted away the cluster of roses, each dancer turning to the audience and making a reverence before falling back to reveal a vision in a flower-starred tunic, beautifully poised on tiptoe, arms arched above her head. The winged god made that exquisite circular motion with his hand that in ballet means "How beautiful you are!" and the two deities advanced toward each other in preparation for a duet.

Here Lisa felt her hand grasped and pressed so painfully that she almost cried out. Graham's voice said hoarsely in her ear. "Look—the red rose! In the middle!"

Lisa turned her eyes wonderingly to the dancer in crimson petals, who was standing together with her companions in the background, having assumed the traditional position indicating modest adulation of the prima ballerina, and saw that it was Katya.

A gasp escaped her. She snatched up the opera glasses that had been lying idly on her lap and stared through them, her heart beating.

Yes, no doubt about it, it was Katya—alive, unhurt and looking just as she had when she was taking a lesson with M. Duroc. Lisa feasted her eyes on the beloved face, its beauty fantastically enhanced by a scandalous amount of cosmetics. Katya's proud little head was cocked to the attentive angle so familiar to Lisa. Her black eyes were enormous; the heavily carmined lips were parted in a smile of delight. To all appearances she was enjoying herself hugely.

A small sound, half a sob of relief, half-laughter, escaped Lisa, and the princess lowered her own glasses to look at her interrogatively. "What is it, Lisa?"

"I am simply amazed by Kolossova's grace. I have never seen her so lovely. Oh, do look at that superb *arabesque*, *ma tante*!"

Nothing seemed as important as keeping her aunt's attention from the dancer in crimson. Lisa gave silent thanks for Kolossova's performance, which was indeed superb and elicited a long ovation after she and her partner finished.

Lisa glanced at Graham, who, oblivious of everything, had his eyes devotedly fixed on the stage on which his bride was now participating in a spirited *pas de six*. A pang pierced her to the heart and was resolutely borne. "This is right and proper," she said to herself. "No more games. I shall never again indulge in fantasies. . . . Thank God that this is so. Thank God that we have found Katya and that she is alive and well."

On stage, Katya was just emerging from a trance as she stood waiting for the *pas de six* that followed the love duet between Flora and Zephyr. A total sense of unreality had separated her from the activity going on around her on the stage: the music, the susurrus of the rising curtain, the burst of welcoming applause; she was only vaguely conscious of the corps de ballet circling them as they held their pose. Another burst of applause greeted Zephyr's entrance. "How handsome Truffaut looks on the stage," she had thought hazily even as, at his imperious gesture of dismissal, her feet took her to the back of the stage in a sustained backward *bourrée* without any volition on her part.

But by the time Kolossova and Truffaut had finished their *pas de deux*, her mind had caught up with her body. She waited for the applause to subside and for Kolossova to float offstage on her partner's arm, with a tiny nod toward them to indicate that she would not return for another bow. Then with a signaling nod of her own, she led the other dancers to the front of the stage, just as she had done at innumerable rehearsals. Her mind was icy clear, oblivious of the audience but sharply aware of every detail of the stage. In a detached way she noted that Masha Dolin was not taking the beat from her.

Am I going too fast?—no, the music says so . . . and now it is commanding the lovely circling *grand jetés*—begin! One—two—three—how I love that soaring leap!—four—five—Tanya is too close for the sixth—no space left. Stop then; wait—*relevé*, *attitude*, *croisé*, *tendu*. Hold. Masha is late with her *enchaînement*; must break in . . . wait for the beat—*now! Plié*, *echappé*, *entrechât*, *passé*. Ah, delightful!" There was a small ruffle of applause as she finished, and she smiled with pleasure. She stretched out her arms and taking their hands, ("Pink rose is all wrong next to my crimson, yellow rose would be better . . .") moved in a sedate circle until the music brought them to their knees, holding hands, their bodies gracefully arched backward, finishing the Six Roses Variation with the opening-flower effect so popular with the Moscow audiences.

Lisa's attention shifted apprehensively to her aunt, who was tapping her fan on the railing before her in time to the spirited music.

"Not bad at all," she said to Lisa. "Of course, Kolossova is incomparable, but these six fillies have been excellently trained."

Lisa waited helplessly, her heart shriveling in anticipation of her aunt's anger when she realized that one of those "fillies" was her niece. She was perfectly capable of rising to her feet in the loge and expressing her feelings in stentorian tones.

But as the ballet went on with the princess showing no signs of recognition, Lisa began to breathe easier. It was possible that they might brush through this without a catastrophe. Aunt Aline had not seen Katya for five years; her eyesight was weak, and she certainly had no thought of encountering a relative on the stage. Surely she would not recognize Katya in these unlikely surroundings!

She gave silent but fervent thanks when intermission came

and Aunt Aline, blissfully ignorant of family disgrace, began to make ready for departure. All of her ached to run backstage in search of Katya; instead she had to attend to her aunt, as had Graham, who was peremptorily called upon to lend his arm. The old woman's lumbago had by now flared up in earnest, and their progress from the loge was of necessity agonizingly slow, as was the ride from the theater to Nikitskaya. It took the combined efforts of the two footmen and Graham to get the princess inside. The delay was maddening; yet the princess's untimely attack of lumbago did in some fashion facilitate things: although unable herself to go to the Golitzin reception, she insisted on the young people doing so, thereby giving them an excuse to depart.

After Lisa had seen her aunt to her bedroom and listened to her complaints and injunctions, she flew to rejoin Graham, who was pacing back and forth in front of the coach as he waited for her. Without another word he helped her into it and followed, after instructing the astonished coachman to go back to the theater. Nearly an hour had passed since they had left it, but ballets were notorious for ending late, and the performance would probably still be going on when they got there.

The ponderous coach started off at its customary slow pace, and Lisa, crumpling her gloves between nervous fingers, begged Graham to make it go faster. The coachman obeyed and the coach accelerated, bumping along the uneven cobblestones.

"We must make sure that he does not report this to your aunt," Graham said. "She must not know what Katya is doing."

Lisa agreed fervently. "And we must devise some scheme to explain her absence when we bring her back with us—something that will stand up to Aunt Aline's questioning. She is not one to be fobbed off with an improbable story. Oh, dear, if she ever found out! She would be so angry! She might even refuse to receive Katya." Graham nodded, not saying anything. The flambeau outside the coach fitfully lit his face. To Lisa's concerned eyes it had a careworn, not to say grim, look. She said falteringly, "Do *you* mind very much?"

His smile was wry. "I should be lying if I denied that."

No, Lisa thought, sighing, it was not exactly the situation in which one would like to see one's future wife, not to mention the future Marchioness of Lyndhurst.

"You see, Lisa, what I cannot understand is why she did not

come to her aunt as she had planned when she started out for Moscow. That would have been the proper—the rational—thing to do. Then there would have been no need for—for what she is doing now." Graham's voice held loathing. "But there is bound to be an explanation."

"Of course." Which was not to say that it would be one that he would like, Lisa thought. For her everything was all too clear. Katya had always wanted to dance; left alone, she would gravitate to the ballet as certainly as a needle to a magnet. She would be undeterred by the knowledge that, in public opinion, ballerinas were respectable only while they were dancing.

Graham's mouth grew grimmer, and she knew, with dismay, that his thoughts had gone back to the mysterious gentleman who, presumably, had brought her to Moscow. She said, "It is possible that she was not sure of Aunt Aline's reception of her. After all that had happened to her, one cannot blame her for not being sure of anyone—or anything . . . Oh, I agree her conduct is open to misconstruction. But one thing I do know, Graham," Lisa's voice strengthened, "no matter how sordid the surroundings in which she finds herself, my sister will rise above them like—like a swan from a muddy pond."

Graham sighed deeply. He said in a shaken voice, "You are the swan, Lisa. You rise above every debasing thought and remain pure. There is no one like you." Her hand was quickly pressed and relinquished as he went on, his voice now carefully schooled: "The main thing is that we have finally found her."

"And this time we really do know where she is." Lisa assayed an unsteady laugh. "This, I fancy, is the end of our disappointments."

"Yes, she can't escape us this time," Graham rejoined, also striving for lightness.

The performance was still going on when they arrived at the theater, though some people had left and were waiting outside for their carriages. Graham sent one of the footmen to look for the back entrance, believing that it would be best to attract as little attention as possible. He helped Lisa out of the coach, and they followed the servant when he came back. A grizzled porter rose from his chair and bowed to them, letting them through.

They made their way backstage to a dimly lit area filled by a variegated crowd: dancers in costume waiting in the wings, *regisseurs* giving instructions to groups, workmen in grimy smocks wrestling with scenery. The sound of the orchestra came muted from the other side of the painted canvas, as did confused glimpses of whirling yet rhythmic movement, punctuated by sporadic clapping. But Katya was not there.

A young man in shirtsleeves who seemed to have a supervisory role noted their presence and courteously conducted them to a small reception room. He was clearly puzzled by Lisa's presence; it was unusual, she gathered, for a respectable female to make an appearance backstage. Besides them, the reception room held a group of officers in bottle-green uniforms trimmed with scarlet, laughing and talking with some girls who were still in costume and heavily made up. A glance told Lisa that Katya was not among them. Nor was she onstage, it seemed. "Monsieur Truffaut and Madame Kolossova are doing their Serbian *pas de deux*," the young man told them. "No, no one else is onstage but they. Forgive me, but I must leave you. I am wanted." He left precipitately before they had a chance to ask him any further questions.

Lisa hovered anxiously at a distance while Graham approached the laughing group of dancers and officers. He asked about Katya, whom he identified merely as the dancer who was the red rose in *Zephyr and Flora*: there was no telling what name she had assumed for her stint in ballet.

"The red rose? Oh, that was Katya Golovin," said one of the dancers, reluctantly turning away from an officer who had been joking with her. She was still dressed as a Watteau shepherdess, but the face under the brim of the French bonnet was that of a Russian peasant girl, snub-nosed and wide-cheeked. "She should be coming here soon; the corps de ballet will be wanted for the finale."

"But she is not in the corps de ballet," another shepherdess chimed in. "You won't catch the Little Countess having anything to do with the corps de ballet now that Monsieur Truffaut has so sweetly promoted her to a *coryphées*."

Lisa, listening with strained attention, thought she detected a spiteful note in that remark.

"He promoted her because she deserved it," the first one countered. "Monsieur Truffaut wouldn't promote an angel from heaven unless that angel knew how to dance. . . . If she is not backstage she is probably in the dressing room. Only the principals are supposed to be performing once *Zephyr and Flora* is over, so neither *coryphées* nor corps de ballet are needed until the finale. That's where she probably is—in the women's dressing room."

"Oh," said Graham, thwarted, and Lisa decided to intervene.

She said to the dancer: "Could you direct me to the dressing room, please?"

The girl, startled by the appearance of a lady of quality in what was evidently the haunt of officers, dropped a curtsy. "Oh, no, madame, it's not for the likes of you. I don't think you ought to go."

One of the young officers immediately clicked his heels and expressed his willingness to go on that errand.

"Yes, you'd like that, wouldn't you? Get along with you," the dancer said, aiming a playful slap at him. "No, we don't need you, thanks all the same . . . Marina," she called to an elderly woman in cap and apron who was shuffling by in her soft slippers with a large wig in her hands. "Marina, would you do something for me, dear soul?"

The woman stopped with a harassed scowl. "I have no time, Mademoiselle Fenya. I need to dress Madame L'Amirale for the next number."

"Just you stop in the dressing room and tell the Little Countess that she's asked for."

The woman shook her head and went on. "She's not there anymore," she said over her shoulder. "I helped her dress an hour ago because she was in a hurry to leave."

"That she was, and no doubt about that," the other dancer remarked *sotto voce*, and again Lisa caught the same undercurrent of malice in her voice. "And she wasn't going home to bed, either. Or at any rate not home. . . ."

Lisa whirled on the speaker. "Where did she go, then? What do you know about it?"

"She knows nothing; she's just a spiteful creature," the dancer called Fenya said angrily. "You must excuse us now, madame, we shall be wanted soon."

Lisa paid her no attention. "What did you mean?" she demanded. "If you know where my sister went—"

"Your *sister?*" The girl blinked. Her pretty, somewhat ferrety face went blank, assuming the look of impenetrable stupidity that Lisa had come to know and fear. "I wouldn't know anything about it, madame."

"Oh," Lisa cried. "Not again! I can't bear it." A great sob escaped her.

Graham's arm shot out, arresting the dancer's retreat. His other hand dove into his pocket, bringing up a twenty-ruble note. The girl's mascaraed eyes widened on it.

"If you will excuse us," he said quietly to the gaping officers and drew her aside. "Well?"

"Don't you listen to Varvara," the girl Fenya said, following them. "She is always telling lies about people and God will punish her for them someday. The Little Countess never goes with any officers, and God knows she has had plenty of opportunities, they are always sending bouquets and notes . . ."

"Well, she seemed to know this one very well," Varvara retorted. "He wasn't one of those whippersnappers, either—an older man, but handsome, I wouldn't have minded knowing him myself. The minute she sees him, she goes running to him, 'Dmitry,' she says, 'is it really you? What are you doing here?'"

"Oh dear God," Lisa whispered.

"Where did he take her?" Graham demanded sternly.

"How should I know? I wasn't standing there eavesdropping, I just—" She broke off as another twenty-ruble note joined the first one in Graham's hand. "I do seem to remember something about Europa. Yes, that's it, the Europa. That's what she was saying as they went out. 'The Europa?' she says. 'Why, that's where Prince Tyomkin was taking Madame Beryllova the other night. It's a lovely place, I hear.' And off she went on his arm, as pleased as punch with herself . . ."

CHAPTER 21

As Prince Dmitry's excellently sprung English carriage made its way over the cobbled streets, Katya showered her escort with questions about Lisa.

"Have you seen her? Did you talk to her? Is she well? Is she terribly anxious about me?"

"Since my answer to your first two questions is negative, I fear I am not in a position to answer your last two."

"You haven't seen Lisa? Why?" Katya sounded almost accusing in her disappointment.

"I do not visit Vorontzov Palace frequently anymore. When I was there last, Lisa had already left Petersburg."

"She had?" Katya stared at him in amazement. "But—but why? Where did she go?"

"I am not perfectly sure," was the answer. "But my impression was that she was going to Moscow."

Katya's eyes grew enormous. "To Moscow? Here? Lisa is coming to Moscow? But then—but then," she stammered joyfully, "that—that must mean that she has received my letters after all, and is coming here to find me. Don't you think so, Prince? What other reason would she have for coming to Moscow? Except for being with me?"

The tall man smiled on her. "At least I can't think of a better one."

"Oh, thank God!" Drawing a breath of relief, Katya crossed herself rapidly several times. "You see, I have been so terribly worried when she did not answer my letters. I have been so stupid! I wrote directly to Lisa, and my letters might very well have fallen into maman's hands. What a disaster that would have been!" Katya said, paling at the thought.

"Yes, a great inconvenience," Prince Dmitry agreed, and Katya couldn't hold back a little trill of laughter at the dry understatement.

"But now I see that all is well, and Lisa is on the way, and I need not think of maman! Oh, thank you, Prince!"

"No need to thank me, my child, since I did not arrange it."

"But you brought the good news. No wonder I was so glad to see you." Her spirits had been extraordinarily lifted when she had seen his erect and elegant figure waiting for her backstage. Someone she knew! Someone from home! She had run to him rejoicing.

She looked at him now with fresh appreciation. He *is* an elegant man, she thought. The redoubtable Prince Dmitry. . . . A bubble of laughter rose in her throat. "If you are here and maman does come for me, will you demolish her with your evil eye?"

"I beg your pardon?"

"When I was little I used to think that your lorgnette was an evil eye, like the Immortal Koshchei's in the fairy tale. That was because people seemed to wilt when you fixed them with it. I seriously considered stealing it for my own use, only Lisa talked me out of it."

"What an abominable little girl you were," Prince Dmitry remarked. He lifted the lorgnette to his eyes, and Katya giggled again. "What is more, I perceive the devil is still in you, in spite of your adversities."

They arrived at the Europa, Moscow's most celebrated inn, and were immediately taken upstairs to a private room.

Katya looked about her with appreciation, almost purring like a kitten at the luxury of it—the tiled stove pouring warmth and comfort into the room, Persian rugs soft under her feet, curtains drawn to keep out the cold October night. A collection of brightly polished daggers and swords hung on one of the walls. A bottle of champagne twinkled in the silver ice bucket. She felt warm and nourished and, now that she knew about Lisa, quite happy.

"My darling Lisa! How I wish she were here right now! When will she be here? Soon?"

"I have no idea. . . . I perceive you do not inquire about your fiancé."

"My—? Oh, you mean Graham."

Prince Dmitry raised his eyebrows. "He *was* betrothed to you, I believe. At least I distinctly remember tendering him my congratulations."

"What a nice man he was," Katya said reminiscently. "Lisa kept saying that I did not value him enough, and I am sure she was right. I suppose he's gone back to England by now."

The prince was silent for a moment, looking at her appraisingly. At last he said, "He is no longer in Petersburg."

It was all very strange, Katya reflected. Here she was, having a midnight supper with the notorious Prince Lunin as though she were one of his "conquests" and not merely the daughter of his old friend. Katya felt a slight *frisson* of excitement. It was easy to see that he was a guest of consequence: the innkeeper himself, attended by two waiters, had waited on them before discreetly withdrawing. The meal had been excellent: caviar, the famous Tarzhok chicken *côtelettes*, cucumber salad—all the things Katya liked. Her exertions had made her ravenous and she ate heartily while the prince watched her with amused pleasure, as though she were a kitten lapping up a saucerful of milk.

Afterward he dismissed the waiter and poured her a glass of champagne with his own hands, wanting to know as he did so how she liked Moscow.

"Moscow?" Katya broke into laughter. "Why, prince, I haven't seen *any* of it!" And that was perfectly true. She hadn't gone to the Kremlin or the Alexandrian Park. She had merely traveled between her boarding house and the Pashkov Theater, with only a visit to the public baths on Saturday and to the church on Sunday.

"A spartan routine," the prince remarked, "for one brought up in luxury. Do you find that being a dancer is worth all those deprivations?" He sounded as though he really wanted to know.

Katya thought about it. She said soberly: "Dancing I love, and have always loved. But it is true that being a dancer is not a pleasant life at all, not at all as I have imagined. It means working very hard—much harder than is necessary, I feel—and being very poor—unless, of course, you have a rich protector. I suppose someone like Kolossova is very well paid and doesn't need a protector. But I should imagine that even she had to have one when she was very young and just starting on her career."

"In effect," Prince Dmitry observed, twirling his glass of

champagne absently between his long, slender fingers, "as you are at present."

"Yes." Katya frowned as she remembered the disagreeable sense of being stranded she had experienced when she had thought that Truffaut was abandoning her, and the undignified relief that had filled her when it turned out not to be so. It was an unpleasant memory and she pushed it away, saying blithely; "Of course, I *will* be a Kolossova eventually. It is only a matter of time. Already I am a *coryphée*, and that after only two weeks!" She sipped her champagne, wrinkling her small nose at the tickling bubbles. "Weren't you amazed when you saw me on the stage, prince?"

"Dumfounded!" Although this was said quite gravely, without a twitch of a smile, Katya had a distinct feeling that he was laughing at her a little. I should imagine, she reflected, looking at his dark face with its drooping eyelids and rather cruel mouth, that very little surprised him.

"Did you recognize me instantly?" she asked.

"It did take me a little time to penetrate the maquillage."

"Yes, and that's another thing I loathe: having all that paint slapped on one. It makes my whole face feel stiff. I don't think I'll ever get used to it. . . . Didn't you think I was *superb*? I mean my performance, of course," she added quickly as he smiled. "I *felt* I was good, and I know Monsieur Truffaut thought so too." As the six *coryphées* had formed the final tableau surrounding the two principals, Zephyr had lowered one heavily made up eyelid in a genial wink and given her a small nod of approbation. "I do hope Monsieur Truffaut won't mind my running away. It is not that I am supposed to perform again. But he does like to see the whole company appearing on the stage for the finale. He says that this gives even the humblest *soubrette* a pride in herself and the company."

"Who is this Monsieur Truffaut?"

"He is the new *regisseur en chef*, brought in from Petersburg."

"I see. And it is important to be in his good graces, I suppose."

"I *am* in his good graces. I told you, he was very pleased with me tonight. I am sure he'll let me have a solo very soon. And it isn't just because . . ." She stopped short.

"Just because?" Prince Dmitry prompted gently.

Katya felt herself blushing and was immediately furious with herself and him. Her chin went up. What business was it of his?

"If you must know, prince, we have an arrangement, Monsieur Truffaut and I."

As soon as she said this, she was annoyed with herself: no reason to tell him any of this! But there had always been something about that unassailable imperturbability of his that made her want to crack his impeccable surface, to startle him into some perceptible emotion. When she was a little girl, the inattentive presence of Prince Dmitry Lunin would for some reason goad her into outrageousness: even then, it seemed, she had wanted to shock him and attract his attention.

"You amaze me." Never before had Katya been looked at with such a bleak and cynical pair of eyes. "It was to be expected, I imagine."

It was a look that made her feel very odd indeed: angry and defiant and strangely desolate all at once. They had been so comfortable together; she had been entirely at ease with him, enjoying herself more than she had in a long time. And then in a trice everything had changed. The friendly room turned inhospitable; she was suddenly alone with a distant, cold-eyed stranger who dared to disapprove of her!

She said icily: "It has been agreed between me and Monsieur Truffaut that I shall be his mistress as soon as he gives me a solo to dance. . . . May I have more champagne, please?" To her intense annoyance her voice shook a little. She told herself fiercely that she abominated people who at first made you feel close and cherished and then turned from charming companions to unapproachable strangers.

Prince Dmitry complied with her request. He also gave her an unreadable look. "Am I to understand that you haven't danced that fatal solo as yet?"

"No. But I shall, soon. And I must say I am looking forward to it," said Katya defiantly, draining the champagne at a gulp. "And to what follows."

If she wanted to enrage him further, her maneuver failed. The odious prince merely smiled faintly. "Are you sure you cannot do better for yourself than that Frenchman?"

Katya's black eyebrows came together. "Don't you look down your nose at my Monsieur Truffaut! He is a dear man, and I am fond of him. He has been keeping his part of the bargain, and I shall keep mine when the time comes."

"You make it sound rather grim."

"Not a bit of it. I am sure I will enjoy it."

"Ah, and that will teach me a lesson, won't it?" His eyes softened. "What a baby you are, my little Katya. I wonder if you know what you are talking about."

"I assure you I do, prince."

"We shall see."

He put down his glass, leaned forward and quite slowly and deliberately kissed her, first on the brow, then on the lips, and then, dipping his sleek, dark head, just above the line of the décolletage at the source of her generous young breasts. The kiss was light but burned. Involuntarily her body swayed toward it, her breath quickening.

Prince Dmitry moved away. His expression was unchanged, but his breath too had quickened perceptibly. "At least," he said, "it is clear that you do have a capacity for delight in love." He sighed, "Yes, you have grown up, after all, on your travels, my little Katya. But you no longer seem little to me."

"I suppose so," Katya said slowly and seriously. "Because you no longer seem old to me."

"Gratifying!" His white teeth flashed under his black mustache. All at once he seemed young and merry.

Katya looked at him long and silently. She was aware of a sudden change: it was as though one had been looking at a pattern, seeing it a certain way, and then there was a shift and you saw it quite differently. Unconsciously her hand went to her breast where that kiss still seemed to burn. For some reason she seemed to see him more clearly than she had ever seen any human being in her life.

"What are you thinking of, my child?" he asked finally.

Katya started. "I was thinking of my mother," she said. "She was much younger than my father, wasn't she?"

"Yes, much," said Prince Dmitry, watching her. "She was close to your own age. And also to mine—at that time."

"Then—wait." She counted it off laboriously on her pretty fingers. "I am not very good at numbers, but it seems to me that there was a much greater interval between the ages of my father and mother than there is between yours and mine."

"Permit me to aid you with your arithmetic," said Prince Dmitry. "I am more than twice your age; your father was nearly three times your mother's."

"But she loved him nevertheless. My grandfather assures me that she did. And he loved her, even though she was a serf and could only be his concubine. . . . It is not a bad thing to be a concubine, it seems."

"It needn't be," said Dmitry, watching her from under his drooping eyelids. "Why, are you considering it?"

Katya nodded. "Yes," she said baldly. "Are you?"

"I have been for these last few years," said Prince Dmitry. He kissed her again.

There was no lightness in this kiss; it lingered and became urgent. Katya, submitting to it, began her usual comparison to Vanya's kisses, and immediately gave it up: this was quite different and even more intoxicating. Closing her eyes, she abandoned herself to it.

"Yes," she said breathlessly, drawing back from him. Her eyes sparkled with pleasure. "Yes, I think I will like it very much indeed. But we must discuss it first." Propping a round white elbow on the table, she looked at him with grave eyes. "I will make conditions, you know."

"That, I believe, is the usual custom," said the prince imperturbably.

"First, I would expect you to help me in my career, which, I am told, is customary for a—a protector to do . . ." She broke off, shaking her head. "No, that is not first, that is second. First is much more important, and I blame myself for not thinking of it immediately."

The prince's lips twitched minutely. "I am burning with impatience to know the nature of this important first."

"I want you to buy my family from my stepmother and give them to me. And I won't be yours unless you do so!"

"I shall make it my business to do so, of course. What a proficient bargainer you are, to be sure."

"That's what Monsieur Truffaut said, too." Katya looked regretful. "This is not fair to him either, is it? I shouldn't imagine that you would be willing to let me go through with that arrangement before we start on ours."

"Astute of you to sense that," said the prince somewhat astringently.

"Then I'll simply have to explain to him before he lets me have a solo. . . . But I am perfectly determined about my family, prince. I want them out of that terrible woman's hands.

In fact, if you could manage to buy the entire village . . ." She stopped, her face lighting up. "I just thought of something. It would be a famous thing for you to do anyhow: you would be buying me too at the same time. Did you think of that?"

"It did occur to me," Prince Dmitry responded wryly. "In fact, *ma petite*, I must tell you. . . ."

He broke off, frowning as a hubbub of voices sounded outside the door to their room. Katya distinguished among them their waiter's voice raised in protest, the deeper tones of the proprietor, and another vaguely familiar voice. A woman spoke up sharply. Katya's head went up; she listened first with incredulity, then with irrepressible joy.

"Lisa!" she shrieked, snatching her hand out of her suitor's. Springing out of her chair, she flew to the door and flung it open. The next moment the two sisters were in each other's arms, laughing and crying.

CHAPTER 22

Lisa, Lisanka, you're here, we're together!"

"My own Katya!" Lisa gazed lovingly into the vivid face between her hands. Yes, here she was at last, real and palpable to the touch, no longer a fugitive ghost. The face was thinner and paler, there was some change yet to be evaluated in the dark eyes: but they looked at her as lovingly as ever, and the blinding smile of delight was the same.

"I knew you'd find me, I told them so and here you are . . . And Monsieur Graham too!" Not letting go of Lisa, she stretched her hand to Graham, who took it and kissed it silently.

"Is it really necessary to advertise our affairs to all of Europe?" Prince Dmitry inquired acidly. He ushered the whole group into the room, dispersed the gaping waiters with one look and shut the door on them, turning the key in the lock and removing it. That done, he resumed his seat, saying to Graham pleasantly: "We have a few things to discuss after the young ladies have abated their raptures."

Graham's gray eyes were cold and contemptuous. "I don't believe we have," he said. "At least I don't intend to stay here and discuss them with you."

"No, I didn't think you would," Prince Dmitry observed calmly. "This is why I have taken the precaution of locking the doors."

Graham, rather pale, said, "I must ask you to give me that key."

"Presently," said the Prince, pocketing it with the utmost sangfroid.

The two girls, their arms about each other, had been listening silently to this exchange. Lisa now broke in:

"Prince Dmitry Ivanich," she said, with cold formality. "I intend to take Katya with me to my aunt's house—"

"My dear Lisa, you can intend all you want, but it can't be done until we come to an understanding."

Lisa's lips curved in scorn. "I believe we *have* come to an understanding—of the sort of man you are, at least."

"Lisa!" Katya was looking at her in shocked bewilderment. "I have never heard you speak so to anyone. Why are you so angry at Dmitry? Surely it can't be because he has taken me out to supper? Why, that is quite *de rigeur* for ballerinas. I told you in my letter—but of course you never received it, you had already left to look for me, my own darling Lisa!" she said, giving her sister another hug. "Were you at the ballet today? Did you see me dance? Wasn't I good?"

"You were wonderful, darling," Lisa said, helplessly. Yes, the same Katya, volatile, self-centered, completely fixed on the impressions of the moment and scornfully oblivious of danger. "But Katya, dearest . . ."

"And the next time there is a performance, Monsieur Truffaut will let me have a solo. I think." Unaccountably she blushed.

"But dearest," Lisa went on, "this will be unnecessary now that we are here. As soon as we leave, we'll go to Aunt Aline—"

"Must we? But yes, of course, we must, we have to talk and you will tell me everything that happened. How did you know we were here?"

"I'll tell you everything when we are at Aunt Aline's."

"Must we go there, really?"

"Yes, we must." And God only knows what I'll tell her, Lisa thought despairingly. But it doesn't signify. The only important thing is to get Katya away from the detestable man who was regarding them with such frightening self-assurance. There was a certain air of ownership in his look at Katya, and it was that that made her say, almost in desperation: "And of course you will marry Monsieur Graham, just as it had been planned before you were sent away. . . ."

"Really?" Katya turned her pretty head to stare at Graham. "Do you still want to? How kind of you! You know that I am a serf, I suppose?"

"Yes, I know, and it makes no difference. We are still betrothed, Katya, and I stand ready to marry you." There was grimness in his voice, and Lisa was at once angrily, agonizingly, shakily proud of him.

To her amazement Katya suddenly broke into ringing laughter. "I am sorry," she said, "this is too bad of me. Only the way you said it reminded me of another proposal I recently had. I wrote to you about my dear Feofil Petrovich Chirkin, didn't I, Lisa? He too was very noble about it." Her eyes danced. With amazement Lisa saw that she had sensed the grim reluctance with which Graham had made his proposal. Why, she thought, this is new, this perceptiveness in her ordinarily self-centered sister. "Dear Graham! But it really isn't necessary."

"I don't think you realize your position, Katya," said Graham wearily. "This is the only way I can protect you . . . and now, sir," he said, rounding on the prince, "if you wish to keep any claim to being a gentleman, you will open the doors for us and allow us to depart."

Prince Dmitry shook his head with a faint smile. "Not until I have shown you a certain document which I believe will make a difference in your plans."

Graham threw him a look of loathing. "I have no desire, sir, to see a piece of paper that gives its unscrupulous holder the right to enslave a helpless woman."

"I don't understand this," Katya said, beginning to show signs of temper. She stamped her little foot. "This is beginning to be like a madhouse! Everybody is behaving so strangely and I simply don't understand any of it. Lisa . . ."

"Yes, I'll tell you," Lisa said. "This man is legally your owner, Katya. He—" with difficulty she made herself go on. "He bought you. From maman."

"He—bought—me?" And suddenly Katya turned quite pale. "I don't believe it," she said in a stiff little voice.

"It *is* unbelievable, isn't it?" Graham said savagely. "That people can engage in traffic with human beings? Yet it is so, to the eternal shame of your country. But I will not submit to it." He turned back to his unsmiling host. "I am going to take Katya away with me. You will have to present your legal claim publicly; and since that will expose you as a mean scoundrel, I don't believe you will do so. So you mustn't worry about it, Katya."

But Katya wasn't listening to him. She had turned to the

prince, her eyes wide and unbelieving. "Is it true, then? Did you really buy me as though I were a—a—"

"An extremely valuable piece of property? Why, yes, I did," said the prince cordially. "And a fine, astute piece of negotiation it was. I wish you would permit me to tell you about it."

"You monster!" Lisa cried out. Graham said nothing. Whirling, he ripped one of the swords hanging on the wall off its mounting and in one swift movement had presented it at his adversary's throat.

"No!" Katya screamed. The prince looked up at his assailant's grim face and his eyebrows lifted. "Attacking an unarmed man? How very un-English, my dear Graham."

"I am rapidly learning to be a Russian," the latter rejoined grimly. "I must trouble you for that key."

The prince shook his head with a faint smile, and Katya screamed again: "No! Don't kill him!"

"I won't," Graham said. "I merely want that key. One of you girls must extract it from his pocket."

"I shall do it," Lisa said steadily.

As she started toward his chair, the prince burst into laughter. It was a sound of pure and unalloyed merriment. "Bravo, Lisa," he said. "I see I have always underestimated you!" He reached into the breast of his coat and brought out a folded square of paper, which he neatly impaled upon the point of the blade that was still presented unflinchingly at his throat.

"Do me the courtesy, my dear Graham, of reading this before you murder me," he said.

Slowly retracting his sword, Graham pulled the document off, shook it open and read it. As he did so, his face went slack with surprise, and the sword he still held went clattering to the ground.

"Oh, what is it?" Lisa cried. Both she and Katya went to him swiftly. Standing at his side and looking over his shoulder, they read the paper which stated in legal terms that Katerina Vassilevna Vorontzov (also known as Katerina Vassilevna Golovin), a female serf belonging to Prince Dmitry Ivanitch Lunin, was hereby given her complete and unconditional freedom.

The tall man rose from his chair and rearranged the folds of his neckcloth, which had been disarrayed by the encounter. He poured himself a glass of champagne and shook his head over it. "Quite flat—and no wonder, in this heated atmosphere." His cold eyes raked the sheepish group before him. "The trouble with young people," he remarked gently, "is that they are so intent on their own heroics that they never stop to listen. And so attached to the romantic prototypes, too: the beautiful heroine, the wicked nobleman pursuing her . . . I am not a good man by any means, but I do stop short of enslaving and debauching the daughter of my old friend."

"Sir," Graham stammered, scarlet, "what can I say? I can only proffer my deepest apologies."

"No, do not. It isn't your fault. Appearances were against me, and we somehow never caught up with each other long enough for explanation. You just missed me in Petersburg; I just missed you in Krasnoye. Altogether a Marivaux farce, with people chasing each other all over the stage. . . ." He turned to Katya. "I am afraid your stepmother feels rather strongly about you—for various reasons." His glance barely touched Lisa and Graham. "It was imperative to get you out of her clutches, and the only way that could be done was to obtain ownership of you. I must say," he added reflectively, "I enjoyed it, brief as it was."

And there it was again, Lisa thought, that same reflective, troubling look that used to make her uneasy whenever she saw it directed on her unaware sister in the days gone by. Was Katya still unconscious of it? she wondered. "I am sorry," she said, "it was wrong of me to have misjudged you, prince. . . ."

"Ah, but you always have, haven't you, my dear Lisa?" His eyes gleamed derisively.

Flushing, Lisa avoided the question. "At least Monsieur Graham didn't," she said. "He was reluctant to believe the worst."

"I was indeed," Graham said. "And I was right, it seems." He hesitated, looking youthfully discomfitted. "As you say, appearances were against you. But at least I should have stopped to listen to you instead of ranting on about the key like a Captain Bombast! Again, my apologies for the drama I have enacted. All I can say in my defense is that this has been a—a *damnable* time. The disappointments—the constant sense of being thwarted—"

"Quite," the prince said. The monosyllable held so much

amused understanding that Lisa's eyes flew suspiciously to his bland face.

"I assure you that I couldn't have ever imagined myself acting so very Russian."

"Perhaps," the prince said, "it is time for you to go back to England."

"Yes, my return there is quite overdue. Well, Katya . . ." Unconsciously he squared his shoulders as he turned to her. The gesture was that of a man conscientiously picking up a burden he had for a moment put down, and Lisa knew a moment of perverse pleasure. In England, he had said, a gentleman does not cry off from his engagement. Nor had she wanted him to do so, when marriage provided the only measure of safety for her sister. But now of course it was different. Lisa wondered how long it would take him to bring himself to defy his English conventions. However, unlike the heroines of her romantic novels, who rejoice in misunderstandings and self-sacrifices and get perverse satisfaction from putting their lovers through hoops, she had no intention of waiting to see what would happen. She would have a private talk with Katya as soon as they were alone.

"Well, Katya," Graham pursued heavily, "it seems you and I must be eternally grateful to the prince. He has made it possible for us to continue with our plans unobstructed . . ." His voice might have held gratitude, indeed, but not much joy, and the prince's smile widened.

With one of her swift movements, Katya was before him. Her small hands smoothed his lapel; her black eyes looked into his with the velvety, caressing look that used to reduce him to jelly. With a throb of delight Lisa saw that he now merely looked harassed.

Katya said softly: "You were a dear to look for me and to want to marry me. But if you don't mind, I would just as soon not. I don't believe I would want to go to England and be the Marchioness of Lyndhurst. It would not suit me at all. What is more," she added with a sudden and unexpected flash of altruism, "I don't believe it would suit you, either. Do you mind very much, dear Graham?"

"Not at all," Graham's answer came with ungallant hurry. He gave a boyish smile, reddening. "That is to say, I am desolated, of course, but I must bow to your decision." He lifted to his lips the little hand that lay coaxingly on his lapel. "You will at least tell me what you intend to do."

"Oh, you need not worry about me," Katya said blithely. "I shall go on dancing and become a prima ballerina, quite as great as Kolossova, and I shall be admired and—and loved, too. . . ." Her quick look in the direction of Prince Dmitry was both radiant and shy. It occurred to Lisa that she had never seen her sister looking so lovely. "I shall have everything I want and be divinely happy!"

"Gently, my child." Prince Dmitry came strolling toward her from the table. "In this world one cannot have everything one wants. A Princess Lunina cannot perform on the public stage."

"Oh," said Lisa. A low laugh escaped her. She said, unknowingly quoting her mother. "So that's how it is!"

But Katya faced the prince indignantly. "But we agreed—we made a bargain!"

"Indeed?"

"When we were talking before—you agreed to my terms, you know you did, Dmitry!"

"Wrong, my love. You made terms—I merely listened!"

"Surely you don't expect me to give up dancing!"

"I shall love to see you dance. But not on the stage."

Katya's bosom rose and fell mutinously. "I am no longer your serf, remember, I shall do as I like."

Prince Dmitry's eyes grew hard. He gave her an ironic little bow. "By all means. But you will do so on your own. You should go far, particularly if you make use of the worthy Monsieur Truffaut."

Katya's face fell, ludicrously. "But I don't want him. I want you!"

There was a heartfelt fervor in her voice. She really does, Lisa thought. She has really fallen in love with that worldly rake who is twice her age.

"Then you are in trouble, *ma petite.*" It was wonderful how attractive and young the middle-aged rake could look when he laughed. "You can have me—at a price!"

"And you want me, too. You know you do."

"Indeed, I do."

"Well, then!" Katya's voice was at its most dulcetly persuasive. "I don't really have to be Princess Lunina, you know. As long as we have each other . . ."

"*Merci du compliment!* Unfortunately, that's how I want you—as Princess Lunina."

"Thank heaven for that," Lisa murmured fervently.

"I have had my share of ballet girls."

"You'll never be able to let me go, you know you won't!"

"Try me."

"Oh, you are an odious tyrant!"

"And you are a spoiled brat, my love."

"Oh," Lisa breathed, fascinated. "I wonder how they will settle it!"

"I neither know nor care," said Graham, taking Lisa's hands in his. His gray eyes looked into hers with the look she loved, and suddenly the sounds of the preposterous argument going on beside them faded from her attention. "I have set my heart," he said, smiling a little, "on bringing a Russian bride to England. Well, my dearest, my dear and only love. . . ?"